Half Moon Harbor

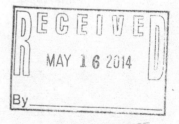

Also by Bestselling Author Donna Kauffman

Half Moon Harbor

DONNA KAUFFMAN

KENSINGTON PUBLISHING CORP.
www.kensingtonbooks.com

KENSINGTON BOOKS are published by

Kensington Publishing Corp.
119 West 40th Street
New York, NY 10018

All Kensington titles, imprints, and distributed lines are available at special quantity discounts for bulk purchases for sales promotions, premiums, fund-raising, educational, or institutional use.

Special book excerpts or customized printings can also be created to fit specific needs. For details, write or phone the office of the Kensington special sales manager: Kensington Publishing Corp., 119 West 40th Street, New York, NY 10018, attn: Special Sales Department; phone 1-800-221-2647.

KENSINGTON and the k logo are Reg. U.S. Pat. & TM Off.

ISBN-13: 978-0-7582-9279-7
ISBN-10: 0-7582-9279-1

First Kensington Trade Paperback Printing: May 2014

10 9 8 7 6 5 4 3 2 1

Printed in the United States of America

First Electronic Edition: May 2014

ISBN-13: 978-0-7582-9280-3
ISBN-10: 0-7582-9280-5

For Terri & Kathy

"Sisters, sisters, there were never such devoted sisters . . ."

ACKNOWLEDGMENTS

A special thank-you to all who helped me with the research on this book, most especially the folks at the Maine Maritime Museum in Bath and the inspiration of the tall ship *Margaret Todd* in Bar Harbor, her captain, and crew. I couldn't have done this without each of you. For the sake of the story, I have made a few tweaks to some of the details you all so helpfully provided. Please forgive me. And of course, any inaccuracies are all mine.

Chapter 1

The morning of Brodie Monaghan's one-year anniversary as a resident in Blueberry Cove, Maine began with a hard-on and a surprise visitor. Unfortunately for him, those events occurred in exactly that order.

Living right on the wharf in Half Moon Harbor, he loved waking to the sounds of herring gulls and the guillemots calling back and forth as the tide eased up past its peak and began its rapid descent. The sun gloriously making its way over the horizon in the wee early hours, accompanied by the low, reverberating thrum of Blue's lobster boats chugging out toward Pelican Bay, was the best alarm clock known to man.

Brodie stretched fully, not minding as the linen sheets and his grandmother's old, faded quilt slid to the hand-hewn cypress floorboards in a tangle. Restless night. Again. He let the chilly May morning air ripple over his heated, bare skin, but it did little to calm down his body's morning state of affairs. He rubbed a hand over his face, felt the scratch of his morning beard, knew it was a match to the shaggy condition of his hair, then glanced down through barely open eyes. "Aye, yes, I know. I've been neglectin' ye, I have."

The part of his anatomy to which he'd directed the comment twitched as if in response, making Brodie grin, even as he sank his head back into his goose-down pillow and let his eyes drift shut. He was considering taking matters into his own hand—a poor substitute, but he was a man who believed in taking gratification where and when he could—when a loud clatter on the docks below brought the rest of his body upright, as well. Grunting, he rolled out of his bed, which was located in the newly added loft of his converted boathouse. Well, one of his boathouses. All of which happened to be situated on his docks. His privately owned docks.

Probably the ruddy pelican again, getting his claws caught up in the frayed old ropes still piled out on the back piers. Damn bird apparently hadn't found a mate this go-round so had chosen to make a summer bachelor pad out of the small boat shed at the end of the central pier. Been making a noisy nuisance out of himself since. "That's likely why the rest of yer flock gave ye the heave-ho," Brodie muttered. "Of course, we'd both likely be in better spirits if we could get ourselves well and truly laid."

Still, he didn't want the great winged beast getting hurt. He'd meant to get the old ropes hauled out the previous fall, before they'd frozen into miniature piles of ice as winter descended, but that season happened earlier in Maine than he'd realized, and then hung around quite a bit longer. It was well into spring with summer just around the bend, but the mornings still had quite the nip to them, and the water was downright frigid. However, in recent weeks the sun had returned consistently enough to fully defrost his happy little patch, and he made a mental note to give Owen a call down at the hardware store and see who might be available to help with removing the old, half-rotted heaps.

Before he could cross the narrow space to spy out the porthole window and see exactly what had happened on the docks below, there was a louder thud, followed by some very inventive swearing. As far as Brodie knew, Auld Eán, as he'd taken to calling the pelican, could grumble like an old man, but hadn't as yet managed that particular feat

His grin returned. Partly because, as an Irishman, he respected anyone who was as passionate in their cussing as he was, but more so because he was fairly certain the colorful curser in question was a woman.

It was respect for the fairer sex more than any modesty on his part that had him grabbing and pulling on the pair of faded green-and-blue plaid pajama bottoms he'd dropped beside the bed before climbing between the sheets. "Down, boy-o," he said to his still invigorated manhood, which also apparently approved of passionate, swearing women. "I promise I'll end the drought and soon enough. But for now, behave. We've company."

He climbed down the circular iron stairs to the open area below. He'd had the main floor converted into kitchen and living space. The corner area, where the picture windows in the east and south walls came together, was dedicated to his drafting table and work desk.

Normally he grinned every time he looked over the newly finished space, sending silent thanks to fellow new Blueberry Cove resident Alex MacFarland for her fine craftsmanship and dedicated work ethic, but for once, his thoughts were mercifully on another woman.

Perhaps I'll get lucky and this one won't already be spoken for.

He flipped up the oversized iron latch, slid open the large plank door that was original to the boathouse, and stepped out onto the docks. And immediately wished he'd also grabbed a sweatshirt. And his wellies. The steady breeze coming off the water was quite brisk. His nipples went stiff, but that was the only thing interested in staying that way. Folding his arms and rubbing his warm palms over his chest, he jogged down the pier and around to the docks on the far side where the noise had come from.

"I should have left you in the car," he heard as he neared the back corner of the boathouse.

Definitely a woman. One with a decent bark, too. Despite the gooseflesh covering his bare torso, his morning mood grew decidedly cheerier.

"Pants are ruined, heel busted. And I'm pretty sure I'll need some help getting these splinters out. *Ouch!* Damn, that one's deep. Seriously, how does someone your size cause so much trouble?"

Brodie slowed his pace. Ah, so she had wee ones. Or a wee one, at least. Those usually came with a father of some sort. Present company excepted. *And doesn't that just figure?*

"I have one moment of weakness—*one*—and this is what happens. I get you."

Just like that, Brodie's smile faded, as did every ounce of his respect. No child should be talked to that way, made to feel unwanted—as if they'd had a choice in the matter—even in the heat of the moment. Especially in the heat of the moment.

He rounded the back corner intent on . . . well, he wasn't sure, exactly, but no one was going to shout down a tiny tot on his docks, or anywhere else in his presence. "Excuse me, miss," he said, taking the short ladder up to the higher pier in a single hop. "This is private property and you'll be wantin' to watch your tone with the wee one if ye don't wish to make a direct exit, seaside."

She hadn't heard him. "Aw, come on now, there's no need for—cut it out with the look, okay? That's what got me into this mess in the first place. You're killing me here. Oh, no. *No!* I didn't mean—don't you even think about—*augh!*"

Brodie took one look at the woman sprawled all over his dock, tangled up in a pile of ropes—and the small, scruffy mutt presently planted on her chest, tail wagging like mad, giving lots of wet, slobbery doggie kisses to his owner, and his goodwill was instantly restored.

"You tell her, laddie," he said with a chuckle. "That's a good boy."

At the sound of Brodie's voice, the wee bit of scruff looked up, spied him, and set off down the dock in a dead dash toward him, barking the whole way.

"Whomper! No! Stop! Down! Something! Hell, what's the right command? He's friendly!" she called out as the dog increased his speed. "But be careful, because he can jump really—"

At that exact moment Whomper launched himself from the dock, and in an amazing display of vertical prowess that would make any of those lads in the NBA quite envious, he landed squarely against Brodie's chest.

"High," she finished, limply.

Brodie instinctively caught and clutched the tiny terror, staggering back a step, but remaining upright in the end. He simultaneously realized two things. One, he still wasn't wearing a shirt, and two, the dog's claws were remarkably sharp. Then he got a whiff of Whomper and realized a third thing. The tiny rascal had apparently found a dead fish he liked . . . and had gotten quite cozy with it.

In danger only of being asphyxiated by the smell of wet canine mixed with fish guts and possibly licked to death, Brodie immediately held the thing away from his body. "Whomper, me boy." He shook his head and grimaced at the stench. "Not even the tide would take you out, mate."

"I'm so sorry," the woman called out. "He's kind of . . . exuberant."

"She's being kind to ye now that ye've gone and made a scene."

His pronouncement was met by bright dark eyes and a lolling tongue, along with a still wagging stub of a tail. Part terrier, part harbor doxy, most likely. His white scruffy fur was marked with the occasional splash of black and brown, yet the wee bit still managed to be quite the dashing rascal. One pointed ear and one with a rakish tilt at the tip didn't hurt matters any, either.

Brodie felt a certain kinship to the mutt, despite being half frozen and smelling like a fishing net left out in the hot sun. "Aye, 'tis a charmer you are, born and bred. Gets you out of a lot of scrapes, does it?" He grinned and gave the little fellow a fast wink when the dog yipped in response. "Yes, I know. Comes in handy, that, eh?" The dog wriggled with renewed adoration.

Still holding him at arm's length, Brodie strode down the dock toward the pup's entangled owner, who was still cussing under her breath as she tried—and failed—to extricate her feet and heeled shoes from the frayed edges of the heavy ropes.

"Might take both of our charms combined to get you out of this one," he murmured to the dog. "That and a hot shower. With lots of something exceedingly sweet-smelling." He shuddered. Their commingled fishiness was impossible not to breathe in. "Good Lord, but we reek."

"I'm really sorry," the woman said, teeth gritted as she worked to get the strap on her shoes free. "He's very well behaved, but only when he wants to be." She glanced up at the dog and gave him an arch look. "Like when luring unsuspecting women into taking him home."

Brodie grinned at the wriggling dog. "Well, mate, I'm finding you more interesting by the moment."

She eyed both dog and man. "Perhaps he'd be happier with a fellow hound to room with, then."

Brodie barked a laugh at that. "I can see why you picked her from the crowd," he told the dog. "Women who know their own minds and aren't afraid to speak them are infinitely more interesting." He bent down and set the pup on the docks. "Now, be a good lad and don't run off whilst I free your mistress here. You've a bit of making up to do, I'd say, but we'll get ourselves cleaned up first, aye?"

Whomper planted his butt on the dock, tail going in a furious spin, panting happily as he looked up at Brodie like he'd caused the sun to rise all by himself. Laughing, Brodie glanced from dog to owner. "You had no chance," he told her as he crouched down beside her. "You realize that." He swiftly pulled the knotted rope fibers free from the buckles on the side of her heels.

She sighed. "I never thought of myself as a sucker for strays, but I guess there's always that exception."

She glanced up just then, and with the angle of his head blocking the bright beams of the rising sun, looked directly into his eyes for the first time.

Suddenly, he was the one all tangled up—only he wasn't quite sure why.

There was nothing extraordinary about her eyes. They were hazel, in fact, not quite distinctly green or blue, and possibly leaning a bit toward brown. Or gray. She was pretty enough in that her features were all lined up just right. Her hair was a shiny sable brown and long enough to likely do justice to a man's pillow when spread across it, but being as all those lovely strands were presently pulled back tightly against her head in a way that took them out of the equation entirely, collectively there wasn't really anything about her that would turn a man's head in a crowd.

And yet, in that singular moment, he couldn't quite look away. Without breaking their gaze, he deftly slipped her shoe with the dangling heel from her hose-clad foot.

"Thank you," she said, and if there was a hint of breathlessness in her tone, he was quite certain he'd imagined it. "I should have worn something more sensible, I guess. I didn't think I'd be encountering any particularly tricky terrain this morning."

He said nothing to that and their gazes continued to hold tight. Then she completely and quite surprisingly dazzled him by flashing a full-on smile. "I guess I was wrong about that. In more ways than one."

His smile spread more slowly, but ended just as broadly as her own.

"I'm Grace Maddox, by the way. Aren't you cold?"

"I passed cold several minutes ago. I would have said I was numb . . . only that smile of yours is like a blast straight from the sun, so that can't be the case now, can it?" He eased up from his crouched position, offering his hand to pull her up next to him. Her fingers were slender, but her grip was quite strong, and there were calluses on her palms. He'd barely registered the surprise of that before she slipped her hand from his and began brushing at her long black coat and crisp linen slacks that now sported a greasy black stain on one knee.

She gave up as quickly as she began, with a roll of her eyes and a wry slant to her mouth. "Given it smells like rotting fish now, the state of my good coat is kind of irrelevant, isn't it?"

He'd taken a step back, telling himself it was to save her from having to smell the fish on him, then realized she was right. She'd been equally tainted. Yet a bit of distance seemed wise, at least until his equilibrium returned.

"I should let you get back to . . . wherever it is you came from," she was saying, "and get warmed up. And cleaned up. I'm really sorry about that. Thank you for the rescue. Please accept my—and Whomper's—apologies for disturbing your sleep."

Brodie ran a hand through his tousled hair, realizing that between the bed head, the morning beard, and pajama pants, he presented quite the rumpled picture. "It's not often I'm awakened by a damsel in distress, but I can't say I minded it." His lips curved. "Your smile was payment enough. Glad I could be of service."

"It just rolls off your tongue, doesn't it? The charm," she added, still smiling when he raised a brow in question. "You're probably not even aware of it, second nature." Her gaze shifted from him to the still perfectly seated dog, that wry arch returning to her brow. "I can definitely see why the two of you bonded."

Brodie chuckled at that, not even trying to refute the assessment, self-aware enough to know the truth in it. He folded his arms and tucked his hands under them as his awareness of the morning chill returned to the point of being beyond ignorable, the action having the unintentional result of pulling her gaze to his chest and arms, and on down over the rest of him, where it appeared she got a bit hung up as well. He grinned, liking that she wasn't as impervious to him as she pretended to be. *Fair's fair,* he thought. And just like that, he wasn't in quite so much of a hurry to find the nearest shower. Not alone, anyway. "What brings you down to my docks?"

Her gaze jerked up to his and the smile blinked away as if it had never been. "Your—?" She looked momentarily confused; then her expression cleared. "Oh, do you live on one of the boats in the harbor here?"

"At one point, I did, indeed. Now I reside in my boathouse. Converted boathouse," he amended, though not sure why it mattered that she know that.

The confusion returned with a frown for added measure. "*Your* boathouse? Which would be . . . ?"

"All of them, actually, but I live in that one." He nodded to the building he'd just come around at the far end of the lower pier, the smallest of the four main boathouses.

His grin began to fade as her frown continued to deepen. "What is it, exactly, that brings you to my docks this fine spring morning?"

"Who are you?" she countered.

"Brodie Monaghan." He sketched a quick, formal bow, despite being half naked and smelling of dead fish, then grinned once more when Whomper barked in approval. "Seventh-generation builder of boats and current owner of Monaghan's Shipbuilders. Such as it is." He nodded to the largest of the boathouses, built by his ancestors' own hands, stationed several piers down, hugging the gentle slope of the land that curved up behind it and the heavy pilings that marched out into the water in front. It had been the first of what had gone on to become the Monaghan family heritage in the Americas.

Due to fire, flood, and the ravages of time, it had been rebuilt from the pilings up several times since its inception in the early 1600s, with timely modifications made each time. But the current structure was still more than a century old, close to two, and showed its age and neglect, as did the weather-beaten company name painted on the side. After decades of disuse and utter lack of maintenance, the proud company logo was barely distinguishable. One of the many things he aimed to change, in due time.

"And you, Grace Maddox . . . who might you be?"

She nodded toward the last in the row of the four main boathouses, nestled at the opposite end of the Monaghan waterfront property from where they were standing. "Owner of that boathouse." She pulled a sheaf of paperwork out of her leather satchel. "As of this morning."

Chapter 2

Grace watched with careful attention as Brodie took the papers from her hand. Careful because she should be paying attention to this potential new headache, but she was having the devil of a time keeping her gaze on the papers and not the exquisitely sculpted chest and fantasy abs directly behind them.

That dilemma was helped not at all by the fact that she was fairly certain he hadn't gotten those muscles by spending time in a fancy gym, but by working with those rough and tough, wide-palmed, workman's hands of his—which she also took care not to ogle. Along with his equally gifted face.

His green-as-emeralds eyes and that clever little cleft in his chin easily put him in the ranks of the drool-worthy. But because the gene pool fairies had apparently been drunk off their collective asses the day they created him and didn't know when to say stop, that pretty, oh so pretty face had to go and be matched with ridiculously sexy dimples that winked out when he smiled. And don't even get her started on that delicious brogue of his.

The ogle avoidance wasn't because she was shy. Far from it. She was quite certain he was well used to turning heads, most of them female, so catching her staring would likely just be yet another casual confirmation of his studliness. That was precisely the point. She wasn't interested in being yet another ogler in what had to be a long line of oglers. Anyone who'd been around her for even a short time would realize that she wasn't much of a joiner. God knows her life would have been much easier if she'd had that mind-set. But those same gene pool fairies who had blessed the Monaghans, or at least this one, with all that natural, gregarious charm had skipped the Maddox family tree entirely when the team player gene had come up for distribution. Her branch had been blessed with an overabundance of the fiercely independent gene, though she wasn't sure *blessing* was the word she'd always have used to describe that particular trait.

True, it had come in more than a little handy during her formative years, but there had been distinct disadvantages, as well. She was trying to rectify that now. Her thoughts drifted to her brother, Ford, but she purposely pulled them back to the matter at hand. Those manly, manly hands . . .

Grace supposed, given the surprising news of her rescuer's name and ancestry, and the fact that it matched the one painted on the side of the main boathouse, she should be grateful he hadn't snatched the mortgage papers away, or ordered her off his docks, or both. It appeared that Cami Weathersby, her Realtor, had some explaining to do, as did a few folks down at the county tax and property offices. Not that Grace was worried that the sale of the boathouse was anything other than legitimate. She'd known from the moment Cami had led her onto the property last week that it was perfect for what she had in mind. Grace was nothing if not focused when she had a goal in her crosshairs, but her excitement hadn't kept her from doing her due diligence on the place. Being an estate attorney came in handy like that.

A former estate attorney.

Grace held her hand out. "I think you'll find all the paperwork in order, but please feel free to check with the county offices. I'd recommend you start with the tax assessor." She slipped the strap of her slim leather messenger bag over her shoulder and tucked her hand in the exterior pocket, wincing as the splinters still embedded in her palm brushed against the stitched leather trim. She handed him her banker's business card. "You can also call my loan officer. Sue—Mrs. Clemmons—seemed really pleased that the place was going to get some attention and was more than happy to work with me on my new business loan."

Privately, Grace was beyond thrilled she'd been able to purchase the property outright, and for what amounted to a steal. It had allowed her to think much more broadly about her plans for the place, which was a good thing since she'd initially planned on buying either an old inn or an older home she could turn into one. She definitely hadn't planned on renovating and completely repurposing a boathouse into an inn. But, based on the outright purchase and her relatively healthy personal portfolio, she'd secured a small business loan. Instead of moving in small stages as her previous, somewhat conservative estimated budget would have allowed, she could more or less leap straight into the deep end and really get moving on the renovation. She couldn't wait to get started. But she didn't think Mr. Monaghan really wanted to hear all about that.

Brodie was still scowling, and it was either a testament to those drunken gene pool fairies or the embarrassing length of time that had passed since her last serious relationship that the expression served to make his strong jaw and chiseled cheekbones stand out more handsomely than before. If that were possible. He was like a walking billboard for steaming hot, up-against-the-nearest-wall fantasy sex. The kind you only saw in movies. Her gaze briefly dipped to his chest again, and it was possible his lilting brogue played through her mind as her little voice added *down and dirty, steaming hot, up-against-the-nearest-wall fantasy sex.* Yeah. She'd buy a ticket to that show. Hell, she wanted to be *in* that show.

He handed the papers back, but didn't reach for the business card. Instead, he took her hand in his, the surprise of his touch making her draw in a quick breath, which, from his glance into her eyes, he'd heard.

He turned his attention to the angry red welt on her palm and the sliver of his dock that was jammed into the center of it, along with several smaller slivers embedded on either side. "Och, but that doesn't look like much fun. You need to get these taken out." He cradled the back of her hand in his wide palm and bent his head to take a closer look. He gently bent her fingers back a bit to better expose the splinters to view and absently rubbed his fingers along hers in a consoling gesture that seemed so natural, she wasn't even sure he knew he was doing it. But of course, a man who looked like he did, who exuded over-the-top sex appeal from every last pore, was likely quite well aware of the effect his touch had on members of the opposite sex.

It took great restraint not to jerk her hand free. The contrast of the gentle strokes and the work-roughened skin of his fingers shot zings of awareness to points front and south, making her want to shift on her feet, maybe press her thighs together a little—or a lot—and wish the soft silk of her bra wasn't clinging quite so snugly to her now-taut nipples.

"I-I plan on doing just that. As soon as I'm near a pair of tweezers."

He lifted his gaze to hers. Up close and real personal, all that deep, sparkling green was every bit as disconcerting to her freshly reawakened erogenous zones as was his touch. And the two together, well . . . She carefully slid her hand free and tucked Sue's business card away.

"Good," he said, making no attempt at all to move back out of her personal space. "As for Monaghan's, as happy as I am to know that the lovely Mrs. Clemmons is smilin' upon ye, as hers is a delightful smile indeed, this place is already getting the attention it needs."

Grace wondered how much money Brodie had charmed out of the older loan officer. She imagined, given the lethal levels of charm he possessed, that the sky had probably been the limit. In an effort to get her equilibrium back, she shifted her gaze and did a slow scan of the waterfront property. Even in its dilapidated condition, it was not insignificant in scope. Monaghan Shipbuilders sat centrally, right in the pocket of the gentle inward curve that had given the harbor its name, and accounted for at least a third of the waterfront real estate. The deep harbor edged into a naturally upward sloping open area of timber-free land, and it was that precise combination, Grace understood from Mrs. Clemmons, who was as proud of the heritage of Blueberry Cove as Brodie appeared to be, that had led the eighteenth-century shipbuilders and town founders to choose the place as their new homestead.

Back then they were building, among other things, magnificent two-masted schooners and three-masted clipper ships, each of significant length and scope, and therefore needed to construct them on land that had to be just the right angle so that, when completed, the ships could slide straight into the deep waters of the harbor and be sailed out into the bay. Personally, she wasn't sure how any of that had been accomplished, especially given the rudimentary equipment they'd had at their disposal at that time, but she didn't doubt Mrs. Clemmons knew what she was talking about.

In fact, as someone who spent a significant amount of time on the water, albeit in a rowing scull, Grace had taken the history to heart, realizing that it was her turn to stake her claim in Half Moon Harbor and build what she hoped would become the future Maddox family heritage. Granted, there wasn't much Maddox family left, but heritage had to start somewhere, right? She'd honor the generations of Monaghans who had poured their hearts and souls into the property, be respectful of those who had come before her, and learn from them where she could. But she planned to stake her claim as well, and hoped they, in the form of the current generation landholder, would respect that.

It was in that moment that the enormity of what she'd done suddenly became very real, in a way it hadn't—or couldn't have—before. She didn't know Brodie well—or at all, actually—but she understood, given his ties to the land, and the people, that she'd need to present a solid front to him when revealing her plans. And she felt anything but solid at the moment.

She anchored her gaze to the waterfront and held it there. The main boathouse was built half on land, half on the substantial pilings that extended into the harbor, creating a wide, heavy pier. From that pier ran a series of smaller docks, anchored and floating. Brodie's smaller boathouse was on the near side of the main building, situated mostly on land and slightly edged out over the water. A smaller dock extended from the side and a wider one where they stood connected to the main dock. The two other boathouses were situated on the far side of the main building. The third in the row, of moderate size and scope, was completely on land, though its condition was the poorest of the four.

"Rome wasn't built in a day, lass, and I'm but one man," he said, the slight defensive edge to his tone making it clear he'd taken her studied appraisal as a judgment before she had voiced a single word.

If he only knew, she thought as her gaze shifted and stayed on the last boathouse in the row. The one that was now all hers. A shot of pure adrenaline—or maybe it was sheer terror—made her heart race. She'd plotted, she'd planned, she'd tried to be methodical and smart . . . mostly because she knew her new life decision was anything but rational. Still, she couldn't truly believe she'd really gone and done it.

Her boathouse hugged land and water and was second in size only to the main boathouse, and then, not by much. A smaller version of the main pier extended directly from the rear decking and was separate from the other docks. On learning from Cami that her ownership included that pier, she'd immediately envisioned sailboat rentals, along with dockage for her guests who traveled by boat. The vision of her future seaside inn teased a smile from the corners of her mouth, and brought a particularly sharp tug near her heart. She was already falling, heart and soul, for the place and its possibilities. She wanted the chance for them to grow into something new together.

Feeling his scrutiny, she continued her visual scan to the rest of the boatyard situated to the side of the open grassy slope that extended up to Harbor Street. It was a long, fenced-in gravel and dirt lot that contained a number of buildings, equipment sheds, a garage or two, and property for dry dock storage. The lot was the only land-based access to the docks and boathouses. Her own car was parked there. She wondered how Brodie would take it when he found out that her purchase had also secured her access to that lot, at least in terms of parking.

She tried to imagine what it had been like, back in the day when the Monaghans had actively been building those big clippers and schooners. It would have been quite an impressive operation, big and bold and proud. Dominant. Run by a powerful family, or one that had surely gained power as the town and their industry took hold and grew.

But now . . . well, now it was barely a shadow of its former glory, and only in property size at that; a tax burden to the county and apparently every kind of burden to the lone Monaghan tasked with taking care of it. She'd have been overwhelmed at the mere thought of tackling such an undertaking. As it was, she was more than a little freaked out by the tiny part she'd signed on for.

"Half Moon Harbor and all of Blueberry Cove that surrounds it were forged from the sweat, bent backs, and hard labor that began with its founders, most of whom were my ancestors," he said as if reading her mind.

She wasn't too sure those green eyes of his couldn't see deep down into the depths of her soul and the hunger there that she'd so recently, finally decided to feed. The problem was, looking back into his green eyes created a whole new kind of hunger. . . .

"They each, to a family, suffered great losses and exhilarating triumphs," he went on, looking at her so intently, so earnestly, she couldn't look away. At least that was her excuse. "It took loss and triumph, I think, for them to continue onward, undeterred and determined. The harbor exists to this day because my greats, men and women both, poured their hearts and souls into creating it, sustaining it."

"And yet, from your accent, I guess I'm safe in assuming you weren't born here in Blueberry Cove."

"I am a direct descendant—"

"Who has lived here for . . . ?"

He folded his arms, clearly annoyed. "Longer than you."

Unfair, really, drawing her attention to those shoulders, those biceps.

"That may be true," she said, trying to keep her eyes on his face. Admittedly, it didn't help all that much. Dear Lord, he was a lot to take in. And she was feeling so very greedy. "However, though my last name might not be

Monaghan, the deed"—she lifted the sheaf of papers—
"has been done. I can assure you I will be completely respectful of your heritage. I'm not here to destroy anything.
Quite the opposite. In fact, given the scope of the place
and the amount of work you have in front of you, you
might even be grateful for the help in restoring it."

"Restoring it now, are you? Are you a shipbuilder,
then? Who are your people? Where have they established
their legacy?"

"I meant restoring the property to something functional, giving it renewed purpose. You certainly didn't
mean to bring all of it back to the same size enterprise it
once was. There isn't the economic demand for something
on that scale, is there?"

"How is it that you're here at all?" he said by way of response.

But she hadn't missed the flicker of something that
looked a lot like the same kind of hunger she felt, the need
to build, create, and sustain something important. And
dammit, she couldn't ignore the responding twinge of
guilt it made her feel, either.

"You mean in Blueberry Cove? I have family here. My
only family." Why had she added that last part? She didn't
want to talk about Ford . . . to this man, or anyone else,
for that matter. At least, not until she'd found her brother
and talked to him first.

"I mean here on my docks. I'm quite certain that this
property wasn't actively for sale, as I've never put it on the
market."

"You didn't have to. The county did that for you."

He opened his mouth, then shut it again. That accent of
his, along with his easy charm, had likely gotten him out
of more than one sticky situation, but after nine long years
spent sitting between bereaved, feuding, and downright
hostile family members as she determined if their dearly

departed loved one's assets were being properly toted up and dispersed, she'd become a pretty shrewd judge of character. There was more going on behind those Emerald Isle eyes of his than one might assume from the rest of the package.

"Then there should have been some kind of notice regarding their change in plans and intent with regards to the property," he said, more to himself than to her, "which I can assure you there was not."

She could see quite clearly that he spoke the truth as he saw it. The sale or even the possibility thereof had come as a shock to him, and not a small insult. It wasn't any of her doing, but the flash of true hurt, of betrayal, she spied on his face gnawed at her nonetheless. Why had the town seen fit to do what they'd done? She didn't know the history of the particular situation, or what his life had been like since he'd put down his own roots, or how the town perceived him. But she knew she didn't want to be part of whatever conflict her purchase seemed likely to unleash.

"I came here to establish roots, meaningful ones," she said, realizing it was probably unwise to give too much, but seemingly unable to stop the floodgates once they'd opened. "I spent most of my life doing what was safe, what wouldn't do me harm, and I was very good at it. Too good, really. I convinced myself that safe equaled happy. Only . . . it didn't. Couldn't.

"Security is a great comfort, but it's ultimately an empty one. I've watched—and helped—countless families going through some of their most challenging times, some torn apart by it, some united. Most of the time it was messy and hard, but . . . real—the bonds, the love, even the anger and sometimes hate. Legacies are not built simply from amassed assets, but from history, moments shared, memories created, futures dreamed of. It's not hollow and it's not separate and alone. All that means . . . something. It's—I don't want to be a bystander any longer, watching, assessing, assisting. I can't do that any longer. I want—no, I need—to reclaim what is left of my family and make something that has meaning, then stand by it, no matter the risks. You have to believe me when I say that I'd never have knowingly intruded on or intentionally thwarted someone who is trying to do the same thing."

"So . . . what is it you're saying then? That you'll undo the deed? Literally?" He jerked his chin toward the papers clutched in her fist.

"I don't know that I could, even if I wanted to. And . . . to be honest, this is the right place for me. I'd pictured something different, and yet the moment I saw it, I knew it was exactly right in more ways than you can know or possibly understand. Or maybe you're the one who would understand best. I meant what I said about honoring the history of this place. Even if I didn't want to, I'd be a fool not to capitalize on it, so trust that if you don't trust me. I plan to keep the integrity and history of it alive . . . because it's smart and because it's the right thing to do."

"So, that would a no then."

"Brodie—Mr. Monaghan—I don't know what else to say. You've—your family—has managed to hold on to this entire place for a very, very long time, but when the last Monaghan walked away from here, however long ago that was, he—or she—had to know they'd abandoned the place. It's fortunate you had as much left to reclaim as you did. From what I understand, the town could have divested itself of the burden at any time over the past several decades. I imagine if anyone had shown the slightest interest, the town council would have."

"Is that what estate attorneys do then? Dismantle the property of families?"

She frowned. "No, that's not what we do—what I did—and how do you know what I used to—" She looked down at the deed papers. He'd looked at them more closely than she'd realized. More going on behind those winking green eyes than it would seem. She looked back to him. "My previous occupation has nothing to do with this."

"Previous, is it? Other than when it provides you with the tools necessary to do exactly what you did, you mean? Dismantling my inheritance might not have been your intent, but it was, in fact, exactly what you did."

"I know it's come as a shock. I can see you're upset and I understand why. But I didn't knowingly do this to you. I had no idea about you, any more than you had any idea about me. I thought the property was abandoned." She didn't want to hurt him any further, but needed him to be realistic. "Once you've had time to think it through, I think you'll see that this could be a good thing. One less part for you to have to deal with, and something that can only bolster whatever it is you hope to do here."

"That's something we'll need to look into then." He turned abruptly and headed back up the dock, glancing back when he reached the ladder down to the lower dock. "You coming?" He slapped his thigh, and Whomper, the traitor, took off toward him like a bullet.

"Coming?" she repeated, her mind going to places it had absolutely, positively no business going.

"Inside," he clarified. "We can defishify ourselves and make a few calls. I'm sure this can all be sorted out." Brodie hopped down the steps and turned to catch Whomper as the dog made the leap off the higher dock, trusting completely that he'd be caught. Brodie's smile returned as he cradled the scruffy mutt in his arms, even as he winced at the smell and gave the dog a healthy scratch between his ears.

"There isn't anything to sort out," Grace called, lifting

the papers in her hand as proof, feeling ridiculous for being jealous of a damn dog.

But Brodie had already turned and continued on his
way to his boathouse.

The boathouse he lived in—where he apparently
walked around half naked. Only a hundred yards or so
away from her boathouse. As that future reality set in, she
also took note that his stride was confident, not angry and
not worried like someone who feared he'd lost a part of
what was his and meant to get it back by whatever means
possible.

Whomper was back on the dock, trotting happily at his
side. *Men.* She should simply walk away, leave the two of
them to each other, and get on with the business at hand,
which was charting out the first steps she needed to take
with her newly acquired property. Her new life. Her new
future.

Her new everything.

But she wasn't looking at her newly acquired future
everything. She was still watching Brodie's broad bare
back and his very fine plaid pajama-bottoms-covered tush
as he neared the point where the pier would take him
around the corner of the boathouse and out of sight.

He paused as he reached it and slapped his chest.
Whomper immediately sprang upward, blissfully happy to
once again be in those manly man arms, clasped to that
equally manly man chest.

Grace sighed, intending it to be one of disgust, but was
forced to acknowledge it had been rather wistful, instead.
She should head back to the bank, then the town municipal building, make absolutely certain that there hadn't
been some kind of small-town misunderstanding about the
property, some hidden handshake deal or verbal agreement. Neither would hold up in court, but she didn't have

the time or need the frustration and financial drain of a potentially lengthy legal battle. Not to mention that regardless of Brodie's personal standing in the community, she was certain that suing a member of one of her newly adopted town's founding families was probably not the best way to go about introducing herself to her new neighbors.

But there was also the part where she reeked of dead fish, was down to only one functioning shoe, and had a splinter in her palm that felt like she'd jabbed a needle into her hand and left it there.

"Okay, so maybe I go talk to the half-naked Irishman some more, get my dog back—or not," she added darkly, "then go clean up before calling my architect, or my banker and the county clerk, depending on how well I do in convincing him this is all going to be a good thing." *Yeah. That'll happen. Right after he pushes me up against the nearest wall, tears my clothes from my body, and has his very sexy Irishman way with me.*

She sighed again, not even caring that it sounded wistful and more than a little needy. She had other things that needed attention first. A whole long laundry list of them, which only began with figuring out how she was going to turn her centuries-old boathouse into a modern-day, functional inn. There was still Ford to consider and deal with. She didn't even know where to begin there. He'd chosen to live a life of seclusion for very good reasons, and she doubted he was going to be all that excited, or even remotely interested, in reuniting with any part of his past. Even if that part was his only living relative. His own sister. But she was going to do whatever it took to at least get him to consider her plea. He might not need or want her in his life, but she needed him in hers. At the very least, he was going to understand how serious she was about reuniting what was left of their family.

So, her poor, neglected libido was going to have to wait, as were her equally neglected and still uncomfortably stiff nipples. She watched Brodie disappear around the corner. *I know he'd be damn good at making that ache go away. Oh so very, very damn good.*

Feeling more foolish by the second, she slid the deed papers back into her bag, slid the straps up on her shoulders again, and clomped unevenly down the pier, broken heel dangling from her fingers by the strap. She considered taking the other one off, but figured she was already risking splinters in the bottom of one foot, so she walked as gingerly as possible, wincing when she felt the expensive silk hose shred as it snagged on the uneven wood planking.

She made it down the pier and around to the side of the boathouse that was built on land, noting with grudging approval the big picture windows he'd had installed facing out toward the harbor and bay beyond. She made a few mental notes, rethinking the northeast facing wall of her own building, then was equally surprised to see the big original panel door still in use as entrance and exit. She liked that, too, she decided. It was charming and unique and admittedly functional.

She glanced up, and her gaze caught and held on the family crest signage that had been painted directly on the restored and freshly painted wood planking of the boathouse. The sign was done in a rich, emerald green with fancy gold and black trim. MONAGHAN SHIPBUILDERS ~ ESTABLISHED 1627, it announced in elegant black script with gold accents. She glanced over her shoulder at the main boathouse, which sat centered in the pocket of the harbor, and realized the sign was a smaller version of what had once been painted so proudly and elegantly on the side of that building.

She looked back to his boathouse and noted that it had

been completely restored, from shake roof to wood plank siding, and he'd mentioned the interior had been remodeled as well. She hadn't gone through any of the rest of the property—until this morning anyway, and then she hadn't made it farther than the docks that connected the boathouses together—so she wasn't sure what else he might have accomplished, but he'd most definitely been busy.

Her attention shifted to the heavy ship mast mounted on the dock nearby. A spar, she thought it was called, complete with lanyard ropes, and all the fittings, but sans sail and abbreviated in overall height. The wood gleamed, as did the brass accoutrements, and the ropes were new and neatly and perfectly knotted, or so it appeared to her, anyway. Her sailing knowledge was limited to what she'd picked up being around others who sailed from the same piers where she'd kept her scull and oars. But it wasn't the ropes or the knots that held her attention. It was the plaque mounted where the beams formed a tee. On it was a stunning, hand-painted rendition of a three-masted clipper ship in full sail. Eighteenth-century model, she supposed, given the established date on the bigger sign on the side of the building.

Hanging below the near side of the cross beam were three rectangular signs, connected by brass hooks, each one hanging beneath the next. The top sign, in the same elegant script as the one on the side of his boathouse, said BRODERICK MONAGHAN VII. The one under that read SHIPBUILDER, IRISHMAN, KEEPER OF THE FLAME. Her heart twinged at that last part. Underneath that, the final sign read BOATS BUILT BY HAND ~ INQUIRE WITHIN.

Below the final sign dangled a smaller wood plaque, painted black with a beautifully rendered family seal or crest in the center. The crest was made up of a blue and gold flag with a knight's head positioned above it. She assumed it was the Monaghan crest. Then she glanced back up at the hand-painted clipper ship, and noted the same crest was painted on a small flag that flew at the top of one of the masts. *Wow.* She couldn't even imagine what it took to build something so majestic . . . and to think it had been Brodie's own ancestors who'd made their legacy doing just that. She wondered what kind of boats he built or planned to build. Obviously nothing on so grand a scale as his ancestors', so . . . what was his goal?

She thought of her own goals, and how overwhelming it felt, launching herself into uncharted waters, trying to build something new while resurrecting the only part of her past that meant anything to her.

Thinking about what Brodie faced, the weight of what he bore on his shoulders, of all who had come before him . . . made her own journey seem miniscule and a little ridiculous by comparison.

She turned, looked back down the curve of the harbor to her boathouse. *And yet, mine is no less important, no less meaningful a mission.* In fact, any time she felt overwhelmed, which she imagined would probably be pretty much all the time, she only had to look out on all he had to accomplish to put her own to-do list in perspective.

She smiled at the thrill that shot straight down her spine, the sensation comprised of equal parts anticipation and terror. She'd initially thought she'd build something brand new, completely original, thinking that was necessary to her new life plan. But as soon as she'd entered the old coastal town, she'd been drawn to its history, its heritage, and decided she wanted to blend old and new. She'd looked at old waterfront houses and even a few abandoned inns, wanting something with character, maybe with its own colorful history, where she could begin to build her own . . . and then she'd walked inside the boathouse right on the water, with a dock of its own, and something about it had called to a place deep inside her. Probably the same place that had pulled her to the Potomac River back in D.C. and to rowing. There was a specific kind of peace that she'd found only on the water, an inner serenity. The water had represented continuity. Security.

She'd felt that same thing when she'd walked into the boathouse, then down the pier that extended into the harbor. In some ways, it couldn't be more different from the river she'd spent so many hours on. But in all the ways that mattered, it had felt the same, standing on that particular spot, feeling physically hugged by the curve of the harbor behind her, and energized by the horizon that spread out in front of her, endless, hopeful, full of promise.

She understood Brodie's disappointment with the town for doing what they'd done, but she told herself that the loss of one boathouse wouldn't diminish one iota the proud and bold legacy the Monaghans still laid claim to in Half Moon Harbor, and the entire Cove for that matter. She needed to make him understand that if anyone was going to co-opt even the tiny part of his heritage that she'd taken over, how fortunate he was that it had fallen to her understanding and careful hands, and not to some developer who might have simply torn it down and started over.

She'd honor his ancestors' intent and put her own stamp on the place. She'd bookend what he'd started. He'd see that for himself in time, and she could only hope he'd approve.

She turned back to the wide plank door, smiling as she noted the throng of small white buoys hanging from the oversized handle, each banded with a different colorful stripe, or rather what once had been bright and colorful, but had clearly seen their share of ocean action. Pot buoys, she knew they were called, for the lobster pots they marked all over the bay. They were a symbol she'd noticed hanging proudly on countless buildings and posts all around Pelican Bay and Blueberry Cove. Most noticeably, they were in the harbor area, so charming and true to the local fishing heritage.

All in all, Brodie had made a really good start with his boathouse renovation, a fine beginning to the daunting task he had ahead. Well, it could do with a bit of landscaping, she thought. Some shrubbery, a flower garden to cheer up and soften the overwhelming masculinity of it all wouldn't have been out of place, but what did she know from boatbuilding businesses?

"About as much as you do about innkeeping," she murmured under her breath. *Not that he has to know about that.*

Chapter 3

Brodie had left the large sliding door partially open, but Grace knocked on the plank closest to the gap just the same. No response. A small brass ship bell had been mounted to the frame of the door panel, but ringing it seemed a bit overkill since he was expecting her. She stuck her head inside, but didn't see man or her traitorous beast. She did, however, see the remarkable transformation of the wide-open interior and eased inside to take a better look.

She turned in a slow circle and took in the smart use of space, the corner work area, and the cypress planking used for the flooring. Original to the place, she knew, as her boathouse had the same. She'd been planning on replacing it, thinking the boards beyond salvation, but whoever had restored these had done a stunning job. The golden wood glowed with renewed warmth and a rich glossy finish. She made a mental note to ask him whom he'd used. *Like he'd tell me.* She sighed, hoping they could sort out their issues without involving anyone else—namely lawyers. Well, more lawyers.

Still caught up in the structure of the place, she moved to the beautiful piece of circular stair ironwork that led up to the thoughtfully executed loft space running across about a third of the open-to-the-rafters interior space.

Also cypress planking, she noted, looking up at the loft flooring, absently wondering where the ironwork had been done or if it was original to the old boathouse structure before the renovation. She stepped back and looked up, and noticed the black wrought iron continued across the open edge of the loft space, creating a simple, yet beautiful railing. So, it was new to the renovation, she thought, making another note to look into local tradesmen and see if it had been done by someone in the area.

The railing itself had been turned into art by the addition of a circular opening in the middle, which had been fitted with a vintage-style brass medallion the size of a dinner plate.

Without thinking, she climbed a few steps to get a closer look at the piece, and realized that while the wrought iron was new, the medallion was not. The patina had turned it a deep sea green, and the brass was pockmarked and pitted from excessive exposure to salt water and weather. The engraved clipper ship, the same as on the painted emblem representing the Monaghan shipbuilding legacy, was no less majestic for the wear and tear. Was it some kind of logo, a stamp of sorts, that they'd put on their ships, perhaps? Or in them? She didn't know anything about ships or what the historical traditions might have been, but the detail work in the medallion was intricate and beautiful. On closer examination, she noted that the flag flying from the center mast appeared to have the same family crest as the one outside, though it was almost impossible to tell for sure, given the degradation of the metal. It made sense, though, since it was exactly the same rendition in every other way. Again she was struck by the enormity of Brodie's legacy. She couldn't even fathom a history so rich and full of carefully documented detail.

From her perch halfway up the twisting staircase, she turned to take in the space as a whole. Whoever had planned and executed it was a smart designer and a talented craftsman. It occurred to her that the craftsman could very well be her erstwhile host. Considering his trade, she imagined it might not be a big leap from building boats to rehabbing a small boathouse. She did another quick scan of the open space, wondering where he'd gone.

She gave a short whistle for her dog. "Whomper? Where are you?" she called, keeping her voice low. Neither man nor beast was anywhere below her on the main level as it was completely open and easy to see into every corner. That meant—she cringed, imagining the little ruffian rolling and rubbing his fish-rot fur all over Brodie's bed linens, then allowed a short, self-deprecating smile as she thought that would at least be a handy solution to her wanting to roll around in Brodie's bed linens.

She turned and took another step up the circular column, pausing to finally slip off her other heel, before climbing a few more. "Whomper," she whispered. "If you're up there causing more trouble, I'm going to leave you to explain yourself."

Nothing. No sounds of anything being destroyed or tangled with. It took a few more steps and another turn around the spiral before she heard a thrumming sound and realized it was coming from the bathroom. The shower was running. She also heard what sounded like . . . "Singing?" She rolled her eyes. "Of course he sings." And beautifully, too, she thought, as his lovely baritone, rich and deep, rose over the sounds of the water as he sang about a bonny lass with a smile like sunshine.

Her traitorous mind had no problem whatsoever imagining him naked in his shower, water cascading, hot and steamy, all over that too-sculpted-to-be-real body, white teeth flashing, dimples dimpling, as he let loose with the chorus. Filling those broad, wide palms of his with soap and rubbing them over those pecs, down those abs, and straight out along his . . . *Dear Lord*. Her grip on the iron rail tightened as her thighs went a bit wobbly, only to go rock stiff a moment later when his voice soared to the high notes . . . and a very distinctive howl rose up along with him.

"Seriously?" She climbed up a few more steps until her chin was level with the loft floorboards. The entire area was open up to the pitched ceiling, with a small porthole window in the side wall, and a bigger circular window set in over the headboard of the wide sea of mattress that dominated the space. Two long rectangular sunroof panels had been installed in the longer side of the roof that slanted toward the water. Warm, dappled light, which she imagined would turn to a golden glow as the sun climbed higher into the sky, flowed in. A large, slowly turning ceiling fan hung from a long pole mounted to the apex of the roof, the blades cleverly made from boat paddles, kept the air in the upper part of the building from getting too still and heavy.

Wide, deep drawers with heavy rope pull handles were built in under the bed. Similar drawers with brass handles had been built in along the base of the short side wall where the ceiling slanted steeply downward. Three wooden poles that looked a lot like boat masts in miniature, each about a few feet long, had been mounted with heavy brass fixtures straight out from where slanted roof met back wall, providing racks for apparel requiring hangers. A bit exposed for her taste, though she did take a moment to skim her gaze over the cotton shirts hanging on the top mast and the folded trousers on hangers that were racked on the pole two below it. All in all, it was a decidedly masculine space that did absolutely nothing to quiet her suddenly needy libido.

She shifted to look to her left and saw that a triangular corner portion of the other end of the loft had been walled off and turned into what was clearly a bathroom. Complete with shower that apparently fit a man and a dog.

She tried not to be charmed by the idea of Brodie and Whomper howling in unison as they scrubbed free of rotting fish remains, but it was damn near impossible. Grinning despite herself, she had turned to head back down the stairs when the water was abruptly shut off and an instant later the bathroom door was flung open.

"On with you now, ye little heathen," Brodie commanded. "Go find your ma."

A split second later, her freshly scrubbed ball of scruff shot out of the bathroom like a sodden bullet, slid to a stop not a foot from her floor-level face, and shook for all he was worth.

"Augh!" she spluttered, unable in her present position to do anything but take the full frontal shower square in the face as she held on to the railing to keep from stumbling down the metal stairs. Spitting at the short strands of dog fur clinging to her cheeks and lips, she was trying to keep her balance on the stairs when the floorboards creaked right next to her—which was when she made mistake number two. She looked up at the man presently towering over her, wrapped in nothing more than a navy blue and white striped terrycloth towel, which, from her vantage point, didn't really cover . . . anything.

"For heaven's sake," she cried, squeezing her eyes shut, but far, far too late to block out confirmation that the genetic fairies hadn't just been drunk off their asses when they'd created him. They'd apparently been high as well. Because . . . well, that kind of generosity in the face of all the other assets bestowed on him was just downright ridiculous.

Unless, of course, I am the one who'd be benefitting from it.

She squeezed her eyes more tightly, hoping to squeeze that thought right out of her head along with it.

"There you are," he said. "We're through if you'd like a quick rinse, and at the risk of being rude, I'd encourage ye to take the offer."

She cracked one eye open in time to see him wrinkle his nose a bit as he shot Whomper a quick wink. She shifted her gaze to her dog, who sat at the top of the stairs, stubby tail wagging for all its worth, eyes shining in eternal glee at the grand adventure the day had turned out to be.

"Speak for yourself," she quietly informed her little beast. Adventure, yes, but grand wasn't quite how she'd have defined it. "I, ah—" She turned away from the dog, then quickly looked down, over, anywhere but up at the man in the towel. Surely from the broad grin once again splitting his handsome face, he'd realized the show he was putting on. Inadvertent or not, that was exactly the kind of man she'd pegged him to be, so she had no reason to be so disappointed at the confirmation.

She decided right then and there that following him inside had been a mistake, one that needed to be immediately rectified. He'd call whoever he needed to call and find out that she was indeed the owner of the boathouse, and they'd eventually come to some sort of détente. Or not.

At the moment, exiting the building seemed mandatory. And she didn't feel the least bit guilty over taking the coward's way out and avoiding further confrontation. "I can clean up where I'm staying. I'll, uh, just get the two of us out of your, um—"

She really shouldn't be stuttering and stammering. It wasn't as if she hadn't seen man parts before, although perhaps none so, generously—um, proportioned. And certainly not from her current vantage point. Exactly. *Jeez, just get on with it already.* "Contact the county offices and they can go over everything. I assure you my paperwork is all in order and, if necessary, we can always—"

"Talk right here, right now," he finished for her. "As you were there, and you've got the papers, you can go over them with me. Then we'll call whoever we must and get this whole thing put to rights."

"There's no rights to put things into," she said, then grimaced at the twisted wording. "What I mean is, there's nothing that needs fixing. I was merely saying that if you need further proof, or you want to find out why they handled things the way they did, that's the direction to take. You really don't need me for that, and it's possible you'll be thankful I'm not there."

"Meaning?"

She might have glanced up. Again. She really had to stop that. And he really had to move. Or she did. To that end, she turned on the stairs, keeping a death grip on the twisted iron railing as she wasn't entirely certain her knees wouldn't betray her sudden, overly avid interest in his genetic, um . . . prowess.

"Meaning you didn't look too happy to find out that neither Sue Clemmons nor Cami saw fit to let you know what was going on with the property. Property you clearly thought was under your control. So maybe it's best if you handle that privately, that's all. It's your personal business, not mine."

"Cami Weathersby?"

Grace paused and turned back, relieved to see he'd moved closer to the railing, which pressed the towel against his legs, and formed a merciful barrier between her gaze and his—*seriously, can't you think about* anything *other than that?* "Uh, yes, Cami Weathersby. Why? Do you know her?"

His smile faded and his expression darkened in a way it hadn't before. She was surprised by how much it changed him. She'd already imagined he woke up smiling, then just went about being charming perfection the rest of the day, leaving a long line of lusting, desirous women in his wake.

"Aye, indeed I do." The darker edge, she realized, was anger. He'd been shocked before, insulted, hurt even, then annoyed and dismissive. But if she wasn't mistaken, he was well and truly pissed.

Frowning, she asked, "Is there something about her I should know?"

"No, but perhaps ye've a point and we should meet at a later time."

For the first time, a trickle of unease slid down her spine. "Why is that?"

"You were right about it being personal business. I need to make a few calls."

The trickle became a steady stream. She had no idea what Brodie might be able to accomplish with a few phone calls and she didn't want to find out. The main problem with being the newest addition to the Blueberry Cove citizen roster was that she had no real contacts beyond those who had helped her achieve the first step in her dream. Worse, she had no knowledge of anyone's background or interpersonal history, not even the few she'd dealt with personally.

Grace gave in. "You know, on second thought, I can barely stand the smell of myself, and I don't need to stink up my car. Why don't I take you up on that offer to rinse off, and then we can head to the county offices together." There was the little matter of her needing to get a change of clothes in there somewhere, but one step at a time.

He looked like he was going to nix the idea and go his own way. He definitely wanted to, she could tell, but hospitality—or her stench—won out. "Help yourself to the shower. I left a pair of track pants, a tee, and a jumper in there for you. You'll likely—"

"Jumper?"

"Oh, erm, a sweater, yes."

"Ah. And track pants. Like a sweat suit, then."

"Aye. They'll swim on you to be certain, but you needed something to wear. I put a large plastic dustbin liner in there to put your smelly things in."

"Thank you," she said, giving herself an internal eye roll as she thought how she'd been drooling over his sea of a bed and imagining the two of them rolling in those white linen sheets . . . all while he'd been thinking of her as a "smelly thing." Which she was. *Yeah, it's past the time to get your head back where it needs to be. On business. And business only.*

She turned and climbed up the stairs again, wincing as she grabbed on to the railing with her splintered palm. "I won't be but a few minutes. Then we can make the calls—"

"Here, let's have another look," he said, taking her good hand before she could dodge the assist and helping her step up onto the loft floor.

"It's okay," she said, damning the hint of breathlessness in her voice. It didn't help that not only was he wearing even less than the last time he'd touched her, but he was framed by the impossibly wide expanse of bed behind him. Made even more inviting by the rumpled pile of old, faded quilts and oversized pillows. *Eyes on the splinters, not on the bed. Or the towel. And for God's sake, stop thinking about what's under it.*

"Come on into the bathroom with me. I've got tweezers there." At her arched eyebrow, he grinned and it so effortlessly transformed him from brooding Irishman back into irrepressible charmer, she couldn't help but be a bit

transfixed by the glow of it. He wiggled his dark eyebrows. "I don't tweeze me brows if that's what yer thinkin'. When you live on the docks, splinters are a part of
life."

"I bet," she managed, trying to ignore how dry her
throat was. And how it was pretty much the only dry part
she had left. She slid her hand free. Not touching was a
good idea. Getting some distance was even better. "I'll
find them. Just wait here and I'll be out fast." She didn't
want him phoning anyone while she was cleaning up, but
she couldn't stand the smell of herself another second.
That he was all clean and soapy-smelling, and it appeared
he'd shaved while he was in there, only made her feel
more gross and uncomfortable.

"Medicine cabinet, top shelf for the tweezers, bottom
shelf for the alcohol. It'll go faster if you allow me." He
nodded to her injured left hand. "You're left-handed."

"How did you—"

"I tend to notice details. It's part of my craft."

Disconcerted that he'd been paying that close attention,
she stammered, "Right. Shipbuilding. Boats by hand. I
saw the sign when I came in."

"And yet you didn't notice it when you were off buying up a piece of my property."

"I—the first thing I looked at was the boathouse at the
other end. It sits apart a little and has its"—she broke off,
not wanting to get into the part where she also owned one
of his piers —"other selling points. The big boathouse in
the middle blocked yours from view, so I didn't see it, or
that it had obviously been renovated." She thought back,
wondering how she could have missed it, and realized that
Cami might have steered her specifically to keep her view
of Brodie's place blocked. But she wasn't entirely sure. She
waved a quick hand. "What you've done is amazing. And
the sign outside—that's impressive artwork. Yours?"

He shook his head. "Not part of my skill set. 'Twas a local, a new local." His gaze darted to the open area below, and she caught a brief, wistful look that she'd have missed if she hadn't been staring at him. *Like a besotted idiot.*

"Same local who did the renovation?"

He blinked, looked back to her, and nodded once, the wistful moment gone, but her curiosity over who had engendered that reaction from him lingered. She wondered if the recipient knew of his interest. Wistful meant unfulfilled, or no longer fulfilling. Hmmm . . . "What's her name?"

"Alex MacFarland," he said almost absently, then instantly sharpened up, and she knew he regretted giving her the information.

Why, she wasn't entirely sure. Presumably because he didn't want to give her any help with her renovation, but it could be more than that. In fact, she'd bet it was.

"How did you know it was—"

"A woman?" she finished for him. *Because I'm not blind. And because I wish a man would look all wistful like that when he thought about me.* "Good guess." She glanced down at the lower level. "If she designed this, she's more than a little talented. Multifaceted."

"She restores lighthouses. By trade. Comes from a long line who've done the same. So she's used to thinking outside the box."

A woman with her own proud heritage. *Figures.* He'd understand and appreciate that quality more than most, so of course he'd been drawn to it. That he'd been so quick to mention it said as much. She nodded, and, glancing back at him, noticed that while his praise was sincere, his expression was carefully professional now. She wouldn't have thought he'd have that kind of cool reserve in him. She'd have bet he tossed his charm around so effortlessly and often that a professional façade would be an unnecessary addition to his arsenal. Although in his line of work, he likely dealt mostly with men. Men who probably secretly wished they were him, while not-so-secretly making sure they kept their women away from him. And not necessarily because they distrusted Brodie.

"Have you started any projects yet? Boats, I mean?" she asked, changing topics, though she doubted she'd forget that wistful look anytime soon. Perversely, discovering his heart had even come close to being compromised, when she'd have bet her most challenging estate probate that he was a woman-of-the-moment, love-'em-and-leave-'em-sighing kind of guy, only served to make her tingly parts that much more, well . . . tingly. *Danger, danger, Grace Maddox.*

"Grab a quick rinse and meet me below," he said by way of response. "I'll tell you whatever you want to know."

That lilting edge of command in his tone, paired with that almost taunting promise, had her imagining all sorts of ways he could convince her to tell him whatever *he* wanted to know. Hell, she might have signed the boathouse back over to him. And she couldn't have rightly said that she'd have even minded if that was the kind of persuasion he was looking to employ in the effort.

If, you know, she didn't reek of dead fish.

"Right." She made a gesture to the door behind her. "I'll—just let me—then we'll talk," she managed. Cheeks hot and nipples hard, she escaped behind the bathroom door, then leaned back against it, feeling like the complete and utter idiot that she was. So cool as he thought wistfully about another woman, so calm as she so casually changed the subject. *See how worldly I am? How unaffected?*

She snorted. "Right. You couldn't be more affected." She nearly jumped out of her skin when a sharp knock came on the other side of the door. Pressing a fist to her pounding heart, she turned around, but didn't open it. "Yes?"

"You'll need towels."

She cracked the door open, which was silly, since she hadn't so much as undone a button. But that didn't keep her from feeling somehow naked and defenseless around him.

He held out a folded set of thick, fluffy towels that matched the color of the deep blue water in the harbor. "Thank you," she said, feeling more foolish by the moment. *For God's sake, get a grip, Grace. For real this time.* If she was going to see her dream through to fruition, she couldn't let the first little obstacle she encountered shake her up just because she wanted said obstacle to throw her on his bed and have his charming Irish way with her.

She took the towels. "I won't take long." She started to close the door, but he kept it open. Her gaze flicked to his hand on the doorknob, then back to his face.

"Why are you here?" he asked, his expression still that of the distant professional.

Except she saw that there was nothing professional or distant in those green eyes of his. Storm-tossed seas came to mind.

"You said you've got family here and you were on about putting down new roots with the intent to build something. Presumably using my boathouse as the foundation. Not a law practice, apparently, as you claim that's no longer your professional intent. So . . . what, then? Is your family in shipping? Boatbuilding?"

She blinked, surprised by the question, though she quickly realized it probably seemed the most logical one for him to ask.

"Storage?" he prodded, when she didn't respond right away.

"An inn," she blurted, knowing it was not how she'd intended to have this particular conversation, being on the defensive. "I'm going to turn your—*my*—boathouse into an inn."

His stormy green eyes went wide. "So, it's an innkeeper you are now, is it?"

He hadn't said it unkindly, or even mockingly. Still, she immediately felt her hackles rise. Probably because he'd have been well within his rights to be both of those things, considering. "Aye," she said, mirroring his accent. "That I am."

Or will be. *Just as soon as I figure out how to get you to stay out of my way.*

She clicked the door closed right in his face. Then leaned her cheek against the freshly painted wood and tried desperately to regroup.

"We'll see about that, Grace Maddox," came his voice—far too softly, far too confidently, and all so very, very Irish—through the closed door and right at her ear . . . as if his lips were pressed directly against it. "We'll just see about that."

Chapter 4

"Innkeeper, my skinny Irish arse," Brodie grumbled, then added a few far more colorful thoughts under his breath as the fragrant steam eased under the closed door to the bathroom and filled the loft air. He caught Whomper giving him a baleful eye while keeping a safe distance near the top of the iron stairs. "Don't go chiding me with that look. You might have turned her head with that woe-is-me mug, but you won't trick me. I wrote the book on those tricks."

Whomper just blinked at him and somehow managed to look even smaller and more vulnerable.

"Och, for the love of—" Brodie slapped his thigh. "Come here before ye break me heart."

Instantly perky, the scruffy mongrel wasted no time in getting a running start and launching himself into Brodie's arms. Laughing, he fell back on the bed, twisting his head this way and that to avoid the tongue bath of adoration Whomper insisted was his due reward. "Enough," he said, finally lifting the still-damp mutt away, then laughing again as Whomper merely dangled, legs akimbo, tongue lolling, simply happy to be with his chosen human of the moment. "If only your mistress were half as affable as you." He plopped the dog on the quilt next to him, then rolled up to sit on the edge of the bed, casting his gaze toward the closed bathroom door.

He hadn't looked at every crossed *t* and dotted *i* on the forms she'd handed him earlier, but they'd looked mighty official and orderly. Given she was a lawyer, the chance of their being anything other than completely valid was slim to none. And given he didn't doubt she was, or had been, a very smart lawyer, he also assumed they were ironclad, no loopholes.

He debated the wisdom of calling Cami Weathersby and inviting her and her husband Ted, who was the leader of the town council, to come join the conversation. He wasn't sure if this was a case of personal vengeance on Cami's part, or another of Ted's big plans to raise the town's profile, or some twisted combination of the two. But though it would seem logical to call them, the fact that they'd taken pains to keep him in the dark about the boathouse sale until it was completed led him to think that perhaps it would be best to come at it from a different angle.

Sue Clemmons was also an unwise choice. Though a darling woman and a source of great assistance over the past year as he'd tried to sort through the labyrinth of ownership documents, deeds, and various and sundry other paperwork that detailed the long and storied history of the Monaghan shipyard property, she'd also not seen fit to let him know that one of his buildings was about to be sold out from under him. Why, he didn't know, which was something he needed to find out first.

"What the hell," he grumbled, disturbed, and yes, hurt, to think that the townsfolk who'd so readily embraced him and his cause, many of whom he called friend as well as neighbor, might not be at all what they seemed.

By the time he heard the water cut off in the shower,

he'd pulled on an old pair of jeans, a clean white tee, and a faded blue hoodie with twin *U's* stamped and peeling off the front. In deference to the morning chill, he'd tucked his bare feet into one of the half dozen pairs of aging boat shoes lying about, only half paying attention if one actually matched the other, not really caring if it did. Then he'd gone down to the main floor, made a pot of strong Irish breakfast tea, and began going over the contracts in more detail.

He heard the creak of floorboards, then the slight groan of metal as Grace started down the steps. "You went in my bag," she said, referring to the papers he was poring over.

Not bothering to look up, he said, "You bought my boathouse without my knowledge or consent. I think the scales of fairness swing in my favor." He flipped another page. "Besides, you offered them to me earlier. Yet another thing I can't say in return."

"I didn't know about you," she repeated.

"And if you had?" He lifted his gaze then, and almost choked on his sip of tea. He hadn't given any thought to what she'd look like post-shower, but not in his wildest dreams—and he was a man who knew from wild dreams—would he have conjured up the vision standing before him.

The navy blue track pants and old faded tee shouldn't have been remotely provocative on her, especially since they shrouded her slight frame. And yet, somehow, all the extra fabric in the pants had pooled around her ankles in a way that left the rest clinging to shapely legs and a much curvier bum than he'd noticed on the docks, thanks to the coat she'd been wearing. Topping that, his old, pale green T-shirt had been turned siren hot by the fact that apparently her undergarments had also been tainted by the fish smell, and she clearly wasn't wearing a bra. His gaze dipped lower again, and he shifted in his seat as his body responded to the realization that she'd probably had to go commando . . . everywhere.

He might have even gotten past the full breasts with those pointy little nipples and the limber thighs and . . . damn. He shifted in his seat again. But there was no getting past the hair. That plain brown, pulled-back-in-a-tail hair was a completely different beast. Released on its own recognizance, it was a damp, wild thing with a life of its own, curls and waves bouncing and coiling about her head like Medusa's snakes. Only a hell of a lot sexier.

"I've made tea," he said, knowing it sounded every bit as inane as he suddenly felt. He started to push back his chair and stand, thinking that doing something, anything, to redirect his attention would be a good idea, only to realize at the last possible moment that standing would reveal certain . . . reactions. While fair was fair given the raging nipples she was sporting, standing seemed rather a bit too . . . aggressive on his part.

"If I had known about you," she said, ignoring the tea comment, "I'd have made a point of meeting you and discussing things before going forward. As I said before, I was led to believe that the entire property had been abandoned decades ago."

"Cami told you that?" he asked, turning his attention back to the papers, willing his body to turn its attention to something else, as well.

"You know, I ran our conversations through my mind while I was in the shower, and I realized that she was careful in how she presented the place, but the intent was for me to believe that it was abandoned and up for grabs." Grace went down the stairs and bent to ruffle the fur on Whomper's head, sending him into blissful, wriggling rapture.

Brodie glanced over in time to see her heart in her eyes as she gave the mutt a scratch behind the ears for good measure.

Only a hint of that indulgent smile remained when she straightened and crossed the room toward the small kitchen, but he knew it would be a very long time before he erased that look from his mind. *Lucky dog.*

She cast him a quick glance, but he was mercifully saved from having to pretend he wasn't looking at the front of his old T-shirt when she skirted the table and went directly to the teapot still sitting on the stove.

"So," she said, filling the empty teacup he'd left on the counter for her, "what did you do to annoy the Cove's number-one Realtor? Or is that advertisement not true, either? She seemed pretty knowledgeable about the area, I will say. Said she was born here."

Caught off guard by the insult, Brodie's mouth dropped open, but it only took him a moment to regroup. "You've concluded after knowing me for less than an hour that it was somehow something I've done. Would this be a broad gender classification I'm being assigned, or have I done something to specifically lead you to that assumption?"

He saw the hint of a smile ghost her lips as she pulled out a chair and set across from him, cradling her teacup between her hands. That reminded him. "Did you get the splinter out?" He nodded to her palm.

"Mostly. I borrowed a few Band-Aids from the medicine cabinet." She lifted her hand and flashed him a palm covered with two small strips. "I hope you don't mind. And no, I wasn't man bashing, merely making an observation based on, well, my observations." A wry smile peeked out more fully around the corners of her teacup and did the damndest thing to him.

He was reaching across the small table for her hand before he even realized his intent—which was to touch her.

Somehow, some way. He gently pried her hand from the teacup, which she set down.

Her lifted eyebrows clearly indicating her surprise at the move. And yet, she didn't pull her hand away. "It's fine."

"Mostly," he echoed, then cradled her hand while tugging the small strips up and off. "Well, ye've gone and butchered it up now, haven't you?"

"I got the biggest one."

A smile threatened at the hint of defensiveness in her tone. Didn't take kindly to having her judgment questioned, this one. It didn't bode well at all for him with the recent turn of events, and yet, his amusement hovered just the same.

"Well, I'm not too proud to say I'm something of an expert at splinter removal. Sit tight." He scooted his chair back, crossed the room, and spryly took the iron stairs a few at a time.

Whomper thumped his tail and whined low, apparently torn on whether to give merry chase or stay by Grace's side.

You picked a good one, you did, Grace. Loyal, he'll be.

"Stay down there with your mistress," Brodie called to the pup, whose tail took on a much merrier wag, eyes shining once again. "I'll be back in a jiff."

Grace looked between the two of them and merely rolled her eyes. But he didn't miss the way she reached down and reassured the mutt with another scratch between the ears.

He gathered from what he'd overheard and her other comments that Whomper was a recent addition to her life, possibly part of the big move and new future plans she was undertaking. He also gathered that acquiring a canine companion hadn't necessarily been part of the original plan and wondered if she'd given real thought to any of it, or if she was on some kind of pre-midlife bender. "First a pet owner and now she fancies herself an innkeeper as well," he murmured under his breath.

He returned to find she'd pressed the strips back across her palm and was rinsing out her teacup in the sink.

"Have a sit-down," he instructed. "We'll get you right as rain."

She turned and leaned against the counter, folding her arms and tucking her hands away for good measure. "Do you always assume people will do whatever you tell them to do?"

She'd said it lightly enough, but his brows rose all the same. "I'm only tryin' to help."

She surprised him once again by laughing. A full-on, heartfelt guffaw.

"I think I've just been insulted."

With her wild hair, casual clothes and all of her carefully constructed defenses nowhere in sight, the woman standing before him was a far cry from the suited-up, laced-up lawyer he'd met on the docks. Of course, there had been the colorful and equally heartfelt swearing. . . . He didn't want to be intrigued by her, and yet there was no escaping it.

She sat down across from him, peeled the bandages back herself, and sporting a fairly self-satisfied grin, plopped her left hand, palm up, on the table between them. "Do your worst."

"Never, lass," he said, taking up her hand again. "Only me best."

She let out a spurt of sound that was more giggle than laugh, and he aimed one arched brow in her direction before bending to the task.

"Oh, don't go being offended," she said, as he tilted her palm this way, then that, trying to find the jutting ends of the little bastards still wedged in the soft flesh of her palm. "I don't doubt your claim. I laughed because you sincerely have no idea how charmed you are, do you? And I don't mean charm*ing*. I know you're well aware of your natural-born assets."

He glanced up briefly at that, but opted to remain silent as he resumed his task. She'd said it kindly enough. And it was true enough.

"What I mean is, you're kind of clueless about the end result of being so blessed. You're so used to rolling through life, flashing those dimples and wielding that brogue of yours, a wink of your green eyes, soliciting smiles wherever you go with this bit of flattering nonsense or that, I'm betting folks fall happily in line with whatever it is you have in mind even when you're not trying to persuade them to your way of thinking. So, you don't really understand resistance, do you? Because it simply doesn't happen to you—which is why it was funny, the look you gave me, as if you couldn't fathom why I wouldn't just plop down and let you dig in the palm of my hand."

"It's no' about charm or gettin' my way." He glanced up briefly again, noting that when her eyes danced with laughter, they turned a particular shade of bluish-green that reminded him of the waters of home. "It's about doing what makes the most sense." He bent his head again and tried not to think of dancing eyes. Or home. He'd agree that a little Irish accent could go a long way toward charming his way into others' good graces. Here in the States. At home, his brogue wasn't special. And neither was he. "Hold still now. This might hurt a little."

He made quick business of plucking out the tiny slivers, and other than a few winces and a sucked-in breath here or there, she didn't so much as flinch. He dabbed a little of the antibiotic he'd brought downstairs with him onto a fresh bandage and gently pressed it to the pink sides of her palm, then put another crossways to help hold it in place. "There." He rubbed the side of his thumb over the calluses that ran across the top of her palm and the bottom pads of her fingers and risked another look at those dancing sea eyes.

"Rowing," she said in answer to his silent question.

That surprised him, though why he wasn't sure. "You row? To where? You live on an island and boat to work, do you?"

She smiled. "I live—lived—in a condo in Old Town, Alexandria. Virginia," she clarified when he didn't nod in understanding. "And though it is across a river from where I worked in D.C., no, I did not row to work. Though, come to think of it, it might have been easier, not to mention faster."

"So, you row out on this river to do what? Drop a line? Do you fish?"

She made a face. "No. Not that I have anything against it. The seafood here is so amazing, it's like I've never tasted fresh fish before. But me, putting bait on a hook? No, that would be my brother, not me. Although I'm not sure even he does that anymore."

She'd mentioned family earlier, that she'd come to Maine for the purpose of reuniting hers. It was on the tip of his tongue to ask about her brother, but something flickered in her eyes. Pain? Regret? Something other than warmth or love, for sure. Whatever it was, it was gone as quickly as it came, but it was enough so that he left the topic alone. For now. "So you row for . . . ?"

She shrugged. "Fun. It's good exercise." She grinned again at his confused expression and made a show of flexing her biceps, which admittedly had a fairly impressive curve to them.

He nodded and tried not to think about her other impressive curves. "So, in a canoe, then. A dinghy or dory or some such. You just row about?"

"You sail about, right? What's the difference? I row in a

scull." She laughed when his eyes widened. "You build boats for a living and you haven't heard of a scull?"

"Oh, aye. Those long, sleek laddies made to glide over the surface of the water, seats that slide so you can move legs and arms in unison to pull the long oars, sending yourself skimming through waters like a dragonfly skating just along the surface. Body, boat, and soul moving as one, master of your direction, and feeling, perhaps, the master of your own destiny as well." He smiled. "Something like that, is it?"

Her lips parted slightly, and he knew he'd captured exactly what drew her to the sport, just as he knew his insight had startled her. He found he rather liked being unexpected. Maybe it was her dinging him on not being used to being thwarted, or that she so obviously thought she had him summed up, but whatever the case, he knew he could get used to finding new ways to surprise her.

"Something like that," she said quietly and started to slide her hand away.

He tightened his hold then, just enough to keep her in his grasp. "Aye, I know of them, though I've never been called upon to build one. Perhaps I was just surprised that you did. Although I suppose I shouldn't be. The regimen of manning such a disciplined vessel and mastering such a sport would probably appeal to one as proper as you."

Her lovely amber-green eyes widened a bit at that. "Why do you think me proper?"

"We're in a small coastal fishing town where the most formal attire is a new pair of wellies, and even that only lasts an excursion or two. Yet, you're out on my docks in your big city coat, fancy shoes, proper leather satchel."

"I had just been at the bank to meet with—"

"Our sweet Sue. Aye, indeed. Who was likely wearin' a jumper made with more heart than skill by her granddaughter's own hands and a comfortable pair of denims."

He grinned, knowing from her expression he had the right of it.

He couldn't say what made him do it, only that it seemed the right thing in that moment. He lifted her hand to his lips, palm up. He didn't kiss the wound in the center of her palm, but instead pressed a soft kiss to the calluses, then rolled her fingertips over them as he let her hand go. "That you've found joy on the water is something I know and respect. It's a lucky thing to know, and an even luckier thing to have. Have you ever sailed?"

She blinked, absently shook her head, and protectively slid her curled hand to her lap, out of view. He knew she was dwelling on the kiss, or how he had described being on the water. Or some combination of the two. Truth be told, so was he. So much so that rising from his seat would once again prove a bit too revelatory. He was going to have to do something about that. The problem was, what he wanted to do and what was the wiser thing regarding his property, were on opposite ends of the solution spectrum.

And she was right . . . he wasn't used to encountering resistance.

Perhaps he'd go about finding a way to have both. "Well, that's something we'll have to rectify then, won't we?"

Chapter 5

"I'm not questioning that the property was legally available for the price of back taxes. I paid them myself. I have the deed in hand." Grace propped the phone between her ear and her shoulder as she raked her free hand through her still-damp hair, then held onto it in a tail in her fist at the back of her head, trying to hold on to her patience, as well. "I just—I was curious why I wasn't made aware of the fact that there is a Monaghan currently living and working on the premises of Monaghan Shipbuilders."

She knew instead of talking to Cami Weathersby, trying to find out what amounted to local gossip, she should be on the phone with her architect, plotting out the first steps toward turning her boathouse into the inn of her dreams. She owned the place, it was hers, the rest was Brodie's problem. But just because she'd pointed out to him that she was on to his charming ways didn't mean she was immune to them herself. Far from it. She'd be reliving that moment when he'd glanced up at her through those ridiculously thick dark lashes of his, just before pressing those warm, hint-of-a-smile lips to her skin for days. Weeks.

She couldn't risk that he'd somehow charmed her attention away from the giant red flag that might be waving right in front of her face. Something was going on between the town and Brodie and, like it or not, Grace owned a piece of the town and was likely going to find herself smack in the middle of it, whether she wanted to be or not. If Brodie was going to try to get the sale overturned—charm and palm kissing aside, she had every reason to believe he would—she had no choice but to arm herself with as much information as she could, right from the start.

"Oh. Well. So, you've met Brodie then," Cami responded.

Did you think I wouldn't notice he lived there? "We've become acquainted," was all Grace said.

There was a pause, and perhaps it felt like a pregnant one because Grace was on high alert.

"The sale went through late yesterday," Cami said.

And in record time, Grace wanted to add, but didn't. She'd assumed they'd pushed it through quickly so the back taxes would get paid and they could dump the property before Grace changed her mind. But that didn't excuse them not alerting Brodie to the impending purchase. Not that they had a legal obligation to do so, but surely an ethical or moral one. In small towns, those often took precedence.

When Cami had set up the list of Cove properties for Grace to look at a mere week ago, the boathouse wasn't even on the printout. In fact, it had seemed almost an afterthought on Cami's part, like something that came up because they were in the area, but she hadn't thought to mention as, surely, Grace wasn't interested in something like that. Cami had talked about the sad condition of the property, adding in the tax issue almost off-handedly. In fact, Grace realized it had been her own idea to stop in and give it a look. Had Cami intended that outcome? Grace really had no way of knowing.

When she'd decided to buy it and brought up the point

that, since it was a tax buyout from the town, Cami wouldn't earn anything on the sale, the perky blonde had waved it off with a smile. She'd seemed very sincere about being happy she was able to do such a big favor for the community. She'd even mentioned that her husband Ted was head of the town council, and that he would also be thrilled to see even part of the property find renewed life. She'd gone on about how her family had ties to the community going back more than five generations and Ted's almost as many. Putting the legacy of the Cove above all else was something they tried to do whenever possible.

Admittedly, at that point Grace had thought Cami sounded a bit disingenuous. It didn't take a law degree to figure out that if the rundown waterfront property showed signs of regeneration, it would only mean good things for property values in the harbor area and therefore a greater likelihood that Cami would make commissions on other local properties that she did represent. But Cami's intent hadn't mattered to Grace at the time.

"Yes, I know," Grace said in response, "and I was really relieved and happy that you were willing to work so quickly to get the paperwork done and processed." That was true enough, though the chirpy tone that had crept into her voice was a bit wince-worthy. "I was so eager to get started, I went right down to the docks after my early appointment this morning with—"

"Sue Clemmons, at the bank, yes. I was in this morning myself and she mentioned it," Cami added quickly.

Grace paused a moment then said, "Yes, well, my hope is to get the ball rolling on the boathouse renovation and take advantage of the good weather while we have it. So you can imagine how surprised I was when I went down there this morning and discovered someone living in the boathouse at the other end of the property. Someone whose last name is the same as the one on the side of the largest boathouse. He says he has claim to the entire property.

"Now," she continued before Cami could speak, "I know the property I purchased is legally mine, but shouldn't he have been informed of the pending sale? I know it went through quickly, but . . ." She trailed off on purpose, hoping she simply sounded naturally inquisitive and not accusatory.

"Brodie was well aware of the situation regarding the property," Cami assured her, all brisk business. "Is he— what did he say, exactly? Is he giving you problems because of this?"

At the honest concern in Cami's voice—though it wasn't so much concern, as, well, avid interest, perhaps?— Grace straightened and let her hair fall back around her shoulders. It felt heavy on her neck, and she felt silly for not putting it up again when she'd gotten back to the room she'd been renting on the outskirts of the Cove. She'd started to pull it up in a ponytail, but couldn't shake the way Brodie's eyes had gone all dark and hot when he'd first spied her on the iron stairs with her hair down and wild. Now she just felt silly and vapid.

"Should he be?" Grace asked, knowing she couldn't keep letting the man distract her. "Am I going to be facing some sort of battle over this?"

"I can't see why he would. If he'd wanted to do something to secure it, he's had plenty of time. As you could see, he hasn't really done anything."

Grace wouldn't say that the total renovation of the boathouse he was using as his residence and office was nothing, but she wasn't going to argue the point.

"The property is yours," Cami stated flatly. "And that's all that matters. We're all excited about this new venture," she went on quickly.

Grace didn't ask who *all* was comprised of, but knowing small towns and how long the waterfront property had been dormant, she imagined word was spreading quickly. She hoped that was a good thing. She wanted to get to know her new neighbors and wanted them to have a positive attitude about her future inn.

"I'm really happy to hear that," Grace said sincerely. "The thing is, living and doing business on the same property, Brodie and I will have to work in some kind of joint fashion, but we don't necessarily share the same overall vision. You can probably understand that he wasn't exactly thrilled to find out part of his property had been sold out from under him. So, being new to town and with you being so connected, what with your family background here and all," Grace added, shamelessly sucking up a little if it meant getting the inside scoop, "I was hoping maybe you could shed some behind-the-scenes light on the situation."

Cami was more than eager to reply. "Well, there's no light to shed, really. I'm not sure what he told you, Grace, but he's been here a full year, and other than fixing up that boathouse he lives in and one of the outbuildings where he's building one of his boats, he hasn't made any real headway or shown any real interest at all in reinvigorating his family's former business. Not in any appreciable way that we can see, anyway. I mean, one boat does not an empire rebuild, you know? The town officials, the council—everyone was excited when he showed up, believe you me, thrilled even, that the eyesore the Monaghan property had become was finally going to get some attention. I know from my husband that they bent over backwards to come up with a payment plan regarding the back taxes, all with the hope of seeing some change come to pass. Only it hasn't."

"Well, a year isn't that long when most of it's winter, and he's only one man. Property of that scope and size is a pretty massive undertaking. I—" Grace broke off, realizing she was actually supporting Brodie's argument. Her plan when she'd called Cami had been to remain neutral, the newcomer eager to work with everyone, wanting her business to be the right fit, etcetera. All true. But something about Cami's explanation, the air of condescension toward Brodie, rubbed Grace the wrong way, and she'd spoken without thinking. "I just want to make sure we're all on the same page. I've explained to Mr. Monaghan that I intend to honor his family's legacy and, if anything, my ownership has lightened his burden somewhat."

"Exactly!" Cami chirped. "Win-win for everybody, just as I said. And don't you worry about his feathers being a little ruffled. I'll speak with my husband and make sure everything is fine there. Frankly, like you, I thought he'd be happy about it; that's why I didn't give it a second thought."

Now Cami, that's not really true, is it? Grace thought, her instincts and Cami's too-eager-to-gloss-things-over chirpiness telling her something else was definitely going on. Grace wasn't looking to be best pals with her Realtor, but she did wish Cami respected her intellect a little more. She'd been quite happy with how quickly Cami had moved everything through, even patting herself on the back for picking someone with Cami's extensive connections. But while Cami's family history was a strength when it came to making things happen, Grace was well aware those same connections could work against her if Cami got it in her mind that maybe Grace wasn't such a good fit for Blueberry Cove after all.

"Well, as I said, we'll be practically living on top of each other and, as someone with a vested interest in launching a new business in town and being part of the hoped-for growth potential for Half Moon Harbor that you spoke of, of course, I want to make sure it all goes as smoothly as possible. For everybody's sake. Win-win." She tried to strike a balance between too-chirpy and giving away her true feelings, which were going to be a little more complicated than she'd initially thought. Maybe a lot more.

"Yes, well, as you said, all on the same page," Cami echoed. "I'm so glad you called me so I could clear up any anxiety you might be feeling."

If muddy waters are clear, Grace thought.

"It's exciting, isn't it? This new project of yours. I hope you don't mind, I've already spread the word a little. I figure we fellow businesswomen should always support each other. Small towns are still such men's clubs, and this far up the coast, it can be even more retrograde, trust me." She laughed in an overly bright way that made Grace wince a little and decide right then and there that no matter the stakes or people involved, she was personally all chirped out.

"If they only knew how easy they were to read, right?" Cami went on. "If we can't work over them, we just work our way right around them."

Sort of like you just worked your way around Brodie. Grace opened her mouth to make some kind of polite response and bring the conversation to a close. She was thankful for Cami's help in securing her inn property, but bosom businesswomen buddies wasn't where she saw things heading.

"Is it true you've retained Langston deVry as your architect?"

Whatever Grace might have said to end the conversation went right out the window. "I—how did you know I'd retained Langston?" She swore under her breath, realizing she'd confirmed Cami's query. But she had retained him, and that wasn't any kind of big secret . . . though she hadn't told a soul in Blueberry Cove about him as yet. In fact, she hadn't even mentioned his name since arriving in town.

"Oh, I don't even remember now." Cami's perky voice

took on an even higher chirpy note, indicating Grace's query had unnerved her a bit. Maybe she wasn't used to dealing with people who actually paid attention to what was being said. "Is he—Langston, I mean—will he be coming to the Cove soon, then?"

Every instinct Grace had went on full alert. There *was* more going on. She just had to figure out what, exactly. "He does such great work," Grace said carefully, saccharine free. "I guess it's not surprising that you've heard of him. Do you know him personally, then?"

"As it happens, Langston is a good friend of my father's. They were Harvard men. Small world, right?"

Grace didn't think of Harvard grads as collectively being all that small a club, but she said nothing.

"With Langston's business being based out of Boston, they've lost touch over the years. You know how that is. When I mentioned it to Daddy, naturally he was excited about the prospect of seeing his old friend again."

"I imagine so," Grace said, still trying to figure out how Cami had even heard whom she'd hired, much less how Langston's connections to one of the Cove's oldest families might affect her plans. Now that Grace thought about it, she had taken a call from him while she'd been waiting for the loan papers to be drawn up. She'd probably said his first name when she'd answered the phone, but she'd been sitting alone by Sue's desk. Who would have overheard that or even cared, much less put two and two together to figure out who Langston was? *What the hell kind of town am I moving to?*

The town where Ford lived. Ultimately, that was really all that mattered.

"I don't know what his plans are," Grace cautioned, "or even if he'll make a stop personally."

"Oh, but you have to get him to pop in. Surely you'll

want him to see the property firsthand. How is it that you know him? Have you worked with him before?"

Grace knew Langston deVry because she'd been the lawyer who had handled the probate when Langston's wife had died suddenly in a car accident shortly after their quickie wedding, and unfortunately before they'd had the chance to sort through all of the his-and-hers details of their personal holdings. As she'd been his fourth wife and a good twenty years his junior, Grace had been surprised to find Langston sincerely and truly devastated by his sudden loss. He'd been in no shape to deal with his late wife's family, who'd all crawled out of the woodwork to see what, if anything, they could lay claim to in her name.

For all that Langston was a very wealthy, highly celebrated, and respected architect who ran a successful firm that operated on more than one continent, with offices on both coasts in the U.S., as well as London and Tokyo, Grace had ended up feeling very protective of him during the long, drawn-out proceedings. It was something she wouldn't have thought he'd take notice of, assuming he expected nothing less from those who worked on his behalf. But notice her he had.

That had been five years ago. He was the nearest thing she had to family. Of course, the path to their friendship had been . . . interesting, to say the least, but with Langston, there could be no other way. His approach to his work mirrored his approach to life, meaning it wasn't exactly linear. He'd even made a move on her at one point, a year or so after his wife's death, despite being almost thirty years her senior. She'd politely declined, which had actually been a turning point—it was rare anyone said no to him, most particularly women—and her independence had served to strengthen what had gone on to become a very trusting and loyal friendship.

She would never categorize him as being particularly fatherly, or even avuncular. He was far too flamboyant and charismatic for that—worldly genius mentor-slash-BFF was more like it, a cross-generational duality only Langston could truly embody. But that hadn't stopped him from trying to match her up with every up-and-comer he could con her into meeting. She was wise to his games and usually managed to sidestep his Cupid maneuvers.

Whatever the label that best described their relationship, she trusted him more than anyone else in her life and often sought his counsel. More in business matters than personal ones, though that didn't stop him from butting in on both. When she'd finally shared her crazy, impossible, totally nutso idea about the big life change she was contemplating, he'd immediately tried to talk her out of it. Normally, that would have been that. She trusted him. He'd done, seen, experienced, so much more than she had. Instead, it perversely made her more determined . . . as if she had to show him she was right.

In typical Langston fashion, once he'd realized he couldn't change her mind, he'd tried to commandeer and orchestrate her big move, but it was something she was determined to do on her own. Though she'd wrestled control of her life back, mostly because he was far too busy to meddle consistently from long distance—he did that particularly well when he put his mind to it—one thing had remained irrevocable. Whatever place she found, whatever property she chose, he was doing the renovation and remodel. No questions, no buts, no nothing.

There was no way she could explain any of that to Cami Weathersby, nor would she have tried. "We were business acquaintances a few years back," was all Grace said.

Cami made appreciative noises. "Working your contacts. Good for you! Well, please feel free to name-drop Daddy if it will help your cause. Brooks Winstock. We'd love to have Langston to dinner," she said brightly. After a pause, she added, "With you, too, of course."

In the privacy of her room, Grace rolled her eyes.

"Well," Cami said, her voice hitting that wince-worthy note again, "this is turning out to be just all kinds of fun! I know you're busy as the proverbial bee, as am I, but I'm so glad we could have this little chat. As always, you can turn to me for anything. Professional or personal. We girls—"

"Stick together," Grace finished, her jaw aching along with her head. "I appreciate it. I'll let you go. Thanks again." She clicked off before so much as another chirp could come through her earpiece. She immediately tossed the Bluetooth device on the bed, then slumped down next to it.

Whomper leaped up on the bed, gave her cheek a quick swipe, then settled next to her as she flopped onto her back, propping his chin on her arm. She glanced down into soulful brown eyes that seemed to say, "I understand. I'm here for you."

She sighed and scratched him behind his ears. Whomper wriggled closer, nudging her hand again to keep her scratching and petting him. She smiled and shook her head. "Clearly I'm helpless against the charms of sparkly-eyed males." Whomper's quick bark, as if in complete agreement, made her laugh out loud. "What have we gotten ourselves into, my furry little friend, huh?"

She needed to call Langston and let him know about his Blueberry Cove connection. For all she knew, he'd be delighted to be reunited with his old college buddy, but forewarned is forearmed. Something neither she nor Brodie had had the luxury of being. She thought about the boathouse. Staring at the ceiling, she tried to clear everything out of her mind, take a step back from what she wanted, and truly consider whether or not it would be the wiser thing to work out some kind of deal where she sold it to Brodie. "Who clearly would have paid the taxes himself if he had the money, so yeah." Not really a solution.

While her investments had held up reasonably well despite economic fluctuations, buying another property outright was beyond her, because it would mean taking on a mortgage in addition to the business loan she'd already gotten. Plus, it might put her business loan in jeopardy if she suddenly became fickle and hopscotched properties.

Even if those realities weren't in play, she'd seen most of the properties on Cami's list before checking out the boathouse, and none of them had been the right fit. There was no second runner-up that had caught her eye or any part of her heart. Certainly nothing had captivated her the way the boathouse had. Going outside the Cove was not really a viable alternative, and not simply because she wanted to be as close to Ford as possible.

She was presently staying at the only inn anywhere near the Cove, and it wasn't even close to the water. She'd booked there to avoid small-town speculation while she looked at properties, which was sort of humorous, since she had confirmation that Cami had spread the word the moment she'd taken interest in the Monaghan property. But Blueberry Cove was tucked along the shores of Pelican Bay, which was located in the Acadia region of Maine. Down East, as the locals called it, was a nautical term—down east referred to the winds and currents used by boat captains out on the water—and was not a geographic term. Pelican Bay was really up north.

The coastal region in that part of Maine was far more rural and sparsely populated than places like Bar Harbor and other points south along the mid-coast region, heading down toward Boothbay and Portland. She was taking a pretty big risk establishing an inn in the more remote region, so moving away from the Pelican Bay area would more or less doom her already narrow window for success. She'd been banking on her family connection in Blueberry Cove to gain the trust and support of the community as she launched her business. Elsewhere, she'd be what the locals called a PFA—Person From Away—and unlikely to gain any such support. As it was, there was no guarantee she'd get support in Blueberry Cove. She was still a PFA, but she'd hoped family would count for something.

Of course, for all she knew, Ford had alienated himself from the locals just as he had from everyone else who cared about him. But he was still in the Cove, that much she knew. The fact that he'd been a resident for more than a decade had to count for something.

She thought about Brodie, whose family stretched back seven generations to the very founding of the town, and how he'd still been screwed over. She smirked in self-deprecation over thinking that her brother's residence of a whopping decade was going to be some kind of insurance.

She scratched Whomper's ears and gave him a little pat. "We are so screwed, little man." She closed her eyes and let out a deep sigh. A smart person would give the property to the Irishman and run, cutting her losses and being thankful the hard lesson hadn't been more costly.

She opened her eyes and tilted her chin, giving the scruffy mutt a sideways glance. "But where has playing it smart gotten me really, eh?"

Sink or swim, she had a connection there, estranged though it might be. Ford had to realize she was serious and understand she was also permanent. In Blueberry Cove . . . and if he'd let her, in his life.

She thought about the questions that had led her to Blueberry Cove and Half Moon Harbor. For the past eight years she'd watched as countless families contended with and found answers to those very same questions. When she died, what was it she'd look back on with the greatest sense of pride? What would she recall with the most tender, the most profound emotions? Would it be a person, a place, a thing? And most important, how would she measure her life? What would be considered a success? A failure? How would she measure the role she'd played in what she'd achieved? Or what she hadn't?

All she knew was that the life she'd been living, the person she'd been content to become, had no decent answer to any of those questions. Not one she could be happy or satisfied with, at any rate. And that, she'd realized, wasn't the kind of someone she wanted to be.

"Well, one thing that won't be an answer to any of those questions is my inn, unless I get up and start making it happen."

Whomper thumped his stubby tail and gave a quick bark.

Grace laughed and scooped him up as she curled herself back upright. "Maybe you'll turn out to be my goodwill ambassador," she said, holding him up so they were nose to nose, leaving his rear legs dangling. "You can go guy bond with Brodie while I try not to destroy the man's heritage in an effort to begin one of my own." She set Whomper on the floor and grabbed her Bluetooth and her phone, punching the speed-dial button for Langston. "Ready or not, Brodie, Ford, the entire town of Blueberry Cove, and the whole rest of my life . . . here I come."

Chapter 6

"Here barely a fortnight, and she's already turned my life upside down. Women, eh?" Brodie ran the pine plank through the surface planer, careful not to let his frustration add weight to the pressure he was exerting on the wood. "Man can't live without them and be truly happy. Or at least not be horny. But living with them? Och. It's almost not worth the happy parts, now is it?" He straightened and looked at the plank with a critical eye. "Of course, what would you know? Confirmed bachelor, I'm guessing. Here I'd been feeling sorry for ye, left out of all the summer shenanigans going on and about. You might have the right of it, after all. Find a nice private spot, make a home, leave all the craziness to the others." Brodie glanced over at Auld Eán. "No words of wisdom, then?"

In response, the large brown pelican tipped his ungainly beak downward, preened at a few feathers along his wing, took his time settling his weight, tucking beak into wing, and finally pulled up one leg as he settled in for a nice morning nap.

"Sleep on it, ye say." Brodie grinned at the snoozing bird, shook his head, and walked over to his tool bench. "Easier said, old man. Especially when I close my eyes, picture that wild hair, and the front of my old T-shirt she was wearing. Add in the way her eyebrow cocks when she's callin' ye out, the dry smile that follows." He walked back over to the measurements marked on the floor, then went back and examined the laminations he'd built up against the false nosepiece. Satisfied, he set about fastening them, taking care to keep the screws clear of where he'd have to shape the wood. Once that was done, he ran his gaze over the edge and toe of the pattern, then collected a drawknife, planes, and his wood rasp to start on the contouring.

He enjoyed the rhythm of the work, that every piece required a different set of eyes, formed a different part, and had a separate function. As he started in with his drawknife, he could appreciate the workmanship—the patience along with the skills he'd worked so hard to achieve—that would go into shaping every piece, then fitting them together to create the larger section, then adding on to that. But his mind was really on running his hands along something even smoother, and a lot softer. "And the laugh. Honest, sexy, uninhibited. Och, mate. The laugh will haunt you every time now, won't it? More provocative than a signature scent is that unique sound."

Brodie focused back on the task at hand. Normally the rhythms of working with his hands while analyzing, sorting, calculating with his mind smoothed out whatever rough edges there might be inside himself. Hours passed, sometimes a full day, and his heart was so into his work, into bringing the spirit of the vessel to life, that he didn't notice much else, didn't think of much else. If his drawing board was the place where he dreamed and let his imagination soar, the balance of time in the workshop was a retreat for the mind and body and a sanctuary for the soul. It was the one place he'd always be welcome, the only place he'd always felt truly at home.

Of late, it hadn't provided much solace or brought him

the much-needed balance he sought. His heart was in the work, that was a constant. But his mind . . . his thoughts, aye, those were elsewhere. A very specific elsewhere. He wrote off the distraction as unavoidable, what with her just several piers down, and all the noise coming from that direction. How could he not be distracted by the very idea that someone other than a Monaghan was putting a hand to what had always been under Monaghan rule?

Except it hasn't been under any rule for a good long spell, has it, lad? his little voice prodded. Close to thirty years it had sat untended, almost the entirety of his lifetime. It was a miracle of fate and whatever else a man might believe in that the property was still lawfully in Monaghan hands at all. And barely that, apparently. "The illusion of ownership is all it is. Or was."

"Your burden was lightened a bit. I thought you'd be happy."

At the first sound of a woman's voice, Brodie was forced to admit his heart had actually skipped a full beat. *That's how far down the slope you've gone sliding, boy-o.*

He could lay blame on the noise coming from the far pier and boathouse, but the distraction was the woman herself. Brodie took a brief moment to gather himself. He set the plane down and brushed his hands off on his pant legs before turning to face his uninvited guest. "Perhaps if you'd taken the time to question me directly, I could have cleared up your unfortunate misunderstanding in that regard."

Cami Weathersby stepped into the boathouse, slipping the thin gold chain strap of her fuchsia-colored, hand-tooled leather messenger bag farther up on the shoulder of her precisely tailored fawn suit. She tucked in her elbows and picked her way across the wood-shaving-strewn floor, clearly unaccustomed to allowing any part of her expensive, overly designed, matching fuchsia heels to come into contact with anything that wasn't, well . . . equally expensive.

"Careful there. Wouldn't want to scuff the red soles on those party shoes of yours on something as common as pier planking."

Her carefully tweezed and perfectly penciled brows lifted ever so slightly, careful not to actually crease the smooth skin of her forehead. If she wondered how he knew she was sporting Christian Louboutins on her dainty feet, she didn't come out and ask.

Six sisters, four nieces, and countless aunties back in Ireland, each with an addiction to one high fashion magazine or another, would have been the answer. But he didn't like to spend too much time thinking about the extended family he'd left behind and he sure as hell wasn't going to share anything about them with this woman.

"Yes, well, perhaps if you'd returned any of my calls, we could have sorted out so many things without my being forced to risk my favorite footwear in your"—she broke off and looked around the interior of the almost century-old boathouse which had been built into the end of the main pier, unable to disguise her complete lack of appreciation for its history and even less for its location—"place of business." She said the last word with just enough of a dubious tone to make it clear she questioned whether or not he truly understood the meaning or the concept.

That boathouse was the fifth such one built on that very spot, starting back with the shipyard's inception. It was actually meant to be used as a toolshed and above-water repair depot for boats already in the water and was not particularly practical for building them because all the materials had to be hauled down the docks. When he was able to complete renovation on the largest boathouse and get the business up and fully operational, that would be the main workshop.

The smaller place had tugged at him when he'd first arrived and docked his boat just outside. It had been convenient back then, since he'd lived on his boat leading up to that first winter, and he'd grown used to it. He liked it—the peace and solitude of being as close to the water as he could get.

"You didn't seem to have any qualms about risking your fancy footwear when you were down here hawking my boathouses to the highest bidder. Perhaps you should have dropped by right then and this terrible inconvenience would never have come to pass."

He thought about how similarly out of place he'd imagined Grace to be on first seeing her on the docks, expensive heels caught up in the old ropes, fancy coat and clothes ruined, completely inappropriate for that environment. And yet, in truth, she'd proven herself to be quite comfortable and at home in that setting. He'd spied her often enough out on the dock that extended from the boathouse on the end—her boathouse now—sitting out on the end of the pier with a morning cup of coffee and more times than not again at sunset. Apparently, it drew her for the same reasons being out over the water drew him. She was a rower. He wondered if she missed being on the water as much as he did. He wondered what else she thought about while she sat out there.

Brodie looked at Cami, who truly was out of her element. While there were any number of tumultuous emotions swimming through his mind and swamping his heart regarding the sale of his family's property, he knew he couldn't let her see a one. After all, that had been the entire purpose of her little stunt. To make him pay. He'd be damned if he'd give her even a hint of satisfaction.

Sliding her bag in front of her, likely to keep it from rubbing against anything filthy, but which also turned it into a handy shield, she moved over to the large, multipaned window that faced the harbor with a view of the bay in the distance. "I'm here now," she said, glancing out at the water.

Her gaze paused briefly on his sailboat, which was once again docked just outside, then down at the floor as she took another careful step, then another, before finally lifting her gaze to look directly at him. She was nothing if not a master at making an entrance, then posing appropriately while delivering whatever carefully constructed verbal slap lay on the tip of her tongue. Of course, where he was concerned, words of an entirely different sort had rolled off that very tongue, not three months past.

He'd underestimated her then. He wouldn't make that mistake again.

"The town leaders, the council, everyone is excited to see a bit of life brought back to the harbor. Grace's inn will turn what has been an eyesore for longer than most of us can recall into something beautiful and hopefully, profitable." Cami glanced around again, making it clear the same could not be said about what he'd done with the property as yet. "In fact, that's why I'm here. Grace was a bit . . . unsettled, when she realized you were still on the property."

Brodie had no idea where this little conversation was headed, but she'd caught him off guard, and he knew by the satisfied gleam that entered her dark brown eyes that she hadn't missed it, either.

"Sounds like she's someone who values transparency in her dealings, too. But then, you know I'm a big proponent of being open and aboveboard." That was about as close as he could tread on the subject they were pretending didn't exist. He'd been raised not to call a woman a cheating whore. Even if it happened to be true.

From the way her eyes narrowed, she hadn't missed his underlying point.

Of course, it was no secret that Ted Weathersby liked to dip his wick, as it were, in places other than his wife. Whether it was an angry game of one-upmanship or they had some kind of open-marriage arrangement, Brodie didn't know, nor did he much care . . . as long as it didn't involve him. Cami had only taken exception to that last part. If her response to his polite refusals—it had taken three of them—was any indication, apparently she didn't hear *no* all that often.

As soon as Grace had mentioned Cami's name as the agent involved in the brokering of the boathouse sale, Brodie had had a pretty damn good idea why it had gone down as it had. But it wasn't the kind of thing he'd ever come out and say, in public or in private, to Cami or anyone else. The host of Monaghan women who had raised him had done a better job than that. There was also the part of him that refused to give her the pleasure of knowing just how deeply she'd plunged her dagger of retribution. Or how concerned he was that she'd do it again. And again. Before he could do a damn thing to stop her.

He simply turned his attention back to the job at hand, knowing the only thing that was going to stop Cami once and for all was the other kind of currency she was comfortable bartering with. Money—which meant he had a boat or three to build.

"If Grace has any concerns, she knows she can come and talk to me," he said, laying down the plane, then making notes and marking off measurements in pencil directly on the wood. "Hell, she's down there tearing my boathouse apart, so I don't think she's really worried about what I think, much less hurting my feelings."

"I didn't think it was possible to hurt a man who kept such a careful guard on his heart."

Brodie could have told her it hadn't been his heart he'd been protecting when he'd turned down her indecent proposal. He could have told her that any man crazy enough to travel across an ocean to lay claim to a centuries-old property that hadn't been operational, much less turned a profit, for decades was a man who wore his heart so vividly on his sleeve that no one with eyes could mistake it.

"Oh, that's right," she went on, injecting a note of faux surprise into her voice. "I forgot. That wall does have a few chinks in it after all. Chinks that Alex MacFarland all but tripped over and fell right into, poor dear, without even noticing. Or caring."

As soon as she'd taken that dripping, calculated tone with him, he'd braced himself for her to volley whatever verbal arsenal she thought she had, and she hadn't disappointed. Hopefully his nonreaction had. Maybe for the first time, Brodie was truly and sincerely thankful that Alex was happily in a relationship with the town police chief, Logan McRae. McRae's family was one of only two whose ties to Blueberry Cove and Pelican Bay were older than the Winstocks, so Cami wouldn't dare take out her vengeful venom on Alex.

Of course, the other family was the Monaghans, but oh, the mighty had fallen and fallen far. And Cami had taken advantage. She was the type who never met an advantage she didn't like to press. Especially if that meant pressing her tight little curves directly against it.

"Poor Brodie." She pursed her perfectly lined and colored lips and ran a lingering gaze along his body, trying for a dismissive smirk when her eyes reached his again, only her dilated pupils told another story.

He kept his amused smile to himself and let her have her moment onstage. Now that he understood her game, it was simply a matter of endurance. He'd never suffered a shortage of that. Another of the few benefits to growing up the only boy in a house full of women. Not that he'd ever admit as much to said women.

"I never would have pegged you for a fool, pining for what he can't have. You always struck me as a smart man who understood exactly what he could have and made good use of it." Cami took another careful step toward him, somehow managing to step over wood pieces and make the movement appear serpentine all at the same time.

He wouldn't have been surprised in the least if a forked tongue had snaked out of her mouth like a fast whip. He'd often wondered how it was in a town as small as Blueberry Cove that no one seemed to see this side of her. Of course, maybe they all did, but, like him, had their reasons for not airing their true opinions in public. Or private. Her family was as old Pelican Bay money as it got and wielded the kind of power that made folks think twice about speaking their true minds.

Cami continued her careful, deliberate approach until Brodie was forced to stop what he was doing and turn as she closed the space between them to mere inches. He held her gaze easily, his demeanor calm, unaffected.

That wasn't entirely true, but it wasn't attraction he was fighting, though she was a damn beautiful woman. It was fury.

"So, the thing is," she said, her gaze dropping deliberately to his mouth, then back to his eyes, "Grace is making some noise about maybe expanding her little enterprise. You've no doubt heard she has Langston deVry as her architect, and Lord only knows who else is in her little black book of connections. I know she had no problem writing a check for that boathouse. Now that she knows the situation with the property, there's nothing to stop her from writing another one." Cami leaned a bit closer and lowered her voice to a whisper. "And another one."

Brodie's gaze never wavered from her eyes, though he was certain that despite the fact that his body hadn't moved so much as a twitch, she hadn't missed the tightening of his jaw.

"Of course," she added, almost purring. "Grace and I, we've grown close. Businesswomen sticking together and all that. Smart, powerful businesswomen." She shifted until her lips were beside his ear. "I could probably convince her that spreading herself thin that way, in a town this small, isn't a wise business decision." She trailed a soft breath along the side of his neck, before lifting her head enough to look him in the eyes again. "If someone were to persuade me to consider it."

Brodie held her gaze, letting the moment stretch out until it was tightly strung as a thin, taut wire. Then he let a slow grin—deep, wicked, knowing—curve his lips and watched as desire punched those black pupils so wide they soaked up almost every last bit of the dark chocolate brown. He heard the small gasp and all but felt her body tense in anticipation, little signs that a man who wasn't too far from her description of someone who took what he could have and made good use of it knew from years of experience.

"You're right about Grace," he said, his voice low, his gaze remaining directly on Cami's. "She is a pretty smart woman. Knows her own mind, which it seems is quite made up on this inn business. She'll do whatever she thinks is best, and I doubt she'll be looking for a second opinion, much less be swayed by one." He took a step back then, picked up a rag, mostly for something to do with his hands, other than wring Cami's slender white neck. "But thank you for the heads up on the threat to what's left of my property," he said quite pointedly holding her gaze. "I'll be sure to take that into consideration as I move forward."

If eyes could turn to hot coals, Cami's would have com-
busted under the pressure of the fury presently seething
within the hard brown depths of hers.

Brodie silently acknowledged that messing with her in
that way—or any way—had probably been unwise. But
she'd once again put herself on the path to certain disappointment. As it was, he thought he should be congratu-
lated for not resorting to physical violence. His lips curved
again as he recalled yet another valuable lesson learned oh
so well at the hands of his sweet, sweet siblings. No matter the provocation, no matter the torture, a man could
never, not ever, lay a hand on a woman in anger. Women,
on the other hand, when provoked in any manner, large
or small, incomprehensible or no, had free rein to do
whatever struck their fancy. Often with whatever was in
easy reach. He knew this to be true because he had the
scars to prove it.

He gave a quick glance at the tools in the immediate
vicinity, something perhaps he should have done sooner,
and had barely gotten out a half sigh of relief that they
were all out of range when she swung her purse off her
shoulder and at his head in a clean, sweeping arc. Fortunately, all those formative years had left him well trained
in the three D's. Deflect, duck, and defend. He blocked
the bag with his forearm and ducked at the same time so
the weight of the trajectory was then on her end, and the
bag went sailing. Brodie turned just as it smashed against
one of the tool shelves, setting up quite a clatter.

It spooked Auld Eán from his deep slumber. The pelican made his disdain for the intrusion quite clear and quite
loud. There was a burst of grumbling squawks and flap-
ping of very long wings.

Cami shrieked in terror in that pitch it seemed only
women and small dogs could achieve, which sent him
ducking again, hands over his ears. Eán opted to take his

cantankerous self someplace where there wasn't such a piercing squeal, and Brodie watched him lift off and calmly flap and glide his way out the big open sliding door and over to the boathouse at the end of the far pier where he'd made his nest. "Can't blame ye, old chap. I'd follow if I could."

"What in heaven's name—" Cami was clutching her chest with one hand and scrabbling over toward the tool bench, gripping whatever came in handy to keep her balance as she went. "Did you know that beast was in here? Of course you knew," she said accusingly as if he'd set the whole thing up on purpose. She snatched up her purse and examined it closely. "If there's so much as a mark on this, you'll be replacing it. A Louis Vuitton limited edition doesn't come cheap."

Brodie could have pointed out that she'd thrown the bag herself, before Eán had ever awoken, but wisely remained silent.

"Perhaps it would be best if you called ahead next time. Then I could arrange more civilized surroundings," Brodie said. Quite pleasantly, he thought. He even managed to hide the broad smile that threatened as he noticed the big black streak on the back of her jacket shoulder where she'd clearly backed into the hoisting chains. It might almost be worth the money it would cost to replace it to see the look on her face when she discovered it. Not to mention the grease smudge on her cheek where she'd pushed her hair back.

"Oh boy," he murmured under his breath, trying not to wince as she brushed off her sleeves with the same grease-smeared fingertips.

Realistically, he doubted she'd be sending him the bill for anything. She'd have to explain why she had grease stains all over her nice little suit and just exactly what *had* she been doing in that boathouse with Brodie Monaghan, anyway? Frankly, he could do without the town speculating on that front. It was enough that she'd confirmed that he'd lost the boathouse to female retribution. It wasn't a stretch to think that she had likely said something innocuous to Sue Clemmons to keep her from alerting him to the sale, which meant that the whole thing hadn't happened because the town was against him.

Just one angry, wealthy, powerful woman scorned. Whom, in his infinite wisdom, he'd just scorned again, bringing the tally to Brodie: 4 Cami: 0. Lord only knew what this one was going to cost him. Clearly she wasn't a woman who believed in the three-strikes-you're-out rule.

Cami slid the chain of her bag back up over her shoulder and managed to pull herself together quite sharply, all things considered. "Oh, there won't be a next time," she said scathingly.

Even better.

"When our paths cross again, you'll be handing your keys over to the tax officers right before you pack up and head back where you came from."

If raw will and desire were anything to measure by, he'd be packed and on a boat to Ireland by morning. Fortunately, wealth plus power didn't always add up to a magic wand that the mighty could simply wave at something they didn't like and make it go away. *Although damn close,* he thought. *Damn close.*

She stumbled on her way to the sliding door and he automatically moved forward to assist, only to be rather viciously waved off. "Don't touch me. Don't ever presume to even *think* about touching me." She made her way to the door, drew herself up rather impressively, then turned and struck an elegant pose in such an offhand, second-nature manner that Brodie wondered if she'd rehearsed it endlessly as a child in front of a mirror or whether she was simply born to it.

"You may have been born into a last name that this town has historical affection for," she stated, her voice crystal clear and once again perfectly poised. "But don't mistake our largesse in tolerating your presence here as any sort of real acceptance. Unless you plan to make a real contribution to the Cove, and by contribution, I mean getting your family's property out of hock and somehow managing to keep the roof from falling in on your head before you turn anything resembling a profit, don't expect those same arms to remain open much longer. Others have arrived here after you, bringing a brand of ingenuity and fire that puts you to shame."

Brodie understood she was referring to Alex. He supposed she could add Grace to that list. It annoyed him that she was right on both counts. Both women had been in the Cove a shorter time than he and both were making faster or at least more immediate headway toward having a real impact on the town's bottom line than he was. Of course, when he'd arrived, he hadn't known the enormity of the obstacle he would be facing. Nor had he been aware it was a race to see who could prove their worth first.

"Flirting and charming the women of whatever little village you came from in Ireland might have been enough to get you by there, but here we demand more. We expect things like character and integrity. Grit, passion. Someone not afraid to bend his back and get the work done." Cami scanned the boathouse interior and appeared to barely restrain herself from shuddering in disgust. "You've been here a full year and what have you got to show for it?"

Had it been anyone else questioning his integrity or his willingness to work, he might have responded differently. In this instance, however, Brodie merely tapped the corner of his mouth with his fingertip. "Careful, there, Mrs.

Weathersby. My sisters tell me that carrying tension at the corners of your mouth is sure to bring about signs of early aging. Something about making your lipstick bleed into tiny wrinkles?" He shrugged. "I don't know that I recall exactly." He smiled lightly. "Just trying to be neighborly."

The screen of civility dropped and ugly venom dripped from her tongue. "So sure of yourself. So certain that Half Moon Harbor is the place you want to spend the rest of your days. Be careful what you wish for, Mr. Monaghan. Your ancestors knew when to give up. And so, one way or the other, will you."

Brodie stood right where he was for several long minutes after Cami departed. The fury he'd felt when she'd first arrived had dissipated somewhere along about the time she'd tried and failed once again to seduce him into being her latest lapdog. At least he understood, with no ambiguity or question, what he was up against.

There was nothing he could do about Cami Weathersby. There was only what he could do for himself and the heritage he'd set himself on the path to restore. "If it's grit and passion she's wanting, a man willing to bend his back—" Brodie bit off the rest and ground down on a tight jaw. Maybe there was still a bit of fury left in him. There was definitely a whole lot of fight.

Question my integrity and character, will you? Coming from a woman with questionable morals and no qualms about playing dirty, the challenge shouldn't have inflamed him as it had. *I'll add in honor, dedication, loyalty.* His family had a very different idea about how he should be expressing those last three and would have sided with Cami on the wisdom of abandoning ship in the States and going home again.

He, on the other hand, had not a single doubt about his path.

To that end, he carefully put his tools away and stored

his notes in a drawer under the tool bench. He walked to the small version of a drafting table he'd erected in the corner of the long, narrow building and flipped the cover page over the drawing of the single-mast sloop he was building. It was only his third such contract since arriving in the Cove, but he'd had to completely overhaul his plans on how he would resurrect a modernized version of the family shipbuilding heritage, and still hadn't quite figured out how he was going to make it all happen.

Building boats to order was a full-time job. Renovating property that had all but crumbled to the ground from disuse was more than a full-time job. It was a career in and of itself. He needed to do one to earn the income to hire folks to manage the other, but as one man, he could only do so much, so quickly. He'd funded the renovation on his boathouse with the first boat he'd built. The second one he'd completed over the winter and just recently delivered would keep him in heating oil and food through the summer months as well as fund the early stages of restoration on the largest boathouse.

He'd accepted it wasn't going to be a speedy process. But he was a patient man, and would take all the more pleasure for bringing the place back to rights with the labor of his own two hands and the sweat of his own bent back, however long that took. At least, that had been the plan.

A quick sweep of the floor and the power circuit flipped off, and all was set to rights. *If only life was as simply tidied up,* he thought as he stepped outside, slid the panel door closed, then bolted and locked it.

Then he did what he should have done the morning after he'd found Grace Maddox tangled up on his dock, waving deed papers in his face. He headed down and across the network of piers to pay her a visit.

He'd meant what he'd said about her being smart and

decisive. He doubted she really wanted to take on additional property so soon, given how much of a learning curve she had in front of her already. If she did have
second-stage plans, however, then he needed to find out
what they were so he could plan accordingly. He'd lost
one boathouse. He didn't intend to lose so much as another parking space to her or anyone else. It was vital he
impress upon her how important his own mission was to
him. She'd been sensitive to that. In fact, apparently she
had gone so far as to discuss with Cami her discomfort
with how the sale had gone down.

At the very least, he needed to make sure they could
stand together against any intrusion Cami might make
with a prospective third, fourth, or fifth buyer whose vision neither he nor Grace could control. Grace wouldn't
want to risk the quaint harbor idyll she envisioned for her
quiet little inn any more than he wanted anyone else messing with his property.

He had to convince her that he was the one least likely
to infringe on that idyll—whether or not it happened to
be true. One part of Grace's learning curve she'd yet to
embrace was that, by their very nature, there was nothing
idyllic or particularly peaceful about shipyards. He had to
make sure he'd secured the deeds to his family's property
before that reality became unavoidably apparent.

Chapter 7

Grace felt him before she saw him. It didn't seem fair that she was so in tune with a man she'd done nothing but try to erase from her mind for the past two weeks. Even worse, her heart picked up an extra beat.

Whomper, of course, had no such conflicting emotions. With a bark of pure glee, he made a mad dash across the plank flooring to the open panel doorway as Brodie entered the cavernous boathouse space.

"There's a lad," he said, wide grin on his too-handsome-for-his-own-good-face. He patted his chest and Whomper accepted the invite without a moment's hesitation, launching himself from floor to arms in a single, well-timed bound.

Grace might have sighed a little inside, thinking how nice it would be to leap into those arms every day.

After a good belly scratch, Brodie plopped Whomper back on the ground and picked up a hank of canvas sail fabric that had been tied into a knot in the middle and clearly chewed on. Grin broadening, he heaved it across the open warehouse space and Whomper tore after it with utter canine abandon. Brodie glanced up and caught her gaze for the first time, and Grace thought, *he makes for a pretty picture, but that's all. Remember that.*

"Top o' the morning," he said, still grinning as he approached.

"Hello yourself," she said, doing everything she could to stamp out all the little butterflies flitting about her heart, not to mention the zips and zings that went straight to her tingly parts. And failed miserably across the board. That grin, those eyes, that accent. She'd hoped she'd romanticized the whole morning-in-his-boathouse chemistry thing. Apparently, she hadn't done it enough justice.

He gave a quick glance around the empty building. "Crew all done for the day? Or have you been making all that noise down here by yourself?"

"Curiosity finally get the better of you?" she asked, smiling despite herself. Damn Irish charm. "Yes, the crew is done for the day. I know it doesn't look like anything yet, but we're in more of the 'figure out what we can restore and tear out what we can't' phase, than doing anything particularly constructive. Or reconstructive, I guess I should say."

Brodie made a slow turn and stared up and around the warehouse-size boathouse. "What in the world made ye look at this place and envision an inn of all things? Why not take over one of the historic old homes and renovate it? Dress up all the bedrooms, install a few extra bathrooms, expand the kitchen a bit. Charming, quaint, historic, traditional."

"Who said I wanted to be traditional?"

"I believe you did. You said you planned to honor the Monaghan history."

"Oh, I do. Very specifically, in fact." She followed his gaze, knowing she saw something completely different from what he saw. "I know it will take longer and involve more, but I'm not afraid of the work." It was what came after the work that terrified her. "I will honor this place's history, and charming will definitely be part of the appeal, but quaint?" She scrunched her nose a bit. "Mmm, not really what I had in mind. If we're going to transform a

boathouse, then I want to do something to reflect its original function." When Langston had sent her rough sketches
of his initial ideas on how they could transform the cavernous, open space into nautical-themed, loft-like spaces,
a thrill like nothing she'd ever experienced shot straight
through her. It was like passing the bar exam on her first
try. Times a hundred. Thousand.

"I came here with the idea to build something. Not just
renovate or restore, but to create. My original plan was to
look at land and build my own inn from the ground up.
Something that was purely mine from the start."

"I'm on board with that idea." The dry note in Brodie's
tone carried humor and a hint of resignation.

Was that what he'd come to tell her? That despite wishing otherwise, he'd resigned himself to the way things
were? She hoped so. She shot him a wry smile in return,
but didn't apologize again. What was done, was done.

"When I got here and saw the historic architecture and
how important preserving traditions were, I wanted to
celebrate that and build on it, instead. I want to find a way
to blend tradition and innovation." She smiled. "Ironically,
when Cami showed me this place, her suggestion was to
tear it down and build myself a brand-new little harborside
inn. The property, the placement, the footprint, all would
have supported that." Grace caught the way his facial expression tightened, but he didn't otherwise say anything.

"From the outside, the property was a long-abandoned,
run-down boatyard—at least as far as I knew—so I actually considered the idea. I wasn't sure it was salvageable.
Then I walked inside." She did a slow turn and gazed up
into the open space, the wide-beamed ceiling area, the
thick, weathered hardwood planks that made up the interior walls, the wide and timeworn cypress boards beneath
their feet, and felt the same wired mix of adrenaline and
fear simultaneously knot up her gut and exhilarate every

nerve ending. Along with all the other tingly bits perco-
lating inside her body, it made for an almost light-headed
rush, and she spoke from her heart, without thinking.

"This place has such character and heart. After Cami
had said it was part of founding the town centuries ago, I
knew I couldn't tear it down. But I couldn't walk away
from it, either. Initially, I think I connected to it because
of my own feelings about being on the water and how that
makes me feel. Though I've never spent time in boathouses this size, I've spent a lot of time in and around
them. There's a comfort there, a security for me. I'll always feel like I'm where I belong."

She continued her slow scan, her thoughts spinning to
the past and to the future. "It all came together from there.
That once there had been meaning to this place, an important, vital one that had helped launch this town and
build it into what it has become today. It's hard to wrap
my head around that, to really understand that kind of
time span.

"I came here because I don't have that history, not the
traditions nor the ties, much less any kind of legacy to pass
forward. Shipbuilding isn't the backbone of this town now,
but the town still thrives. Past, present, and future, all
wound together, each part vital to the other. I knew there
had to be a way to take what had once been so important
and make it useful again. In doing so, I can create my own
place in the legacy and history of this town. Preserve and
renew."

Her gaze landed back on Brodie and she felt immediately abashed at gushing the way she had. "I know I'm the
last person you think should be spouting about the impor-
tance of this place. It probably seems the height of patron-
ization or . . . or worse. But I assure you, it's not. I know
you don't care what I think or feel, and I get that, but
surely my motivation, my passion, seeing the possibilities

and feeling the drive to do something about it, is something you can relate to."

"Aye." He continued to look at her, his gaze so direct and intense it was as if he'd pinned her right to the spot where she stood.

She didn't know what he was thinking, if the emotion she could see banked in those storm-tossed-sea eyes was because he related to her professed passion, or if it was barely restrained fury that she had the audacity to think she had any right to be there.

He abruptly went back to looking around, and she let out a breath she didn't know she'd been holding. It was as if he'd physically released her, and she felt surprised that she hadn't stumbled at the force of it.

He shifted his gaze to her. "I don't know that my vision is quite as . . . creative as yours."

Her mouth dropped open, surprised by the dry humor, the casual observation. Stunned, actually. Given what she'd seen in his eyes, she'd expected derision at worst, dismissal at best. She noted the tension hadn't left his jaw or the set of his shoulders.

She could understand that. It couldn't be easy for him, but he was clearly trying to find a balance. She wanted that, too. "I've spent the past two weeks asking myself what kind of crazy person does this, but I guess the crazy person turned out to be me."

There was no trace of humor. The set of his jaw, the impenetrable look that was still in those green eyes, and the way he naturally commanded attention made her body tighten all over again—not necessarily in a bad way. Her fingertips tingled and twitched. There was something primal about the way he looked at her, and animal attraction was part of the equation. A really, really strong part. *Dammit.*

"You know I come from a long line of shipbuilders," he

said at length, finally glancing away again, but not releasing the tension between them. His legs were braced apart, the balance in his hips. His folded arms showcased the musculature of his shoulders, his chest, and the bunched-up curve of his biceps. "In my case, you could say the passion for what I do, for what I create, is in the blood. I don't know that it makes me or my ancestors any less crazy for pursuing our dream, but . . . I'm merely following the course they've already laid out for me, doing what I do best." His gaze lifted, locked on hers again, and though his tone was casual, conversational, the flash in those green eyes felt anything but. "Is that how it is with you, Grace? Long line of innkeepers dotting your family tree and you're abandoning a law career to embrace your true nature?"

"I-I don't know, to be honest." She hoped she didn't sound as breathless as he was so effortlessly making her feel. "I mean, yes, I'm giving up estate law to run an inn. But I don't know anything about what my relatives did or didn't do."

Whatever answer he'd been expecting, that apparently hadn't been it; he looked surprised. "You said you had family here in Maine. So what is it they do, then?"

She paused for several long seconds, trying to decide what she wanted to tell him, but it was hard to think, hard to process the bigger picture with Brodie's penetrating gaze feeling as visceral as a physical touch. *What is really on your mind? Why have you really come to see me?*

For the past two weeks, Grace hadn't heard a peep from anyone at the county municipal building, Sue at the bank, Cami, or anyone else on the town council regarding the sale, so she'd assumed all was well with her ownership. If Brodie had made a flap of any kind, it hadn't filtered down to her, so she'd decided to let sleeping dogs lie and focus on her own business.

Not that that had kept her from thinking about him.

Thoughts of him, of their conversation, his sexy brogue, the mischievous glint in his eyes, and that knowing smile invaded her brain. The way he'd rubbed his thumb over her palm, those ridiculously thick eyelashes he'd peered through before kissing her hand . . . all of that had plagued her waking hours. She was more than a little ashamed to admit it had interrupted a fair share of her sleeping ones, as well. Given the hundreds of details she was trying to keep track of every day and the sheer exhaustion she'd felt when she'd fallen into bed at night, the frequency and manner in which he still dominated her thoughts should have been impossible.

Looking at him and feeling every fiber of her being respond to him as if he'd kept her on edge the entire time—maybe her constant thoughts of him had done just that—it was just as well he'd stayed away. Everyone in town knew about the sale of the boathouse. Once she'd hired the guys who were helping her do the preliminary assessment and clear out the unsalvageable, it hadn't been a full day before folks began stopping in to say hello and introduce themselves. *Get a peek at what the crazy lady from D.C. was up to,* she'd thought at first, but they'd all been polite and not overtly nosy. Mostly curious.

No one had asked if she and Brodie were working together or getting along. No one had commented on the two of them together in any way, for that matter, which was a relief, but also kind of odd considering she'd bought a piece of property that had never been out of Monaghan possession before. Maybe Mainers were so well mannered they kept their speculation private. She wasn't sure.

She'd done her own bit of poking and prodding, of course, trying to figure out how Brodie fit into the fabric of the town. At the moment, that was as unclear as it had been the day they'd met. Well, except if her visitors were female—age didn't matter—a certain wistful little look would pass through their eyes if she managed to find a way to inject his name into the conversation.

The silence between Grace and Brodie grew awkward, but she didn't want to talk about her family, such as it was, and she didn't know what else to say. Since her arrival, she'd done a bit of digging on Ford, mostly accessing county records, that kind of thing, but hadn't reached out to him yet. It turned out her brother didn't own a cell phone and there were no landlines on Sandpiper Island, where he was presently living and working. She knew it would be better to simply show up than try to contact him first and give him a chance to reject her straight out. Again. Given the location, showing up was going to take some doing.

Instead, she'd opted to get her project underway so he'd know she wasn't going anywhere and he'd have to deal with her at some point. He'd shut her out of his life completely for the past thirteen years. Longer, if she counted his time overseas. And she counted all of it. Every last day. He'd probably think her insane, making the leap into the unknown as she had. But to her mind, it wasn't any different from the one he'd made when he'd relocated and started his life completely over.

Maybe that was the other family trait they shared . . . impulsive, big-ass life changes. But, impulsive or not, he'd stuck by his choice and he'd find out she was going to stick by hers. And stick by him. Like it or not, he was damn well stuck with her. The sooner he accepted that, accepted her, the better off they'd both be. She firmly believed that. She had to. She'd just bet her entire future on it.

Yeah. She really didn't want to talk about her brother yet.

"Just one family member," she finally said, knowing she had to say something. "And he's not a lawyer or an inn-keeper. He's a scientist."

Brodie nodded at that, but didn't otherwise comment on it.

She waited for him to ask questions about Ford. Hell, he might even know him. She hadn't thought about that. No one had mentioned her brother to her, though, so she doubted anyone had made the connection. Not yet, anyway. Maybe the fact that Ford spent most of his time out on a little island in the middle of Pelican Bay had something to do with that.

But if he didn't question her about Ford, then surely Brodie would wonder why on earth she'd gone from law to innkeeping. Knowing her answer was not going to help matters at all, she held her breath and tried to figure out how best to explain her new direction.

Instead, he asked, "So, you're not familiar with any other branches on your family tree, I take it?"

Relieved, she shook her head, then made herself smile, feeling silly for letting him get to her the way he was. When it came to dealing with the opposite sex, she was neither naïve nor prudish . . . nor shy, for that matter. Yet he made her feel completely out of her depth. "It's probably more like a small bush, at best, anyway."

His grin made a quick, flashing return. "We're on opposite ends of that orchard then. Sometimes I wish my branches were a wee bit more twig-like rather than hanging heavy with so much fruit. I suppose that comes from thinking the grass is greener under someone else's tree."

"It's funny, I spent a lot of years telling myself how lucky I was not to have to deal with—well, to beat the analogy to death—a bunch of wild growing fruit. Watching families argue and fight with each other more days than not . . . I counted myself lucky to be out of that. But"— she lifted a shoulder—"I've come to realize that strong roots are better than shallow ones or the lack of any at all.

A dear friend helped me see that every plant starts as a seedling, and just because I wasn't born to an already deeply rooted tree doesn't mean I can't plant one of my own." She rolled her eyes. "I think we can retire that metaphor for good, now."

"Well, at risk of taking it one step too far, I'll add that it's been my experience that sometimes big trees expect their fruit to fall directly under it and flourish where they land. I suppose had I fallen from my tree a century or two earlier, that axiom would have held up quite well." He lifted his shoulders in a half shrug, as if he was going to complete that thought, then chose to let it go.

"Your family wasn't happy with your move here?"

He suddenly looked as uncomfortable as she had felt when he'd asked about her family. That flash of vulnerability was surprising. Her heart immediately softened, even as she knew his reaction should have made her more wary. She didn't want to feel more connected to him, more drawn to him.

"Let's just say they felt my talents could have been better put to use back in County Donegal," he said when the conversational pause once again grew to an uncomfortable length.

"Is your family in shipbuilding back in Ireland, then? Did they expect you to stay there?"

He didn't pause, but spoke immediately. "The Donegal Monaghans moved away from that industry several generations ago. Over the past century or so, economic times, war, any number of other things, shifted my family toward a new path, and new traditions were formed long before I came along."

"And yet you embraced the heritage of your more distant ancestors. Your family didn't think that was still honorable in some way?"

"Oh, it wasn't about their not respecting our past so much as feeling that my energies should be spent supporting the current focus of the clan."

"Which is?"

The grin that split his face was as unexpected as the quick punch it sent straight to her libido. "Restaurants. Pubs and taverns mostly."

"Oh," she said, surprised, not understanding the broad grin.

"Hand in hand with that"—his eyes fairly glittered— "we've also spawned a long line of boardinghouse owners and innkeepers. We're quite good at it, in fact. Of course, the fact that we're champs at procreation doesn't hurt. Put enough Monaghan feet on the ground and hands to working and I'm fairly certain we could do anything we've a mind to."

Grace's mouth dropped open, then snapped shut, a flush heating up her cheeks. What an idiot he must think her, waxing rhapsodic about her little dream inn, admitting she knew nothing about innkeeping. Hell, she felt like an idiot. She *was* an idiot. "You want to build boats. So you came all the way to America to get away from the pubs and the innkeeping to relaunch that part of your family's heritage and traditions, only to have someone step in and turn part of it into . . ." She shook her head. "Wow."

"Indeed," he said dryly.

She tried a laugh. "Maybe it's a sign of some kind?" she asked faintly, trying to match his humor. "Fate trying to tell you something?"

"The thought did cross my mind."

She shook off her shock, trying to assimilate what his revelation meant in the grand scheme of things. "You said that shipbuilding hasn't been a family industry in Ireland for several generations. So . . . how did you come to be a boatbuilder then? Who taught you?"

"The family on this side of the pond were pretty removed from those back home, and that has been the case
for some time. No one had crossed over from Ireland to
join the stateside Monaghans for several generations,
though a handful had come back our way over time, having either given up on the venture here, or wanting to explore their Irish roots, then staying on once they had. All
of that was before my time. Growing up, I didn't even
know about this part of our family tree."

"Not at all? Really? And yet—"

"Here I am," he finished for her. "I know. I was raised
in kitchens, busing and waiting tables, cooking, eventually
working behind the pub bar when I was old enough. I
knew our Irish heritage, every last limb and twig of it, like
I lived and breathed. I worked with descendants from
every part of it. We were a big, close, loud, noisy lot.
There was no escaping the clan, and for a long time, I did-
n't want to. I still don't, truth be told. Not the family part.
Just the family business." An affectionate, somewhat wistful smile crossed his face and there was humor in the twinkle in his eyes. "I don't miss the noise and general chaos
much, either, I'll admit. Privacy was a rare commodity in
my world."

She could see that he was being bare-bones honest with
her. He couldn't know it, but that openness, that honesty—
she'd seen quite clearly moments ago that his work wasn't
something he appeared to naturally talk about—really
struck a chord inside her. Rather than make her uncomfortable or feel guilty about the situation between them,
the more he shared, the more she felt . . . well, trustful of
him. That had to be an even more dangerous thing than
attraction.

Didn't it?

"What changed?" she asked, compelled to hear the rest,
as if knowing was imperative. Maybe it was. Maybe it

would help her gain objectivity about the situation, about him and his effect on her so she could focus on the work at hand. Except it didn't feel like it was about smart business. It felt . . . personal. Very personal.

"My grandfather was a wee lad when the shipbuilding part of our ancestry was coming to its final end, but he had an uncle—my great-great—who kept his hand in. I never knew him. He passed before I was born. He'd picked the craft up from his own father, and so on. He taught my grandfather the love of being on the water, of boats, of fishing—which is how the transition came about for the Monaghans way back when. We went from building ships to building fishing boats to working on them in the lean times. That led to cooking the catch and . . . well, we seemed to find our niche there and flourished in a new direction."

"But for you . . . it was being on the water?" Grace had seen the light come into his eyes as he spoke of it, so it wasn't really a question so much as she wanted to hear him talk about it more. To see more of that light.

"Aye, indeed. We'd fish, and my grandfather would tell me tales of my greats and my great-greats. He talked of the tall ships, the schooners, the clippers our ancestors built, and how his own uncle built great sailing boats and had passed those skills to him." Brodie grinned at what was obviously a fond memory. "I was begging him to teach me how to build a boat before I could even ride a bike."

"And he did? Your grandfather taught you? That sounds pretty wonderful, actually, for both of you."

"It was, truly. I never knew my father really. He was gone for good before I'd turned six, so my grandfather was the man of the family. My best memories are of time spent with him in the shed behind his house. He'd turned it into his own workshop. He built wee boats then, little dinghies, a dory or small, single-mast sailboat. He had even taken to doing miniatures as a pastime. All of it fascinated me. I was happy to learn any of it. Started the fire in me, he did. As I got older, the passion grew and took real shape from reading the journals my ancestors had kept, going over the chests full of plans and charts that my grandfather had saved. They'd all come down to him from his uncle and from his uncle's father before him."

"Did you—were you able to bring any of them with you? I mean, I assume all of that passed on to you then? Or is your grandfather still alive?"

Brodie shook his head. "No, he passed on when I was but twelve. It was more a hobby to me then, something we shared on the side of regular day-to-day life. My real life was in the kitchen, not in his work shed. My family didn't even own anyplace where a real boat could be built. My grandfather's place was sold off when he became infirm and moved to a full-time-care facility. I was far too young then for them to be holding on to it for me. Though I know those were his wishes."

Brodie broke eye contact briefly and a gruff note entered his voice. "Senility is a cruel thing, robbed him of so much at the end. Felt like it robbed me, too. But he passed to a better place and my memories now are of the good moments. Of those, we had many." He looked directly at her once more. "And aye, I did come into possession of a fair number of his things and have held on to them all, though only a small portion came with me. I put the rest in storage along with most of my other worldlies back in Donegal."

"How long have you been here?"

A brief twinkle lit his eyes again, an edge of . . . something else there, as well. Something deeper. Given how it made those tingly parts respond, she thought it might be better not to figure out exactly what those deeper things might be.

"'Twas a year to the day, that morning we first met."

"Oh. Well." The corners of her mouth twisted downward. "Happy anniversary, only not so much. I'm sorry for that."

"As you say, fate takes us in hand, and we've but to figure out what best to do with wherever it guides us."

She gave a short laugh. "It all sounds ever so much more doable when you say it with that lilting accent."

"That and a merry twinkle in yer eye will get ye far in this world, lass, indeed it will," he said, his brogue deepening with every word. "And don't you be forgettin' it."

She shook her head, still smiling, and felt a bit of warmth creep into her cheeks as his gaze lingered along with that very twinkle he spoke of aimed directly her way. "So, you came here to bring back the family business," she said, wondering if there was anything that would help her feel more bulletproof to his charms. *Good luck with that.* The more she knew about him, the more vulnerable to them she became. "I guess it must have been pretty exciting to discover the Monaghan shipbuilding legacy hadn't died out on this side of the pond, as you called it. Well, not as far back as it had on your side, at any rate. How did you find out? From your grandfather before he passed?"

Brodie shook his head. "No, his stories were all from our side. I don't know that he knew, as it would have been up to his uncle to tell him. Who knows what the politics of the family were back then in that regard."

"So, how did you find out? How old were you?"

"Just going on eighteen. When I say my grandfather left trunks of old documents and such, I wasn't kidding. When he passed, I was still in school, and when I wasn't, I was working in the kitchens, so free time was a rare commodity. It took me some time to even make a dent in them."

"Were you building anything then? Oh, right, you said your family didn't have any kind of outbuilding and had sold off your grandfather's place. That must have been hard. Reading about boats, and not being able to get your hands on them."

A quick grin flashed and the dimples winked out. "Oh, I kept my hand in. Not that my family knew, but aye. In a school chum's shed, we'd begun building our own sailboat, following some plans of my great-great-uncle that I'd modified. Of course, even modified, it was a big two-master. Once we'd gotten the hull built, I don't know how we planned on actually finishing the thing. I lived right on the water, but Trevor lived a good kilometer or so inland. We weren't even old enough to drive and neither of us had a boat trailer." He laughed. "But it was a good lesson, a good challenge."

"What did you do with it?"

He shrugged. "Nothing we could do. It was kind of like that old wreck you buy as a lad, thinking to fix it up and get it running, only you never do, so it sits on blocks in the garage for a lifetime or two."

"Surely your friend's family noticed they had a half-built sailboat in their shed."

"Trev's family had a good bit more money than we did. We were doing well enough, but we also had several times over the number of mouths to feed as Trevor's parents did—only child that he was. So the shed we used, which was more a garage, really, was but one of a number of out-buildings on his family property. I think they were just thankful he had something to do to keep him busy and out of the hair of the household staff." Brodie laughed. "Of course, I wanted to spend any free second I could over at his place, and all he wanted to do was spend every breathing second in our tavern. He'd do anything, any job, didn't even want to be paid. He was just starved for the noise and chaos and the people, while I craved the peace and solitude of that stifling shed."

Grace shook her head and smiled with him. "I can't really imagine the kind of life you led. The family, all of it."

"You were cut more from Trevor's cloth then?"

"Hardly. We had no money, no outbuildings, no property at all that we actually owned." Her laugh was dry. "And the only household staff we had was me."

"Cinderella, were you?" Brodie grinned at that.

But it was compassion she saw in his eyes. It shouldn't have stung—it wasn't pity, after all—but it did, more than she wanted to admit.

She shook her head. "No. No evil stepsisters." She found a smile from somewhere, not really wanting to think about her situation growing up and kicking herself for opening that door. He'd been so open and honest about his, though, it was only fair.

"Well, I've got six I would have gladly lent you for the asking," he joked.

"You have six stepsisters?"

"Oh no. They're full-blood siblings." He grinned. "Though, you ask me, I'd say they could lay claim to the evil part often enough."

Grace laughed at that, though it was envy she felt, more than sympathy. "Six sisters. I can't—I can't even fathom what that would be like. Any brothers?"

"If only I'd been so fortunate," he said on a heartfelt sigh. "I might've had a fightin' chance. As it was, I'm often surprised I made it to puberty."

"Were you the youngest?" Grace grinned broadly. Brodie being the baby of the apparently sprawling Monaghan clan explained a great deal about his natural-born charisma.

"Right in the middle." The most disarming bit of flush came to his cheeks, proving that he could, indeed, be even more attractive and adorable. "Three younger, three older. My mother had four sisters and my father three more.

Most of whom worked in the business or close enough to it, all of whom made it their business to make my life a miserable matriarchal hell."

Grace snickered at that. "That explains even more."

"Even more of what?"

"Oh, we've already discussed how you're pretty darn charming, especially with members of the opposite sex. The ladies who have stopped in to see what was going on with the boathouse all but swoon at the mere mention of your name."

His grin flashed again. "You've been mentioning me, have you?"

"See?" she said, eyes widening. "You can't help yourself. All I meant was that if you were drowning in the estrogen ocean for all of your formative years, that's probably a large part of why you understand women so well. Or understand how to get to them, anyway."

He cocked his head, his smile so slow and devilish it made her throat go dry. And other parts of her go quite decidedly in the other direction. "Who said I understand how to get to women?"

"No one. I mean, I did." Why was she so flustered? "I mean . . . it's pretty obvious you aren't shy about using your genetic gifts. You know your strengths and don't mind playing to them. It's smart, really. I definitely don't blame you for it."

"Good to know." His gaze zeroed right back in on hers, bringing all those primal parts sinuously back to life.

He shocked her by taking a step closer, and suddenly the huge empty boathouse felt a whole lot smaller. Stifling even. In a really earthy, steamy, hothouse kind of way.

He held her gaze, then dropped his to her mouth, before finding his way back up to her eyes. "What would you say your strengths are then, Grace? What cards do you play when you want to get your way?"

Chapter 8

What in bloody hell am I doing? Listening to the poor deprived head in his trousers, rather than the bobbling idiot perched on his shoulders. Yet, despite that bit of knowledge, Brodie remained right where he stood, deep in her personal space. Deeper still in the danger zone.

"Why did you come to the boathouse today?" she asked, the words a bit strained with a breathless quality that may have been mostly wishful thinking on his part.

His body was perfectly happy to respond to the promise of it, nonetheless.

"Is that your answer then?" He smiled. "Blunt speech, direct confrontation if necessary?" He noted that her throat worked and the finest of tensions tightened that lovely jawline of hers.

"I've found being direct cuts down on time lost to needless discussion." Her gaze was riveted to his. "And avoids potential misunderstandings."

"Well, there are discussions and then there are conversations. They aren't always the same thing, you know. Dialogue doesn't always have to have a bigger purpose. Sometimes it can simply be enjoyable in its own right. The give-and-take . . . ebb and flow. A harmless bit of banter now and again." His smile spread. "Surely you've heard of it."

Not an hour earlier, Brodie had been in close proximity to another woman, one far more classically beautiful than this one. He'd watched her eyes grow dark with desire and felt nothing. Grace Maddox, on the other hand—who, truth be told, was likely a far greater threat to his achieving his goals than Cami Weathersby could ever hope to be—drew one breathy note and his body went instantly rigid at the idea of what other little sounds he might elicit from her.

Why *had* he come to the boathouse? To see if that morning a fortnight ago had just been an odd blip on his physical radar? Given the state he'd been in just before finding her sprawled on his docks, it was quite probable that his rather primal reaction to her had been more about timing than any real response. At least he'd wanted to believe that.

So how was he going to explain away what she was doing to him now?

He lifted a hand and ran a fingertip along a wave of her hair down below her chin, stopping just above where it rested on the faded camp shirt she wore. "It suits you down, you know."

The most delightful spots of pink bloomed in her fair cheeks, which in turn delighted him. *So,* he thought, *not used to wearin' it down, are ye, then?* He could think of only one reason why she would have made the change, and the fit of his jeans grew a mite more uncomfortable as the image of her descending his wrought-iron stairs, hair all damp and in wild disarray, played through his mind.

Spurred by the memory and the way her eyes grew darker under his continued study, he wound a tendril around one finger, then brushed the back of it along her cheek. He felt more than heard the intake of breath, and his pulse jumped another notch along with it. "Chameleon eyes. Amber, then gray, then the most stormy of greens. If

I knew your rhythms better, perhaps I'd be able to match color to mood."

To his surprise, rather than sway her further into the sweet tension building between them, the comment made her roll those hazel eyes of hers and tugged a wry smile from one corner of her mouth.

"You're very smooth with that," she said, the self-deprecation in her tone making it an admission that she wasn't immune to his charm.

"And you're quite hard on a charmer like me," he said, completely unrepentant.

"Someone needs to be."

That surprised a laugh out of him, even as he was quick to note neither of them had shifted so much as a millimeter away from the other and her hair was still wrapped around his finger.

"I've been nothing but kind," he said, smiling down into her upturned face, tempted, so tempted to lower his mouth the few inches it would take to seal his lips to hers. "I offer up my personal shower and exceptional tweezing skills. Even go so far as to bathe your fish-loving scruff of a wee dog."

"For which we were—and are—very grateful. Although you have to admit that some of that was motivated by self-preservation. We all smelled pretty bad." Her lips curved in that way they did, with that little twist nudging at something inside him he didn't have a name for and was likely better off not knowing.

Yet self-preservation slowed him not in the least. "Indeed. I was going to mention how much sweeter your scent was, but I knew you'd see right through my shallow, shallow ploy."

The eyebrow arch was the other thing he'd missed and he grinned when she deployed it. She was sharp, too sharp, missing nothing, calling him on everything, and if he was any judge, enjoying herself in the process.

"So is that it, then?" she asked, injecting a hint of his own lilt into the words, her efforts making his smile grow. "You came here to shallowly see if you could charm me into . . . what? Signing the boathouse back over to you?"

He shouldn't have been surprised she'd think exactly that, so it shouldn't have pricked his pride. Yet it did. He let the curl wind off his finger and let his hand fall to his side, but his tone remained light. And he stayed right where he stood. "You made it quite clear your intent was to move forward, and you've wasted no time doing so. Your passionate speech the day we met, and again just now didn't go unnoticed."

"So . . . why the visit?"

"You made a point of saying we'd have to find a way to work together, or at least side by side."

"I don't know that I meant that quite so literally."

His grin spread again as he laughed. "You call me the charmer, but you undersell your own allure. You're not to be underestimated, Grace Maddox."

She laughed with him. "I'm glad you figured that out, although it's the brainy part I rely on, not so much the beauty—which is a good thing, given their relative distribution in my gene pool."

"Fishing, are we?"

"What?" She looked confused for a moment, then understanding dawned. "Oh. No. I wasn't asking—I don't . . . that's not something I'd do."

"No," he said more quietly. "I imagine you don't." His lips curved. "Else you wouldn't be giving me such a hard time on it. A bit of pot and kettle, otherwise."

"Right."

Despite her straightforward speech, she seemed . . . flustered. He found he rather liked that and wondered how long it had been since someone had flustered her a little. Or a lot. He reached up again, rubbed at a smudge on her cheek with the side of his thumb. "You could rely on both. Makes me wonder if the person who underestimates you most . . . is you."

He felt the finest of tremors race under her skin and let his hand drop away. Not because he minded disconcerting her, but because he liked it rather too much.

"I just walked away from a very secure career and significant annual paycheck to turn a two-hundred-year-old boathouse into an inn, which I then intend to run. Both things I have zero experience doing. I'm either grossly overestimating myself, deluding myself, or both."

"The risks we take with time and money are nothing in the face of the risks we take with our hearts and souls."

She tilted her head at that and smiled. "Nice quote. Who said it?"

His grin returned slow and deep, and he noted her gaze drop to his mouth . . . and saw her throat work again. He had to curl his fingers into his palm to keep from sliding them under that waterfall of hair and pulling her mouth up under his.

"It's the accent," she added dryly. "Makes everything you say sound profound."

That got a chuckle out of him. She managed that quite frequently, he thought. It felt . . . good. In turn, it made him realize that most of his laughter lately was in reaction to the smiles and guffaws he elicited in others. 'Twas rather nice to be provoked to laughter by someone else.

"I don't know about profound, but it's the truth as I see it. Do you?"

"Do I . . . ?"

"Think true risk is putting yourself on the line, and no' simply your bank balance?"

She laughed, and he noticed how it brought a light to her eyes, made them crinkle at the corners. Something his sisters would have rushed off to put this or that cream on in an attempt to smooth them out. Not Grace. She seemed unconcerned about that sort of thing. There'd been a time when the fresh and natural approach wouldn't have turned his head, but at the moment, it had his full, undivided attention.

Perhaps the briny, fresh sea air in Maine had changed him after all. Alex MacFarland had turned his head not soon after his arrival and she was certainly a far cry from primped and polished, almost tomboy. Grace, however, wasn't that. On first glance in her tailored coat, office shoes, and city-girl satchel, he'd thought her a little buttoned up, definitely out of her element.

He'd watched her perched out on the end of the pier the past few weeks, dressed much the same as she was in army green khakis, a thin, figure-hugging lemon yellow tee, and unbuttoned plaid camp shirt. With her hair down around her shoulders and the most becoming flush on her cheeks, she didn't look the least bit repressed. Her natural, earthy air, the way she moved, her laugh, the arch of her brow, and the wry twist at the corner of her mouth all spoke of a woman very in tune with herself, the essence of female. She held her own when she looked at him.

"I think putting my bank account on the line *is* risking myself," she said, seemingly unaware of his frank appraisal.

She was woman incarnate, in her very own, particular way, and it had quite the effect on him. He shifted his weight, but it did little to ease the growing discomfort in the fit of his denims.

"It will certainly be putting me in a very different position in life if I do this and fail. But yes . . . risking heart and soul is more terrifying." She looked up and around the place again, and he saw the yearning . . . and the fear.

Och, Grace, but your heart is already caught up in your dreams, isn't it? As much as he didn't really want to see that, to know that, he understood such dreams too intimately not to acknowledge their power.

"You can always earn more money," she added, though she wasn't looking at him, but taking in the world that would be her future.

"Aye," he agreed, watching her. "But there are only so many pieces of your heart to be given away."

Pain flashed over her face and through those ever-changing eyes.

He touched her cheek without thinking about it, compelled by her expressiveness, her frankness. And her complete and utter lack of concern regarding what he thought of her. "Did someone cast your heart aside, Grace Maddox?"

Her gaze moved right to his, and the responding smile was softer, more wistful, and a good bit sad, like nothing he'd seen from her thus far. That glimpse of vulnerability pulled at something completely different inside him. Something he was in no hurry to put a name to. *Och, my blunt, outspoken little warrior, no' so bulletproof after all, are ye now?*

He tipped her chin up. "Was he blind then? And dumb to boot?"

A quick smile as she shook her head just slightly, but she didn't pull away. Her gaze seemed lost in his, drenched with emotions she didn't put words to.

Even knowing her thoughts were somewhere else, on someone else, Brodie drank from the well of her gaze like a man desperate to quench his thirst after a long stint in the desert. He wondered what it would feel like to inspire such depth of emotion in a woman.

"It wasn't like—it's not what you think." She went to duck her chin, but he kept his finger under her chin and her eyes on his. He was not ready to lose that connection, though he realized it for the selfish gesture it was.

"Ye want me to hunt the dragon down for you?" he offered, intending it to sound like a tease, to lift the sadness from her eyes. The question came out sounding far more serious.

Her gaze searched his. "I almost think you mean that." She smiled again, though he noted it didn't reach her eyes. "I appreciate the offer, but I came here to hunt him myself."

Brodie went still, then started to pull back. *Idiot. Do you really think a woman like her would be available for the taking?* Was that the truth of it? Did he want her to be available? And would it be to simply slake the thirst of his too long ignored physical needs? Or for more than that?

"I'm talking about my brother," she added, making Brodie wonder what she'd just seen in his expression. "And it's not his fault. There were . . . circumstances. A lot of circumstances."

He was relieved—more, he thought, than he should have been—and disconcerted to realize that the revelation only left him feeling a stronger connection to her. He, better than anyone, understood that particular brand of pain. "Aye. Family can break yer heart like no one else can."

She looked into his eyes in a way she hadn't as yet, as if she were really seeing him. Perhaps she was. He felt . . . exposed.

She cast her gaze downward and laughed shortly. It sounded a bit thick, and there was little humor in it. "Aye, indeed."

"Och, Grace, now yer breakin' me heart. Come here." Had he thought about it, there were a dozen, a hundred reasons, why he should have kept his hands and his mouth off her. But he was thinking only of the damsel in a bit of distress in his arms. He did what he knew he could do, even if it was the only thing he could do. He consoled her.

Had she turned away or given any indication his attention wasn't welcome, he'd have come to his senses and stopped. He almost wished she had. Almost. Instead, she trembled ever so slightly under his touch. One palm cupped her cheek, his thumb stroking the curve of her chin as he lifted her mouth to fit his. She let go the softest of sighs. And he was lost.

He sank his other hand into that mane of hair and pulled her in. The feel and fit of her, so right and perfect, pressing against him had him sighing a bit himself.

She opened her mouth under his, lips parting, accepting, taking. She tasted sweet, her lips even softer than he'd have thought. The hunger for more grew fast and fierce.

He groaned a little as she moved fully against him, so easily, so naturally. Her palms smoothed over his chest and pressed against his shoulders. Rather than push him away, it was as if she was steadying herself. He teased his tongue into her mouth, and she groaned, giving herself over to the moment, over to him. Her hands moved to the back of his neck, her fingertips teasing up his nape, and into his hair as he took the kiss deeper. His response was a growl as she kissed him back, dueled with his tongue, incited him, excited him, matching him thrust for thrust.

Lost completely, pulse thrumming, he moved his mouth from hers, kissing, nipping along her jaw. She tipped her head back, gasping as he found the softest of spots beneath her ear, kissing the pulse point there, teasing her earlobe with his teeth. She moaned when he shifted his thumb from tracing the curve of her chin to brushing it along her bottom lip, tugging, pressing at the softest, fullest part.

She nipped at it, making him twitch hard and pull her into the frame of his hips. With a little growl of her own, she pressed against him as he slid one finger into her mouth, his hips jerking when she sucked on it. Nipping down the curve of her neck, he slid his hand down, cupping the soft curve of her, pressing her against the rigid length of him as he nudged aside her camp shirt and left a string of kisses along the open V neckline of her T-shirt.

She moved into him easily, sinuously, arching in, letting her head fall to the side, the soft gasps, the twitch of her hips, slowly killing him in the most exquisite way possible. He slid his finger from her mouth, then slid two back in, pushed himself right to the edge when she took them almost greedily. He didn't know where her moans ended and his began as he slid his hand under the edge of her tee and slid his palm up along her spine, finding the hooks of her bra. Her fingers curled into his hair, holding, pulling, demanding. Growling yet again, he slid his fingers free and turned her head, taking her mouth hungrily, greedy for more. She met him, dueled with him, taking his tongue, possessing it, then giving him hers and demanding he do the same.

He slid damp fingers along her jaw, down her neck and onward over the front of her shirt. She moaned, writhed a little as he ran his fingertips over her nipples, so hard and full he could feel them through the layers of shirt, tee, and bra. He wanted his tongue on them, wanted to taste, to tease, to wring more from her, for her.

He hiked her up on his body, urging her to wrap her legs around his waist, mindlessly wondering if there was something, anything to push her up against, or lay her down upon.

A sudden clearing of a throat instantly paralyzed them. Then a gruff voice said, "Well, if this is how you conduct interviews, I'm surprised there isn't a line around the harbor, begging to be hired on."

Chapter 9

A bucket of frigid seawater tossed directly on her couldn't have had a more bracing effect.

Grace unwrapped herself from Brodie, all but springing backward in fact, one hand flying to her mouth, the other to the front of her shirt. She stumbled, her knees like jelly, and would have probably fallen if Brodie hadn't moved immediately toward her. He took her gently by the elbows, pulling her to him, then shifted her behind him as he turned toward their surprise visitor.

That his instincts had been immediately to assist and protect, to shield her from this sudden intrusion, did absolutely nothing to help her regain her equilibrium. Every one of her X chromosomes all but quivered in response to his XY alpha display. As if she hadn't gotten enough alpha from him already. That was the single most carnal thing she'd ever experienced. And that included actual sex. *Holy . . . wow.*

"Langston," she finally managed to rasp out. Putting her hand on Brodie's shoulder, she moved next to him. "It's okay. He's a friend."

Still feeling wildly out of sync with the sudden change of events, she took a short, steadying breath and turned to look at her dear friend, mentor, and architect. "I . . .

didn't know you were coming up. I thought you were at some conference thing in Prague."

Brodie kept his hand bracing the small of her back and didn't move away. Nor did he seem the least bit embarrassed or abashed by the sudden intrusion. Or that they'd been caught about a breath away from getting naked.

The rightful way he stood by her side even after their intruder had been identified should have annoyed her or . . . something. It didn't.

"My favorite person went and bought herself a two-hundred-year-old boathouse that I get to play with and you thought I wouldn't come see my new toy in person?"

My new toy. Grace's mind went immediately to the man at her side. She specifically didn't look at him for fear he might see something of her thought on her face and grin. *Lord help me,* she thought, because she'd have grinned right back.

She dragged her mind from those thoughts and back to Langston. "Marnie sent me your sketches and told me you'd be away through next week. I told her to let you know I wouldn't be ready to go through them until after you got back."

"Yes, she told me how excited you were about them."

"I told her not to mention that. I couldn't help saying something, they really are amazing . . . but I wanted you to hear it from me first."

"Last I checked, she works for me, not for you, so of course she told me."

With a dry smile aimed at Langston, she then turned to Brodie. "This is Langston deVry, an old friend and also my architect for the inn. Langston, this is Brodie Monaghan. The shipyard property has been in his family since the town was founded in the mid-eighteenth century."

"Earlier—1715, actually," Brodie said, glancing down at

her. "Although Blueberry Cove wasn't properly recognized until 1734, the McCraes and Monaghans were already well in business by then. This yard was originally built in 1765. Big storm destroyed the two main piers in the early 1800s and did its fair share of damage to this place, as well. Half of the north wall and most of the east one were all she left behind. Rebuilt it, though. Shakes on both the exterior walls and roof have likely been replaced more times than you can count since then, of course." He tapped his heel on the floorboards. "These are original cypress, dating back to before the turn of the nineteenth century for sure, if not original to this building. Same with the interior wood on the rear wall."

Grace met his gaze, wishing she knew what was going through his mind as he talked about the provenance of the building, its place in his family's history. When he wanted to be inscrutable, he did a good job of it.

Langston shifted a shrewd look from one to the other, but Brodie took a half step forward and reached out his hand before Langston could give voice to whatever was on his mind. Grace was sure he'd be certain to share it with her later, however. Whether she wanted to hear it or not.

"Pleasure to make the acquaintance, Mr. deVry. I've seen photos of your work. Always appreciate someone who is unafraid to build on old tradition with new vision. Grace is fortunate indeed to have such a talented friend."

Langston's surprised expression likely matched her own. With a delighted smile, he gave Brodie's proffered hand a quick, firm shake. "Langston, please. I'm glad to hear it. I think you'll approve of what our girl here has in mind for the place."

Grace winced a bit at the "our girl" reference. It didn't go unnoticed when Brodie didn't directly respond to the comment, but after a noncommittal nod and a polite smile, he turned to face her, moving just enough between her and Langston so that whatever he planned to say would remain private between them. "You're okay?"

That he was still putting concern for her first, especially given the fact that her role in the hijacking of part of his heritage had just been thrust between them again, took all those hot and heavy moments and added something decent and thoughtful. Making them—and him—a hundred times more dangerous to her general well-being. She wasn't sure if she should be encouraged and take his consideration as a sign of détente . . . or be wary of being led into some kind of seduction. She knew better than to think that what had just happened between them— exploded between them—automatically changed anything.

"I am," she said, wishing he'd grin or wink or do something Brodie-like to indicate what was going on behind that searching gaze of his. "Thank you," she added sincerely. "For asking. I appreciate that."

His lips curved a bit then, and she made the unfortunate discovery that his being Brodie-like was a hundred times more lethal now that she knew exactly what kind of havoc that mouth of his could really wreak.

"If you're certain of that, then I'll leave you two to your business. I've work of my own needing some attention." He sounded casual and natural, as if conferring on their schedules was something they did routinely. "I'll be back 'round later."

"Wait. I—that is, what we were just—I mean, I don't know what you—"

"Stop your stammering, luv. I won't be coming by to collect on some imagined promise I thought ye just made. It was a moment. And a mighty damn fine one." He lowered his voice to a rough whisper that put every nerve bundle in her erogenous zones right back on red alert.

"I'm no' expecting anything. Hopeful maybe," he added, dimples flashing as the grin deepened, "but I'd be lying if I said otherwise."

"I don't know what you—"

"Shh." He placed a quick finger to her lips.

Just that brief touch, along with the vivid memories it evoked, not to mention her twitchy nerve bundles, made her knees tremble and all points north and south put the welcome mat right back out again.

"Maybe I'm simply interested in finding out what deVry has in mind for the auld place."

"Is that why you came by?"

"I didn't know he was on board, but yes, I was curious to find out how you were going to get from big, empty cavern to inn. Having seen his work, I'll admit my curiosity has grown. Are ye willing to share?"

Am I ever. "Um . . ." She had to clear her throat and put some starch back in her knees. "They're rough sketches, and everything might change once he's looked at the place in person, but—"

"Go talk with your friend, Grace. I'll be by when my work is done. And we'll see what we see." He leaned in, stole a quick kiss, then looked as surprised that he'd done so as she. Turned out that brief flash of vulnerability was far more devastating to her equilibrium than any sexy whisper or impulsive kiss.

"Seemed the natural thing to do," he said, although she wondered if the explanation might have been more for his benefit than hers.

He turned around, giving Langston a nod. "Good to meet you." And startled her again when he gave his thigh a hearty slap. "Where are ye, laddie?" he called out.

Scuffling sounds erupted in the corner behind an old stack of lobster traps. Whomper came trotting out with a half-chewed pot buoy proudly clenched in his teeth, tail wagging hopefully. He paused as he took in the newcomer and shrank back a step.

"Come on, Mischief," Brodie said. "Keep me company. Bring your new friend there with ye."

Whomper took another long, baleful look at Langston, but his adoration for Brodie was stronger, and another thigh pat had him bounding gleefully to Brodie's side. Not so much as a glance in her direction, Grace noted with a roll of her eyes. *Men.*

She laughed when Brodie shot her a wink and a shrug and watched the two incorrigible males depart, shaking her head as she realized they had a similar confident swagger. She briefly wondered if she would look back and realize that was the moment she'd lost complete control of her life.

"Well, I see you've fit right in with the local population."

Grace flushed straight to her roots. "Langston, I—"

He walked into the middle of the big, open space, the light of amusement making his sky blue eyes that much bluer. "Now, now, don't go blustering and blushing. I was beginning to worry that you'd chucked your old life so you could come up here and hide out forever. Good to see that's not the case." After a quick but thorough study of her face, he turned his astute eye to the boathouse interior. "Caught you a bit off guard, too, if I do say."

"You're the one person who knows I came up here to reconnect with Ford, to build . . . well, to build a life, a future. Hopefully one that includes him. Then I'll figure out what comes next. I wasn't—I'm not—looking for anything else at the moment." She sighed. That had been the truth. Now . . . now she didn't know what she wanted. Or didn't want.

"The truth is I was hiding before, in my old life. Now . . . I feel like I've finally really come out, joined the world at large. I can no longer hide behind the comfort of knowing I can always predict what will happen next. That's exciting. And scary as hell. I need to take it one step at a time."

He glanced her way, a bit of the devil in his eyes. "You didn't look all that scared a moment ago." He waved off her visible mortification at being caught doing something so completely out of character. "I'm saying that's a good thing. You stay too closed off. I understand why. I haven't forgotten what you've told me about your childhood, growing up being moved from distant relative to distant relative after your mother passed. You were barely school age."

"Relative is probably a . . . relative term. When I said distant, I was being . . . kind. To myself."

Langston reached out, took her arm and squeezed it gently, then let it go. "I knew what you meant. Something equivalent to off-the-books foster care."

"At best."

"I know you had to feel abandoned, by your mom, by Ford."

"He's thirteen years older than I am. He enlisted when Mom died, so it—"

"Hurt you all the same. I know as an adult you understand why he made the choices he did. Then, anyway. It's easy to say that you don't take those choices personally. Much harder to actually do. Especially when you're a five-year-old little girl who pretty much lost her entire family in the span of a few short weeks."

"Ford wasn't really in my life much before that, at least, not from his perspective." From Grace's perspective, she'd worshiped her older brother. He'd been everything to her. In fact, she had stronger memories of him than she did of her own mother. Her mother hadn't been well before she'd had Grace, and afterward her condition had only worsened. Grace hadn't known then, but her mother had battled severe depression as well as prescription addiction. She was thankful neither of those had been part of her own life and, as far as she knew, not Ford's life, either. At least up through his time in the military, anyway.

She'd never known her father. As far as she knew he'd taken off before she was born and might have been nothing more than a one-night stand. No one ever talked about him. By the time she was old enough to ask more specific questions, she'd been shuttled so many times she wasn't living with anyone who'd even directly known her mom, much less known who had knocked her up. Grace wasn't even sure if she and Ford had the same father, though she knew they resembled each other pretty strongly . . . or had as children.

Her direct memories of her mother were mostly of her being closed away in a dark room, always needing rest and for the house to be quiet. There were occasional trips to the hospital, some stays longer than others. Through it all, there had been other adults in and out of the house who had helped out, but it had been Ford who had mostly taken care of her, though he'd made it clear he didn't appreciate the responsibility.

Not that that had mattered to Grace. He might have thought she was a drag and a burden, but he'd been there for her, gotten her dressed, brushed her hair, made her meals, and when she'd told him she was afraid of the dark, he'd sat in her room and told her silly stories until he was sure she was asleep before he left her room at night. He'd even made a nightlight out of a battery-operated camping lantern he'd found in the garage. Then, right before her fifth birthday, their mom had gone into the hospital again and hadn't come out.

Ford had just turned eighteen. He'd told Grace he'd joined the Army and had to go fight for their country in some desert far, far away. She'd be proud of him. He'd promised he'd be back to see her. Except he hadn't come back. Well, he had in body, but in spirit, he'd been a stranger to her. To everyone, really. He'd found out where she was living and had stuck around long enough to make sure she was okay. She'd convinced him she was, praying he'd realize that she was anything but—then he was gone again, back overseas. She'd been nine then. And so the routine went.

She knew exactly how many tours he'd gone on, though she hadn't always known where. She'd been so proud of him when he'd made it into the Army Rangers Special Forces. She'd bragged to anyone who would listen, but she hardly ever heard from him. She got postcards occasionally, fewer and fewer from that point on, and had treasured them as if they were worth a royal fortune. To her, they had been. As she'd gotten older, into her teen years, she'd wondered how she could love him so much and be so angry with him at the same time.

She'd been eighteen and legally independent—though she'd been on her own in every way that mattered far earlier than that—when he'd finally retired from the military and come back for good. By then, they were more estranged than not, and she was a pissed-off teenager who hadn't been all that forgiving when he'd finally come to see her. He'd moved around some after that, and she'd lost track of him, mostly because when Ford didn't want to be found, there wasn't any finding him. She'd only found out he'd settled in Maine by accident. A woman he'd been seeing had gone to the trouble of tracking Grace down and sending her a note, telling her where Ford was and what he was doing with his life, asking her to please come up and see him.

The fact that it was some strange woman asking and not Ford himself told her all she needed to know about how welcome a visit from her would be. She'd been about to graduate with her bachelor's degree and start law school and had long since decided she was better off alone. She'd told herself to stop thinking about him or wanting what she couldn't have. But the note had shaken her up. More than she'd wanted to admit. She'd finally compromised by sending him an invitation to her graduation, not sure which she was dreading more—that he'd come and be all happy in some new life . . . or that he'd stay away and reject her once again.

He hadn't come. No note. No phone call. So, she'd never gone to Maine. She had no idea what had happened to the woman. For all Grace knew, Ford had a passel of kids and multiple ex-wives. She only knew he was still in Maine because she'd done a little digging on him through a lawyer friend of hers who had a variety of contacts and verified that the address on his tax forms still listed him as living in Blueberry Cove, Maine. He filed as single and didn't list any dependants, not that that necessarily meant he didn't have any. Under occupation, it said *scientist* and that his employer was an organization that funded endangered wildlife study and rehabilitation. She couldn't really picture him doing that, but then she probably wouldn't recognize her brother if she bumped into him on the street.

"I know how important it is to you, to do what you're doing," Langston said, breaking gently into her thoughts. "You know I worry about you doing all this and getting your hopes up—"

"I'm—I know this isn't going to be some magical reunion. We've talked about that. I know it may end up that my brother and I simply reside in the same place and that's as good as it will ever get. But . . . it's more than I had. I fully believe it would be a good thing for Ford to know me, to have me in his life, but this is ultimately the most selfish thing I've ever done. It's all for me. I don't belong anywhere, Langston. If I'd come here and it had felt off or wrong or ridiculous or . . . or as foolish as it sounds when I try to explain it to anyone, I'd have gone back. Or done something else."

"But . . . I'm guessing that wasn't the case."

She shook her head, and knew her heart was in her eyes because his expression softened and the worry she knew he still felt was exposed. "It was . . . well, it was simply right. The water here . . . so much of it, everywhere you look, the bays, the inlets, the ocean. It's so blue. So beautiful. It fills my heart, makes it pound. I can't even explain it. How is it I've never been here and it's the closest thing to home I've ever felt? Maybe it was that way for Ford, too. Maybe the water has some meaning to him, like it does to me. Or maybe it's nothing like that and there is nothing that connects us but the same zip code. It doesn't matter. What matters is I like it here. I like the water. I also like the quiet of the place, the slower, more deliberate pace. There is such a strong history here. The Cove has endurance and fortitude over centuries of time, and yet it feels intimate and personal, not cold and statistical, like a footnote in some history book. I'm liking the people, too, as I get to know them. And they seem to be welcoming me. I want to be here and I'm already falling in love with Blueberry Cove and the harbor and this scary new life. I haven't a freaking clue what the hell I'm doing . . . not a one, Lang, and I just don't care."

She smiled at her friend. For the first time since arriving in Maine, since signing her name on a dotted line and taking out a loan for a business she had no idea if she could run, but desperately wanting to find out, she let every bit of her hopes and dreams show. "I hope this life will eventually involve Ford, too. He was the catalyst to all of it. When I finally admitted I didn't want to forget him, that

I wanted—needed—to find him, reunite my family, this whole hair-brained idea took root and it wouldn't let go. Or I couldn't let it go. But he's not all of this. It's become so much more."

Langston's smile deepened and the worry abated as a more typical gleam of excitement filled his eyes. "I can see that. You know I'll worry anyway, just as you know I'll do whatever I can to support you."

"That means more to me than you will ever know. I realize we haven't known each other long in the big-picture scheme of things, but you know you're my other real family." Her eyes got a little glassy when he nodded, and the honest affection he had for her shone very clearly in his eyes. "I'm scared, Lang. To death, actually. Like, a thousand times a day I wonder what the hell I've done. But the fear is almost like this kind of cool, energizing thing. It makes me feel . . . alive," she said, being as honest and frank as she'd ever been. "Hitting the big three-o and then being passed over for partner—a position I'd worked my whole career for, lobbied hard for, and damn well deserved—should have crushed me. Devastated me. And . . . all I felt was relief."

She paced and looked around the open space, but her thoughts were on her life as it had been, a mere ten months ago. God, it felt like a lifetime ago already. "I couldn't ignore that. I had to . . . well, to figure out why, to reassess. Everything. To ask myself if that was all there was. And if not . . . then what did I really want? What I realized I wanted was family. Not the biological clock kind, though that's probably in the mix somewhere, I suppose, but I wanted back the one I already have." She looked at him again and grinned. "You know, you played a part in the decision, too."

He looked honestly surprised. "I can't fathom how. I was the one who tried to talk you out of it."

She laughed. "You have to admit that's pretty funny coming from the guy who lives for challenges. Your favorite hobby is taking risks."

"Yes, but the difference is, it's my nature. I don't know any other way to be. I didn't think that was at all the case with you. I was trying to be a good friend."

"And you were. That's just it. You've become so dear to me, and—" She broke off and her smile turned wry. "Don't let this alarm you or anything, but I trust you. I let myself rely on you—which speaks huge loud volumes you probably don't even realize. And, well, that was part of what made me want to reach out to Ford. To see if maybe we could establish something. Anything. I know what it can be like, because I have that with you. So it gave me the confidence to try. You know?"

"You humble me, Grace."

She could see in his expression that he meant that sincerely.

"You're one of the few people I feel the need to take care of, besides myself, of course." He flashed a smile. "I'm glad you feel you can trust me, rely on me. Because you can. Even if it means surrendering your life in the city and moving to the back of the beyond. An innkeeper? I'll admit I still don't see that part. You're a brilliant lawyer, so good at reading people, assessing what they need, and handling challenging emotional environments deftly. Your firm has to feel the loss. I'm sure they're kicking themselves ten times over for letting you go."

Grace grinned. "Well, it would be a lie if I said I didn't hope they suffered at least a little. Thank you for all the kind words. I'm not sure I live up to that lofty a height, but if I was good at defusing tensions and reading people, it was because I didn't feel an emotional attachment to them. I used to be proud of my ability to remain detached and objective. It did make me good at my job. It also made me removed and distant, even from myself." She lifted a hand when he started to respond. "I'm not going back into estate law. But I am hoping I can take parts of what I learned from it and apply it to my new life. If I'm good at reading people, helping them, assessing their needs, then that has to come in handy when it comes to running an inn, wouldn't you say?"

He nodded, though she could tell it was with some reluctance. They'd had this particular discussion before, more than once, since she'd made her decision to leave Harneker and Swift, the prestigious D.C. law firm that had hired her straight out of law school.

"You still haven't ever really explained where the sudden burning desire to open an inn came from."

Grace fully intended to sidestep that question again, and every time it came up. In fact, she'd probably never admit out loud to anyone how she'd come up with the idea for an inn. Maybe on the twentieth anniversary of its opening or something, she thought with a private smile, when it would all seem so amusing. And not completely nuts. "I know this is all a little crazy and I probably sound ridiculous to you, trying to describe any of it," she said by way of response.

"No. What you sound is happy." Langston's smile had grown and the deep affection in his gaze made her eyes grow a bit misty again. "That is a good thing, indeed." He gave her a look up and down. "It's only been a few weeks since I saw you and already I almost don't recognize you. I didn't think you owned anything that wasn't black and tailored."

She laughed. "Actually, I didn't." She gave a quick turn. "The latest in boathouse renovation wear. Sure to turn heads in Milan next season."

"Well, I don't know if it's the clothes, this new thing you're doing with your hair, or the high color in your cheeks, but so far, it appears Maine . . . or maybe it's certain people who live in Maine"—his eyes twinkled—"agrees with you."

Her cheeks bloomed again, so she deflected revisiting what she'd been doing with Brodie, which conveniently meant she didn't have to think about whether she was going to do any of it again with Brodie, by saying, "You're one to talk. Check out the new duds. How very . . . Lauren-Does-the-Hamptons of you."

Langston stood a full head and a fair amount of very thick shoulders taller than her own five-foot-seven and was built like the linebacker he'd been in college—if linebackers wore exquisitely tailored Italian suits and hand-tooled leather shoes. For all his bear of a chest and shoulders, he was surprisingly trim at the waist, with strong legs and, she hated to admit she'd noticed on more than one occasion, a pretty fine ass. All of which would have made him appear far more youthful than his sixty-some years, except for the lion's mane of shocking white hair he sported. He was ridiculously vain about the thick, wavy mass, which he wore to the shoulders, always meticulously groomed, as was his neatly trimmed, equally white Fu Manchu beard and mustache. It had become his signature, of sorts.

Given that architects were essentially artists, Grace figured it was a fairly mild eccentricity. However, only the lion's mane resembled the man she knew. He was decked out in pleated, white canvas trousers, tailored to fit his athlete's frame, with a thin, braided leather belt, under which he'd tucked a rich, melon-colored silk shirt with white bone buttons. The sleeves had been casually rolled up over his heavy forearms, and he'd topped off the ensemble with a thin ocean-blue sweater tied jauntily around his neck. Something only Langston could pull off with aplomb, given his size.

He held out his arms, thoroughly enjoying her once-over. "I thought I captured the essence of coastal Maine brilliantly. I wanted the sweater to match the color of the water here. So brilliant a blue, as you said, very inspiring indeed. I think Sven did a remarkable job, don't you?"

She laughed, shaking her head. "Considering what you pay him, I'm surprised he didn't find a way to spin the water itself into a sweater. You're such a clothes hound."

"Darling, I appreciate great talent. People pay me ridiculous sums to create their perfect nest, and I'm thankful every day I have the God-given talent to do that. I enjoy discovering great talent in others, and giving them the same opportunities. Worth every penny."

"Says the man who has accumulated many, many pennies."

"What's the point in accumulating them if you don't do something interesting and fun once you have them?" He glanced around. "Something you would know a little bit about now, as well. *Ho ragione?*"

"Yes, you're right," she said, exhausting most of what little Italian she knew. That wee bit she had him to thank for. He'd taken her to Fashion Week in Milan three years ago, claiming he needed her estate skills to help him assess certain purchases he wanted to make while there, when she'd known all along it was because he'd been between girlfriends and really just wanted someone along who wasn't on his payroll. Regardless, she'd been thrilled to go. "You're always right."

"And that is why I love you. You'll tell me that without my having to pay you to say it."

"Oh, please. People all over the world gush about you

on a regular basis. It's amazing your ego isn't the size of all Europe combined. Except, wait . . ." She shot him a dry look.

He barked out a laugh. "And that's the other reason I love you." He held out a hand, beckoning her in for a hug.

Grace went willingly, not realizing how much she needed one of his patented bear hugs until she was wrapped up against his big, lumberjack-sized chest. "I'm really glad you came up."

Langston laughed again, squeezed her a bit, then set her back. "Well, perhaps you might have wished I'd had Scotty plot a slightly later flight plan." A devilish gleam livened his eyes. "Say, tomorrow morning? After breakfast in bed?"

She swatted at him. "I'll never live that down, and okay—maybe it's deserved. Although I will submit that I was in my own boathouse where I had at least some expectation of privacy. You could have knocked."

"Darling, the hounds of hell could have been howling and you'd never have heard them. Besides, you're renovating one of the most historic buildings in town, and the panel door is wide open. Don't tell me half the town hasn't trooped in and out of here on a regular basis since you showed up."

"Oh, sure. Be logical." But she grinned as she said it.

He lifted her hand, pressed a gallant kiss on the back of it, then gave her his most brilliant smile. "There's nothing logical about a passion like that, my dear." He winked. "That's often the best part."

Grace laughed and tugged her hand free. "Says the guy who's been married five times."

His smile spread to a broad grin, completely unabashed. "It beats being lonely and alone."

Langston had married a fifth time about eighteen months after his wife Ava's death, which was about six months after Grace had turned down his advances. He'd even acknowledged at the time that it was a rebound and probably a very bad idea, yet he had no regrets then, or nine months later when she'd demanded a divorce, unable to deal with the knowledge that she would never measure up to his lost love. Of course, from all accounts, former wife number five was quite happy with her very generous divorce settlement and was already dating an Italian count or some such, last Langston had mentioned. So who was Grace to judge? It was more shocking he hadn't married again in the three years since.

The closest she'd come to marriage was when Barney in accounting had gotten drunk at the annual Christmas party and blurted out his undying love for her. Fortunately, she'd caught him by the elbow before he'd gotten down on one knee.

Grace wasn't opposed to marriage or to being married, though she'd grown up without any role model for a good one. She'd dated, and like any normal person, she had general hopes of someday walking down the aisle. She guessed.

She'd spent so much of her life trying to figure out what family meant to her, what it should mean, and what she wanted it to mean, that she'd long since given up on forcing any kind of traditional boundaries or definitions. Ford was her family. And Langston factored in there. More recently, she had Whomper counting on her. That was about as nontraditional as it got. And yet, it was family all the same.

She wanted to have a partner, children, to spend the latter part of her life creating and enjoying the kind of family she'd so wished she'd had in the first half of her life. Beyond that, it didn't much matter how it was framed. She supposed she'd always assumed when someone came along who made her think in the long term, she'd decide how she felt about saying the *I do* part and go from there. That her thoughts strayed immediately to a brash, green-eyed, sexy Irishman did little to help clarify the issue.

Grace lifted an eyebrow. "You do know you don't have to marry them to not be alone, right?"

Langston lifted a beefy shoulder. "I'm an eternal optimist. Sue me. When I said my vows, I believed in them with my whole heart. What life chooses to do after that, it does. If you sit around waiting for a guarantee, you're going to do a lot of sitting and no living." His smile shifted, grew less teasing, more tender. Approval and admiration were in his gaze as he took a shrewd, assessing look at the building around them.

She wasn't ashamed to admit that both of those meant the world to her.

"But then," he said, his gaze resting fondly back on hers. "I don't have to tell you that any longer, now do I?"

"No," she said, grinning with delight. "Not anymore."

"That's my girl." He clapped his hands together. "So, let's play with your new toy, shall we?"

I'd love to, but my new toy is in his boathouse, she thought, then looked away when her face went hot all over again. How long was it going to take before she didn't have Brodie on the brain? Okay, Brodie and sex. Preferably together.

She quickly gestured to the huge, open space. "So," she said, perhaps a tad overly brightly, "what do you think? Will your plans work? I loved, loved them. I can't believe you made my general loft concept work. It was really just a whim."

"The best things are, my dear."

Oh, if you only knew. The whole idea of building and running an inn had, at best, been conceived on a whim. *Apparently it's like a virus, and it's spreading. I seem to be doing a lot of things on a whim these days.*

After seeing the loft design and the open lower area that Brodie had done in his boathouse, Grace had wondered aloud to Langston if there was some way to incorporate that open-air, loft-type feel with the rooms in her inn. To her delight he'd been captivated by the idea. But even knowing how brilliant he was, Grace had been blown away by the rough sketches he'd scanned and e-mailed her a few days later.

He'd designed a series of cantilevered loft spaces, layered around the perimeter of the boathouse interior in a sort of circular pattern, angling upward from the floor all the way to the open ceiling area. Each loft would look down over an open hearth floor plan on the ground floor in the center of the boathouse, designed to bring a homey feel to the place, while creating a tucked away, aerie-nest feeling for each of the individual rooms. He'd designed each loft with angled screened louvered walls made of a special kind of fabric that would imitate the feel of nautical boat sails, and could be made transparent or opaque from the inside by sliding them over one another in layers, though they were always opaque from outside view.

The angle and design of the room allowed for complete privacy in the bed and bath area. Depending on which side of the building, porthole windows or bigger were to be on the exterior walls, all with at least some view of the water. Because of the way the boathouse was situated all the rooms encompassed at least one corner of the building. He'd also created an open balcony feel at the front of each loft, where out by the railing there would be a low, intimate table and comfortable chairs for dining, reading, and conversation.

On the ground floor, in the rear of the space, would be her personal rooms, a small office, and a kitchen for preparing breakfasts and small tray foods for afternoon snacks, evening aperitifs, and the like. He'd even sketched out a plan to include tables on the deck out front, looking out over the docks, so guests could snack or sip wine there, or inside at the small, intimate groupings of chairs and low tables arranged around the central woodstove hearth.

He'd also suggested a theme for the rooms that would echo a high-end stateroom or captain's quarters, such as one might have found on a historic ocean liner or passenger ship. Updated, of course, with modern amenities. Grace had loved all of it, and only hoped his vision worked with the reality of the place. She envisioned a sort of crisp, New England elegance with touches of nautical, seashore whimsy. She wanted each room to have the latest comforts in bed and bath, but imbue it all with a warm, inviting spirit.

The whole thing was definitely high concept, and not inexpensive to deliver, but if they could pull it off, it would make for a very unique travel experience for her guests and set her place apart from the gazillion other inns that dotted the lengthy Maine coastline. She hoped that would be the key to enticing folks to come a bit farther north than they might have otherwise decided to travel.

She found herself wondering what Brodie would think of it, if he'd be upset that she'd played off the same basic theme he'd gone with, or be happy she'd found a way to take his personal vision and expand on it.

"Speaking of whims and whimsy," Langston said, pulling her away from fantasizing about her future inn. "Have you been to that fabulous antique store a few blocks up? It's utterly enchanting."

Grace didn't have to ask which antique shop. There seemed to be more antique shops in Maine than people, but in Blueberry Cove, there was only one. And it was a doozy. "I meant to tell you about Mossy Cup. I knew you'd be fascinated by the tree."

The shop was yet another historic place. Dating back to the town's origins, it had been in business, uninterrupted, since the 1700s. If that alone weren't enough of a draw, the building was constructed around an actual mossy cup oak tree, which grew straight up through the middle, with its leafy branches extending directly through the roof and creating an umbrella over the place. It was like a life-sized shop for those cookie-baking elves.

"It's really incredible, isn't it? Did you go inside?" She smiled. "I hear the owner, Eula March, is really something. I haven't had the pleasure as yet, but the word is she's a bit cantankerous, and something of a mystic or . . . well, I'm not sure entirely. You'd probably love her."

"I did stop, yes. There was a sign on the door, however. Closed till after lunch. But I got out and walked around the place. From what I could see of the pieces in the window, she does impeccable restoration work. And you're right, I have to get inside and see how they built the place around that gorgeous tree. It makes the mind spin."

She could all but see the wheels turning. It made her smile. She knew the feeling. It was how she felt every time she looked around the boathouse and tried to imagine what it would look like when his drawings were realized.

"Perhaps we should come back and take a stroll there after dinner," he said. "See what she has that might work in here."

She laughed. "Oh, we're a long, long way from picking out furniture." But she had to admit, she was dying to start planning that part. Now that the general theme had been established, she could really let herself begin to think about it. "Besides, if I let you in there, I'll lose you for days, I can already tell."

"Quite true." He winked at her, completely unrepentant. "When I got the photos you sent, I did do some tweaking on the plans I sent you. I brought the updated version with me for you to look over." At her glance around and behind him, he lifted empty hands. "I left them back at the house."

"House? What house? You've already checked in somewhere?"

"I leased a place out by the Point, on the bay. Lovely view of the old lighthouse. Marnie found it. A real gem."

"You . . . leased a house? Already? Are you staying then?" She knew what his schedule was like, so she was sure there was no way he could be doing that.

He pretended to look offended. "You don't want me around and underfoot? Well, I suppose given the greeting I received, I can understand that." He was the only man she knew who could give an aggrieved sigh and a naughty wink at the same time, and make both of them work.

"Oh, stop with the sad violins already. I would love it if you were around and underfoot, and you know it," she said dryly, making him grin like a mischievous child who had just gotten what he wanted. "But I'm aware what your life is like, so we both know that's not going to happen."

"True, but I do plan to make it up here during the construction phase whenever I can, and of course I'll be coming to visit once the place is done. After all, if my favorite person insists on living in Maine, then I suppose I'll have to come to Maine to see her."

"Your favorite person will be running an inn. What, you can't stay in my place? You're designing it."

"You know I like my privacy. And loads of space. I'd have to rent out the whole thing." He smiled and let the ego that was always simmering just below the surface rise to the top. "Besides, a Langston deVry inn will always be booked. Folks will be lining up to see what I've done with this place. I've already let the word drop to a few of the architectural digests."

"You—did?" Grace's eyes popped wide. "Langston, that's—thank you!"

"Darling, you didn't think I was doing this exclusively for you, did you? It will be a new kind of feather in my cap. We'll both reap the rewards. Now, let's go swing by wherever it is you're staying and get your things so we can move you out to the house." He pulled two sets of keys from his pants pocket. "Here. It's yours for the duration. Longer if you need an escape once you're living here."

"You can't just buy me a house."

"I didn't buy you a house." He grinned. "I leased one. If you like it, though, just tell me and . . . merry Christmas to you."

Grace tried to stare him down, knowing it was fruitless.

For all that Langston was a polished, worldly sophisticate with his prestigious Ivy League degree and offices on more than one continent . . . he was still, at heart, a big kid who happened to be able to play in a very big sandbox while simultaneously owning—or leasing—all the candy stores he wanted. He got so passionate about things that he sometimes forgot that not everyone appreciated or even wanted him bulldozing in and simply making his visions for them happen.

She thought that was probably a large part of his marriage and divorce record.

He jangled the keys. "Come now, don't waste time. Let's go have dinner and make plans for this place, shall we?"

Most times when he got a little—or a lot—out of line, he'd back down, grudgingly, if she really put her foot down. Today, however, was not one of those times. He leveled at her his big-time-boss-man-architect gaze, reminding her why he was also a huge global business success.

"You say it's for convenience, but I'm thinking it's just a means of keeping a closer eye on me."

"You said you think of me as family. Well, that's what family does. It goes both ways."

She laughed even as she took the gentle admonishment to heart. "Is this where the *be careful what you wish for* warning comes into play?"

"I think you're beginning to understand, yes." He smiled, but all the affection he had for her was plain to see as well. "I want to know you're happy and safe here. So, just say, 'thank you, Langston.' "

"Thank you, Langston." It was sincere. She raised a hand, though, when he beamed. He loved winning almost as much as he loved doing whatever he damn well pleased, which might be the same thing, she realized. "But you're going to make some kind of lease agreement with me. I won't be a kept woman," she added, with a dramatic air.

"More's the pity," he tossed back, and they both laughed. "Well, now that that's settled, shall we?" He crooked an arm in invitation. "I have Carlos already out at the house, preparing us dinner."

"You brought Carlos with you to—never mind." She shook her head. "Of course you did. And that sounds fabulous."

They had climbed into his jaunty rental—how he fit his frame into the little sports car she had no idea—when she remembered. "Oh, wait. Whomper!"

"What on earth is a whomper?"

"Not a what, more a who. My dog. You met him when you came in."

"You have a dog?"

She laughed. "You say that like I've suddenly contracted a highly contagious virus."

Langston gave a little shudder. "Only a slight overstatement, I'm sure. I guess I never saw you as a pet owner. What breed is the thing, anyway? Surely not pedigreed."

She nudged her elbow into his side. "I forget what a snob you can be sometimes."

"I've nothing against animal cohabitation. Cats can be lovely, self-sufficient companions. Why couldn't you get something in an exotic Siamese?"

She laughed again. "Wow. For the record, I never saw me as a pet owner, either. I assure you, it wasn't planned. I was at the local farmers' market and they were doing these shelter adoptions. It was an uncustomary moment of weakness."

"See? I'm not the only one who sees the value in not being alone or lonely."

"I never thought I was either of those things."

"Don't fool yourself. With a lack of family, you made your work your steady companion and when that was gone? How long did you wait to fill the void?" She glanced away and he said, "Exactly. Maybe you're more like me than you're wiling to admit." He glanced at her as he settled in and pulled the seat belt across his chest. "Any regrets?"

Grace rolled her eyes. "A hundred times a day."

When Langston gave her hand a knowing pat, she laughed, and relented. "We haven't been apart since I got him. And I never thought I'd say this, but it feels weird going off to dinner without checking on him first."

"Will you be seeing your man later? He looked pretty comfortable with taking over doggie duty."

Brodie had, she thought, seeming not to care how long the pup stayed with him. She'd go over and get Whomper the minute she got back from dinner. "He's not my man," she told Langston, trying not to think about what else she might get from Brodie after dinner. "Trust me. Guys like Brodie Monaghan aren't any woman's man."

Langston nodded, then let his silence speak volumes.

Grace was tempted to continue to push her point, but even she realized it would sound a bit like "she doth protest too much."

She clicked on her seat belt and took a moment to glance down the curve of the harbor to Brodie's boathouse. She thought again about that look she'd seen in his eyes when he'd spoken of the woman who'd renovated his boathouse. Maybe he had been one woman's man at some point. Maybe it had been Alex MacFarland. But she had chosen her man, and it hadn't been Brodie. Grace had heard that Alex was living with the town's police chief out on Pelican Point.

Grace wondered what it would be like having Brodie Monaghan want to be her man . . . and what woman had been strong enough to send him away.

Chapter 10

Brodie let the door swing shut behind him as he entered the Rusty Puffin. It was Blueberry Cove's only pub, and an authentic Irish one at that. Since it wasn't quite nine in the morning, he hadn't come by for a pint. "Fergus?" he called out when he saw no one was behind bar.

"Back here, laddie," came a shout from the kitchen, which was situated on the other side of the wall behind the bar. Fergus's shout was followed by a loud, metallic clang, a particularly inventive string of swearwords, another clang, then "Aw, bloody hell."

"Hold up there," Brodie shouted over the din. He was grinning as he ducked under the bar and pushed through the swinging door to the kitchen. "What have ye—oh Lord."

He walked over to stand next to his fellow Irishman and mirrored the older man's hands-on-hips pose, as they stared at the antiquated and dismantled grill. "Ye should have called me over sooner."

"I believe that's exactly what I did," Fergus grumbled. "Took your sweet time. Had to try something." He gave Brodie a once-over. "Thought maybe you'd found someone to keep you warm this morning, but given that pinched look on your puss, I'm guessing the drought continues."

Every time Brodie thought he'd gotten used to Fergus's all-knowing-all-seeing fey Irish ways, he was proven wrong. He thought his cheeks had grown blush proof when he'd discovered the joys of sex at the ripe young age of sixteen. The family tavern's new barmaid had been three years his senior and light-years more experienced. Och, the things she'd shown him. Apparently, however, he'd been wrong about being blush proof, too. "What you think you know about my current sex life is not up for discussion."

A stout fireplug of a man, Fergus had a thick shock of black wavy hair surprisingly free of so much as a single strand of gray. His bright blue eyes were the color of the summer sky, and his bushy beard and thick brows, both threaded with white and gray, belied his seventy-plus years of age. He gave Brodie a sideways glance. "These days it'd be a brief story anyway, short list of characters and not much plot to speak of." Barking out a hoarse laugh, he clapped his beefy palm to Brodie's back with a reassuring thump. "Dinnae worry, lad, boy with a face as pretty as yours, the slump can't last for long."

Brodie merely shook his head and accepted the advice, knowing it would go better on him if he resisted the urge to offer so much as a token defense. He was well aware of the reputation he'd earned since coming to the Cove. Was it wrong that he found women of all ages the most delightful creatures made by God's own hand? He couldn't see how. To his mind, any time spent in the wonderment of their company, especially if one could coax a pretty smile or a bright laugh, was a moment never to be regretted.

If he didn't exert a great deal of energy—or *any* energy— disabusing those who assumed that a bit of a flirt and some good Irish charm were synonymous with bedding every beauty he'd flashed a grin at, well, folks were going to believe what they were going to believe anyhow. Naturally, if a woman of his acquaintance wanted it made clear that her good name hadn't gotten a bit of Irish tarnish on it, then he'd gallantly stepped up and corroborated her story—regardless of the truth between them. Some women rather liked creating a bit of buzz, letting folks assume what they would. In those cases, he was happy to not kiss and let the gossips say he did.

The reality of his reputation and the idea that there was always some speculation about who he was or wasn't seeing . . . turned his thoughts instantly to Grace. Normal enough, given what they'd been doing the last time he'd seen her. He'd thought of little else since. It was the protective nature of his feelings, the immediate and rather strong desire to protect her privacy, that was a bit disconcerting. Grace would likely tell him right where to step off for presuming he was in charge of defending her honor in any way, shape, or form.

But he remembered the way she'd looked at him when she'd thanked him sincerely for taking a moment to make sure she was okay after their spontaneous moment of . . . well, unbridled lust was what they'd been having before being rudely and somewhat embarrassingly—to her mind—intruded upon by her old friend. Brodie could presume she was so used to taking care of herself that it had been a surprise for anyone else to assume the role. Or perhaps it was because she dated knuckle-dragging jerks who didn't know how to treat a lady. Somehow, though, he didn't see Grace falling into that pattern. Her self-esteem seemed pretty healthy.

And yet, she gave you a go. He ignored his little voice. Or tried to. He wasn't a bad bloke. He respected women. Hell, he'd never have survived childhood if he hadn't learned their merit early on. The surprise of it was that he was a bit bothered by the fact that once Grace learned of his reputation, it might reflect poorly on him. Why that should matter when the woman had all but stolen his family heritage out from under him, he couldn't fathom. And yet, it mattered all the same.

All the more reason to change the topic with Fergus giving him the once-over. "Speaking of my charming ways, why don't I see if I can coax a wrench or two into fixing her up." Brodie nodded toward the grill. "Maybe she can be resuscitated one last time."

Fergus's attention was pulled back to the matter at hand and a scowl crossed his ruddy face. "For all ye've a bit of magic with the fairer sex, I'm fair to certain your luck will meet its match with this flaming—"

"Now, now," Brodie said with a chuckle of his own. "Why don't you head on out front and do whatever it is that needs doin' and leave her to me. I'll set her right or put her out of her misery once and for all. Leave me to determine which it will be and it will go much easier on you."

"You know I just replaced the damn furnace not six months back, and now this one wants to act like she's—" Fergus bit the rest off in an uncustomary show of restraint.

Brodie clapped his hand on his friend's broad shoulder. "Women. Can't live with 'em, can't run a decent pub without 'em. I'll come out and give you the final score in a bit." He gave the array of ancient parts littering the floor a wary look. "But you might want to take a peek at the budget."

Fergus swore under his breath as he stalked to the door. "I've business to discuss with ye when you're done."

Brodie's brow climbed. "Do ye now? What would be the topic?"

"Put Ms. Humpty there back together again first. Before I lose what's left of me patience."

Brodie shifted his gaze downward to hide a grin. Fergus

was a man of many talents, patience not making even the long list. "Aye, sir. I'll be out in a bit then."

He waited until the door swung shut and Fergus was on the other side of it before looking back at the old grill. It had probably been pulling duty since just after prohibition ended. "Darlin', I think this is where you and I might have to end this beautiful relationship."

It wasn't his first time grappling with the damn thing. Far from. Brodie had met Fergus McCrae on his second day in Blueberry Cove. Looking for a bit of home across the pond, he'd wandered into the pub, hoping for a decent ale and a bit of conversation. Back home, his family's tavern had been the center of information in the village. Well, the tavern and the salon where the ladies had their hair and nails done. He knew a little about that, seeing as it was his mother's aunt who'd been running the place since before he was born.

Every time Brodie had bitched about being stuck working in the family business, Auntie Aideen had offered to let him come do shampoos at her shop. At the time, however, it had seemed a fate worse than death, even when compared to working in the family pub. Looking back now, he realized maybe he should have thought the offer through a bit better. Having his hands in a woman's long, silky hair, relaxing her, making her happy? Yeah, he'd definitely dropped the ball there.

His thoughts ran once again to the only long, silky hair to beckon him in recent memory. Certain indelible images came to mind when he thought of Grace Maddox. Despite the numerous new ones added to the repertoire after their hedonistic *pas de deux* earlier that week, the one of her descending his stairs that first morning, with those wild, damp locks dancing about her fair face, would likely always hold a spot near the top of the list. Och, but sinking his hands in all that silk and under running water? It wasn't a sink in the back of his dear auld auntie's beauty shop that came to mind.

"I don't hear any work being done back there, boy-o," Fergus hollered from the front.

"All in good time, my fine friend," Brodie called back, grinning once again. There were parts of home he didn't miss, but only the Irish could be irascible and lovable in equal measure, and he missed that natural ebb and flow.

Fergus was a character of the highest caliber. From their first meeting, he had become a fast friend, in part due to the two of them being the only direct Irish imports in a town full of Irish descendants. The relationship had long since grown beyond their obvious ties.

Fergus had come to Blueberry Cove close to twenty years earlier, another in the very long list of McCraes to do so, beginning with the ones who'd helped found the town along with Brodie's own forebears. As it happened, Fergus's cousin some number of times removed had taken on the burden of raising his son and daughter-in-law's four children after the pair had been killed in a tragic car accident.

As Brodie well knew, only one of those now-grown McCrae children had stayed on in the Cove, the three girls having gone off to seek their fame and fortune elsewhere. Brodie had met Logan McCrae, of course. In the span of a year's time there wasn't anyone left in the Cove he didn't at least have a nodding acquaintance with. As police chief, it was Logan's business to know everyone, and though Brodie hadn't had any reason to connect with him for professional reasons, they had developed something of a personal connection, albeit one neither had chosen.

About six months after his arrival, Brodie had found his head turned by the latest newcomer in town, Alex MacFarland. Problem was, she'd caught Logan's eye even sooner. Despite having inherited more of the irascible trait than charm from his Irish forebears, at least to Brodie's mind, Logan McCrae had caught Alex's eye early on, as well.

None of that would have mattered a whit to Brodie, as women in general were fun to look at, even more fun to flirt and banter with, and on occasion take home. That was where it usually ended. Rebuilding and relaunching the Monaghans' boatbuilding business was a monumental task. He wasn't looking for anything more complicated.

Alex had been different, though. He had given it a lot of thought since, and wondered if it was merely that they were both fish out of water that had been the draw . . . or if it was because she didn't fit neatly into any kind of category of women he'd ever had the pleasure of meeting. Whatever the case, she'd lingered on and on in his mind and in his life, even after she'd gently but firmly turned down his advances.

She'd overseen the renovation of his boathouse, so even after she'd declared herself off-limits, he'd been subjected to being around her daily. While he respected her choice completely and had made the requested full retreat . . . that time spent together had formed the unshakable feeling in him that she was the one who'd gotten away.

The one. He'd heard the stories and the songs that had been sung in his family's tavern about "the one." He'd seen it often enough in his large and boisterous family, as well as in and around the village at home, to know and believe the concept existed. Yet, despite being quite in favor of spending as much time in the company of the fairer sex as possible, he'd never once felt that for himself. Until Alex.

When the renovation had been completed, she'd gone back to her work on the Pelican Point lighthouse restoration, eventually moving in with Logan. Brodie had been left with the ghost of her smile, her laugh—her essence, so to speak—haunting his boathouse. He'd spent more than a few restless nights wondering if he'd ever feel completely at home there. It felt like some part of what made it a true home was missing.

He frowned. All this maudlin bitching and moaning and carrying on . . . for a woman he'd never so much as kissed.

So it had been. The heart wanted what it wanted, even after being shut down and flat-out denied. He'd flirted, bantered, dated since, but it was as if a bar had been set. He wasn't particularly satisfied or even interested in starting something unless the potential to meet that bar was present. Crazy and frustrating as all hell. What was wrong with his old life, he wanted to know? There it was, his new truth, a new knowledge gained that he had to accept—since what had once been enough for him clearly wasn't acceptable any longer.

Six months had ticked by with agonizing slowness and he'd begun to think he was ruined for good . . . then he'd awoken three weeks ago to the sound of a woman swearing down on his dock. . . .

He grinned as he sorted through Fergus's extensive toolbox, looking for the right size socket. Funny how he hadn't thought of Alex MacFarland in . . . well, in three weeks. And when he thought of his boathouse, all he pictured was that moment on the iron steps. His grin turned wry and tone self-deprecating as he muttered, "Perhaps ye might want a mental image that doesna' include a woman in your home who otherwise wants nothing to do with your pale Irish ass."

Except that wasn't entirely true. Oh, Grace Maddox wanted him. They'd sealed that truth the afternoon in her boathouse. *Her* boathouse. He grimaced. That he'd even thought of it that way was a step in a direction he still wished he didn't have to take.

Problem was, that direction also led him to Grace.

Who, since their blistering hot interlude, had yet to make time in her oh-so-busy schedule to so much as wave in his general direction. Other than a message left on his business voice mail asking him to leave Whomper back at her boathouse—*her* boathouse—with a bowl of fresh water and a bit of dog food that same night, he'd only heard her voice two other times. Both times also via voice mail, both times turning down his invitation to dinner, invites which he'd been forced to leave on her voice mail because she couldn't even be bothered to answer his damn calls.

He'd been sorely tempted to simply show up on her doorstep again, but he told himself to have some pride, a shred of dignity. If she wasn't interested, he wasn't about to grovel, for God's sake.

Brodie found the right socket, fixed it to the wrench, then parked his bum in front of the open base of the unit and wedged his shoulder in so he could reach the connectors on the back and make sure they were cranked completely off before he went any further. Grace probably had the right idea anyway, he thought, as he'd told himself numerous times already. Starting something up wasn't a good notion, not when they were destined to be close neighbors for at least some length of time. Privately, Brodie questioned her future as an innkeeper. It was long hours, hard work, and not nearly as romantic or heartwarming as was painted in novels and movies.

Coming from a small Irish village, he'd been in the position to live in close quarters with women he'd dated but no longer saw romantically . . . and he'd always been able to find a way to keep the friendship, even if the more personal liaison had frittered out. It always had. But that was then. Things were different. He was different. Only he wasn't exactly sure yet where those differences began and ended. He wasn't interested in easy liaisons, casual dalliances. He wanted . . . well, he wanted to feel like he had when he thought about Alex. He wanted to feel like he wanted . . . something more.

Grace had certainly captured his full attention . . . in a way that made whatever fledgling feelings he'd had for Alex seem dim and unformed in comparison. He credited that to the fact that the attraction in this case was mutual. Bordering on downright explosive. He'd have to be dead not to have her constantly on his mind. She'd proven he was far from that.

That left him where? Wanting what . . . exactly? If wandering around his boathouse like a pathetic sad sack these past months had been bad after the nonstarter his relationship with Alex had been . . . what in the world would it be like living within spitting distance of Grace if things went in the same direction? He doubted it would turn into the friendly, platonic arrangement he'd enjoyed back in Ireland, and had managed with Alex.

Oh, if only his sisters could see him, the merry amusement they'd have at his expense.

"Coming to America might have had its saving graces after all," he muttered as he bent to the task at hand. *Now I just have to figure out how to save myself from Grace.*

Brodie emerged from the kitchen a little more than two hours later without any answers to his most pressing questions, but he was smiling as he wiped his hands on an old work rag. He found Fergus behind his cluttered wooden desk in his equally cluttered office at the back of the pub. "I've managed to sweet-talk your recalcitrant little fire pistol into keeping her flame alive a wee bit longer. However, I'd be thinking about trading up in the near future. Way up."

Fergus looked up from the pile of receipts he'd been tallying on a small calculator. He slid off the pair of bifocals that had been perched on his nose and rubbed the spots on the bridge where they'd been resting. "Och, and that's good to hear. I've got a few other pressing concerns that need tending to before I deal with that headache."

"Well, I'll let you get back to it then. I'll see about dropping in later for a pint when I've reached my limit with the current work in progress."

"Park yer bum for a moment longer if you can spare it." Fergus pointed the arm of his glasses at the seat positioned on the other side of his desk, just inside the door.

Brodie looked at the stack of books, folders, and catalogs that filled the beat-up leather chair and grinned. "I'm no' sure I should dare to squeeze any more of me into the space left in this room." He looked around the small office.

The walls and built-in shelves were all original wood, stained dark from heat, smoke, time, and God knew what else. The shelves lined the wall top to bottom on one side, every last inch of them crammed with books, binders, framed photos, bowling trophies, a few hand-fletched darts, and every other thing the old man had saved and held on to over the past two decades—which appeared to be everything. Old oak file drawer units filled the other wall, crammed to bulging if the partially opened drawers were any indication. Stuff was stacked just as high on top. The floor, the desk, and the chair bore the weight of more files, more books, various and sundry wholesale catalogs. "It's a wonder you know what's what and what's where. I'm guessing you keep your accountant on a running open tab at the bar to bribe him into even coming in here."

Fergus snorted. "I'm my own accountant. Ran my own businesses just fine back home and I'll do the same here, thank you very much. Just move that stack"—he glanced around and shrugged—"somewhere. Have a sit down."

"We can go out to the bar. It's still early yet."

"I'd rather talk here."

Brodie frowned. "Aye, then." He shifted the stack in the chair to the open doorway, then took a seat. "Is everything okay? Whatever the problem is, ye've only to ask and I'll do whatever it is I can."

Fergus smiled and true affection shone from his eyes. "Aye, you're a good laddie, you are, and I'm proud to call you friend. But the problem here isn't mine. 'Tis yours."

Good lord, now what? "What is it you've heard?"

"Heard you up and lost a piece of your heritage to the newcomer."

Brodie wasn't surprised word had spread. In fact, he'd assumed everyone knew by nightfall the day the deed had been signed over. His brows lifted a bit at the hint of censure. "The local grapevine must be slipping. Happened three weeks ago. The property was gone before I knew the deal was even in the works."

"Och, give me a wee bit more credit than that, boy-o. I'm aware the sale was a done deal inside a week of when she first laid eyes on it. In a town this size, hard to believe pulling off something like that would be possible. Unless of course the motivation was there." He tapped his glasses on the open file on his desk. "I can think of only one person who might have had the power and the inclination."

Brodie wasn't surprised that Fergus might have put together what Brodie knew to be fact. Cami Weathersby's extracurricular proclivities were high on the list of the town's worst-kept secrets. He had thought, however, that his rejection of her advances had been a private matter and had remained such. He couldn't imagine she'd have advertised her failure to land him in her bed. "How would this particular . . . motivation as you call it, have become public knowledge?"

"Oh, I didn't say it was common knowledge, lad. But I might know a bit or two more than your average citizen, mostly because I pay attention. You've a smile, a wink, and a spare moment for a pretty face, whether they're in a stroller or using a walker to get themselves about. To you, every woman has a pretty face. It's a part of you as much as breathing; a harmless diversion at worst, at best, a lovely example of our Irish charm."

Fergus smiled briefly. "However, if one were to pay attention, one might have noticed that there is a rather exceedingly attractive face in our wee village who hasn't been able to command much more than a polite nod from your general direction." He sighed. "Seeing as she's used to the opposite sex generally treating her like royalty—some would say she gauges a good part of her self-worth on her ability to command her royal subjects—my sense is that where you're concerned, perhaps a bit of the 'evil queen' is showing." Fergus made quotation marks with his fingers.

"Aye, well, there's no supposing to it." Brodie wouldn't have confirmed or denied it to anyone else, but Fergus wasn't just anyone. And Brodie knew he'd keep what was said between them private. "She visited me in my workshop a week or so back and made it quite clear that I had myself to blame for the transaction."

Fergus looked surprised at that. "Did she now? What leverage would there be in that? Unless it was merely to gloat."

"You have the right of it, there. But she also let it slip that Grace was considering snapping up yet another of the buildings, the largest one that sits right next to her first purchase, in order to expand on the inn she is in the process of creating."

"I imagine she wanted you to shift your allegiance to her and she'd protect your, shall we say, vested and divested interests?"

Brodie choked a little on that last part, but managed to say, "Essentially . . . aye. My favors for her favors."

"Ye turned her down, I imagine."

"I did. If my previous rejections set her on a path to see me stripped of my heritage, I honestly don't know what Plan B will consist of. But I can assume it won't be pretty."

Fergus studied him for a long moment. "I was going to say that explains the pinched look I commented on earlier, but you've another matter concerning you, don't you." He didn't make it a question. "How are you getting along with the newcomer? I've yet to make her acquaintance, but I hear she's related to Ford."

That got Brodie's full attention. "You know her brother? Is that his name?"

Fergus's bushy eyebrows climbed quite high on his forehead. "Whew, that's quite a concerned look yer sportin' there, my boy. If I didn't know better, I'd say . . ." He trailed off, then his face split wide in a devilish grin. "Och, but you've gotten yourself into a tricky mess now, haven't you, laddie? Does Cami realize she's competin' with her own client?"

"There is no competition. Of any kind. With anyone."

"Maybe not to your mind, boy-o. Or perhaps even Miss Grace's mind. I suspect if Miss Camille were to get a gander at your expression at the moment, she might have a somewhat different take on the matter, however. Do ye think Grace will leave your property be if she has a reason to not ruffle your feathers?"

"Grace is a strong, independent woman who will do whatever she thinks is best for her plans. I'm not a factor in those decisions, nor would she let me be."

The twinkle in Fergus's eyes could only be described as merry, bordering on downright gleeful. "Wouldn't she now? Oh, I wouldn't be so certain. That you're not taking credit for your charm is also interesting."

Brodie frowned, angry and hurt at the insult. "I'm not using her. I wouldn't do that. Not her or anyone else."

"Oh, pipe down." Fergus was completely unabashed by Brodie's outburst. "You know I wouldn't accuse you of such. My point is that if you're involving yourself in any manner with Grace Maddox, I think you'd be a fool to believe it won't influence her, even if you or she wish it otherwise. There is not a single doubt that if word were to get out, so much as a whisper—in a village this size, I can't see that not happening—then Cami's very pretty head will likely explode. There's no telling what she'll do."

"There is nothing happening with Grace. If there were and it mattered, I would warn her about Cami. As it stands, there's no point. She'd just think it a ploy to win her trust and divert her from purchasing the other boathouse. As it is, I think it's all moot. I think Cami was bluffing. As I said, Grace is a smart businesswoman. I don't think she would risk taking on the extra real estate at this point in her little venture, even at rock-bottom prices."

"Oh, my concern wasn't that Cami would try to sell the place to Grace. If she finds out there's even a hint of smoke to that fire, my bet is she would want to stick it to both of you. There's nothing keeping her from finding yet another buyer. Especially now that she could pitch the building as part of a harborside renewal project or some such. With you launching the sailboat business and Grace opening an inn, that property will become a lot more attractive. For that matter, it could happen even without Cami's interference."

"I know. I've thought about that. But I can only expand as fast as I am. I wasn't planning on having to commit to a complete overhaul. Building boats by hand isn't something you can expedite. I've had three under contract, two delivered. I've made headway on the third and have a few nibbles on what's to come next, but not enough to hire on or expand. Barely enough to make meager headway. It's a healthy start and as good or better than I anticipated. If not for the state of the place, I'd be in fine shape. The Monaghan shipyard didn't spring up overnight, nor did it fall to total disrepair in that same time span. It will take time, patience, and a lot of diligence, blood, sweat, and probably a few tears or at least some colorful language to pull her back to something resembling a new life. It won't be what was there before, but it will be something I can put my name on, my family name on, with pride. I just need time. Time I thought I had."

Fergus leaned his heavy forearms on his desk . . . and grinned. "Well, laddie, perhaps I can help you with that."

Brodie looked sincerely surprised at the comment and the confidence with which Fergus had made it. "How?"

"I've word that there's a bit of chatter about courting more of the tourist trade."

"We're too far up the coast for that. We're a fishing village. Tourism here, what little I've seen, is a distant, distant second."

"Aye, perhaps. But it is some part of our economy, and chatter is it might be ripe for expanding upon. Frankly, I think folks are right. With a Monaghan back at the helm of the historic shipbuilding business and Grace wanting to put in an inn that I hear is being designed by a world-famous architect, well . . . that chatter will only increase."

"How does this involve me? I mean, yes, my family has historic ties to the whole bay area, but the shipyard is hardly a tourist attraction. Don't tell me you want me to make it into some kind of maritime museum or such. Maine has more than a few of those, quite good ones in fact. All more geographically desirable and more than capable of handling the tourist demand for that sort of thing."

"No' a museum, lad, though it's something to think on as an aside to your own business. Don't discount it at any rate. But this is a far grander scheme than that, and a far more profitable one for you. You've heard of the tall ships that some of the tourist towns have commissioned and use to take folks out on the water?" At Brodie's nod, Fergus said, "Well, talk is someone with deep pockets is thinking of commissioning a schooner to sail here in Pelican Bay. In this case, a wood-hull, no-auxiliary-power, full-on replica of an eighteenth-century flagship. Who better to build her than a Monaghan?"

Brodie slumped back in his chair, momentarily speechless. He had to take a moment to absorb the impact of the idea. "There is no one better suited. I was born to do that. I would kill to be the one to do that." He looked at Fergus, energized and crushed at the same time. "I don't have the . . . I'm not set up for anything of that scope. I don't know that I ever would be. I . . . there's no' exactly a big demand for ships these days."

"Your forebears built the very same right on the plot of land you now call home. Nothing has changed about the lay of the land, the deep harbor. Where else could it be built, lad, if not right here?"

Brodie's pulse was pounding so hard it was almost impossible to sit still. "Where is the chatter coming from? Who's putting up the money for it? Do they really think they can develop a tourist trade this far north? If they want the attraction to be water based, they'd have to work with someone in Half Moon Harbor to make that a possibility. All the other businesses running out of the harbor are for commercial fishing, which would mean—"

"Working with you." Fergus slid a card out from under the blotter on his desk. "Aye. I said the very thing to the gentleman I heard talking over his grand scheme. It's possible he wasn't intentionally including me in his conversation, but who pays attention to the barkeep?"

"You have his card?"

"Not only that, I have his word that he'll contact you.

In fact, he was already planning on it. We were of the same mind in regard to you being the right one . . . the only one. I believe the contract is yours if you can find a way to make it happen. That would pretty much solve the rest of your problems about getting your property out of hock and back into proper Monaghan ownership."

"I—I can't even believe—ha!" Brodie sat back, well and truly gobsmacked. He laughed, a slight manic edge to it. "It will take me a moment to wrap my head around it. It's like a dream come true and winning the lottery on the same day." He leaned forward and reached for the card. "Who is it?"

"Well, that might be the sticky part."

Brodie frowned and turned the card over, read the name engraved on the front. And the bottom dropped out of his stomach.

Fergus hesitated only a moment. "Brooks Winstock."

Brodie looked up. "Cami's father."

Chapter 11

Grace headed down the main pier toward the large boathouse built out over the water, way at the end. She'd never been inside it, but she knew Brodie used it as his workshop. She'd seen him walk there most every morning, had heard the sounds of power tools coming from there when she sat on the end of her pier with her coffee in the mornings, and had viewed him hauling lumber and other supplies there from time to time while working on her own boathouse. Lately, she'd seen a light on there well into the night. Not that she'd been watching morning and night or anything.

She'd seen him head in that direction just after sunrise. Sunrise happened early in Maine, which had taken some getting used to. It had become her favorite time of the day, though. Most of the world was still quiet, asleep. The morning air was crisp and cool. The sounds of the gulls starting their morning hunt for fish mixed in with the banter of the osprey pair who'd nested for the summer atop the light pole that stood between her boathouse and the parking lot. She didn't think she'd ever be less than awed by the extreme changes in high and low tides so far north, and enjoyed listening to the lobstermen talk, their voices carrying easily over the water as they set up their boats with traps and buoys before chugging out from

Blue's, a commercial fishing enterprise situated just past the Monaghan property.

And, okay, she might have paid more attention than she should have to Brodie's boathouses . . . the one he lived in and the one he worked in. She hadn't spoken to him since what she'd come to think of as *that* afternoon, which was two weeks ago. He'd invited her to dinner a few times in the days immediately following, but had quickly given up when she hadn't responded. It hadn't been an intentional slight on her part. Other than a quick trip back to get Whomper from her boathouse after Brodie had dropped him off that evening, she'd ended up spending a good part of the following two days holed up with Langston at the rental house, working and reworking the plans, alternately arguing, listening, and ultimately compromising. Her cell phone signal out there was poor to nonexistent, so she'd missed both of Brodie's calls.

By the time she and Langston were done hammering out all the details and Grace had returned and resumed work at the boathouse, she'd decided it would be wiser to focus on the steep hill she'd just begun to climb rather than her attraction to Brodie. In order to give the renovation her full, undivided attention, she should probably steer clear of her sexy Irish neighbor and those clever hands of his. And that accent. Also, his amazingly talented mouth.

Yeah. Wiser.

That didn't mean she didn't think about what had happened *that* afternoon. Often. Too often. The very fact that just one time together still had the power to distract her the way it did made her stick to the decision to leave well enough alone. When her unintentional silence had resulted in his calls stopping . . . she'd left it at that, and turned her attention where it needed to be.

After all the haranguing and wrangling back and forth with Langston, whose vision was inarguably brilliant but hadn't always lined up with hers, Grace was happy with the final plans for the inn—thrilled, really—and couldn't wait to begin the actual work. It was just a matter of getting through what felt like the endless delays as new problems cropped up on a daily basis. Sometimes hourly. Some of the issues even had issues.

There were continuing problems with the foundation, the wiring throughout was faulty, and neither that nor the plumbing was even close to current code standards. Many of the original cypress boards could be salvaged but would have to be taken up and shipped out to be worked on, and the new planks she needed to fill in the gaps would have to be ordered and shipped in from out of state. Way out of state. And on it went.

She was starting to worry that they wouldn't make enough progress to be under the new roof and ready to begin interior work before the weather turned. Winter came early to Maine.

She'd had to divest more and more of her investment portfolio to cover the additional repairs, causing more than a few sleepless nights as she worried that she'd go broke before she ever got the inn finished. Admittedly, Cami's suggestion to tear the place down and start from scratch had played through her mind more than once.

But even if she'd had a change of heart about the historic building—which she truly hadn't—she couldn't imagine doing anything other than building the marvelously unique loft plan that Langston had designed. So onward she pushed. To that end, she'd been staying at the boathouse full-time. Despite having keys to the amazing waterfront house that Langston had rented and spent all of two nights in, she'd been bunking at her boathouse. She told herself it was because she was too exhausted by nightfall to make the drive out to the Point. But, truth be told, even though the cavernous building was still more torn up and run down than anything resembling reconstruction . . . it was hers. And she liked being there. No . . . she loved being there. So did Whomper, who had free rein of the place as well as the docks.

She felt too disconnected when she was out on the Point, and not just because her phone didn't work out there. She knew that staying on the boathouse property day and night wasn't getting it done any faster, but she just . . . felt better when she was there. Given the gorgeous summer weather, with warm sunny days and brisk nights, she hadn't needed much more than a cot, a cooler, a small cookstove, and a lamp that ran off the work generator her crews were using for their power tools, all of which she'd picked up at Hartley's, the fabulous local hardware store.

Stepping into Hartley's was like stepping back in time. A true vintage hardware store like she'd only seen in old movies, with everything from nails and lumber to kitchen utensils and Red Flyer wagons. Owen Hartley had been a godsend in more ways than she could have ever hoped. Late forties or early fifties, she guessed, average height, trim physique, ginger-haired and somewhat mild-mannered in demeanor, he'd also turned out to be the town historian and had all sorts of connections with local contractors. He'd been a tremendous help in hiring her initial demo crew. He'd also assured her that when the time came and she needed to install fixtures and such, he could help her with the more traditional, antique, and period pieces she might be interested in. He promised that if he couldn't track down the parts personally, he surely would knew of someone who could. Between Langston and Owen, she felt she had two fairy godfathers watching over her.

She smiled at the fanciful notion. Langston would love the comparison, but she wasn't sure the hardware store owner would feel the same.

Rounding out her stay-cation villa, as she'd come to call it, was a heavy work hose and sprayer nozzle that ran off well water and connected to the fixture at the back of the building as her make-do shower . . . and the port-o-potty she'd had installed out in the parking lot for the crew took care of the rest. It was sort of like camping indoors. Well, except for the fact that half the roof was now down to exposed beams. So, indoor-outdoor camping. When she couldn't stand herself any longer, she'd head out to the Point and live like a real person for a day—or more typically a short evening and a night—then come back to her place.

Her place. Her smile spread to a grin as she strode down the long pier and resisted the urge to hug herself. Again. She still couldn't get over how drastically her life had changed in such a short time. The idea of pulling on panty hose and wearing tailored suits and sensible pumps for eight to ten hours a day sounded like torture to her now. Well, not that it hadn't been before, but she'd grown so used to the business uniform she'd simply donned it out of habit. She had thought she'd miss the people, the sounds, the day-to-day conversations with coworkers and just, well, the general "noise" that comprised her former world. But it was exactly the opposite. It was as if everything had slowed down and she could finally breathe. Think. Clear her head. The way she'd only been able to do out on the river, back in D.C.

There was noise in Blueberry Cove, just an entirely different kind. She wasn't referring to the loud and chaotic noise that came from the work being done to the boathouse. She was thinking about the day-to-day interactions she had, talking with the locals—her new neighbors—and not just when they stopped by, but everywhere she went. It was a completely different rhythm. Folks weren't in a hurry. They took a moment to say hello, and when they asked after you, they were sincere in wanting to hear your reply.

Grace had wondered if that sort of thing would drive her crazy. How would her hurry-up-and-get-it-done-racing-always-racing mentality of living in the city work with the slow pace and Nosy Nellies that were the norm of small-town life in the Cove? She couldn't lie, the slow pace had, at times, tried her patience right to the limit and then some. It had definitely taken some getting used to, especially as she felt she was racing under the deadline of winter to get the boathouse to a certain point in the renovation . . . and no one else seemed to share her focused intensity in making that a reality, no matter what hourly rate she was willing to pay.

Ultimately, though, as the days passed, her internal rhythms had slowly begun to shift to match the external ones . . . and she realized just how much she'd needed to slow down, to stop and smell the proverbial roses. Or, in her case, the gorgeous stalks of purple, pink, and white lupines that bloomed and blossomed any and everywhere in summertime Maine. Most especially the thriving patch that filled much of the long sloping hill that curved upward behind the Monaghan property, all the way to Harbor Street. She never tired of looking at them, gently swaying in the breeze that always came off the water.

So, she mused, watching yet another fishing boat chug away from the docks at Blue's, was it more grand adventure or insane leap off a cliff? She laughed. *Both. For sure.* She'd never worked so physically hard in her life. She'd thought rowing had made her stronger, fitter, but ripping out old warped boards, prying off and taking down hundreds—thousands—of rotting shakes, hauling more loads of demolition detritus than she could count out to the big construction trash trailer she'd also had hauled in, not to mention pile after pile of junk that had found its way into the boathouse over decades that had turned it into the world's biggest crap-filled garage, was a whole different kind of workout.

Still, it was progress. Every shingle, every old lobster trap, every warped board they hauled out of there was one step closer to the time when they'd start the real renovation, start making Langston's gorgeous plans come to life. In the meantime, she tried to enjoy the process, knowing it would make the end result all the more meaningful to her because she'd done it with her own hands.

She also knew that sinking herself heart and soul into the arduous, slow-moving process was making it a lot easier to procrastinate on making any headway on her other reason for coming to Maine. Her main reason, as it were. She figured at some point she'd know when it was time. The right time. If there was ever going to be such a thing. Maybe it was when she'd finally feel confident enough, work up enough nerve, to take that critical first step. But the days were turning into weeks, and that "right day" hadn't happened.

She'd finally admitted that she was simply going to have to make it the right time.

She'd been in Blueberry Cove just shy of six weeks, a boathouse owner for exactly a month. Though she'd come to know many locals from their visits to the boathouse and from her trips to the town grocery, handling her account at the bank, stopping in at the post office from time to time to pick up the plans from Langston or other paperwork stemming from her investment dealings, as well as frequent trips to the library to take advantage of the free Wi-Fi . . . not a single soul had said a word to her about Ford.

That had helped to foster her belief that she could take her time and do things in her own way, when she was ready. She knew that his living and working on Sandpiper might be part of why no one had made the connection, but as far as she knew, he didn't live out there year-round, only during the summer months when the island became the nesting ground for seals, puffins, arctic terns, razorbills, and other seafowl. Otherwise, he kept a place on the outskirts of town in the opposite direction from the Point, heading around the harbor to the east side of the bay.

She knew about the latter because that was the address he used on his tax returns, though she hadn't gone and found the place. She'd learned the rest after stumbling across some brochures and a little sign posted at the post office soliciting tax-deductible donations that went toward the work being done by the scientists and interns on the island every summer. Her heart had pounded as she'd read through the brochure front to back, but there hadn't been any specific mention of her brother. Still, the organization advertised was the same one he listed as his employer, so she had to assume that's where he was.

Of course, she knew it was only a matter of time before someone pieced the connection together, but it had only struck her a morning or two ago during her coffee time on the pier, that possibly they already had. What if they knew exactly who she was in relation to Ford, but had thought they should mention her arrival to him before making any comment to her? It stood to reason they'd be more protective of him than of her.

She'd spent the past two days trying to figure out the best way to get out to Sandpiper Island. Whale-watching boat tours went out into the bay, but none of the brochures or websites mentioned trips to Sandpiper. She assumed due to the sensitive work the scientists were doing with endangered species that tourists weren't welcome, and understandably so.

She was fairly certain that being related to one of the scientists wasn't necessarily going to gain her any advantage. But having Ford find out from someone else that she'd up and moved her entire life to the very same small town he had been calling home for the past dozen or so years was far worse than anything that might happen if he heard it from her directly. She shouldn't have waited as long as she had. She'd just assumed that if no one was saying anything, no one knew. She should have thought that through a little better. *But hey, why start thinking things through at this late date?*

She glanced out toward the horizon, her nerves returning and starting to jangle in earnest as she drew closer to the boathouse. It was bad enough that she was scared about what was going to happen with Ford, possibly even as soon as that very day. It didn't help that she had to deal with Brodie on top of anticipating what would happen when she saw her brother for the first time in fifteen years.

Fifteen years. She'd been sixteen the last time they'd been together. It had been June then, too. Angry teenager or not, it hadn't been one of her finer moments.

She shut off thoughts of that day and focused on the current glorious June morning. *New day. New life. New start.* It was Saturday, and the crew had the weekend off so they could head up to Machiasport to participate in some sort of river race regatta. She'd thought about going herself, taking a much-needed day off to enjoy the river races and the country fair type thing she'd heard went hand in hand with the event. Then she'd seen Brodie head out to the boathouse, and another idea had taken root. One she couldn't set aside, at least not until she pursued it and got either a solution to her transportation problem, or more likely, a curt "maybe when the bay freezes over." With the crew off for two days, there would be no better time to find some way to get out to Sandpiper Island.

She watched Whomper scamper on ahead and hoped he'd do his job as ambassador for her surprise visit. Just because she'd decided Brodie was off-limits didn't mean her dog had. The traitor would disappear for hours at a time and, after a frantic round of calling and whistling for him the first time it had happened, dread filling her as she imagined him either leaping off a pier and drowning, or hit by a truck up on Harbor Street . . . she now knew that when the construction noise got to be too much for him, he'd head on over to visit Brodie, either at his boathouse office or his workshop one.

Brodie hadn't called to complain, and Whomper trotted over quite happily and confidently whenever the mood struck him and always came back in much the same mood . . . so she assumed that at least his visits were welcome. For all that she hadn't contacted Brodie in the past two weeks . . . he hadn't so much as stopped by to see how things were going, either. She'd told herself it was better that way all around. Personally and professionally.

She knew, lingering fantasies about *that* afternoon notwithstanding, at some point they'd have to find a way to deal with each other. The longer they waited to meet again, the more awkward it might become.

"Well, we're about to put an end to that moratorium," she murmured under her breath. Even more than that, if her reason for seeing him went as planned, they'd be spending more than a few minutes together, which only added more tension to the nerve bundle.

She'd been planning her little speech all morning. "Hi," she practiced under her breath. "I know I've been avoiding you since we almost had hot monkey sex in the boathouse I bought out from under you, but I need a ride out to Sandpiper Island to find my long-lost brother. Got a few hours to spare?" *Yeah. That's going to go over really well.*

She heard strains of music mixed in with the noise of a power saw before she reached the open panel door situated on the opposite end of the boathouse from the side

that faced her pier. She'd spent many mornings being alternately thankful and frustrated that she couldn't look
into his workshop, see what he was working on. *Okay,
okay, see him doing the work. Preferably shirtless.*

Yeah, she really didn't need that visual on the brain at
the moment. But even that vivid image was mercifully
erased a heartbeat later when Whomper came tearing out
of the boathouse, a chunk of cut wood clenched in his
jaws. He gleefully tore past her and headed at a mad dash
back toward her boathouse, where, given the chance, he'd
spend at least the next hour chewing on it, then another
one determining the exact right spot to bury it.

"So much for my goodwill ambassador," she called out
to his rapidly retreating form, then shook her head with a
resigned smile, deciding not to call him back. She'd go get
him if the boat ride panned out for the day.

She turned back to the workshop and was startled to a
stop again by the sudden emergence of a large pelican,
long brown wings unfolding as it lofted itself through the
open panel door and out across the water. She laughed.
"And I thought I had work distractions."

She took a moment, hand propped over her forehead to
shield her eyes from the sun as she watched the big, ungainly thing make its way out to the other, smaller dock-
side boathouse at the far end of the network of piers. His
displeasure at being disturbed was made obvious by the series of grumbling squawks as he flew. It wasn't her first en-
counter with the crotchety old bird.

She'd noticed early on in her morning coffee-drinking
sojourns that the pelican had made a summer nest out at
the small boathouse . . . and made regular visits to see
Brodie when he was working in his boathouse. She'd like
to pretend that she hadn't been jealous of the damn thing,
hanging out in Brodie's workshop. Or that she hadn't been
charmed by the idea of Brodie and Big Brown, as she'd

come to think of the bird, hanging out together while he built boats. She hadn't seen a single other pelican during her time in Maine, so she wasn't sure what the deal was with the big guy, but she'd enjoyed marking his daily rituals as she'd been developing her own.

She stepped around the corner of the boathouse, forcing her thoughts back to the matter at hand, and exactly how to broach the favor she needed from the probably brooding Irishman, but whatever words might have come to mind fled as she stepped into the open doorway . . . and got her first glimpse of the man at work.

The pelican hadn't taken off because of Whomper tearing out in reaction to the loud noise of the saw. Quite possibly it was because the other occupant of the boathouse had started singing along—loudly—with the oldies tune playing on whatever sound system Brodie had rigged up. Not because the man couldn't sing. She'd found that out the first day when he'd showered with her dog. More, probably, because he wasn't exactly shy with his vocals.

The song playing was the one about a green tambourine, but his singing wasn't the only thing that wasn't shy or retiring. What had stopped her in her tracks was the decidedly uninhibited hip action the sexy, not remotely brooding Irishman had added to his performance.

Wearing jeans that looked older than she was, he had his back to her so she could see just how magnificently the worn, faded denim and torn pockets enhanced his very fine, Irish ass as he rocked from side to side in what could only be described as a wicked, oh so very wicked swivel that made her think about just how wicked other parts of him could be. Wicked things . . . and tongue . . . she knew of firsthand.

He was measuring a long piece of wood, making pencil marks as he belted out a line about how money fed his music machine. All Grace knew was that she was suddenly hungry herself. Starved. The old white T-shirt, sleeves hacked off sometime in the past century, did absolutely nothing to hide the play of muscles across his back or the flex and bunch of his shoulders and biceps. Hell, even his forearm flexors made her hormones flutter as he measured, marked, measured . . . and never missed a single, hip-thrusting beat to the tambourine-punctuated refrain.

Grace resisted the rather insistent primal urge to strip naked and jump him . . . but dear Lord, she wanted to.

Then the swirling, sensual tune ended and segued right into . . .

Oh for heaven's sake. "Hanky Panky?" Really?

She knew she had to say something, if for no other reason than to save herself from thinking about hot monkey boathouse sex every time an oldies pop tune came on the radio for the rest of her natural life. But before she could figure out a way to announce her presence, he turned around as he sang the line about a pretty little girl sitting all alone . . . with a grin so sexy, so knowing, and so . . . intent it made her pulse stutter. He crossed the short distance between them, slid the pencil behind his ear, and grabbed her hand, twirling her smoothly into a spin, then wrapping her up against him, back to front, then back out again . . .

And they were dancing, and he was singing, and dammit, he'd known she was there the whole time. Watching the show. Worse, she was laughing. And not exactly extricating herself from their continued spin and swivel.

So much for keeping my physical distance.

She'd been sure he'd be angry with her, or at least distant and dismissive. She hadn't envisioned anything like this. Grinning, laughing, singing . . . and dancing like they'd been doing it for years.

She knew she had to stop, had to explain why she'd come, but as she caught her breath, the music changed again, and suddenly Tommy James was singing about somewhere over yonder and how good it was to find crystal blue persuasion. Brodie had spun her back into him, catching her neatly up against his chest, face-to-face. He curled her arm, his hand still in hers, around her back to hold her there as they swayed to the beat. His sexy grin didn't shift a flicker, but the devilish twinkle in his eyes turned decidedly darker when she gasped as her hips bumped his.

His gaze dropped to her mouth and before she could decide just how bad an idea that was going to be, he slid his free hand beneath her hair and drew her mouth closer, tilting her head back so her lips were softly parted for the taking. Her eyelids started to drift shut as she awaited what she knew was going to be the pure carnal bliss of his mouth on hers, but his gaze flicked back up at the last possible second, locking with her eyes.

"Did you miss this as much as I have?" he asked, shocking her with the admission. "All of it," he wanted to know. "No' just this part."

She wondered if he saw the truth in her gaze, if there would be any point in even trying to deny it. Or pretending she wanted to. Her throat worked, but no words came out. His gaze dipped down, and she felt his fingers twitch on the sensitive skin at her nape as he caught the movement of her throat, then looked straight back to her eyes. He was still swaying with her to the slow groove of the music, keeping her hips locked to his. So many things she should say or do, boundaries she should set.

What she did, however, was tip her chin down just a fraction . . . in a nod of assent.

"Thank God," he murmured. Then claimed her.

Chapter 12

He'd thought about this moment. Hell, he'd even dreamed about it. About how he'd like it to go, at any rate. Every last vivid, highly specific, erotically charged detail.

He'd spent every day since that afternoon in her boat-house convincing himself that those thoughts had to remain just that—thoughts. It was why he'd stayed away. Why he'd told himself it was smart, smart indeed, of her to do the same. Both on the same page, they were, and wiser for it. Good for them. He might have to live with the fact that she'd sneaked a piece of his heritage away when he wasn't looking . . . but that was the only thing of his she would—or should—get her hands on.

Aye, and look where that brilliant bit of hard-and-fast rule making got you. Lasted all of what, three seconds? Four, tops?

But Grace Maddox was back in his arms again, and frankly, he didn't give a flat, flying damn about the rest.

Like an animal sensing its mate, he'd known she was in the doorway even before her shadow had fallen over him. He wasn't sure what bit of mischief had made him play with her, thinking to make her blush perhaps, with his song and dance. If his sisters knew that not only was he listening to the oldies music he'd found in their CD player, but seducing a woman with it? Didn't bear thinking of.

When she'd stood there watching him, and he'd felt that sweet, sweet tension build all over again, the joke had ultimately been on him.

When he'd turned, grinned, and pulled her into the dance, he'd expected that wry, arched brow, a laugh, and a shove. Something that would give him a much-needed reminder of all the good reasons he'd stayed away from her. Instead the music and that undeniable, palpable . . . *thing* they had, had spun them in a very different direction . . . a direction that made it clear her thoughts and dreams hadn't been so far off from his.

Even then, he hadn't thought she'd admit it, despite the truth right there in her eyes, for all to see.

One tiny dip of a chin later . . . and he hadn't stood a chance.

He sank into her mouth and drank her in as if she was the prize sip of water at the end of a very long, very hot race.

Bless Tommy James and every one of his Shondells, as the lad sang about crimson and clover, and Brodie kept Grace's hips melded to his while the beat slowed down. They continued to sway to the music, oblivious to the sawdust, the wood shavings, and scraps littering the floor as they moved in the narrow space between boat and workbench. She fit him all too perfectly; moving with him, she took him as ardently and helplessly as he took her. Mating her mouth to his, the fit perfect, each lured the other into a tango of taking and giving that moved in sync with the thrust and shift of their hips.

She let go of the hand he had pressed to the small of her back, and slid her palms over his shoulders, around his neck, then drove her fingertips up into his hair, raking his scalp, making his body shudder and surge, greedy for every sensation she could give him. He kept her wrapped tight against him, one arm banded around her waist, keep-

ing them toe to toe, hip melded to hip, as he sank his free
hand into that thick wave of silk and brought her mouth
under his so he could take the kiss even deeper.

He felt that same full-body shudder vibrate through her
as he slid his hand around to cup her cheek, rubbing the
side of his thumb along her jaw, and he knew she was
thinking about the afternoon in her boathouse. He sure as
hell was.

He lifted her off her feet, but didn't need to urge her to
wrap those strong legs of hers around his waist. All that
rowing, sliding fore and aft as she moved the scull across
the water, had given her sleekly curved hamstrings, dia-
mond calves, and the sweetest ass he'd had the pleasure to
ogle, which he shamelessly had as she'd strolled out on her
pier every dawn wearing snug gray leggings. Occasionally
she'd don his very own sweatshirt, the one he'd left for her
the morning she'd used his shower, what seemed a lifetime
ago.

The idea of her showering in his boathouse two feet
from his bed, and him not joining her, seemed ludicrous.
Did she think the same thing every morning when she slid
his old college sweatshirt over her head? The thought of
her bunking in her boathouse the past two weeks, much
the same as he had while his own had undergone renovation, had driven him close to crazy. So close, yet forever
so far away. Something he'd have to get used to, he'd told
himself, as she'd be living there full-time when her inn
opened. He wondered why the hell he'd waited so long.

"Hold on," he said, his voice gruff with need. "We're
not doing this here."

He knew where he wanted her, where he'd wanted
only her. That she didn't play coy or pretend not to know
what he'd meant by *this* cemented his decision. That was
the blunt, no-time-for-games Grace he'd missed. Aye, and
he respected her all the more for it.

He carried her through the open panel door, up the pier, and across a dock to the next pier, where his double-masted schooner was moored. He kicked the stepladder over until it lined up right with the rail, then climbed aboard with Grace still wrapped around him.

She lifted her head from where she'd been doing the most devilish things to the side of his neck with her teeth and tongue. "This is . . . yours?"

"Whose did you think it was?"

"I don't know. It's so big and elegant and . . . I guess I thought some of the locals docked their boats here." She looked around, then her eyes went wide and her gaze swung back to his. "Did you—you *built* this?"

"I had help putting her all together, of course, but, aye, she's mine from paper to water, down to the last futtock and cross-spall." He let her feet slip to the deck.

"Your own design, too, then?" Grace kept her arms around his neck, but shifted enough to take in the schooner, stem to stern to top of the double masts, before looking back at him. "Those marks on the floor, out in the boathouse? Those are the measurements for the boat you're building now, right?"

He nodded. "It's called the laying down, yes."

"I thought it looked huge, but that one is going to be much smaller than this. I can't imagine the process— where you'd even begin—for something so grand."

"The same place. Process doesn't vary so much. The scope and the detail simply expand on the basic concepts."

She looked back to him. "You've got a very special gift, that ye do," she said, softly mirroring his accent and smiling up into his eyes. "She's beautiful, Brodie. Stunning. Truly." Her sincerity and awe were all right there in her eyes.

Brodie felt something flip over inside his chest, and perhaps his fingers trembled just the slightest bit as he pushed the windblown tendrils from her forehead. "Aye, she is that," he said, his voice low, his gaze never wavering from hers.

Her gray-green eyes, already full to capacity with the want and need of what they'd both come for, shifted, softened, and the most delightful color stole into her cheeks.

His grin was slow as it spread fully out to the corners of his mouth. "How is it I can all but rip yer clothes straight from that lovely body of yours in my dusty old workshop, and you're with me every step of the way. But pay you a compliment, and you get all rosy on me?" He stroked her cheek.

Her own grin was that wry twist he'd so missed seeing, and the eyebrow arch that went with it filled him with the same pleasure he'd get upon seeing an old friend. "We both know you're so full of the blarney you can't help yourself . . . it just spills out of you. But every once in a while, I have to admit, the things you say . . . I want to fall for it. I do."

He deserved her skepticism, he knew that. There was no way she'd been in Blueberry Cove for six long weeks and not heard every story there was to tell about him and all of his rumored dalliances. Even though only a small fraction of them were the full truth, it was indeed a fact that he enjoyed bringing color to a pretty cheek, and a flutter to shyly averted eyelashes, even if the bulk of the time his intent was far from romantic, but simply . . . his nature. Fergus was right in saying that it made no difference if they were in strollers or using walkers, making a woman of any age feel good about herself made him happy. Where was the shame or sin in that?

Still, that didn't mean her reaction didn't twinge at him. "I've no way to make you believe that I mean what I say, other than to give you more words." He wrapped her up against him again and smiled against her lips as he kissed her. "Maybe showing you would be more convincing."

She laughed against his mouth as she kissed him back. "Well, just to be fair and to eradicate any lingering doubt . . . you may have a point."

"Oh, lass," he said, bumping hips with her. "I've that, indeed."

She made him groan and his body jerk—hard—when she shocked him with a little nip to his lower lip as she pushed her hips right back. "Well, if you need to . . . press your advantage in order to . . . fully make your point, far be it from me to stop—"

Whatever might have come after that ended on a loud squeal as he scooped her straight off her feet and slid her right over his shoulder. He'd never once been motivated to do that, not a single time in his entire life, but it seemed like the most natural thing in the world to carry her off to his lair.

"What are you doing?" She beat on his back, but she was laughing so hard, the pounding wasn't even a remotely effectual deterrent.

"Well lass, it was that or drag you to me cave by your lovely, lovely hair."

"Well, when you put it that way . . ." She made him hoot with laughter when she slid her hands down, grabbed his bum, and squeezed. "Have I mentioned that I have a whole new appreciation for worn denim jeans?" She fingered the tear in his back pocket. "At least now I'll know for sure."

"Mind your head," he instructed as he ducked down through the hatch and took the short ladder down facing front, careful to guard her head as he took her below-decks. "For sure about what?" he asked, bending so she could regain her footing once again.

She grinned as she reached around and pinched his arse, and it was as unrepentant a smile as he'd ever seen. "Boxers? Or briefs?"

"Spent some time on that, have ye?" he asked, backing her up as he moved toward her.

She nodded, the twinkle in her eyes daring him and desiring him.

He didn't think he'd ever been so turned on in his entire life. "Yer aware that I'm a full-blooded Irishman, and as such, have worn the plaid a time or two in my life."

"You own a kilt?"

He barked out a laugh at the pure unadulterated lust that completely consumed her expression. "Och, lassie, but had I been aware of even of a hint of your interest, I'd have come down wearing nothing but a bit of the plaid that first morning. We might have dispensed with all this parry and thrust we've been doing."

"Speak for yourself. I myself happen to enjoy a little parry and thrust." She grinned. "Okay, a lot of parry and, definitely the thrust." She pretended to look confused. "Are we talking about the same thing?" She squealed when he scooped her up again, keeping her in his arms. "Is this an Irish thing, too? Carting innocent women about?"

"Darlin', there's nothing innocent about the look in your eyes. Though I can honestly say I've never carried a woman off to bed." He angled them both down a narrow passageway to the master stateroom, ducked through the hatch, then tossed her gently on the bed . . . and followed her immediately down until he had her stretched out beneath him. He slid her hands above her head and linked them with his own until his nose touched hers. He dropped a hard, fast kiss on her lips, groaned when she pumped her hips up into his, then looked down into her storm-tossed, gray-green eyes. "But then, you provoke me to say and do all sorts of things I've never done before."

She looked into his eyes, and the barest hint of that wry smile ghosted the corners of her mouth, but her eyes were never more serious. "I almost believe that, too."

His expression turned serious. "Grace, I know ye've reason to doubt my sincerity, given the flirt and banter between us, but I'll no' take kindly to my integrity being questioned. I don't tell lies, no' ever, for any reason. If I say something, I mean it in the spirit given. Making a woman smile is never, and will never be, a bad thing to my mind. But simply because I enjoy bringing a bit of sunshine to someone's day, does no' mean I have an interest in anything else." He took a moment, a breath, then said the rest, wanting it out in the open between them, needing it there.

He spoke quietly and never so earnestly. "When I tell ye I want you, crave you, think of you endlessly, my words are sincere. It's no' simply to have you here, beneath me . . . but also the conversation, the laughter, the way you take me to task and seem to see me as I really am . . . even that wry tip to your eyebrow. I'm never anything but sincere. You've no reason to trust that, but I'm asking it of ye, all the same. Your faith will never be misplaced. That I can guarantee."

Grace blinked, and he saw the surface of her eyes grow a bit glassy.

"Och, now don't go and do that. I wasn't—I was simply trying to—"

She shut him up with a kiss. Her hands still trapped in his, she lifted her head to meld their mouths. "Okay, I believe you," she said against his lips. "I do."

He kissed her back, pressing her head down into the bed. When he lifted his head, she slid her fingers free and brought her palms to his face, held his gaze, searching for . . . something. He wished he knew what else he could say, or do, but knew there was nothing that would prove the truth of his words but time. And faith.

As if reading his mind, or perhaps his expression, she said, "Trust isn't an easy thing for me. Not just in giving it, but in myself, my own judgment. I let myself want things, and . . ." She drifted off with the slightest shake to her head, then tried to look away.

He gently coaxed her, prodding her face back to his until she looked at him again. "I can't promise ye I won't disappoint. I can promise ye I'll always speak the truth. It might not be what you want to hear, but . . . this is uncharted territory for me, as well. I can't say what I have to offer . . . only that I'm wanting to find out what can be. Might not be the smartest thing, certainly no' the safest, but it seems to be a truth that's not going away with time or distance. I don't want to ignore it any longer." He brushed her hair back from her face, emotions he had no name for all tangled up inside him, scaring the bejesus out of him. Yet, he knew in that moment there wasn't a single other place he'd rather be.

"No chart here, either," she finally said, and there was a husky note to the words. And not a small hint of trepidation in her eyes. "I—will very probably disappoint. But the truth telling part I can do, too. And I will. That you can count on."

"So, you're saying—"

"It's not going away for me, either. And, so . . . yes. Let's find out . . . whatever there is to find." She pressed a hand to his shoulder when he grinned, still serious. "There's something I need to say first."

He nodded. "Anything. I want to hear it."

"I came out to your workshop today to ask a favor. I figured you were probably mad at me for blowing off your dinner invites, then basically retreating from the field without comment. That afternoon . . . after you left, I went out to the house Langston rented on the Point to go over the plans. No phone service, so I didn't get your messages until I got back. By then, you'd stopped asking and I thought it would be best to just . . ."

"Aye. I did, as well. I wasn't angry." He smiled when she rolled her eyes. "Okay, a wee bit put out, but only for a moment. Eventually, I came to realize that you were a bit smarter than me and simply put it together faster."

"And yet here we are, anyway."

His smile widened. "Why do ye think I steered clear? I knew it was my only hope." He brushed her cheek with his fingertips and had a moment of wonder at how they went from animal lust to laughter, back to teasing, then on to the serious . . . and yet the ebb and flow all felt quite natural. "What was the favor?"

"Oh . . . we can talk about it later. It's . . . complicated. I just didn't want you to think . . . you know . . . after we . . . do whatever we do here, that you'd think I purposely waited until afterward to ask."

He hooted a laugh and she mock punched him in the shoulder. He rolled to his back and carried her with him until she was sprawled over him, her hair hanging down in silky waves as she looked daggers at him, even as her lips were already curving. "Darlin', if you're ever a mind to use me for your own nefarious purposes"—he flung his arms wide till they were splayed on the bed on either side of him—"please, have your way with me first, then ask what ye will. I'd have said yes no matter, but I'm always open to a little needless coercion if you're of a mood for it."

"Very funny," she said, pushing at his chest, then squealed when he took her wrists captive and rolled her again, stretching her arms once more over her head, trapping them there.

"We'll talk favors later."

"It's not about the boathouse. I wouldn't ask for your help with that. I respect how hard it is that I—"

"I'm learning to live with the boathouse deal and, well, there's another long story that probably needs to be shared between us and the sooner the better." He leaned in, kissed one corner of her mouth, then the other when she frowned. "But right now, I say we put the business of the world aside for an hour, maybe two, and spend some time on that other part."

She smiled and he felt her relax beneath him. "That part where we figure out what can be?"

"Make a start on it, at any rate."

Her oh-so-expressive eyebrow lifted in an elegant arch. "Would that involve us being naked? In the actual, not metaphorical, sense?"

"It was my fervent hope and desire, aye," he said, allowing more of his weight to press her into the bed.

He watched her throat work and that husky note went deeper still when she replied. "Well . . . just so you know, I'm a big fan of hands-on knowledge." Her gaze dropped quite deliberately to his mouth. "Amongst other body parts."

He chuckled even as his body all but growled. "I'm quite good with my hands, if I do say so. I'll let you be the judge on the other body parts."

"Aye, aye, Captain."

"Well then, cast off, Mate"—he leaned in to nip her bottom lip—"and let's see where the tide takes us."

Chapter 13

She should feel guilty. The most important thing she had to do—her sole mission in life when she'd woken up that morning—was to find Ford, tell him about her move to Maine and her desire for them to find each other again, to be a family.

So, where was she? In bed with Brodie Monaghan.

A man who swore honesty when he told her he was serious about finding out what might be between them, then in the next breath admitted straight out that he'd probably disappoint her.

Though that double standard would likely send most women running . . . she wasn't most women. She wasn't looking for a one-night stand—or morning, as the case may be—but since she was just as curious as he about what was going on between them and just as likely to be the one doing the disappointing when it was all said and done, his declaration was a relief. She'd rather hear that than some promise of undying . . . whatever.

When Brodie started dropping kisses along the side of her neck as he slid his body—and his hands—down her arms and slowly over every part of her, she sent a silent apology to her brother . . . and let him.

No more words. Actions would speak for them. *And damn,* she thought, *Brodie was saying . . . a lot.*

He pushed her T-shirt up, smoothing his palms over her stomach as his fingers brushed the curve of her breasts through her simple, white cotton bra. *Gah.* So much for turning him on with her sexy underthings.

"Pull your shirt off for me, luv," he said, slipping his hands under her and making quick work of her bra hooks.

The fact that his lips had been pressed against her navel as he said it, had her fumbling to yank her T-shirt over her head. "Fair's fair," she managed on a short gasp, as he peeled her bra down her arms, then tossed it . . . somewhere.

He chuckled, the sound a warm vibration against her belly as he lifted his hands long enough to grab the back of his T-shirt and pull it over his head. It followed her bra. "Anything else you want to take turns doing?" He looked up at her, green eyes dancing, and popped the button on her jeans.

"I—"

He slid her zipper down . . . and trailed the movement with his tongue.

Her head fell back to the bed. It was possible her eyes might have rolled upward, too. "Let me get back to you on that," she breathed, then gasped again as he tugged jeans and panties straight down her legs and off. She felt his bare torso pressed against her thighs as he returned to what he'd been doing . . . which was the most amazing thing with his tongue as he—"Oh . . . God. Don't . . . okay, you can keep doing that. A lot of that."

He chuckled again, and she absently wondered if the vibration from his laughter while he was . . . *oh yeah, he could make me come that way. Twice.*

Her fingers curled into the bedspread, then gripped hard as he wasted no time proving her right. He slid one hand up over her stomach, found her oh-so-needy nipples and gave them some much-needed attention while his tongue and fingers found other things to occupy themselves with.

Her hips bucked hard off the bed when he went from teasing and toying, to sliding in and . . . "Yes!" She arched again, and again, heels and fingers digging into the bunk mattress as he took her screaming up and over, no pause, no sweet climb, just . . . stars. There was something to be said for seeing stars during an orgasm. She was an instant fan. *Holy wow, indeed.*

And he was nothing if not . . . well, *relentless* was the word that came to mind. He wasn't content with merely getting her there. No, oh no. He seemed to take an inordinate amount of pleasure in keeping her there. And there. And there.

She let him do that, too.

"I . . . can't . . ." She couldn't string together more than two words, and even those had come with an effort, so she stopped trying and pushed at his head.

He simply growled, making her twitch—hard—and moan when he left her with one last body-trembling kiss, before working his way back up her belly. "Oh, aye, but you could," he said, murmuring against her breasts, where he paused to take a leisurely detour that had her squirming all over again.

Just as she thought he might take a turn south again, he continued his sinful journey up, along her collarbone, to the soft spot just below her ear. He pressed a kiss against the throb of her pulse and nipped her ear.

She reveled in the weight of him on top of her, all deliciously warm and—"You're naked. All of you."

"I am indeed. Fair being fair." He kissed the side of her neck.

"I like fair." She let her head drop to the side so he could keep doing what he was doing to her neck. "I love fair."

He slid broad, warm palms along her arms, and pulled her hands in next to her head, then wove his fingers through hers.

Despite the fact that they'd just been about as carnal as two people could be, or at least well on their way to it, there was an intimacy to that particular gesture that pinged an entirely different place inside her. It was then she opened her eyes, and found him staring right into hers.

"Hi," she said, thinking it was the most inane thing to say, yet felt exactly right. The way he was looking at her, into her, made her feel exposed in that moment in a way she'd never been before, vulnerable, and not because she had no clothes on.

His responding smile was beautiful. And perfect. Not teasing, not mischievous, simply . . . happy. "Hi, yourself."

That was when she realized just how deeply in trouble she was . . . because her heart stood right up and waved a welcome banner. Her heart never did that. Run, hide, make up endless excuses to never come out and play. That was her heart. It didn't take a rocket scientist or a therapist to figure out why, so she'd never pushed it. She'd either be inspired to get over her past, someday, by someone . . . or she wouldn't. But she was pretty sure unless he did something phenomenally stupid inside the next five seconds, there wasn't a damn thing she could do to stop her heart from going straight past "let's see what we see" to "please don't hurt me"—which turned out to be about a million times scarier than she'd thought it would be. And she'd spent a lifetime being terrified of being vulnerable to wanting anyone. Ever.

Please, please, just let it be the pheromone fog making me feel this way.

He leaned in and kissed her. It was sweet, simple, honest. She whimpered a little as her heart teetered closer to the edge.

"I've a sad, sorry confession to make," he said when he lifted his head, still smiling, but with clear regret on his face.

Oh God. Here comes the phenomenally stupid thing. I should be happy. Why aren't I happy?

"I don't have any condoms here on the boat. So, unless you . . . ?"

She wanted to laugh out loud at herself. That was it? *I am such a goner.* She shook her head. "So, not the love boat, then, I guess?" She'd meant it as a tease, but she saw that same thing come into his eyes as when he'd said he didn't take kindly to having his integrity questioned. "I'm kidding," she said quickly. "Not that there would be anything wrong with it, even if it was. You're a grown, single man with a gorgeous, sexy boat."

He grinned instantly at that, and it honestly took her breath away. "I like how you use the fun adjectives for the boat rather than for me. Perhaps I should have carried you out here sooner. Wearing but a kilt."

"I would be lying if I said the very idea of that didn't make me . . ." She let the image play through her mind, sighed a little bit, and definitely wriggled under the weight of him.

He gave a low chuckle. "I'll keep that in mind."

"Do that," she replied.

"I'm sorry it appears I've already been the disappointment I feared I'd become. Admittedly I had thought to do well at this part."

She laughed, surprised, but in a good way—a very good way—that they were lying naked, entwined on his bed with several intense orgasms between them—okay, her orgasms, but still. Rather than be disappointed that things appeared to have come to an early end, she was almost enjoying this part as much. Maybe more. It was very . . . real.

As it turned out, that didn't help stifle the banner-waving thing one bit.

The fact that he didn't even question that they'd have to wait, that the caretaker/protector side of him was showing once again, was probably what gave her the courage to say, "Well, there might be other circumstances that could change . . . things."

He merely lifted a brow in response.

"I appreciate you putting protection above . . . anything else."

"It would never be any other way."

Something about the way he'd said it had her looking at him more closely. "Never?"

He gave a single shake of the head. "For the protection of my partner, aye. And, in all honesty, myself as well."

"Is there . . . a reason? Specifically? I mean—"

"If you're asking whether or not my wild and wanton ways have landed me with a sexually contracted disease, the answer is no. As I said, I've never once no' taken care."

"It wasn't a commentary on you." She smiled, unlinking their hands long enough to touch his cheek. "You're very sensitive about that."

"I never have been before," he said, sounding a little disconcerted. "Never felt the need to apologize, as, truth be told, I've nothing to apologize for. My reputation is exaggerated, but aye, I've not been overly concerned about correcting assumptions."

"And yet . . . ?"

She felt some of the tension in him relax. "And yet, with you, I . . . don't know. I don't want you thinking poorly of me, I guess. I enjoy women, I do. And that's a good and healthy thing to my mind. But I'm no' some indiscriminate bastard who—"

She pressed her finger over his lips, silencing him. "I didn't say you were. You're a flirt, a charmer. It's a natural thing for you. But I'm . . . it didn't go unnoticed that it's your instinct to protect and put your partner first." Her smile spread to a grin. "Might I say a hearty thank you for that?"

He smiled at that, too, but it didn't fully reach his eyes.

"Brodie, I don't know you, not well, not yet. But I'm not indiscriminate, either. What I do know of you . . . I value. Or I wouldn't be here, with you . . . like this."

He took her fingers, brought them to his lips, and kissed them. "That's good to know, then. Thank you."

She smiled, still a little surprised by the serious turn they'd taken once again, that her opinion seemed to matter so much to him. And that it seemed to surprise him, too.

"I'm on the pill," she said, watching his face. "Not for birth control, so much as it helps keep certain things on a more normal course, as it were."

"I've six sisters, remember? You needn't explain it to me."

She grinned then. "I guess not. You poor, poor man."

"Finally," he said with mock angst, "somebody appreciates the hell I lived through. Monthly. I'm all for anything that makes that easier. For both of us."

She wriggled under him. "It might make other things easier, too."

His eyebrows lifted, but he was still serious when he spoke. "Grace, we don't have to—"

"I know. If you'd feel better waiting, I understand. I can tell you that I haven't had a partner in over a year. Not since before I left the firm. No one serious in my life for far longer than that. Never, actually. So, I always used protection, too. Like I said, the pill was for other reasons. In fact, I've never told anyone I was even on it. I'm healthy. I've made sure of it."

"Och, Grace," he said, pushing the hair from her face once again.

The brush of his work-roughened fingers somehow felt all the more tender for their less than smooth surface. Brodie was a study in contrasts, a little rougher underneath than his smooth surface might indicate. She'd known he had depth, had seen it that first day, but the nuances of him, the way he effortlessly charmed one moment, then wore his soft Irish vulnerabilities on his sleeve the next drew her in. He drew her in.

"I'm sorry there hasn't been someone you've wanted for your own, yet selfish enough to admit I'm thankful for it all the same."

She lifted a shoulder. "There's been a time or two when I thought . . . maybe. But it never went that far, or that deep. It hasn't been something that I've put a lot of pressure on myself to find. I have . . ." *Issues.* She trailed off, not really wanting to get into anything more about the particular whys and wherefores. *Not here, at any rate. Not now.*

"I know you said you have no extended family, and I'm guessing things with your brother . . . well, that's for another time, perhaps. My story might have been quite the opposite. Too many rather than no' enough." He smiled down into her eyes again, in that way that made her heart flutter. "Childhood stories we can share some other time, aye?"

"Aye," she said softly. "What about you? Special someones?" She knew exactly what she was asking, and whom she was wondering about. Any other time, any other man, she'd have kicked herself for inserting potential old flame conversation right in the middle of a new flame being built. But, with him . . . it was important to know. *Better now,* she thought.

"As a young man, my fancy was caught often, I'll admit. Never for long. But never unfaithful, either. I was never set on hurting anyone. When I arrived here, it was something of a relief, really. There was no history, no family looking over me shoulder, documenting my every wink and kiss. I think I enjoyed a few dalliances purely because I could and simply be myself. Again, nothing serious. No' because I would have minded. I think I figured I simply wasn't cut out for it." He smiled, then dipped his chin. "Then . . . about a year ago . . ."

She knew where he was going, whom he was likely thinking of. It was why she'd asked, after all. She appreciated his honesty in being open about his social life and thought he'd probably left a lot of disappointed women in his wake, but she also believed that he'd probably never led them to believe it would be otherwise, either. Hadn't he already warned her of the same?

She was just about to open her mouth and let him off the hook, despite being more curious to know the true story, when he spoke first.

"I told you about Alex MacFarland doing the remodel on my boathouse. Well, she turned my head straight around, right from the start. It was . . . a first." He grinned. "She also turned me down flat. Not so much as a kiss was shared between us. Turned out her head had been turned right around, too . . . but by someone other than me."

"Must have been hard," Grace said, truly surprised by the twinge of jealousy she felt, hearing him talk so fondly of someone else, realizing how ridiculous that was, since he wasn't with Alex, and was currently naked in bed with her. Still . . . "Working with her, having unrequited feelings."

"Aye, it was," he said with simple, open honesty. "We've gone on to manage a friendship, and I'm sincere in my happiness that she's found what she wants. Who she wants. It threw me, though, first that I felt what I did at all, and then again when it didn't simply go away."

Grace nodded, thinking she might not have fully understood before, but having met him and experienced the feelings he so effortlessly elicited in her . . . yeah, it made sense.

"Once those feelings are known to ye, then going back to the easy but empty is . . . well, it didn't draw me." He laughed shortly. "Frustrated the hell out of me, to be honest. But I couldn't shake the idea that there was more to be had . . . and I wanted to be the one having it." He gave a short shake of his head, looked at her, then ducked his chin. "And I am now the exact sort of bastard I swore I'd never be. Talking of another woman at the worst possible time, in the worst possible position—"

"I asked," Grace said, interrupting him. "And . . . I already knew."

"Small towns," he said, still looking abashed.

"No, before that. When you spoke of her . . . I knew. Or suspected. I only asked because I wanted—maybe I needed—to hear what the story was behind that look in your eyes when you said her name." Grace lifted a shoulder. "Maybe it shouldn't matter." She shifted her gaze. "But I guess it does."

He lifted her chin with a fingertip. "I know ye said you don't fish for compliments, so I'll take it that you're not looking now."

She shook her head, held his gaze directly as she did.

"Good. So you'll know that I mean what I'm about to say, aside from this conversation. And because we had this conversation, you'll know I understand exactly what I'm saying. For that reason alone, I'm glad you asked."

"Okay," she said, unsure if she really wanted to know what he was about to tell her, or if she'd forever wish she'd kept her damn mouth shut. At least until after they'd enjoyed the happy perk of being on birth control—which was what had started the whole conversation to begin with.

He took her face in his hands, wove his fingers into her hair, and did that thing he did, that soothing stroke of his thumbs. It made her heart race and calmed something inside her, all at the same time.

"Grace Maddox, you've no' been in my world for that long a time, and we've spent only a wee bit of it in each other's company. Yet, it's a profound impact ye've had on me. From the moment I heard you cursing on my docks, my head was turned." He grinned, delighted apparently, as she felt the warmth bloom on her cheeks. "All the moments since have only served to tighten that hold." He paused, held her gaze, then said the rest. "You're the woman I can't get out of my mind. You're the proof that I was right—there's more to be had."

He made her heart pound. She didn't know what to say to that. The declaration thrilled her when it should have terrified her. As he said the words, every one of them echoed the same truth inside her. He was simply braver. She was still trying to admit the truth of them to herself, and he'd put it right out there. She didn't know if she'd ever be that brave, be that vulnerable.

"Then let's get back to finding out what more there might be," she said, hoping she wouldn't see disappointment in his eyes for not responding out loud with the same declaration. Actions, she thought, would have to speak for her.

Instead of disappointment, what she saw was relief. Had he really been worried she'd reject him? Of course, the only other time he'd felt such emotions, he'd been turned down flat.

She spoke before she lost her nerve. "You've turned my head, too." When his gaze sharpened, surprise and a deeper, banked emotion swimming in all that emerald green, she added, "Only you."

"Come here," he said, leaning in and kissing her, taking

her mouth with slow and thorough certainty as he gathered her up in his arms and moved his weight between her legs.

Her heart tipped right over as he sheltered her . . . and claimed her.

"Lift up for me," he said, urging her hips higher. "Hold on." There was no hesitation, no fumbling, just a solid, single thrust.

"Brodie," she whispered, gasping, moaning, wrapping herself more tightly around him. All of him.

"I've got you." He groaned and buried his face in the curve of her neck. "You feel . . ."

Like you're mine. She closed her eyes and held on to him.

He started to move inside her, letting her find her pace with him until they were in perfect, unified, glorious sync with each other.

For all they'd teased and bantered and laughed their way into his bed, there was nothing lighthearted about this. It was earthy and primal; mating, pure and simple, raw and complex.

By the time she felt his body gathering, tightening, knowing it would be the first time he'd truly come inside someone—inside her—she let every last barrier crumble, giving as fully to him as she was able, as if nothing less than all of her would be enough to match what he was giving her.

He growled, a long, low rumble of release, thrusting so deep inside her as he came . . . and she reveled in every vibration of it, glorying in it right along with him.

He held her for long moments afterward, trembling as aftershocks rocked them both. Finally, he slid from her and rolled his weight to the bed beside her, pulling her with him, settling her next to him, half sprawled over him as he tucked her head beneath his chin, his fingers still buried in her hair.

She listened to the thundering beat of his heart, her cheek pressed to his chest. He absently stroked her cheek and she felt him press a long, soft kiss to the top of her head. Her heart tipped past the edge and went into full free fall.

What have I done? What have I gone and done?

Chapter 14

Brodie took a lingering look at the woman presently slumbering in his bunk, then ducked through the hatch and made his way to the galley. He was satisfyingly fatigued, voraciously hungry, and more than a little disconcerted. In an effort to ignore that last part, he focused on the hunger issue. A quick look at the cupboards proved he'd have to go raid his boathouse for something resembling real sustenance. He brewed a quick pot of tea and took an insulated mug of it topside, already engaging in the internal battle of *just go with it, don't overthink it . . .* knowing he was going to lose that one handily.

A short yap had him glancing over at the dock where Whomper wriggled in glee upon spying him, but remained in a very proper sit. "Well, aren't you the repentant lad after running off with my newly planed pine mold piece. Don't suppose you brought that back with you?" He glanced past the pup, but there was no trace of the hand-carved piece that had taken him a good hour to make that morning. He looked back to Whomper, who ducked his chin but kept soulful eyes pinned on Brodie. "Heartbreaker," he muttered, then slapped his chest. "Permission to come aboard."

Whomper didn't have to be told twice, but merely launched himself straight from the dock. Brodie barely had time to set his mug on the rail before catching the ball of scruff against his bare chest.

He winced. "All that digging, you'd think ye'd have no claws left, laddie." He chuckled as Whomper set about making up with him by trying to lick his face clean off. "Okay, okay, all is forgiven. Down, boy-o." He set the pup on the deck and retrieved his tea. Whomper set off investigating all corners of the deck, making Brodie smile again. The mutt had natural sea legs and seemed quite sure-footed on the gently rocking deck. He did a quick scan, but didn't see anything that would bring the dog any harm, so left him to his explorations, took his tea, and climbed up to the helm, where he sat and looked out over the horizon toward the bay.

He had to tell her, of course. About the situation with Cami.

Brodie cursed under his breath, hating that there was a situation of any kind that even needed discussing where that woman was involved. But involve herself she had, and quite ingeniously. If the chance to build a historic, wood-hull schooner wasn't such a once-in-a-lifetime opportunity—what greater one for a modern-day ship-builder could there ever be?—he wouldn't have even re-turned Brooks Winstock's phone call.

He'd told himself he'd simply find a way to separate the two things. It wasn't like his rejection of the man's daughter would have any bearing on the business dealings they might have. Hell, Cami was a married woman, so Brodie had been pretty damn certain Winstock wouldn't know about the rejection in the first place. Of course, the man would have to be blind, deaf, and dumb not to have at least heard the rumors about his only child's extracurricular activities, but Winstock was calling him, not the other way around; Brodie had assumed if it was known, it wouldn't be mentioned. Gentlemen didn't, after all.

His only true concern was that Cami would see the business link to her family as an opportunity to make yet another attempt to leverage herself into his bed . . . or upon hearing about the deal, she would exact her retribution by making sure Brodie was dropped from the project altogether.

"Boy, did you read that wrong," he muttered, sipping his tea. He was deep in thought, trying to figure out the best way to explain the situation, when a woman's voice broke into his ruminations. He smiled.

"I know you probably have a gazillion pairs," Grace said as she climbed up to join him. "But I figured you probably didn't give it to him as a chew toy." She held up a half-mangled boat shoe.

Brodie reached for the shoe. "Does the wee bit have to have something clamped in his jaws at all times? I'm starting to think he's got a problem."

"Don't ask me. I've just been thankful the boathouse has a huge pile of old pot buoys shoved in the back corner. I figure it'll take him a while to work through the stack."

Brodie chuckled and tossed the shoe to the deck. "Come," he said, levering his feet off the console and motioning her to sit on his lap. "Limited seating up here."

He'd pulled on his jeans but nothing more and saw she'd pulled on her khaki shorts and tee . . . and nothing more, either. He smiled approvingly. And, fatigued or not, the rest of his body smiled, too.

She stayed at the top of the ladder. "I was thinking I'd go and find something for lunch. I looked in your galley, but—"

"I did, too. Like minds," he said with a grin. "I'm sure I could find something back up at the boathouse." He started to stand, but she waved him back to his seat.

"I'll go. I didn't mean to interrupt. Just didn't want you

thinking I'd up and vanished. Want me to take Whomper with me?"

He didn't want her to go anywhere. The sun was in his eyes, so her face was in shadow, and he couldn't read her expression. Her tone was casual enough, her body relaxed, but . . . something wasn't right. Or it wasn't the same, anyway. "Grace—"

"Not yet," she said quickly. Then her face creased in a half smile and he saw that she was nervous. Of all things. "I'm just—that was . . ." She looked embarrassed, but kept the smile on her face. "Let me go get us some lunch. Okay?"

He might not have had experience with long-term relationships, but he knew enough about women in general to know that pushing was never a good idea, and more likely to reap a result opposite the one sought. But he really didn't want her to go, at least not without first figuring out where her head had gone once he'd left her alone in his bed.

"Want some help?"

"I've got it." She started to climb back down the ladder rail.

"Grace?"

She paused, then levered herself up just enough so she could see him. "Yes?"

"It's going to be okay."

"What will?" she asked, looking wary.

Brilliant. You idiot. But he couldn't seem to help himself. She wasn't okay, and so he'd had to say something. "I don't know," he admitted. "Whatever isn't, at the moment. We'll figure it out."

She held his gaze for a long, silent moment, and he kicked himself all over again. "I usually figure things out by myself," she said at length.

"So you said. I'm just saying . . . maybe give sharing the

load a go." He smiled then. "Could be, I'll be no help whatsoever, but I'll do my best to try."

"It's just lunch," she said, trying for a glib tone. Failing.

"Okay," he said, matching her smile, knowing he'd done exactly what he'd known not to do. He'd pushed. Better he should stop while he was behind.

She climbed down and he heard her give a stern warning to the pup before climbing to the dock. He turned and watched her walk away. "I don't know what I'm doing, either," he called, not all that loudly, but knowing his voice would carry to her.

She turned, walked backward a few steps, looking at him. Then she shot him a quick, real smile, along with a sharp first mate salute, and turned back toward the shore.

He saluted her back, then sighed and slumped his shoulders. "Permission to break my heart," he murmured, watching her retreat.

Not pushing might be the right thing to do, but sitting there watching her walk away felt like a really wrong thing to do.

A minute later he was smiling as he downed the rest of his tea. Decision made, he hopped down to the main deck, then went below and gathered up whatever bits and pieces they'd left behind. Back above deck, he whistled for the dog, who'd found his way up on the foredeck, and Brodie wondered just how much rope he probably had to replace. "Come on, Mischief," he said, patting his chest. Whomper sprang up and Brodie bent to capture him against his chest.

"Let's go find your mistress, shall we?" He hopped to the dock and put Whomper down, smiling as the pup tore off toward the boathouse. He might not know what the hell he was doing, but she'd already admitted that neither did she. So chances were she was falling back on what felt comfortable. And that was building walls and figuring things out alone. And where had that gotten her? Sticking with what was safe, that's where.

Nothing about what was happening between them—or what could happen—felt like it was anything close to safe.

He was good at letting things go when the going got tough, at moving on when things looked like they might get complicated. At least where women were concerned. And where had that gotten him?

If they had a chance to get past the early part and explore new ground, better to break the pattern right from the start.

He knew she thought his natural charm got him his way more often than not, so it seemed a smart thing would be to use his best skill to set things on the right path before they had a chance to go all wrong. "Go with your strength, mate." His grin began to falter as a few knots started to twist in his gut. "Go with your strength."

She wasn't in his boathouse. He found her in hers. "I know I don't keep the pantry stocked as I should, but it's embarrassing to think you've got more in that cooler than I have in my whole kitchen."

Whomper had dashed in first, so she wasn't startled by Brodie's entrance, but she did take a moment to slowly lower the lid of the cooler and close it with a purposeful little click. She lifted a can of dog food with a plastic lid snapped to the top. "Thought I'd feed Whomper, since we were eating."

Brodie glanced down to the dog. "You didn't tell her?" He looked back at Grace and smiled at the arched brow and questioning expression. Some of the knots loosened a bit. "I picked up a bit of kibble and a box of biscuits. Seeing as he was hanging about." He lifted a shoulder. "I should have mentioned it. But you and I weren't exactly on speaking terms."

She was too far away for him to see if the revelation softened her up in any way. He glanced down at Whomper again. "I think we're in trouble, mate."

"Only because you don't listen any better than he does," she said. "Are you that afraid of what I might fix for lunch? Just because I've been living out of a cooler doesn't mean I can't put together a decent meal."

She walked closer and he was further relieved to see the wink of humor in her eyes.

"It wasn't your ability to construct a good lunch that concerned me." He closed the remaining distance, aware that what happened in the next few minutes could very well keep the door to their continued journey open . . . or slam it shut in his face. He took the can from her hand and set it—"What in the world is that?"

She glanced down. "Just what it looks like. A suitcase table."

"Right." He looked at her. "Why?"

"I needed a little table. There was an old suitcase in the rubble of stuff, and a few old legs and brackets from some long-ago piece of furniture so I screwed them into the bottom of the suitcase and . . . table. Kitchen counter. Desk. It's very all-purpose."

"Clever."

She smiled. "I thought so."

He reached for her arms and very gently shuffled her forward until she was right up in his personal space. "I admire your amazing ability to build things out of odd bits, but what concerned me was your ability to construct some really sturdy walls while you made a few sandwiches."

Up close, there was no hiding that his words surprised her. "I wasn't—"

It was his turn to lift a questioning brow, which halted her denial cold. She looked him in the eye and didn't seem all that pleased by his remarkable insight. The knots reformed and his inner voice launched into another tirade of self-recrimination.

She let out a half laugh, shook her head, and gave him that classic wry grin of hers. "Okay. So maybe I was. Trying to, anyway. It's—"

"Safer. I know. Trust me." He rubbed his hands up and down her arms, then nudged her a bit closer still and put his arms around her. "You can, though, you know. Trust me."

"I'd like to," she said in typical direct fashion. "I want to. It's not an instant thing with me. I told you that."

"And I listened." Her eyebrow climbed and he smiled. "I did. Then I let you walk off, back to the Land of Safety. I almost stayed on the boat, telling myself it was because you wanted me to, asked me to. But I realized I was doing the same thing you were. Retreating, letting things slide and go where they may. But where has that gotten me? Where has it gotten you?"

"Brodie—"

"Just . . . allow me to complete the thought. Then you can kick me out. Though, fair warning." He nodded at the can of dog food. "I feed him much better than you do. He'll likely follow."

"You're threatening to hold my dog hostage?" she said, but he could see she was fighting a smile.

That was when he knew he'd done the right thing and the tension in his gut finally went away. "I'm saying he might choose self-imposed exile."

"You do realize I might think of that as a win-win scenario."

Brodie looked at the dog. "Did you hear that, mate? She's saying she's better off without us."

On cue, Whomper lay down and put his chin on his paws, big eyes solemnly on Grace. Brodie looked back at Grace and did his best human impression of the same.

She smacked his shoulders with open palms, but was laughing as she said, "Oh my God. You are truly incorrigible." She looked at Whomper. "Both of you."

The dog gave a few tentative tail thumps, but kept his chin down.

She looked at Brodie. "I don't know what to do with you." Her expression sobered slightly, but her gaze stayed easily on his. It was as earnest and honest as he'd ever seen it. "I can't impress upon you enough the depths to which I mean that." She let him pull her hands from his shoulders and kiss her knuckles. "I really have no idea what I'm doing."

"Me either. But it seems to me that our best bet is to figure it out together. Unless you really have no desire to try and figure out what the answers are and would rather brainstorm ways to convince yourself you shouldn't go for it. Then I could simply let you do that as I wouldn't have to risk anything, either. I wouldn't even have to take the blame."

"I can't imagine your problem is that women are trying to get away from you."

"Sure and I'm fun to play with, but smart women soon figure I'm, at best, catch and release, and they go off looking for bigger fish. Or better ones, anyway."

Grace held his gaze for one sober moment, then burst out laughing.

"What? What did I say? I'm telling the truth."

"Oh, I don't doubt it. The truth as you see it." She was still laugh-snorting, and her eyes had teared up with the effort to squelch it. "Luv," she said in a dead-on impersonation of his accent, "women would cart ye home to their mamas in a heartbeat if they thought they could get you there . . . and that their papas wouldn't shoot you dead on sight."

"Meaning?" he asked archly . . . but her laughter was contagious.

"Meaning you flirted shamelessly with me until you got me, then the very next thing you did was warn me that you'd disappoint me. The women didn't have to release you, because A, if they were smart, as you say, then they knew pretty much right off that they'd never really caught you, and B, it didn't matter, because you were wriggling off the hook before they could even set it."

He opened his mouth to shoot her down . . . then closed it again.

She shot him a smug smile. "I rest my case."

"So . . . what if I don't want to wriggle off your hook? What do I do then?"

Her smug smile froze and she searched his suddenly very serious expression.

"See? Uncharted waters. Both of us. In all of those depths that you said I couldn't imagine. Well, I can imagine. That's all I was trying to say."

It was her turn to open her mouth then shut it again. Only there was no smug smile from him this time.

"You really do listen," she finally said.

"I try."

"Why me?" she asked.

"Why me?" he countered.

Her eyes went wide and she made a gesture at him, head to toe. "Seriously?"

"If anything, with you I think that works against me, not for."

"Well. I wouldn't go that far." Heat stole into her cheeks again.

He hooted a laugh and tugged her the rest of the way into his arms, pushing his fingers into her hair as he tipped her face up to his. "You don't suffer fools, you curse like a sailor, and with your hair loose you look like a goddess emerging from the sea. I was lost before I had a chance."

"Remind me never to get you a pair of glasses," she said dryly.

"To me, you are all those things. That's all that really matters, is it not?"

"Brodie . . ." She trailed off, sighed, but her gaze never left his.

"Let me ask you this. You said you don't know what to do with me. Would you rather just do without me, then?"

Her felt her body soften and the tension went out of her shoulders. She shook her head. "No. I just—"

He pressed his lips against hers and said against them, "No just-ing. And no more words." He took her mouth in a soul-searing kiss that said everything he wasn't willing to put into words. Yet. "Kiss me back," he murmured. "Show me what ye canno' tell me."

She pressed her lips to his in a hard kiss, but whatever her plan, it quickly shifted to something far deeper, more real. At least, when she softened completely into him, then slid her arms around his neck and kissed him like he was the last man she'd ever see, it felt like that to him.

When they broke off for air, she buried her face in his neck . . . and simply hung on.

And maybe, he thought, that was what you did with each other, for each other. You just . . . hung on.

"So," he said, nuzzling her neck, keeping her wrapped up against his chest. "Tell me about this favor you need of me. We'll start there, okay?" *And then I'll tell you about how Brooks Winstock is trying to buy his daughter a stud pony with a tall ship.*

Yeah. He hoped it was a really big favor. Though he wasn't sure there was a wish he could grant that was big enough to keep Grace hanging on after he got done telling her about that.

Chapter 15

G race pulled her hair back and shoved it in the baseball cap Brodie had given her, squinting into the morning sun as the boat chugged over the open water toward Sandpiper Island. It was probably better that he'd gotten her a lift out to the island on one of Blue's workboats than on his sailboat. The day was going to be complicated enough. She didn't need to also be thinking about Brodie.

"Like that's not exactly what you're doing anyway," she murmured, tipping her face to the salt spray as she perched near the front of the boat. She was the sole passenger and appreciated the alone time as she tried to get herself ready for what was to come.

She knew Brodie was right, knew that she'd have likely done exactly what he'd predicted she'd do—find a list of reasons to not pursue things with him and go with the safe exit. Of course, the list wasn't hard to come by. "But saying no to him is damn near impossible."

The real question is . . . do you want to say no to him?

Despite his pushing her yesterday after they'd left his sailboat, if she told him she didn't want to see him any longer, no matter what her reasons were, he would respect them. That was part of why she was really making sure she thought things through. Running away because she was too scared to try was one thing. But pursuing something she knew would be a bad idea in the long run, just because he'd goaded her into it, was also something she didn't want to do. It wouldn't be fair to her, or to him.

She just needed to think, clear her head, and try to figure out what she really wanted and what would be the best choice. And if they had a chance in hell of being the same thing. She knew damn well what she wanted. He was smart, hot, aggressive in all the right ways, and spoke with a sexy Irish accent. *Why can't it be that simple?*

That was the other question. Could it be that simple? He was right next door. They wanted to spend time together, see if there was something worth pursuing. He seemed to have gotten a grip on the fact that she'd bought some of his property out from under him. Not to mention he was endlessly fascinating, sharply focused, intuitive, funny, and ridiculously good in bed.

She sighed. "Honestly, what's wrong with me that I'm not flinging myself in his arms and promising my undying love already?"

She leaned back against the rail, thankful that the wind on the water snatched her words away before they could find their way back to the boat captain. Robie was in his mid-sixties, she'd guess, stocky, with a burly white beard and a Mainer accent so thick she could barely understand him. He was quick with a laugh—though she couldn't say what exactly he found so funny—and willing to take her out to Sandpiper with no questions asked.

She was very thankful for that as she looked out to the bay and the island that was steadily looming closer. Why wasn't she flinging herself at Brodie? *Because I haven't even figured out how to have an ongoing, healthy relationship with my own brother yet. What makes me think I can handle one with Brodie?*

He hadn't taken her out to Sandpiper because of some business meetings he had in town. He'd seemed nervous and excited about them, but hadn't told her anything more. Instead, after she'd asked her favor, he'd asked if she wanted to talk about her brother or her family or . . . any of her other reasons for coming to Maine besides building an inn.

She'd been surprised to realize just how much she wanted to tell him, partly because she wanted him to understand where her insecurities came from. More stunningly, to her anyway, was because she knew he'd truly listen.

Langston had been a dear friend and very supportive and understanding of her childhood story, but more in the sympathetic way friends are for friends. Grace couldn't help but think Brodie would have a more personal ability to relate. Not because his situation mirrored hers in any way—if anything, it seemed the total opposite—but because he seemed to have a real sense of self, of people, of life.

The idea that he'd truly connect to her because of her story, not despite it, was thrillingly seductive . . . and scary as all hell. Because that connection to her would only deepen her connection to him.

Her feelings for Langston were purely those of friendship, of family chosen; there was no risk that he would abandon her, or not love her back because of her past. The demands of maintaining their friendship didn't come close to what it would take to establish an intimate, strong, committed relationship with Brodie.

The potential reward of having that kind of deep, meaningful relationship with someone was tantalizing. The flip side was risking being rejected, abandoned by someone she loved deeply. Again. She didn't know if she had it in her to try, much less risk failure.

She'd ended up begging off staying with Brodie the

night before and had opted to go out to the house on the Point, take a much-needed shower, sleep in a real bed. Alone. Well, except for Whomper, whom she'd admittedly snuggled with a bit too tightly.

She sighed and finally pushed away all those questions that threatened to plague her and drive her straight to crazy town. She shoved all thoughts of her suddenly complicated personal life aside and focused instead on the more complicated situation that lay ahead.

Today was the Big Day. The biggest. Whatever happened with Ford would help her figure it all out. Or at least be a giant step in that general direction. Any directional help would be appreciated at the moment.

As the boat drew nearer, she turned her attention to the island. It wasn't huge, and rather than being long and flat, it was round and hilly. She knew from the research she'd done during her Wi-Fi time at the library that, from above, it was actually heart-shaped. She'd smiled at the whimsy of it at the time, hoping it was more good omen than some kind of karmic irony.

From the side they were approaching, the island appeared to be nothing but tall pines and rocky shore, jutting out from a pointed bluff that shaped the bottom of the heart.

They rounded the north side, which formed the top of the left side of the heart, comprised mostly of a jumble of rocks and boulders like children's blocks that rolled out to the sea. Tucked between the twin heart tops was a beautiful, calm, sheltered cove. It was there, on the rocks and boulders lining the natural harbor, that the seabirds came to nest each May, lay their eggs, and raise their young, until they all took off for life at sea once again in the middle of August. She knew the island was also home to harbor seals and other predatory seabirds like the black-headed gulls and common eider ducks, each hoping to help raise their own young by feeding on the nests of the more vulnerable. Ford worked with a small band of scientists and interns, studying the habits of the endangered birds, namely the puffins, arctic terns, and razorbills, in hopes of finding ways to encourage better breeding results.

She had no desire to intrude on their delicate research and had questioned Robie about the best way to approach the island with that in mind. She'd learned there was only one dock and it was tucked safely in a pocket of the harbor. Blue's, in addition to being a commercial fishing company, also helped out by running workboats out to some of the islands in Pelican Bay over the summer months, which included ferrying the scientists and interns to and from Sandpiper, as well as delivering supplies, food, mail, and anything else that needed to get to or from the island.

There was no schedule. It wasn't advertised, as the work was private and the public wasn't invited. Someone on the island contacted Blue's when they needed something. A run had just been made the week before, so there'd been nothing scheduled when Brodie had inquired for her.

As it turned out, he hadn't even batted an eye when she'd asked her favor. He'd known exactly what to do, whom to contact. She kicked herself for waiting so long, but tried to cut herself some slack. It had seemed so impossible and overwhelming when she'd first arrived. She'd just bought a two-hundred-year-old boathouse that she had no idea how to turn into a business she had no idea how to run, so her learning curve had been steep.

The captain had said runs were usually called in last minute and simply squeezed in with whatever fisherman could get the job done at the time, so she'd scheduled her own run and offered to pay them well for the trouble. She was thankful that Brodie had convinced Robie to take her out without specifically mentioning why when they radioed ahead, just that they had a package to deliver for Ford.

"Something tells me he's not going to think it's Christmas in July when he sees what's in the box," she muttered.

As they chugged around the tumble of boulders at the top of the heart, her stomach knotted tighter, and tighter still, until she really thought she might be sick. *It might be better if I could be sick, so I can breathe without wanting to beg Robie to turn around before it's too late.*

They came around the last jut of rocks and she got her first look at the small, natural harbor. It was nothing short of gorgeous. The water was such a deep blue it made her heart twist. Framed by the tumble of gray and brown rocks, then backed by the deep green of the tall, soldierly pines, it looked for all the world like they were protecting the island in a giant group hug. The sky above was a startling light blue, with white puffy clouds floating by. It was so postcard perfect, it felt surreal. Or maybe she was just having an out-of-body experience because she so desperately wished to be anywhere but in her own body.

She moved to the center of the boat as they neared the dock, then nervously pulled off her baseball cap and shook out her hair, smoothing her T-shirt, her khaki pants, the thin, button-up sweater she'd pulled on as the temperatures had dipped out on the water. She realized she was twisting Brodie's ball cap into a knot, then noticed something tucked inside the hatband as she smoothed it back out. She pulled out the small, folded piece of paper, crumpled but otherwise looking none the worse for wear. It wasn't old or worn; she turned it over and saw her name had been printed on the other side, in neat blueprint-type script. The only time she'd seen that kind of printing had been on Langston's plans. But Langston hadn't had his hands on this cap. Nor had she seen him since his one visit to Blueberry.

No, there was only one person who could have stuck that note in the hat. She smiled, her heart tilting already as she unfolded it. She read the small, neatly printed script.

> *I asked around and folks here have only good things to say about your brother. I have only good things to say about you. It may not go easy, and it may not go as you hope, but good people will do good things. It will come together eventually. Have faith in him. I do in you. Brodie*

Tears sprang instantly to her eyes. He hadn't said a word about knowing anything about Ford, only asking if she wanted to talk about him. He'd backed off when she'd declined his offer . . . then found his own way to say what he thought needed to be said. *And this is the man I'm considering walking away from? Really?*

"Your package is right here," she heard Robie say.

She quickly wiped her eyes and shoved the note into her pocket. She glanced at the captain, who was looking not at her, but up at the dock. With the tide half out, it was a good ladder climb up to the pier. Her gaze followed his to the man standing up there, staring down at her. He was a complete stranger, and yet she'd know him anywhere. No matter how many years had passed.

"Hi, Ford." She tried a smile, failed spectacularly. But she didn't throw up, so there was that. When his expression didn't so much as flicker, she lifted her hands, then let them fall to her sides. "Surprise."

Chapter 16

Dammit, he should have gone with her. Shouldn't he? "Why don't they make friggin' handbooks for these things?" he asked Whomper, who looked up from the bone he was working on and wagged his stubby tail, eyes gleaming as he bestowed all of his canine adoration on Brodie for a few moments, then went back to his treat. "If relationships with women were only as simple as the one between man and dog," he told the little ball of scruff. *Bugger it all.* This was exactly why he steered clear of them.

He paced his boathouse, checking the old, brass ship's clock mounted to the wall between the kitchen and lounge area for the dozenth time. Was she out there yet? Was her brother welcoming her? Or making her wish she'd never set foot in Maine? From what little she'd told him, it was likely the latter. Added to that, Winstock was late for their meeting, leaving him too long with his own thoughts.

He'd understood Grace's need to take a little time the night before to get ready for the day she'd been planning for such a very long time. He'd appreciated that she'd shared with him as much as she had, especially given it was a topic that she hadn't shared with anyone since her arrival.

Not that it had kept the locals from burning up the

grapevine speculating about it. He hadn't mentioned that to her, though, as she didn't seem to be aware of the gossip and he didn't want to put any additional weight on the proceedings. He knew she'd been making acquaintances with many of her new neighbors, but she'd spent the lion's share of her time in the boathouse working her cute little bum off, so it wasn't all that surprising that she hadn't heard. Nor was the fact that no one had brought it up directly with her.

For all that being in a small village made it possible for everyone to know everyone else's business, in the year he'd spent there, he'd come to learn that Mainers had their own quirks. They might gossip and speculate about a person among those who were so inclined to join the conversation, but otherwise they were a private lot who didn't butt in.

He'd also understood Grace's desire to head out to Sandpiper alone to reunite with her brother. It wasn't Brodie's place to be part of that meeting. He didn't even know what place he had in her life as yet. So no one was more surprised than he that he'd wanted to be part of it in the first place. Familial drama was something he'd always happily avoided; his own, as well as everyone else's.

That hadn't kept him from spending the night and all of the morning thinking about it, about her. Had she found his note? Was she pissed at him for being that presumptuous? Or had the note given her the peace of mind he'd have tried to provide had he gone along for the ride? Somewhere about three in the morning, he'd come to realize that it wasn't so much about wanting to be a part of the reunion as it was wanting to do whatever it took to protect Grace from being hurt by her brother. It was hard to just sit by and do nothing.

That was also new.

He heard footsteps on the pier out front. *Winstock. Hopefully alone.*

Some quirks were a bit harder to respect. Like a father who not only was willing to look the other way when his only child conducted herself in a manner that was about as unbecoming as it got, but was willing to facilitate his little princess's every whim, to boot. Even if her whim was wanting a man other than the one she'd married. Brodie shook his head. *Who the hell does that?*

He tried to imagine his mother, aunts, or any of his sisters putting up with that kind of bullshit, much less pimp themselves out to support it, and the idea was so outrageous it was comical. But there was nothing funny about the arrangement Brooks Winstock was trying to rope him into.

Their meeting was to go over the plans Brodie had drawn up for the schooner. Plans he'd enjoyed laboring over, often well into the wee hours, for nights on end. Every detail, large and small, bore his own personal stamp, as well as exhaustive research into his ancestors' work on building the same exact ship. He was excited by the end result and hoped that Winstock would be just as excited.

Brodie also hoped he had completely misread the older gentleman in regards to his desire to tie their contract to some sort of verbal agreement that suited the desires of his daughter. Or, at the very least, that Brooks was willing to pretend it had never been mentioned, when it became clear that Brodie wasn't going to be manipulated that way.

The schooner was a once-in-a-lifetime opportunity, one no sane man would give up. But would a sane man enter into a devil's bargain for it? He shook his head again. *Not this man.*

A quick, sharp rap on the door had Whomper up and racing to greet the newcomer, while Brodie took a deep breath as he raked a hand through his hair, then crossed the room to slide the panel door open. "Down, boy-o," he said to the pup, who instantly plopped his butt on the floor, tail still spinning furiously as he looked up to Brodie for approval. Brodie flashed him a quick grin, thinking Grace would be proud of the progress they were making turning the wee scruff into a gentleman. Because he was dog sitting and because he'd wanted home-turf advantage, he'd requested that the meeting take place in his boathouse rather than at Winstock's offices in town or at his requested location, his yacht club situated a good hour and a half south of Blueberry Cove on Frenchman Bay off Bar Harbor. Where the money lived.

Something Winstock was looking to change.

Brodie flipped the latch and rolled the door open. "Mr. Winstock, good morning. Thanks for meeting me here."

"Please, it's Brooks." The older gentleman stepped into the boathouse, then looked down as Whomper danced around his feet, sniffing and panting. "Well now, who might this young fellow be?" he said, flashing a quick grin and reaching down to give the dog a good healthy scratch behind the ears.

"This is Master Whomper," Brodie said, thinking Winstock couldn't be all bad if he was a dog person. *There has to be a workable solution here somewhere.*

The older gentleman straightened and took a look around. He was tall, lean, perpetually tanned, with a thick head of white hair, neatly groomed, and casually elegant in pleated trousers and a navy blue golf shirt sporting his club's insignia on the pocket. "Nice work on the remodel. Yours?"

Brodie shook his head. "My skill set runs more toward things that float. Alex MacFarland did the planning and oversaw the work. She's the one presently doing the restoration on—"

"The lighthouse. Yes, I know."

Brodie's attention sharpened at the subtle note of disdain in the man's tone. Another time he might have pushed a little to see what the issue was, but he had his own issues with the man to deal with.

"Surprised you worked with her, after the way she treated you," Winstock said.

Okay, so I guess we're going to deal with this one, too. "I'm sorry. I don't follow. She does exceptional work, she had the time, and she's been nothing but professional with me. And everyone else she's dealt with, far as I know."

"Way I heard it, she let the town believe you two were an item to serve her own purposes. She led my son-in-law Ted on a merry chase as well. Made something of a fool of both of you when it came out she'd been shacking up with the police chief the whole time."

Brodie's hackles rose, but he kept his voice calm. "I can't speak for your son-in-law, but Alex was nothing but straightforward with me in our dealings. I can't help what the gossips wanted it to be. She and Logan McRae seem quite well suited, and I count Alex as a good friend. I'm happy for her."

Winstock shot him a somewhat patronizing smile. "Yet, I note you don't have equally generous words for Chief McRae."

"I don't know the man personally, but I trust Alex's judgment. Folks who do know him have nothing but respect for him."

Winstock nodded, but the damn condescending smile never left his face.

Brodie wasn't sure which annoyed him more—that the man was insulting Alex or that he'd hit a bit close to home with Brodie's lack of generous support of Logan McCrae. The police chief was a hard-ass, at least to Brodie's mind, but he didn't have to be buddies with the guy to respect that he made Alex happy.

"No man likes to be cuckolded," Winstock said.

Annoyance was shifting quickly to outright anger, and Brodie was having a hard time containing it. "There was nothing between us, so that wouldn't apply. Since Ted Weathersby is married to your daughter, I fail to see how the attentions, or lack thereof, of another woman cuckolded him, either."

Rather than anger the man, the comment seemed to amuse him.

If money bought that kind of privilege, it was a status perk Brodie was happy to be missing. *What is wrong with you people?*

He waited a beat, expecting Winstock to use the opening to delve into his sordid expectations where Brodie and his daughter were concerned, which would have been fine by him. Better to implode the deal sooner than later . . . because there was no deal if Cami was any part of the transaction.

Winstock, however, went straight to business. "Enough chitchat then. I'll be blunt. I know I told you that I was taking several bids under consideration for this contract. Assuming you're as talented as your forebears when it comes to shipbuilding and we agree on your design and the bid on the work, I'd like you to be the one to build my tall ship. As I told you when we first spoke, it's long past time we took advantage of the modern age of social media and the like and expanded the appeal of our small town to the tourist trade. We're ignoring a huge potential influx in capital that would only benefit the Cove."

"I'm guessing the town council is already on board with the idea of bringing a tall ship sailing business to Blueberry Cove?"

"I did mention that the head of the council is my son-in-law," Winstock said with a chuckle. "Naturally, I'll want to operate the business out of Half Moon Harbor."

Brodie's attention sharpened. Winstock had just made it very clear he had no problem manipulating his family connections to get what he wanted, and damn the consequences. He happened to be right that the town would benefit economically from the enterprise, but that was only a good thing if the town was willing to take on the rest of the issues that came with being a tourist destination. Higher traffic volume, property tax increases, and the like.

That Winstock was looking to use Half Moon Harbor as a base for the enterprise wasn't a surprise. If he wanted the enterprise in Blueberry Cove, where else would he go? But the more Brodie understood the nature of the man and how he did business, the more wary Brodie became of tying himself to Winstock in any way that extended beyond building the man a boat. Even a really, really big one.

"What, exactly, did you have in mind?" Brodie asked.

"Seeing as you have the largest single piece of real estate on the waterfront and it sits right in the pocket of the deep harbor, it's also prime real estate for my proposed venture. Blue owns the only other harbor property with direct access to the deepest part of the harbor, which would be mandatory for a ship the size and scope of what we're doing. Frankly, a commercial fishing business isn't the sort of combination I think would work well with the clientele I have in mind. Naturally, if charter trips on the schooner book well, we can talk about the rest."

An unease of an entirely different sort put Brodie's instincts on full alert. Winstock was one of the most powerful men in all of Pelican Bay, if not *the* most powerful. In any dealings they had, the leverage would always be on his side. Bottom line, Brodie wanted to build the tall ship to have the experience of taking on and completing such a magnificent piece of work . . . as a pretty impressive entry on his personal résumé . . . and as a memory. He didn't have to be buddies with, or even respect, Brooks Winstock to do business with him . . . but he didn't want to hate himself in the morning, either. Nor did he want to wake up one morning and find he'd been screwed out of the rest of his heritage.

And I thought being expected to screw Cami as part of the deal was the worst problem I could have.

"Maybe we should detail the entire proposal now," Brodie said.

"A bit ahead of ourselves. I've yet to see your plans for the ship."

"You won't find anyone who can design a ship that is a true wood-hull replication of an eighteenth-century three-masted schooner, but me. One of the very same kind that my own ancestors built right here on this land. Having that particular historic tie can only bolster your marketing plans, especially if you're wanting to work a deal to operate your charters from my docks."

"Well, that does bring up another interesting bit of business."

Now we finally get down to it.

"I understand you're in a bit of arrears on the taxes on the property. Lost a prime piece of it recently, if I'm not mistaken."

"Given your daughter arranged the sale, no, you would not be mistaken." Brodie worked to unclench his jaw, certain that Winstock was baiting him on purpose and annoyed with himself for giving him even the slightest satisfaction.

"Yes, indeed. I understand that you were unaware of that deal. My daughter is a shrewd businesswoman."

She's a vindictive bitch. "She made no commission on that deal."

"No, but by putting the deal together she got the attention of numerous other interests who now realize the property has value and is fair game."

Brodie didn't bother to mention she'd make no commission on them, either. He had a sinking suspicion he'd already been played. Rather than having to screw Cami, it looked like she was going to do all the screwing while keeping her clothes on for a change.

"The sharks are circling, Mr. Monaghan. Were you not aware of that?"

And you're the head shark. Brodie's gut knotted as he realized the real situation he was in.

"Camille said she spoke to you regarding the property's newfound potential now that Ms. Maddox is building her inn."

And you're building a tall ship to run charters here, which your daughter had to know about. "She did."

"So, why don't we get past all this posturing and simply say what needs saying?" Winstock's smile turned a shade nasty.

For the first time, Brodie saw the true family resemblance between father and daughter and fought to keep a civil tongue and a blank expression. "I'd appreciate that."

"I want you to build me a boat. A big one. I want to operate charter cruises on that boat with your docks as home port. I want to come to a mutually beneficial agreement with you on the possible future repurposing of the largest boathouse that is central to your harbor property."

There it is. Brodie tried not to show his relief. He'd half expected Winstock to whip out a folder containing papers showing he'd already bought up the rest of his property and was going to do whatever he damn well pleased with it. Saying he wanted some kind of agreement meant that hadn't happened. Yet. "Repurpose into . . . ?"

"A yacht club."

So those were Brodie's negotiating parameters. Winstock wanted a ship built by a Monaghan and all the marketing perks that went with that historic tie-in to sell the idea of a yacht club in Blueberry Cove to the deep-pocketed clients he'd need to make a place like that successful.

Brodie's bid amount on the ship had just doubled. He would have to include the cost of getting his property out of tax hock as part of the deal. It was his only chance at retaining control. Collectively, it was no small amount. Tacking that number on to the actual cost to build the schooner would normally have put him well out of the running, but Winstock had tipped his hand, making it clear Brodie's bid was the only one he was truly considering.

Brodie had no other choice but to play hardball. Otherwise, he might as well sign the deeds over to the man right then and there.

The yacht club didn't surprise him, either. It made perfect sense that Winstock wanted to trade on his standing in the Pelican Bay region to leverage his hometown into something rivaling the money towns that dotted the midcoast region from Boothbay to Bar Harbor. He didn't want to drive an hour and a half to get to his yacht club. He wanted one right there in the Cove.

Yeah, right in the middle of Monaghan's old shipyard and Blue's commercial fishing business. Brodie didn't see it. Blueberry Cove was fiercely proud of its fishing and shipbuilding industry, of its workingman roots. Upgrading one building into some kind of fancy private club didn't alter the fact that it would be surrounded by working-class folks going about their daily blue-collar business. Blueberry Cove had never courted the tourist trade beyond what came naturally from being a coastal, harbor-based town, and had never identified itself as such. Did Brooks Winstock really think he could change all that?

Did Brodie want to be any part of Winstock getting even a toehold on a prime piece of harbor property? That would be only the beginning of his plans. No way was he not going to go after the rest of Monaghan's and Blue's until he had the high-dollar harbor resort he wanted.

"I know your son-in-law is town council leader, but I'm not certain the town wants to attract that kind of clientele—"

"The town will see the dramatic increases in revenues we can obtain by courting that demographic, and it will raise property values as well as strengthen our economic base."

"Raise folks' taxes, too, and not just the ones with businesses of the sort that would benefit from increased foot traffic."

Winstock waved his objection off. "It's all quid pro quo, with significant emphasis on pro. I doubt anyone will quibble."

And I don't doubt you'd find a way to silence any naysayers.

Brodie was realizing just exactly how deep in with the devil he'd have to go, and even though building the tall ship would fulfill his personal dreams and get him out of the precarious financial position he was in, he wasn't selling his soul for it. It was bad enough that he'd pissed off the man's daughter. Schooner or no schooner, doing the same to the father would be unwise in the extreme. If it already wasn't too late for that.

Brodie took a stab at treading carefully. "I appreciate that you have good intentions for the town."

Winstock surprised him by laughing. "Now, young man, this is hardly the time to start kissing my ass. Blunt got you this far. Let's stick with that, shall we? Providing your plans live up to your hype, do we have an agreement?" The man looked supremely smug, as if it was a done deal and he was merely waiting for Brodie to catch up with the program.

Brodie realized that was, for all intents and purposes, exactly where he stood. Either he agreed to Winstock's plans in order to secure the contract and buy back his property, or he nixed the deal . . . and Winstock bought up his property and got someone else to build the schooner. True, the old man would lose the direct Monaghan tie-in, but Brodie knew better than to think that gave him any significant negotiating room.

Still, he had to at least try. "I have my own plans for the boathouse and shipyard property. However, my docks could accommodate the schooner and I think a charter business would blend in quite well here. Beyond that, my family's business and the fishing companies that occupy most of the harbor's property are all generations old and attached to their way of life in more than a simply economic way."

Winstock's expression hardened slightly. Clearly, despite his request for blunt talk, he hadn't expected Brodie to do anything but lie down and roll over. "Your family abandoned its business interests here when it became clear that times had changed to the point that there was no business to be had. It's admirable, indeed, for you to try to resurrect Monaghan's, and I have nothing but respect for the effort. You can be quite proud that your family managed to keep such a stronghold in the Cove for as long as they did. But surely you have already come to realize that there isn't a demand for a business the size and scope of the previous one."

"I do. My vision is different in that—"

"In that it won't do for you or the town, what I can do—what we could do, together," Winstock said, growing impatient. "I want to keep the Monaghan name on this property, but that's not central to my needs."

And there is the other shoe dropping.

"We'll have the schooner charters and an inn designed

by one of our country's premier architects, not to mention my family name on the club. The Winstocks might not have been a founding family, but we were damn close. I can make a go of it with that. However, I would like to anchor the improvements in the history of Blueberry Cove. I'd think you would be proud to see your ancestry being honored. My plans will provide you a future to continue the Monaghans' proud traditions in this new enterprise. Nothing you can do would come close to securing you the future I'm offering you."

"So, you're saying you want to lease the docks and main boathouse from me?" Brodie wanted him to lay it out straight.

"We can talk particulars later. You'll still have the boathouse between the club and the inn being built on the end, as well as the shipyard beyond it. Some of that would have to be co-opted as the parking lot for the club, of course, but then you'll have to do that in part for the inn, anyway. More than enough room for you to build your boats. The type of clientele I'll be bringing in is the exact type of customer base that would likely be looking for your particular services. A more symbiotic arrangement I couldn't imagine." He smiled, quite delighted with himself.

Brodie could have pointed out that building a four-masted schooner wasn't exactly going to be a tranquil proposition for potential yacht owners thinking about tying up at Monaghan's docks. It would be noisy, chaotic, and impossible to ignore. In and of itself, he could see it being a tourist draw; watching a tall ship being built would be fascinating to folks. If there would be a way to allow viewing without interrupting the work flow or putting anyone in danger, he'd be willing to discuss that. But even after the schooner was built and his own personal enterprise was launched, it was nonetheless a loud, messy trade . . . even with the work being done indoors. A working shipyard, even if the end product was high-quality, hand-built sailboats and yachts, was hardly the setting for a bluenose yacht club.

Rather than go there, he went for the even more obvious mismatch. "And Blue's?"

"What about Blue's?"

"How will your fancy clientele feel about sharing their harbor space with a commercial fishing operation and a bunch of lobster fishermen? They leave early and aren't the most genteel lot when they come back in with their catch."

Winstock waved a hand. "Local color. The real Maine coast. A hundred ways to spin that. I'm not concerned." His gaze sharpened again. "I'm not trying to trick you out of your property or pull a fast one. I want you on board with this vision. It's the best of both worlds."

"You'll have to forgive me if I'm not entirely trusting regarding ulterior motives." Brodie had nothing left to lose by angering the man. Winstock had him over a barrel, and he knew it.

"Now, I understand that the way Cami handled the sale of your boathouse to Ms. Maddox has, perhaps, created a sense of distrust, but I'm coming straight at you, being up front, all my cards on the table. That's how I conduct business. Always have, always will."

And if I believe that, I'm sure you've got some swampland to sell me, too. "I appreciate that, but I was raised in a family full of shrewd businessmen and women, and I'd be less than the Monaghan they raised me to be if I weren't at least a wee bit skeptical. In our experience, things that look too good to be true are usually exactly that."

Winstock chuckled. "Smart family. Not surprising given their long tenure here."

"And a much longer one in my homeland," Brodie reminded him. "Before I agree to anything, with even so much as a handshake, I'll want to know all the details." He'd have to make the boat deal and dock lease separate from any of Winstock's bigger plans. That would give him time to make Winstock understand that the yacht club enterprise wasn't going to work, thereby leaving his property intact. Perhaps he could convince Winstock to locate the club in a different part of the harbor. The bigger yachts could anchor out anyway, and their owners would come in on skiffs. A different location would provide a more tranquil, peaceful environment to such a well-heeled clientele.

"Well now, I appreciate your directness and would hope we can always be this open and honest." Winstock perched on the arm of Brodie's couch, all folksy and let's be buddies. "So, let me be completely forthcoming. There is another small part to this dealing that needs to be discussed. Perhaps it will give you peace of mind where my daughter is concerned."

Bloody hell. Brodie had hoped with all the rest of the posturing and grand planning that the heavily hinted at sordid little addendum to their agreement was no longer part of the deal. *Isn't it enough you want to co-opt my heritage? You want a piece of me to go with it?*

"Mr. Winstock—Brooks," he amended when the man gave him what was probably meant to be an avuncular look, which made Brodie's stomach turn over. "I'm not sure what Cami might have said to you regarding any . . . dealings we've had, but—"

"First, let me be clear about one thing. You mentioned Ted's situation earlier, regarding his feelings about his treatment by Alex MacFarland. Cami has also mentioned to me that the two of you have had some conversations of a rather . . . personal nature since your arrival here." Winstock lifted a hand to stall whatever Brodie might have said. It was a wasted gesture, as Brodie had not the first clue what an appropriate response to that comment would have sounded like. "While I'm sure the partnership between my daughter and her husband might be seen by some as . . ."

Unsavory? Morally bankrupt?

"Outside the norm," Winstock continued, seeming to be choosing his words carefully, "it seems to work for them." He paused, then lifted a shoulder in a casual shrug, apparently assuming the hard part was over now that he'd put that out there. "Given my own dismal failure on the marital front, I'm hardly one to preach about how things should be in order to achieve long-term relationship success. It's a small town, so you've probably heard the story, but Camille's mother walked away from us when my daughter was hardly out of diapers. Felt tied down, she said. She needed more. What more I couldn't imagine, as she had everything a woman could ever want. Off she went, however, and never looked back."

Winstock waved a dismissive hand, as if it were water so far under the bridge that it no longer mattered. "Now, Camille is a dedicated, dutiful, wonderful daughter. A man couldn't ask for more, and I couldn't be prouder of her." His face creased then in what Brodie supposed was meant to be a self-deprecating smile, but simply looked awkward. "My daughter is also headstrong, just like her mother, and somewhat restless by nature. Rather than destroy the harmony of her marriage by running off in search of God knows what, she and Ted have come to an . . . agreement.

"I don't pretend to be happy with or even approving of this arrangement, but it does seem to work for them. Over time, I've come to realize that perhaps if I'd been as open-minded, my own marriage might have survived my wife's restless nature." He took a stab at looking sheepish, which didn't sit right on his smooth, aquiline features any more than the self-deprecating look had earlier. Clearly, the man didn't have even a passing acquaintance with either emotion. "Don't go telling my daughter I said so, now, or I'll disavow any knowledge of this conversation."

Oh, not to worry there, Brodie thought, trying to maintain a blank expression through it all. He tried to imagine a man—any man—suggesting such an arrangement to any of the women in his family. The bloke would be lucky to walk upright ever again. He'd certainly never be siring any children.

"This is an awkward conversation for any father to have, so hopefully sharing a bit of insight into our past history brings some understanding to the situation. I'm sure you felt duty bound to turn down my daughter's . . . overtures, and I respect that. You were only doing what you thought was right."

So that's how it's going to spin? Brodie didn't know if he wanted to puke or punch the man in the face.

"Now that you see it's all aboveboard and out in the open, at least between her and Ted—you're a respectable man, so naturally you'll be discreet in regards to the rest of the community—the two of you can pursue your . . . private interests. You won't have to worry about interference from Ted or from me. In fact, to be honest, I'd be a lot more comfortable knowing she was in your care than someone else's."

Because you have my ass and the rest of my family heritage in a sling, Brodie thought in disgust. Knowing there was no chance in hell his real emotions weren't plastered all over his face, he turned and whistled for Whomper, who dutifully trotted over with the remnants of his bone still clenched in his teeth.

Brodie leaned down and rubbed the dog's head, buying some much-needed time to pull himself together and find the right words to tell this disgusting excuse for a man and worse excuse for a father exactly what he could do with his suggestion.

"When did you get the pup?" Winstock asked, all jovial now that the nasty business of pimping out his daughter had been dealt with.

"He's not mine," Brodie said. "I'm dog sitting for Grace."

Just like that, tension snapped back into the air. "Ah. Cozy arrangement. I didn't realize you'd come to any kind of . . . personal détente."

Brodie lifted his gaze from dog to man, wondering just what the hell the man meant by that and what he thought he knew about any dealings Brodie did or didn't have with Grace. "She bought the property fairly, and I'm going to have to come to terms with her operating a business a stone's throw from mine, so it seemed best to work things out. She's smart, good head for business. It could be worse."

Winstock smiled, but it didn't reach his eyes, which were shrewdly assessing Brodie at the moment. "Yes, indeed. Good to see you have a strong sense of doing what is best for the big picture," he said pointedly. "It will stand you in good stead in our little endeavor."

There was nothing little about it, Brodie wanted to shout. To Winstock it was simply something to play at, like a new toy, or a new hobby. To Brodie it was his entire livelihood, his entire life, dangling on a very precarious string of whimsy.

"Good. I'd like to think I can stay focused on what's important." He decided he wasn't going to address the Cami issue one way or the other. Let Winstock believe he'd achieved his goal in securing Brodie for his business needs and his daughter's more prurient ones. They'd sign a contract, Brodie would secure his property to keep it out of either Winstock's possession, then Cami could go whining to Daddy all she wanted when she didn't get her prize stud to go along with her father's latest business deal.

Brodie would have to hope that Winstock wouldn't screw over their deal, that he'd want his new enterprise to happen more than he'd want to shut up his spoiled brat of a daughter. She could find another play toy. Winstock needed Half Moon Harbor and Brodie's spot on it to make his new deal happen. Once those deeds were in Brodie's hand, he would breathe a lot easier. Cami would cease to be an issue for him.

Winstock held Brodie's gaze directly for another long beat, and Brodie let him. Finally feeling there was a chance he could get out with his pride and integrity intact, he shot the older gentleman a purposely broad smile that likely didn't reach his eyes, either. He pointed to his drafting table. "Take a look at the plans?"

Chapter 17

Grace's heart was in her throat, tears threatening the corners of her eyes, and she didn't think she could say another word, or even take another breath, until her brother reacted to her arrival. *Do something. Say something.*

Ford lifted his gaze from Grace to Robie, who merely lifted a shoulder as if to say *I just deliver 'em. Don't look at me.*

When the moment spun out, the captain finally shoved a lobster trap over to the side of the boat so it lined up beneath the ladder up to the dock. "Come on," he said to her, careful not to look at Ford again. "Just step up and grab the ladder."

Grace finally tore her gaze from her brother long enough to look at the captain, then to where he was motioning. She pushed the strap of her bag up higher on her shoulder and walked to the side of the boat feeling almost as if she was having a whole new kind of out-of-body experience. Had she really done it? Her brother was right there. Mere feet away.

She had a moment of pure, unadulterated panic. What on earth could she possibly say to him that would change anything? He was a complete and total stranger and clearly not happy to see her. *Dear God, what have I done? What the hell was I thinking?*

The captain saw something of her rising hysteria and took her elbow in a firm grip in the guise of helping her up on the trap toward the ladder. "Listen, missy," he said in a gruff mutter, "you want to go back to the mainland, just say the word and we'll turn around. Otherwise, I'm not back out here until tomorrow."

Grace gaped. "What? Tomorrow? I thought you were coming back later today—"

"Eel season was extended to this weekend, first time in thirty years. Buyers are on the docks tonight. It's the last night. Going rate is three hundred fifty a pound."

Her eyes went wide at that. "Dollars? For eels?"

"In Japan, Taiwan, China they're a delicacy, so yes ma'am. Man's gotta earn a livin'. I'll be back out here at noon tomorrow. You be here on the dock, ready to go. Or radio Blue by eleven at the latest not to bother coming if you plan to stay." He glanced up toward Ford, then back to her. "What's it to be?"

Grace's heart was thumping so hard she could barely hear herself think, much less scope out plans that included what she was going to do the next day. She didn't even know how she was going to handle the next five minutes. Not only that, she had work crews scheduled to come back in the morning. "Go," she blurted. "I'll be—I'm staying. Tonight. I'll see you tomorrow, or I'll radio, or—or something."

The man looked dubious. "You sure?"

"Not even close," Grace said, then turned, grabbed the ladder as if it was a life raft, and started to climb before she changed her mind. If she didn't go through with it now, she'd never work up the nerve again. She'd taken the crucial first step. *He's going to at least hear me out, dammit.*

She slung her bag farther onto her back and continued the rest of the way up the ladder, clinging as much to the tiny surge of anger as she was to the rungs. *He can do that much.*

The boat was already pushing clear, the engines rumbling louder as the captain moved away from the pier by the time she reached the top. Mostly to give herself a moment to catch her breath . . . and get a hold on her sanity . . . she turned and waved at the captain. He gave her a nod, then the boat swung in a wide arc and he chugged across the open water, heading back toward Half Moon Harbor.

She took another steadying breath that sounded a lot more like a gulp, and turned around, forcing herself to look at her brother. "I'm sorry. You probably feel ambushed." She'd thought her heart would explode with joy . . . or shatter into a million pieces. Neither happened. It felt more like she'd entered some weird purgatory or limbo, where nothing was quite real. Yet. "I was afraid if I let you know I was coming, you'd find a way to keep me from getting out here."

He looked at her for the longest moment.

Face-to-face, with a clear view of him, all of him, she still couldn't read him. In fact, she had to search for the brother she knew, the one who'd worn his hair in a military buzz, with that hard but fresh-faced jaw, stiff neck and even stiffer broad shoulders. At least that's who he'd been when he'd gone off to war.

He'd come back different, but she'd done her best to block those memories. Instantly, they all came rushing back, flashes from childhood. Him making her grilled cheese sandwiches for breakfast, reading her old beat-up copies of *Mrs. Piggle Wiggle* and *Captain Underpants* that had somehow found their way to the shelves in the family room of their house, though neither of them knew why or how. Memories of him saying good-bye to her when he got on the bus that would take him to Fort Jackson in South Carolina for basic training. Memories of him showing up suddenly with no warning at the latest in a long line of houses and strangers she'd been shuffled off to, looking so handsome and rugged . . . with eyes so empty and sad.

Memories of the last day she'd seen him, when she'd screamed at him to get out, that if he loved her, he'd never have left her to live such an awful, horrible life. Screaming that she hated him.

They stared at each other without speaking. He looked . . . distant. Unapproachable. And yet, maybe it was because she'd distorted reality over the years, or maybe it was because he'd found peace in his new life, but forty-four looked a lot better on him than twenty-two had. Or twenty-nine. He was still ruggedly handsome, but he'd matured into his good looks. The haunted eyes were gone, the sadness, too . . . though it was hard to tell, honestly. It was more a feeling than anything specific she saw.

He was tall, a few inches over six feet. She'd always thought he was this giant hero, and was almost surprised to discover she hadn't exaggerated the height part. He was still broad in the shoulder, trim in the waist, but in his short-sleeved T-shirt and loose jeans, his physique looked more sinewy and lean than the pumped-up muscle he'd had back in his Army days.

"Why would I do that?" he asked finally, his voice so gruff, so quiet, she could barely make out the words.

The sound of his voice, after so, so long, made her heart skip . . . and suddenly purgatory was over and seeing him was very, very real. "Because of what I said. What I did. Ford, I know you must—"

"No," he said, cutting her off almost angrily. He seemed to catch himself, steady himself, but his tone was still tight when he added, "You don't know what I must. You don't know anything."

"I know you don't want me here, or . . . in your life. I left you alone, even convinced myself I was doing it for you, because you obviously wanted it that way. But the truth is . . . I was afraid. Scared to death, really. You'd walked away once and I . . . I didn't—couldn't—give you the chance to do that to me again. And . . . yeah," she added more quietly, squinting against the sun as she crumpled Brodie's baseball hat into a ball in her hands. "Because I was still mad. At myself and at you. Even when I knew it wasn't fair, I still was."

There was another long silence; then he said, "What changed?"

"Me." Grace shrugged then let her arms go limp. Truth was, she could have easily crumpled to a little heap on the dock or dissolved into tears, or both, the emotion of the moment was so suffocating, so . . . choking. "I guess I grew up. I had a career—a very good one as an estate lawyer. I've spent the past eight years doing probate for the final wills and testaments of my clients, which is akin to tiptoeing through a minefield of seeing that the deceased's wishes are carried through in the spirit of the will and the letter of the law while simultaneously watching families tear each other apart, or fall apart, even when they didn't want to, and I . . ." Her words trailed off.

She should have all the right words; she'd only imagined this moment a hundred times, a thousand. But it was coming out all stilted and disjointed and not at all the way she'd planned. "I thought I was the lucky one because I'd never have to go through what they were going through. I'd already lost my family, lost everything, so I was bulletproof to that particular pain. It was what made me so good at my job, I think. I understood their loss, but I was distanced from it personally, unaffected. Smug in my own safe little cocoon. So very lucky."

"You were always pretty smart. Sounds like that didn't change."

Her expression sharpened, her focus tightened. She was unsure of his meaning, so she took his comment at face value. "For a long time, no, it didn't. Then I realized that safe doesn't always equal happy. It's just . . . safe. My family wasn't gone. It was just tucked away somewhere. And I wasn't okay with that. When I was finally honest with myself, I knew I had never been okay with that. I'd just accepted it. Partly because I didn't know what else to do, and partly because not accepting it meant . . . well, it meant doing something crazy like this. Something crazy that could end up hurting me all over again. Maybe I just had to wait until I was strong enough, or confident enough"—she let out a half laugh, only the sound was a bit choked—"or crazy enough, desperate enough, that being hurt didn't matter. Not compared with the pain of never even trying." Grace looked at her brother, really looked at him, and tried to find something, anything, of the guy she'd so worshiped as a child. "I should have tried sooner, Ford. And frankly, you should have, too. We should have had each other all this time, in whatever way we could. It would have been better than having nothing at all."

"That's where you'd be wrong." He paused, planted his hands on his hips, looked up at the sky for a long moment, then finally back at her. "For a long time, it was better I wasn't around anybody."

"And when that time was over?"

"You had your life. It was good. You were good. You didn't need me."

"First of all, you don't know a damn thing about my life. Or what—or who—I needed. I know I yelled at you, screamed at you, when you came back that last time. I've regretted it so—" Her voice broke, and she worked hard to get a grip. Losing it now wouldn't help either of them. "I wish I'd been more mature, less angry. But I was a pissed-off teenager. I didn't mean what I said."

"Sure you did. And you were right. You should have been pissed off at me. Then and now. I did abandon you, Grace. I deserved everything you threw at me."

"Then, perhaps. But"—she lifted her hands, gesturing toward the island behind him—"now? Now you're not that man, not that guy. When did that happen? And why didn't you come back? Apologize if you felt you should have. Or at the very least, just made sure I was okay."

He held her gaze for the longest time, and she searched his face, looking for . . . something. Anything. She wasn't finding it.

"I should have come to see you, when your girlfriend asked me to," she said. "And you should have come seen me graduate. She reached out for you and that kind of pissed me off all over again. To know you were back in the world, doing okay. You never even bothered to let me know. But I got past it. I mean, I didn't come, but I did send that invitation." She folded her arms and finally looked away, blinking back tears of regret, of sadness, of anger. "You should have come or at least sent a damn note."

When the silence spun out again, she looked back at him. He was frowning and looking confused.

"What?" she finally asked, her voice flinty from anger and the threat of tears.

He unfolded his arms, lifted his hands in a confused gesture, then let them drop, propping them on his hips again. "I don't know what in the hell you're talking about. What girlfriend? And I never got any damn graduation invitation."

"I-I got a letter, telling me you were here, what you

were doing. She said you'd told her about me, and that she knew you'd never reach out, so she was asking me to make the first move, take the first step."

He shook his head, raked one hand through his long, shaggy hair. Grace almost smiled at the gesture. It was the first familiar thing he'd done, and she flashed back to one of her earliest memories of him, when he was in high school and he'd grown his hair long because he hadn't played sports in his junior year . . . or his senior year. It had gotten even longer over that last summer before their mother died. She knew he hadn't played sports because he'd been taking care of her, taking her to preschool and then kindergarten, picking her up from the sitter every day after school. He couldn't make practice, much less the games, because he had to take care of her. He'd get exasperated, at her, at their mom, at . . . well, at life. And he used to rake his hand through his hair, just like that.

"I guess you were an angry teenager, too," she said quietly, having something of a small epiphany. "All this time, I thought about you abandoning me, walking away. But I guess—" She stopped, her breath hitching. She made herself take a long, slow breath in, then let it out the same way. She looked at him again. "If I was an angry teenager, I can only imagine how you felt when you were that age. Actually, no, that's not true. I can't. I only had me to be responsible for. You had your whole life to live . . . and you were saddled with me. And Mom. You must have resented the hell out of me. I mean, I thought a lot about the burden I was to you, but I never thought about it in the context of your being a teenager then." She shook her head. "I-I couldn't not be a little kid, had no choice in the role I played way back then, but still . . . I should have put it all together sooner. It might have helped me understand better. Be less . . . angry."

"I don't know what the hell you're talking about. Not

the part about my feelings as a teenager. Yeah, sure, I was angry at the whole damn world. But that wasn't your fault. I mean, I never blamed you. Hell, I took all of that on my own shoulders. Who sent you that note? What was her name?"

"I—don't remember. I was, what, twenty-one? That was ten years ago. Who was your girlfriend ten years ago?"

"I didn't have a girlfriend. Ten years ago I'd only been here for—" He broke off, then swore under his breath, something that sounded like, "Dammit, Dee." He paused, raked his hair again, then asked, "So, what invitation did you send? Your graduation from Mason? Or Georgetown?"

Her gaze flew to his as he lifted his head and her heart stuttered, stumbled. "GMU, before I started Georgetown. How did you know where—" She couldn't finish the question.

He didn't say anything for a long moment, then swore under his breath again. "You didn't need me in your life again, Grace. I was just figuring out how to survive back then, and . . . I'd already let you down once. Badly. Unforgivably. But that didn't mean . . . ah, hell." He turned and paced a few steps away. Propping both of his hands on his head, he stood and stared at the island for several long minutes.

Grace didn't say anything, mostly because her throat had closed over completely. He'd . . . what? Kept track of her? But had never come to her? She didn't know whether to feel joy that he really had cared enough to keep up on what she was doing . . . or get pissed off all over again that he'd done it all from a distance, and left her thinking . . . well, all the five thousand different things she'd been thinking all these years—ranging from he didn't care to he hated her.

He finally turned around. "When I started getting my shit together, really together, I tracked you down. I intended to come back, to make things right, which . . . I quickly realized was a complete joke. There was no making right what I did to you. I figured it was best, that you were better off. You were in college then and you were doing great. Then it was law school, and . . . well, you'd figured it out, you had this huge life ahead, and I guess I felt like you'd accomplished all of that despite what I did. The last thing you needed was me, coming back and possibly turning everything to shit."

"How can you say that?" she asked, voice wavering.

"Because I was deep in the shit, Gracie. I was . . . I used to use the phrase 'in a bad place' but that's bullshit. I was in hell. Trust me, it was better that I left you to continue the life you'd made for yourself. I thought you wanted it that way. I mean, why wouldn't you?"

Gracie. No one had ever called her that but him. Tears finally trickled from the corners of her eyes. "So we both fucked up. Repeatedly." She stopped talking and pressed her fingers to her eyes. She had to do something, anything, to stop the tears. Once they started, she knew it would be a full-on, cathartic, big sloppy cry. Now was not the time for that. This was her one chance, and she needed to get the words out. "I quit my job. I was good at it . . . but it was sucking what soul I had left right out of me. I came to Maine, to Blueberry Cove, to start over."

Shock crossed his face, then it became that careful mask again, Despite the fact that he was a good ten yards away from her, she could feel him withdrawing again.

"I want something different. I want family, a place that feels like home. I want friends, a life that I actually enjoy, a reason to smile every day. And dammit, I want you."

"So you just . . . up and moved here?"

She lifted her hands and let them drop by her sides. "This is the only place I can have all those things at once. I-I bought a boathouse. I'm turning it into an inn."

He plowed both hands in his hair, looking at her as if she'd lost her mind, but not saying anything. Maybe wisely so.

"I don't know the first damn thing about running an inn. And if that's not crazy enough? I got the idea because I read a book about a woman who'd gone searching for meaning in her life and that's what she did. It just . . . it resonated with me, somewhere so deep inside I . . . I don't know. I couldn't get it out of my head. It became my fantasy dream life. I did all this research, half hoping it would bring me back to earth, back to reality. Half hoping it would, I don't know, give me the nerve to just go and do what I knew I really, really wanted to do. Needed to do. But I had spent all that time getting my degree, passing the bar. I had this great job. I had money in the bank. Who walks away from that because they read some stupid book and got this wild hair up their ass? I mean, honestly . . . I thought maybe I was losing my mind." She let out a laugh that held a lot of emotion, but almost none of it humor. "I thought maybe I was becoming like Mom."

"You're nothing like Mom." He said it quite fervently, almost angrily.

Grace lifted her hand to her throat as if by touching it she could make the ache swelling inside go away. "See, that's just it, Ford. I don't really remember her. I don't know what I'm like. Or who I'm like." She shook her head and looked away, out over the water. "I've never told a single soul about Mom. About . . . worrying that something like that would happen to me. That maybe it was happening to you and that's why . . ." She let the sentence drift off, and dipped her chin, then shook her head. When she lifted it again, she was smiling. It was a forced smile, but dammit, she wanted to be done crying, done feeling sad. And angry. And lonely. "I sure as hell never told anyone I changed my whole life around because of some stupid damn book I picked up at the library. I didn't even go there looking for it. I was there doing research on one of our cases and somebody was returning it just as I was checking out. It had a lighthouse on the cover, and it just"—she rolled her eyes—"looked peaceful. And tranquil. It reminded me of you. Of you being in Maine. Maybe with a lighthouse like that. I don't know. It was completely insane. More so when I started reading it and it was like a story of what my life could be, if only I was brave enough to do what I wanted, instead of what was safe."

Ford didn't say anything to that. In fact, he was silent for so long, she wasn't sure there was going to be anything left for them to say.

Then he said, "If there's one thing I've learned, it's that there's good crazy and just plain crazy crazy. You ditching it all for a new life in some place you've never been, to come all the way to Maine, sight unseen, lock, stock, and barrel, yeah. That's crazy crazy. But what the hell do I know? Maybe you know better, and it's the good kind."

Her heart picked up speed again, and she hated that she was willing to cling to the tiniest crumb of acceptance from him. But she wanted . . . something. A way in. Maybe that was what he was offering . . . in his own way. She didn't know. For all that he was her brother, and they definitely had a shared past that neither of them would ever forget, or be able to fully bury . . . the truth was, the man standing in front of her was a complete and total stranger. She didn't even know where to start with that. With him. Their shared past didn't seem like such a good starting point. So . . . where then? And how?

"What kind of crazy was it when you came here and

decided to stay?" she asked, knowing that whatever path they took going forward, being open, honest, and unafraid was mandatory or why bother? She wanted to know her brother and have him back in her life, be a part of his, or . . . not. She didn't want some surface, pretend, superficial bullshit deal.

"Crazy crazy. But I guess now, looking back, that described *me* more than anything else. So I honestly don't know. Maybe a little of both."

"And now?"

He folded his arms, then dropped them to his sides, finally shoving his hands in his pockets. "Now it's the good kind. Or at least, not so crazy."

"Well . . . that's good." *It's a place to start, anyway.* "Who's Dee? Or who was she?"

Just like that, his expression became shuttered again.

There was being straightforward and honest, and there was pushing too far, too soon. Grace lifted both hands, palms out. "Never mind. Another time. Or never. It's not really my business."

"She runs the diner. In the Cove. She wasn't my girlfriend. Just . . . a friend. I guess."

He seemed almost a little . . . confused by who or what she'd been to him, so, despite being ridiculously curious to know the whole story, Grace let it go. She gestured to the island behind her. "What brought you out here?"

"Solitude. Quiet."

She smiled at that and looked up at the sky, shielding her eyes from the sun. Birds were everywhere. Big ones, small ones, white, gray, black. On the rocks, floating on the water, dotting the harbor coastline, perched in the trees, and filling the sky. And they were anything but quiet. Between their constant calling and the waves pounding the pier and the rocky coastline, it was far more turbulent and chaotic than peaceful.

He followed her gaze. "You get used to it. It's like white noise now."

"And it's not people."

"No," he said, more quietly. "It's not people."

It occurred to her that they had kept a good distance from each other the entire time they'd been talking. Initially, it had seemed, well, normal, given the situation. Suddenly it felt awkward. She couldn't exactly run to him and hug him. She just . . . wanted to. He was still a stranger, but she felt like the cathartic, awful, horrible part was over. He hadn't ordered her gone or walked away. He'd let her rant. He'd listened. He'd even opened up. A little, anyway.

Most important, they were talking. And . . . that's all she could hope for, really. Only time would tell where it might lead, if it would matter. If *they* would matter again. To each other.

"There are a few others out here," she said. "Researchers and interns, right? I read the brochure," she added, when he glanced at her.

"From mid–May to end of August, yes. Then everybody goes. The people, and the birds."

"And you?"

He looked back to the island. He was quiet for a long moment. "I stay."

She watched him for another silent moment. He tensed when he talked to her, and she understood that. She was tense, too. But when he looked at the island or talked about the birds, he relaxed. Or some part of him did, anyway.

"So . . . this is your safe place," she said, realizing she'd said it out loud when he looked sharply back at her. "For some people that's a good thing. It was for me. For a really long time that safe place was my job and being on the river. I'm a rower. I think both of those things probably saved me. But . . . not anymore." She looked away from him then, because she had the distinct impression that she'd hurt him somehow. "I'm glad you found your place, Ford. I really am."

She wanted to go to him then. It was almost like a physical ache, the need to hug him, to just . . . connect. In more than only words shared. But she couldn't seem to make herself take that first step, and she realized then that the hard part, the cathartic part, wasn't over. In fact, they'd only uncovered the tip of that iceberg . . . because hugging your own brother should be easy. Natural.

It wasn't—which meant she was still afraid of being hurt. Of rejection. She knew that, for today anyway, she was going to take the winning parts, the good parts, and be happy. And not push for more. Risk . . . wanting more.

She had just opened her mouth to ask him if he could show her the island, show her what he was doing, thinking that might be the best way to build a bridge between their past . . . and their possible future . . . when a voice called out from the other end of the pier.

"Hey, Doc? We need you to come check on one of the blinds."

A young girl who appeared to be in her early twenties, dressed in khaki pants and a long-sleeved shirt, came trotting down the dock toward them. On her head was a hard hat, of all things. "I think we have a problem with—oh, hey." She stopped short once she spied Grace. Ford had apparently blocked her from view.

"Hi," she said, friendly, smiling. She looked at Ford. "Sorry, I didn't see you were talking." She extended her hand to Grace. "I'm Annie. Welcome to Sandpiper."

"Hi," Grace said, smiling back at her, but her mind spinning in a dozen other directions. "Thanks. I'm Grace," she added clumsily.

"Are you joining the ranks?" she asked brightly.

Grace looked at Ford, then back at her. "Uh, no. I'm just . . ."

"It's okay, Annie," Ford told the young girl. "I'll be back up in a minute."

The young girl looked between the two of them and seemed to realize for the first time that maybe she'd intruded. "Oh, right. Sorry. Well, welcome anyway," she told Grace. "I'll—yeah, I'm going now." She shot Ford a curious look, not intimidated by him, but certainly respectful, then trotted back up the pier.

Grace knew it shouldn't be weird that people who knew Ford would be completely at ease around him, and yet, it totally was. He was this . . . enigma to her. Standing there talking to him hadn't changed that sense at all. If anything, it had reinforced it. Of course he worked with people. He wasn't a total recluse. No matter that he sure as hell acted like one, at least with her, anyway. It was also stupid and irrational to be jealous of the people who worked with him, who knew him, who could be so comfortable and casual around him . . . but she was.

All of that took a giant step back to the one thing her brain was still stuck on. "Doc?" she asked him. "Is that like a . . . nickname?"

For the first time since she'd climbed up to the pier and laid eyes on her long-lost brother, a tiny hint of a smile ghosted the corners of his mouth. "You didn't get all the brains in the family, you know."

Her eyes went wide. "So you're a real . . . I mean, you actually went and got a doctorate?"

"I did, yeah." He seemed embarrassed. And the humor was gone. "I . . . need to get back to work. It's—this is the busiest we get, and time is short. It's—" He paused, looked away again, and swore under his breath again.

"No, I get it. I didn't exactly make an appointment or give you a heads-up. I . . . I appreciate that you took the time you did." *Just . . . don't let me walk away,* she silently begged. *Well then, don't let him, you idiot. Stop waiting for other people to save you.* "I want to see you again. I'd like to see the island. See what it is you do. When . . . whenever you can fit it in." She braced her hand on her forehead again as the sun peeked out from behind a passing cloud. When the silence spun out, she said, "I'm staying, Ford. I'm here. And I'm not leaving. Blueberry Cove, I mean."

He held her gaze for a long time. "Okay."

"Okay, you'll show me the island? Okay, that I'm living in Maine now?"

That ghost of humor flickered across his face, then was gone again. "Just . . . okay. For now."

"Doc? There's a problem with the generator in Cabin 2! Cam is down in Grid 30 through Grid 42." The shout came from a young man who'd just climbed up to the pier from the rocks on the other side, about twenty yards closer to shore.

"Go do your work," Grace said, hugging his words, his acceptance to her heart as if he'd just made an undying declaration of brotherly love, tentative though they were. "I'll just—uh, well, I don't know what I'll do. You can put me to work, too, if I can help in some way."

He glanced at the young man hanging at the ladder that led back down to the rocks. "How are you with mechanical things?"

She grinned, and it felt . . . tremendous. "Yeah, um . . . what else do you have?"

"Doesn't matter," he said, looking past her out to the open water. "I think your ride is here."

"My—what?" She spun around. A single-mast sloop was dropping anchor in the harbor. She'd seen the boat before, moored one pier over from Brodie's two-masted schooner. She'd thought it belonged to someone else, as she had the schooner, but she realized it had to be his, too.

She turned back to Ford and saw he was walking back down the pier. "Wait," she called out.

He paused and looked over his shoulder.

She had a moment of hesitation, of debating whether it was the wise thing to do, what he'd think about it, then thought *screw that* and started walking toward him. He didn't turn to face her, much less walk toward her, but he didn't walk away. Then she was jogging and then running and all she could think was *I'm finally running toward something, not away from it.* She didn't bother to look for acceptance or even willingness. She wrapped her arms around his shoulders and hugged him tightly, so many emotions going through her mind. It was weird to feel like she was hugging a total stranger, but she was. Tall and rangy, his body was hard and lean . . . and completely stiff and unyielding. But in her heart, she knew she was holding on to the one person she'd loved from the very first day of her life.

"Hug me back, dammit," she whispered fiercely. "Just because I was mad at you a million years ago doesn't mean I don't love you. Then and now."

"God, Gracie, don't say that."

"Too late, I already did." She held on for another moment, then finally started to let go.

A heartbeat later he wrapped his arms around her and hugged her so tightly she lost her breath. She squeezed her eyes shut against the instant onslaught of tears, thinking this was everything, *everything,* she'd come to Maine for . . . and so much more than she'd ever hoped she'd actually get. "I missed you so much," she said, barely getting the words past the lump in her throat.

Then he let her go just as abruptly as he'd hugged her, turned before she could see his face, and headed down the pier.

That's okay, she told herself. It was a start. And left no doubt in her mind or her heart that he still loved her, too. Everything else was workable, if they had that. "I want to come back and see the island," she called out to his retreating back. "If you don't want me just showing up like an annoying baby sister, invite me. Just tell Blue's when and I'll be here."

He didn't make any signal that he'd heard her, but she knew he had. Hell, the whole island probably had.

"If you come in to Blueberry Cove, I bought one of Monaghan's boathouses in Half Moon Harbor. Last one on the left as you come in from the water. No advance warning necessary. Just . . . come." Her bravery faltered then and she fell silent. She waited, for what she wasn't sure, hand still propped on her forehead against the bright sunshine.

The young man at the ladder was staring unabashedly at her. As he realized Ford was at the ladder, he quickly climbed down so Ford could climb down after him. Her brother disappeared below the dock without so much as a single wave, but she hadn't expected otherwise.

Her gaze skimmed past the ladder to the rocky shore. Two girls in hard hats were out on the boulders. Both of them had stopped what they were doing and were also openly staring at her. She assumed her shouts had carried to them and had no idea what they'd make of her showing up on the island, much less what she'd said to their boss. She assumed he was their boss. They seemed to come running to him when they needed something, anyway. It was a good bet that her presence was going to make things challenging for him, having to explain. Or maybe he simply wouldn't. She sincerely doubted he'd told anyone that he had a sister. That might have worried her before, but that hug . . . She closed her eyes just for a moment and relived every too-short second of it. She'd waited so long. So damn long.

Tears continued to trickle down her cheeks as she turned to look out at the harbor and Brodie's sailboat. She couldn't see anybody on board and silently thanked him for giving her the space she'd asked for and having her back at the same time. She remembered when she'd first met him, she'd had him pegged for a love-'em-and-leave-'em charmer, a looking-out-for-number-one kind of guy.

She hadn't been so wrong about the love-'em-and-leave-'em part—he'd admitted that very thing to her . . . right before making her eyes roll back in her head as she came for the third or fourth time. But she was realizing she'd been wrong about the rest. He was proving himself to be a pretty stand-up guy. Or more specifically, a stand-up-for-her guy. *All those sisters must have taught him something.*

She lifted his baseball cap, which she realized was still crushed in her hand, and waved it from the end of the dock. She still hadn't seen any sign of him above deck. He must have been watching from belowdecks because a minute after she'd waved, he lowered an inflatable skiff into the water off the side of the boat before hopping in and skimming over the water, heading her way.

She watched him man the small speedboat over the waves with an ease that revealed how much time he'd spent on the water. The wind ruffled his thick, sun-streaked hair, while black shades covered his green eyes. Even from a distance she admired the play of muscles in his bare arms and shoulders and how the sleeveless T-shirt was plastered against a chest and torso she was intimately familiar with.

She'd just proven to herself, to Ford, hell, to the world, that she was willing to do whatever it took, even if it was hard. She felt strong and whole, finally able to take risks and put herself out there for what was truly important. "And here comes Brodie Monaghan to my rescue," she murmured, wiping away the last of her tears. "Who'd have thought it?"

He throttled down and let the boat drift and bump up against the pier pilings. At the top of the ladder, she looked down at him and found him grinning up at her.

"Ahoy, lass. Need a lift?"

And who'd have thought I'd really like it?

Chapter 18

Even before Grace had gotten fully in the boat, Brodie could see that she'd been crying. *Shit.* He really wanted to figure out this whole relationship deal, do the right thing, but tears were his Kryptonite. He'd known that long before he'd even had his first kiss, courtesy of six sisters who, when quick wit and collective strength weren't enough to get their way, had swiftly learned the value of a well-timed tear tracking down a fair, freckled cheek.

"I wasn't tryin' to intrude," he said, as he helped her jump lightly from ladder to boat.

"No, no. You didn't. In fact, you were remarkably timely." She balanced herself quickly and moved to sit in the front as he took up his position by the engine again, revved it back up before turning neatly and heading back over the water toward his sailboat.

He watched her look back to the island, but wasn't sure from the expression on her face if things had gone as she'd hoped. Better? Worse?

"How did you—what made you come out?" she shouted back to him over the sound of the motor and the wind.

"I was over at Blue's docks, chatting with the guys coming in with the last eel catch, when Robie radioed that he was heading out and not going back to Sandpiper until tomorrow. He didn't seem real clear on whether that was okay with you or not. So . . . I thought I'd head out, anchor, and"—he lifted a shoulder—"be there for the ride back whenever you were ready."

"Thank you." Never more sincere, she smiled, holding his gaze. "I know you've got a lot going on, so I really appreciate that."

He nodded, feeling a bit of anticipatory dread start to curl in his gut. He had come out for exactly the reason he'd said . . . and because he was hoping the time they'd spend alone on his boat, away from any and all distractions, would give him a chance to explain about the schooner deal. And about Cami.

Even with Grace spending all of her time knee-deep in the boathouse renovation, there was no way she wouldn't hear about it. With no idea how Cami would react when he didn't agree to her being a signing bonus, he had to make certain Grace heard the news from him first.

But with her face freshly tear-streaked, he wasn't so sure his timing was all that great. Not that he had much choice.

He angled the skiff along the back of the sailboat.

"The *Margaret Mary,*" Grace said, reading the name on the back.

"My dear, departed mum," he replied with a smile.

Smiling in return, Grace leaned out and grabbed the handle mounted to the back. He liked seeing how comfortable she was on the water. Not surprising given her hobby, but her natural grace and balance definitely stirred more than his professional respect. Her tear-streaked cheeks didn't keep him from eyeing her curvy little bum as she climbed from skiff to deck, either. She didn't typically dress in a manner that overtly showed her figure off, but he rather liked the way her khaki cropped pants and loose polo shirt left most things to the imagination. Well, not that he'd cry foul if she suddenly decided to wear something a bit more snug with an occasional plunging neckline, but as she hopped onto the deck, showing off the flex and play of strong, shapely calves, he was okay with her keeping all the rest of what was strong and shapely for his eyes only.

He tied up and joined her on the deck as Whomper trotted over and gave her a warm, wriggling welcome.

"Hey, there. Check out the new first mate!" Grace knelt down and gave him a good head scratch, then laughed as she added a belly scratch to the deal when he rolled over, still wriggling in delight. She scooped him up and hugged him, burying her face in his fur, keeping it there for a few extra seconds until he started to squirm. "Okay, okay. Go back to your duties." Her laugh was a bit watery sounding as she let him go and stood again.

"Hey." Brodie stood behind her. He touched her arm and turned her. "It's okay, you know."

"What is?" she asked, a sniffle escaping even though she was clearly trying to pretend she wasn't teary-eyed and emotional.

"It was a big thing ye did." He reached up and gently touched her cheek, rubbing away a tear or two. "A very emotional thing. I'm no expert on tears. In fact, they scare the life out of me. But I'm thinkin' you shouldn't have to work at keeping them at bay. Maybe letting them go is the thing to do."

"You say you're not good at relationship stuff," she said, turning a little pink when her snuffle ended up as a rather inelegant snort. "But if that's true, you do a damn good imitation of someone who is."

"I just don't want to see you struggle with this more than you have to. Tears kill me. In fact, I'd do just about anything to keep you from crying, so this is largely selfish on my part. If letting them out gets us to a no-more-crying place faster, then let 'em rip. That's what I say."

She laughed and sniffled at the same time. "You're so

full of shit." Her smile started to crumple as the threat of real tears started to win the battle. "And I can't tell you how much I appreciate that."

"Och, darling lass, come here." He pulled her into his arms and held on tight, sighing when her arms snaked around his waist and she held him just as tightly.

"I don't know why I'm crying," she said, her forehead pressed into his shoulder, even as her own shoulders began to shake. "It went so much better than I'd hoped."

Brodie had arrived and dropped anchor just in time to see the two siblings hug on the docks. Or more to the point, in time to see Grace run and hug her brother as he walked away. It had taken surprising restraint for Brodie to keep from heading straight to the pier and taking Ford Maddox on, demanding to know why he couldn't find it in his heart to take better care of what she was offering him. Brodie had no idea what the real backstory was between the two, and for all he knew, Ford was well within his rights to hold himself separate and apart.

But from what Brodie knew of Grace, the kind of person she was, and what she'd sacrificed and risked to start over in the Cove for the sole sake of reuniting her family, he had a hard time believing Ford would have a moral leg to stand on. *And he'd have an even harder time if I took him out at the knees,* he remembered thinking.

Then Ford had reciprocated. If the way he'd grabbed and held on to his sister was any indication, he did it with fierce emotion. He'd walked away, leaving her standing there. Grace had continued to talk to him, though Ford hadn't looked back.

Still, it was a beginning. One she seemed pleased with.

Brodie couldn't help but wonder if she would be equally open-minded with his news. He'd be happy with anything short of gunfire.

Grace pulled herself together and wiped at her eyes, but

he kept her in his arms. "We don't have to head right back. Take your time." He leaned back a bit and tipped his head so he could look into her eyes. "Do you want to talk about it?"

She shook her head and said, "Yes," at the same time, making him smile and her croak out another watery laugh.

"I actually understand that better than you can imagine. I remember getting so mad at my younger sisters. They'd torment the hell out of me, then pull the innocent act when I finally retaliated. I'd get the punishment while they got the 'there, there's.' Infuriating enough, but then I'd go off to bang on wood at my grandfather's and he'd make me talk about it."

"The horror," Grace said, smiling at him, her hands on his shoulders, her fingertips toying with the hair brushing his neck.

"Talking about my *feelings*," Brodie said with a mock shudder. "Some of the best conversations I had with him started that way. He shared a lot of wisdom with me, which of course I didn't come to appreciate or even understand until much later."

"And here I was crediting your sisters with your enlightenment, but maybe it's the Monaghan men who really have it together."

His eyebrows lifted a bit at that, but he merely grinned and shook his head. "No' that it's completely unheard of for an Irishman to wear his heart on his sleeve, but usually you have to ply him with a pint or three to get him maudlin and pouring his heart out." He brushed her hair from her cheek, then rubbed away one last tear track. "I'm pretty sure I'm simply winging it, as they say, but my grandfather would be proud indeed to think he had any hand in helping me figure out relationships, women, and how to keep both of them happy and functioning together in the same sentence. He was married to my grandmother for forty years before she passed and never stopped loving her."

"That alone sounds like quite a testament to figuring out women and relationships," Grace said, her smile turning wistful. "I wasn't so fortunate. In fact, I can say with fair certainty that you know way more about family, women, and relationships than I do. Well, other than being a woman myself."

He framed her face, held her gaze, and realized that when they stood like that, connecting gazes like that, no matter what position they happened to be in at the time, something simply . . . settled in him. As if everything was always bouncing around inside his mind, ideas spinning in ten different directions, except in those moments. Then he felt, well . . . grounded. Like there was a foundation underneath everything. It didn't stop the constant hamster wheel of work and design and the myriad demands of life in general that were always running through his mind, but it made him feel that at least they wouldn't run away with him. There was a stepping-off point. A reason to slow down, to put things in perspective. An entirely new perspective.

"You can tell me anythin'," he said, searching her eyes, wanting, needing some kind of confirmation, some sign that he wasn't alone in thinking they could build something solid and sound between them. "Ye know that, right?" He tipped her face up to his and dropped a kiss on one salty cheek, then the other. "I may not always have the right words in response, but it won't be for not wanting to understand or offer support."

He felt the shaky breath she took even more than he heard it.

She'd closed her eyes when he'd kissed her tear tracks, and it took a moment longer before she opened them again. "You know, I thought the scariest thing I could ever do in my adult life was going to see my brother. Don't get me wrong, it was pretty terrifying. Amazing and thrilling and . . . so many other things," she added in a rush, smiling even as her eyes went glassy all over again. "And yet, terrifying all the same. But . . . uh . . ." She trailed off, looked down briefly, and cleared the tightness from her throat.

Brodie gently tipped up her chin. "Grace," he said quietly, "it's been a big day. Ye don't need to—"

"I do. I need you to know that you—this—scares me, too. More, even. My brother will always be my brother, no matter what happens between us. But you . . ." She searched his gaze as if struggling to find the right words and maybe looking for the same confirmation he was. "You're becoming someone I find myself counting on." She looked at her hands locked around his neck and pressed her fingers to the nape of his neck, then looked back at him. "Leaning on."

He felt like something perfect blossomed all big and warm inside his chest. "Is that such a bad thing?" he asked, his voice a bit gruff.

"I-I don't know. If you'd asked me a year ago or even a month ago, I'd have said absolutely. Counting on anyone but myself is just asking to make things harder later. Better to always be in charge of myself, handle everything myself. Then the only one who can disappoint me, is me."

"I have a passing knowledge of that feeling," he said, a smile teasing the corners of his mouth.

"See, that's part of it, too. In so many ways, we're very, very different. Our backgrounds, the way we are with other people—you're so naturally social and outgoing and I'm perfectly happy to be in my office alone, no people. You charm people as naturally as breathing, where I refer to it as having to make nice."

He did smile then and slid his hands down her back to her waist, drawing her closer. "Oh, I don't know. I've found ye to be a pretty friendly sort."

She tugged on a piece of his hair and made a face at him.

"Ow!" He chuckled.

"It's a good thing one of the things we have in common is our sense of humor," she added archly.

"Aye, indeed." He rubbed the back of his neck, then quickly pulled her in again when she would have ducked away. "Tell me the rest then."

"In other ways, we're a lot alike. Not so obvious or tangible ways, but . . . we get each other. You wouldn't think we would, and yet . . . you do. Get me, I mean. And I think I get you, too. At least you make me feel like I do."

He walked her back a few steps until they were under the awning and her hips bumped up against the teak panel next to the hatch that led belowdecks. He was smiling, but when he spoke, the words had never been so heartfelt. "When you look at me, Grace, you look into me. Past all the stuff that most folks see . . . and then you keep looking. Disconcerting is what it is." He cupped her cheek. "But I've never felt anything like I do when you keep looking . . . and you're okay with what you see."

Instead of melting, she thumped his chest. "And see? That's exactly what I mean."

He leaned back, eyes wide. "What? What about that could possibly be wrong?"

"It's not. It's impossibly right. That's what I mean. You're impossible. I've got this inn to build, which is turning into a major undertaking, then I have to figure out how to run the damn thing and make a success out of it. I'm completely swamped with all this emotional baggage with my brother, which we've only taken the tiniest first step in dealing with. Then you come along with your charming laugh and your sexy-as-hell dimples, flashing green eyes, a body that won't quit, hands that—well, I can't even go there—and on top of all that, you're a good guy." She thumped his shoulder with her palm again. "A really, really good guy."

"Um . . . how dare I?" He was honestly confused.

"How am I not supposed to fall for you? How am I supposed to remain strong and in control and independent and not need anyone but myself when you're out there having my back every damn second and making me want to get you naked half the time?"

His heart resumed beating as her meaning began to sink in. He smiled. It might have been a grin. Hell, he was only a breath shy of letting out a war whoop. "Only half the time, luv? Then I'm clearly not doing something right."

"Oooh," she said, pummeling her open palms on his shoulders, openly laughing because he'd picked her up and was bodily stuffing her through the hatch.

"Mind your head," he told her, then followed her down the ladder.

She wriggled free when they got to the tiny galley, but he snagged her hand and walked backward toward the single berth, tugging her along with him.

"Brodie, we can't," she said, but her eyes were dancing. "I mean, we're out here in plain view of the island. My brother is on that island."

Brodie reeled her in, then turned neatly and captured her in the narrow passageway between his body and the wall. "Not exactly plain view . . . unless they have infrared tracking. Then we'll show up." He leaned in and kissed the side of her neck.

She gasped, then moaned softly as he continued the gentle assault up to the lobe of her ear, then along the line of her jaw, finally letting her head roll to the side to give him greater access.

"Heat-seeking devices," he murmured against her chin, then pulled her bottom lip into his mouth, taking her mouth completely when she moaned more deeply.

He drew her hands up the wall, pinning wrists beside her head as he took the kiss deeper, until they were both groaning.

"You still want me to lift anchor?" he asked against her damp lips.

She shook her head, slid her hands down until her palms were under his, and tugged his hands to her breasts. "I was kind of hoping for the opposite."

"See?" He grinned against her mouth. "You get me, too."

"Win-win."

She squealed when he scooped her up against him, conveniently bringing his mouth level with those very same breasts she'd been offering him.

"Brodie—"

He closed his mouth over one and suckled it, shirt and all. "Hmm?"

"Nothing," she gasped.

He dipped so she didn't hit her head on the hatch into the master berth that occupied the entire front end of the boat, then took them both straight down on the bed.

"We really have to stop meeting like this," she said, as he made quick work of her shirt and bra and she did the same with his T-shirt.

"We do?" He rolled to his back, taking her with him until she straddled him; then he popped the button of her pants.

"I'm not saying it's not negotiable." She gasped as he tugged her zipper in one short rip, then slid her out of her pants and panties by moving her up his body, over his chest, right to his—

"Good argument." Panting, she arched her back and

grabbed hold of the headboard bolted to the wall as he teased her, then slid his tongue over her. "Excellent . . . point," she panted, moving on him, groaning as he slid his tongue into her. "So many . . . excellent points." The conversation ended on a long, very satisfied groan as those strong calves clamped against his shoulders while she shuddered against him.

She was still shuddering as he slid her back down his body . . . and directly onto him. "I—Brodie—I can't yet, it's too—"

"Shh," he said, easing into her, groaning himself. She was so tight, still twitching. "Don't let it stop, give up a little control," he urged, nuzzling the side of her neck, then pushed the rest of the way in. "And let yourself—"

She cried out as she arched into him, then convulsed around him all over again. She fell against him, her moans muffled against his shoulder as she clung to him and continued to come apart for him.

"Aye, *yes.*" He held her, wrapped up against his chest, and let her move as she wanted, as she needed, gritting his teeth with restraint. She felt so damn good.

She nipped his earlobe, and his will snapped. He rolled over, pulling her under him, and took her mouth as he took her. She lifted into him, took him, held him, and kissed him like he was the only thing keeping her connected to her next breath. He understood the feeling.

When he came, growling, having given up every last shred of control, she bit his chin and growled back, "Aye, *yes!*"

Chapter 19

Grace pulled her leather satchel more tightly under her arm and pushed open the door to Delia's. It was a small, old-fashioned diner perched on the high side of Harbor Street, just past Blue's. The dining area and deck faced the water. Ostensibly, she was there to grab lunch and make use of the free Wi-Fi. She enjoyed the peace and quiet of the library, but the diner was filled with a fair number of familiar faces . . . as well as tourists. The chatter and clink of silverware on dishes and ice in glasses, along with the vibrant hum of conversation was inviting, rather than intrusive. Free Wi-Fi and good food.

None of that mattered much since her stomach was so tense she'd be lucky to get down a glass of water at the moment.

As she made her way to a free table in the back corner, some of the conversations paused and a few heads turned. All of them, she noted, belonged to the locals. As she settled into a booth seat, she saw a woman—Jean Reisters, if Grace recalled her name correctly, who ran the jewelry store across from Owen's hardware store—tug on the arm of the redhead who was presently laughing loudly and taking orders from a table full of tourists.

The redhead glanced at Jean, then over her shoulder . . .

right at Grace. Her smile faltered for a moment, then broadened. She said something to Jean, then turned back to the table she was waiting on and finished taking their order.

Grace realized she was staring, so she turned her attention to getting her laptop out and looking over the menu, trying not to feel as if all eyes were on her, except she was pretty sure a good number of them were. *Have folks heard about me and Brodie? Has his trip out to Sandpiper to get me made the local grapevine?*

She wouldn't be surprised if it had. No doubt he was one of the Cove's most eligible bachelors, so there would be talk about who he was . . . well, sleeping with, she supposed would be the way it would be seen. That was pretty much the only way it could be seen, given they hadn't exactly dated like normal people. The fact that she'd bought property that had been in his family's possession since the town's inception might have something to do with the tongues presently wagging, as well. *Maybe I should have stuck with the library after all.*

Except she wasn't really there for a working lunch.

"Hi. Grace, right?"

Startled from her thoughts, Grace turned from where she'd been staring, unseeing, out the front window, and found the redheaded waitress standing beside her table. She was a little taller than average height, with curves bordering on the knockout variety that even her deli apron couldn't hide. Her gorgeous natural red hair was pulled back in an easy knot with just a few strands escaping and curling around her face. Grace guessed the woman was in her early forties or thereabouts. When she smiled, openly friendly and welcoming, Grace thought maybe she'd misjudged by a handful of years.

Only at the last moment did she notice the smile didn't

quite reach the waitress's pretty aquamarine eyes. Not that they weren't welcoming, exactly, but . . . nervous maybe? That made no sense at all.

Grace tensed as she realized what the problem might be. *Please don't tell me you're some former flame of Brodie's still carrying a torch. Gah. Why didn't I just call instead?*

Belatedly, she realized she was staring. "Yes, hi. Yes, I'm Grace. Grace Maddox. I'm sorry. Have we met? I'm—I've met so many people since I got here, and they've all been so great. I'm very sorry if I've forgotten your name." She knew she'd never met the woman, but made a stab at a polite opening. *Please don't stab me back with a lobster fork.*

"No, no we haven't met. But I've been hoping to. I was just letting you find your way here, in your own time."

Grace frowned, confused.

"I'm sorry. You really don't know who I am, do you?" The waitress took a seat in the booth across from Grace, who could feel everyone's eyes on them. "I'm Delia. O'Reilly. I own the diner."

"Oh!" It was Grace's turn to smile uncomfortably. "I–I was actually hoping we could talk." She braved a quick glance around, forced a smile for the room filled with people who weren't even pretending not to stare. "Maybe . . . not here. I know you're busy—really busy," she added with another darting glance at the other tables. "Just let me know when is good and I could come back. Maybe after you close or—"

Delia reached across the table and placed her hand on Grace's arm, instantly quieting her. Her smile was as open as before, real emotion in her eyes, more than Grace could read. "It's okay. I want to talk with you, too. You're here about Ford, right?"

The breath and tension went out of Grace in a whoosh. "Yes. So, you're . . . Dee, right? He called you Dee."

Delia's expression softened immediately, and there was even more emotion in her eyes, but Grace wasn't sure what any of it meant. Then Delia grinned, and her tone was wry and also more relaxed when she laughed. "If that's all he called me, I'd be surprised."

"No, he didn't say—well, anything, actually. I had to piece it together. I just—did you send me a letter?" Grace shook her head, her own smile coming more naturally, as did the self-deprecating note in her voice. "It was a long time ago, so I know it's crazy to think—"

"Ten years almost to the day, come to think of it." Delia squeezed Grace's arm, her smile softer and sincerely friendly. "What took you so long?"

Grace wasn't sure who was more surprised when tears stung her eyes. God, she was so tired of crying. "It's a long story," she said, her voice dropping to a whisper.

"Now, come on, there'll be none of that. All that matters is that you're here now. And you've seen your brother. At least, I heard that Robie took you out to Sandpiper yesterday." Delia paused and seemed to realize they had an audience. "I'm glad you came to see me, Grace. I would love to talk with you. Tell you what. I'll admit I've been dyin' to see what you're doing to Brodie's boathouse, but I've stayed away because, well . . . we can get into that later, too. How about I drop by this evening once I get the night shift going? They can handle things for an hour or two without me."

Grace smiled and forced even breaths, willing the tears to stay at bay. "That would be great. Though I'll warn you, I haven't done all that much to the place yet. We're still getting it prepped for the rebuild."

"I heard Langston deVry designed the remodel. I don't guess you'd be willing to show me the plans?" Her smile turned conspiratorial as she leaned across the table. "Everyone is dying—*dying*—to find out what's what with your little soon-to-be inn. I'd kill to be the first. Or at least before Fergus McRae, at any rate."

Grace knew Fergus ran the Rusty Puffin tavern and was related to the police chief. She also knew as a somewhat less direct transplant from Ireland, that he was close to Brodie. She'd learned from talking to the locals that Delia's diner and the tavern were the two main gathering spots for locals, and therefore, the two main grapevines in town with the respective owners being the head grapes, so to speak.

Grace smiled, the knots in her stomach finally easing completely. On first impression, she liked Delia. A lot. Thank God. "Well, since you asked and Fergus hasn't, probably only because I haven't made it in to the tavern yet, then I guess you win."

"I'll take a default win," Delia said with a laugh. "I'm not proud. Say around eight-thirty?"

Grace nodded. "That would be great."

Delia started to slide out of the booth, then paused. "Because I'm going to get grilled on this as soon as you leave—not that you have to leave—"

"I-I think I'm going to head back to the boathouse. I have work crews there. And . . ." She glanced around, then back to Delia and made a kind of *ack* face, which made Delia laugh.

"And you're all done being on center stage. I get that, but you might have to get used to it. Not so much because of your brother. Who we all love and respect," she hurried to add, when Grace's smile faltered. "No, it's more about a certain sexy Irish shipbuilder who might have sailed the seven seas to your rescue yesterday." She placed her hand over her heart. "If I was only about a dozen years younger. Hell, half a dozen." She cracked out a laugh, and the crow's-feet that winked from the corners of her eyes and the lines next to her mouth told Grace she spent a lot more time laughing than anything else. "Who am I kidding? If I thought even a fraction of that charming Irish blarney he sends my way was serious, I'd jump him right here in this booth today."

Grace laughed even as she felt her face go flame red. "So, the whole town . . . ?"

"Oh yeah. Half are jealous, the other half just want every last steamy detail. Okay, so all of them are jealous." She winked. "But only half of them would admit to it."

Grace pressed her hands to her warm cheeks.

"I'm not talking about the hot blush, though that speaks volumes on its own." Delia's smile turned sweeter, softer. "I'm talking about that look in your eyes." She leaned across the table. "I'll let you in on a not-so-little secret. When he talks about you, his eyes do that same thing." She grinned as Grace's eyebrows rose, and the flush spread to her neck.

"He . . . talks? About me? In a good way?"

Delia frowned. "Well, of course in a good way. To be honest, it's been a hoot to watch. When he first moved here, I had him pegged as a bachelor lifer. You know the kind, loves all women, so can't commit to any one of them. Then I saw him get all googly-eyed over Alex and—well, shit. I'm sorry. There I go, talking out of school."

"It's okay. I know about Alex."

Delia lifted a brow and gave her an entirely new considering look. "Huh," she said, then murmured, "Well, I'll be damned."

Grace's eyebrow furrowed with the unspoken question.

"Alex MacFarland caught his eye briefly, but I'd make a guess that you've grabbed something a lot more valuable. If he's telling you about other women he's cared for . . ." Delia trailed off, but her blue eyes were lit up in pure delight. "Why would you think he'd say anything bad about you? Oh!" The light dawned. "The boathouse. Yeah, well, I'm sure he was none too happy with that in the beginning, but honey, he doesn't hold that against you. That all goes on Cami Weathersby's doorstep." She leaned forward again, voice dropping. "Not that I'm all that surprised she did it. *Conniving* is her middle name. And the woman holds a grudge."

"A grudge? Against Brodie? For what?"

"He didn't tell you? He tells you about Alex, but not—" Delia broke off, rolled her eyes. "Men. They can be such idiots. Well, it's not my place to tell, but I'd ask him about it. He probably doesn't think there's anything to say, and from his viewpoint, there isn't. But considering the deal he's got going on with her father . . . that's exciting, isn't it?" At the blank expression on Grace's face, she blanched. "Well, shit again. I don't usually stick my foot that deep in it."

"He did mention yesterday that he had something to talk to me about, but I ended up falling asleep and slept the entire boat trip back in." Grace felt the heat climb to her cheeks again. "I . . . didn't get much sleep the night before, and the whole meeting thing with Ford . . ."

She just gave up and let it go. If everyone knew she was spending time with Brodie, there was no point in pretending some of that time wasn't spent having sex. She probably had slept more due to the sleepless night before followed by the emotionally exhausting reunion with her brother than because she and Brodie had ended up in bed again.

Actually, it was more how safe and cared for Brodie had made her feel than what they'd been doing that had lulled her into such a deep sleep. She hadn't even woken when the boat engines started up With no wind, Brodie had motored them back to the harbor. She'd gotten back to find two workers had stopped by to let her know that another member of her crew had gotten hurt trying to take advantage of the last night of eel season. She'd spent the rest of the afternoon finding a replacement for him and the evening in talks with Langston about starting the next phase of construction. She'd finally begged off dinner with Brodie, headed out to the Point house with Whomper, simply crashed out cold until morning.

She hadn't been able to stop thinking about the whole letter thing and was stuck on Ford's mention of Dee, so that had been her mission upon waking. After a night in a decent bed, followed by a long shower and a big breakfast, she'd headed back to Half Moon to figure out how best to approach her.

"It's been a busy morning, and Brodie and I haven't had the chance to talk," Grace finished somewhat lamely.

Delia slid out of the booth and put her hand on Grace's arm. "Well, I'll let the two of you sort that out. I think it's all good news, but with Camille in the mix, there's always room for catastrophe." She squeezed Grace's arm gently. "Don't let her do anything to screw things up between you and Brodie. He's a good man. Sometimes when the ones you think will never fall do, they fall good and hard. And stay there. Trust me," she added with a flashy grin. "I've got a pretty good eye for these things."

"Thank you," Grace said, scrambling to assimilate a whole new host of information she hadn't anticipated. She'd come hoping to gain greater insight into her brother and what he'd been doing for the past thirteen years. She hadn't been prepared for other bombshells. Or potential bombshells. "Are we still on for tonight?"

"I'm game if you are. Why don't you give me a shout when you've talked with Brodie and have your day figured out. We can talk another time." Delia patted Grace's arm, squeezed one last time. "About your brother, and what I know about him? Don't worry. It's all good stuff. Okay?"

"Okay," Grace said, letting out an unsteady breath. "Thank you." She looked up at Delia and smiled. "I mean that."

"I know you do," Delia said with a sincere smile. "I'm glad you came in." She looked over at the still packed tables, grabbed her order pad, and slid the pencil out from behind her ear. "The natives are getting restless. Talk to you soon." Then she hustled off.

There was no music blaring as Grace stepped into the open doorway of Brodie's workshop. Big Brown was nowhere to be seen. She had stopped by her boathouse first and left her satchel and checked on Whomper, who was happily keeping the construction crew company as they worked on the roof and putting new shakes on the exterior. Apparently outside noise wasn't as scary as inside noise.

She leaned against the doorframe and watched Brodie do his version of inside work. He was in yet another pair of old jeans, sawdust-covered boat shoes, a long-sleeved tee. The hull of the sailboat he was building was taking shape, and she marveled that he'd constructed it by hand. It wasn't anywhere near as big as his two-master—he'd need the big boathouse for that—but it was gorgeous. The curve of the wood, the slope of the design seemed more like a piece of art, with the functional element a mere bonus. She hadn't talked to him about how he envisioned Monaghan's Shipbuilders as a company, moving forward. Was he planning to be a one-man crew, building boats to order? Or was he hoping to take on other craftsmen with like skills? Or teach them? She didn't know. In fact, there was far more about him that she didn't know, than that she did.

But she wanted to know. She wanted to know everything about him.

Specifically, she wanted to know everything about him and the Winstocks.

She waited to knock on the doorframe until he'd put down the hand lathe and picked up a towel to brush the sawdust from his forearms and chest before pulling off the work goggles he'd been wearing.

He glanced up, surprised to see her, a grin instantly creasing his face. "Top of the morning to ye." He wiped his hands on the same cloth, then tossed it aside before walking over to her. He took her hand and gently tugged her closer. "I'd pull ye all the way in, but I'm no' exactly user-friendly at the moment." He glanced down at his damp and dusty self.

She smiled, despite the butterflies in her stomach. Nervous ones. Not that she was worried he was going to tell her something that would change things between them, but she'd feel a lot better once she knew what was going on, what he hadn't told her. And why. She leaned in and kissed him, then moaned a little as he instantly claimed her mouth, taking the kiss deep and hot. Her entire body went up in flames as it always did with him. She wondered if that part would ever change . . . and couldn't imagine it would as long as both of them were still breathing.

"Hi," she said, smiling, breathing a bit more heavily when he finally lifted his head.

He smiled right back into her upturned face. "Hi, yourself. To what do I owe the honor? I've been hearing the nail guns going all day. Shakes going up and on. That's good. Means you'll start on the real work soon, right?"

She nodded. "This week, if all goes well and no other

catastrophe befalls me. I heard from Langston. He plans to come end of the week or beginning of next to help me plot the best course of action. I've got Owen compiling a list of various subcontractors for me."

"New guy doing okay?"

She nodded, pleased that he remembered and thought to ask. "I don't think it's particularly challenging work today. Mostly just tedious and endless. I also heard from Shep, the guy who was injured. He's okay, just needed some stitches from a fall he took on the boat. Cut his head." She smiled. "Apparently his is pretty hard. They say he didn't even have a concussion. He'll be back in a day or two providing he can keep it bandaged properly."

Brodie gave her a look that told her what he thought about sissy things like bandages, but wisely said nothing on that. "Sounds like Owen is helping you out pretty well. He's a good man. And a walking encyclopedia of the locals and local history. He knows more about Monaghan Shipbuilders than I do."

"He's been a huge help. A lifeline, really. I like him. Such a nice guy. Met his daughter, Lauren. She's home from college for the summer and working at the store with him." Grace smiled. "She's nothing like him. He's this quiet, sort of nondescript, unassuming guy, and she's tall, vivacious, very outgoing, lots of laughter. Pretty blonde hair while his is kind of spongy red. I guess she must take after her mom. I really like her, too. They're good together, father and daughter, it seems. That's a really nice thing."

"Aye, 'tis. He's been the sole parent to her after her mum passed when she was little. Happened long before I arrived, of course, but I've heard the story all the same. Cancer, I believe. And yes, apparently she was a stunner. Owen used to take a fair share of ribbing from what I've heard about how he managed to snag such a heavenly creature. But I think the envy went a lot further than her good looks. Apparently, they were childhood sweethearts whose bond only grew stronger with time."

"That's so wonderful to hear. But all the more tragic then, that she died so young. I wonder if that's why he's never remarried."

Brodie lifted a shoulder. "I couldn't say. He's been busy raising his daughter, so that could be the better part of it. He's done a good job of it, too, from what I know. She got a scholarship to university, full tuition, so clearly he did something right."

Grace nodded, smiled, trying not to let her thoughts drift to her conversation with Ford—that he hadn't known she'd invited him to her college graduation . . . but that he'd been well aware of her path through school. She wasn't sure how she felt about all of that yet. It was good—great—to know he hadn't truly abandoned her, at least not from his perspective, and yet, at the same time, he'd never given her the comfort of knowing he was still invested, that he still cared. Cared at all. That anger-love thing boiled up all over again, confusing her. She really wanted to move beyond the emotional roller coaster of their past to start working on what came next . . . only it wasn't that simple or that easy.

Brodie's smile shifted and he tipped her chin up with a single fingertip. "What else is going on over there? You didn't come down to make idle chitchat or steal a kiss, did ye now?"

It was funny how much she didn't know about him . . . and yet how quickly they'd come to *know* each other. "Well, the kiss was pretty nice. I might have to find reasons to come down here more often."

He traced that same finger along her jaw and dipped his head to kiss her again. It wasn't that all-claiming, all-consuming kind of carnal kiss. It was tender, sweet, which she hadn't honestly thought he had in him. Of course, he did. It unraveled her in completely different, yet far more powerful ways. The man she was coming to know, falling for, had a heart as big as the moon. He'd been so good at spreading it around and over everyone he knew, he had never focused on only one person. Her heart squeezed tightly with the realization of just how much she wanted to be that one person.

"That's all the reason I'll ever need," he told her, lifting his head, something deep and sparkling in his eyes. Now that was new. "So . . . what is it that's got you concerned?"

The corners of her mouth curved and her eyebrow lifted. "How do you know it's something *concerning*?"

"Because there's a bit of worry dimming the light in your eyes. Is it something to do with your brother? Do ye need to go back out to the island?"

"No, no. Nothing about him. Well, that's not entirely true. I did . . . I met someone this morning who knows him. Knew him. Well, I guess she still knows him. We're going to talk more later."

Brodie's eyebrows rose. "A woman, is it? They were close, you say?"

"Once upon a time, I think so, yes. He mentioned her name, and . . . it's a long story. But it's Delia. O'Reilly. She's—"

"Owner of the diner, and a finer woman you'll never know." Brodie said it matter-of-factly and quite sincerely, though his expression was still one of concern for Grace.

Grace flashed a grin at that. "Aye, and she thinks pretty highly of you as well, laddie," she said, doing her best Irish brogue. She reached around and pinched his butt. "She likes the low parts, too. Just sayin'." Her face split wide as she watched him actually squirm ever so slightly and get a hint of color in his tanned cheeks. "Why, Brodie Monaghan, I didn't know you could blush."

"It's no' a blush, it's . . ." He chuckled then, but looked even more disconcerted. "It's a fine woman she is, and I've flirted shamelessly with her I have, but she's rather like . . . well, no' a sister, perhaps, but she reminds me of a lot of the women in my family back home. She's family to me. Or has felt as such. So . . ."

"Yeah," Grace finished. "Maybe a little bit awkward."

Brodie held his forefinger and thumb close together. "Wee bit," he said, with a grin and a little wince.

She laughed at his aggrieved expression. "I'm sorry. I'd say I wish I hadn't told you, because I truly don't want to make things uncomfortable between you. I like her a lot, too, and I hope there's a friendship there for me. But seeing you squirm a little might almost be worth it. And I'm betting Delia would agree."

"Och, don't go tellin' her now. I'll never hear the end. The woman is as bold as she is loyal. You've got to swear on it."

Grace started to grin, then saw he was quite serious and laughed outright. "You are so adorable right now." Her breath came out of her on a whoosh, followed by a squeal and choking laughter when he scooped her right over his shoulder and carted her out on the docks.

"Adorable am I?" he asked, but she was laughing too hard to respond.

"You can't just cart me off to your sailboat cave every time I—Brodie, I'm serious. Put me down." But her laughter hardly made the threat carry any weight. Unlike him, who seemed to have no problem whatsoever carrying her. "You realize the whole town knows about us. They know you came out to get me yesterday."

"So?" He paused before stopping entirely and sliding her down his body until her feet touched the pier. "Is that a concern for you? I should have thought. I'd never want to make ye feel compromised or—"

She cupped his face and looked into his eyes, surprised by what she saw there. "Do you think I'm, what, ashamed of being with you? Because you have some reputation as a ladies' man? No. No, I don't care what anyone else thinks. They'll say what they're going to say. Honestly, your reputation only adds to your considerable charm. If anything, I'll be more the target of envy than anything else." She smiled. "I can live with that."

He smiled, but it was clear he was still thinking about what she'd said.

Hands still framing his face, she tipped his chin down so she could look squarely into his eyes. "What we have, or whatever we will have, is ours. No one else's. If you're okay with that, I'm okay with that. Unless you think it will harm your business interests, or mine. Frankly, if this town is that small-minded, maybe I need to rethink my business plan."

"No, they're lovely folks here. They welcomed me, and from what I can see, they've welcomed you just as heartily. They'll talk and they love their gossip, but no. Ye don't have to worry about that, I don't think."

The actual reason she'd come to see him came back to mind, and she couldn't believe she'd gotten so sidetracked. Well, she could, but still. "Actually, that is partly what I came to talk to you about. Now, don't hold this against Delia. She assumed since you told me about Alex, that you told me about this, but—"

"How on earth does Delia O'Reilly know what I did or didn't tell you about Alex?"

Grace's cheeks warmed a little. "Uh, because I might have mentioned it."

To her surprise, he grinned. "Getting quite cozy, the two of you."

"Why are you grinning like that?"

"Well, knowing Delia, she grilled ye a bit on the goings-on between us, if, as you say, tongues have been wagging. I'm no' unhappy for her to know and spread about that there's something more between us than there might have been for me before."

"How do you know that's what I told her?"

He reached around and pinched her butt, making her squeak, but she was grinning. "Okay, okay. So maybe Delia did immediately jump to that conclusion. But then that led her to also mention—"

"Camille." Brodie's expression immediately changed to one of dawning understanding. "Christ."

"Well, she used somewhat different words to describe her, but yes."

He lifted his eyebrows and let out a short laugh. "Well, as I said, Delia is loyal to those she cares about, and that care doesn't extend much to the Winstocks." He sighed in resignation. "What else did she tell you?"

"Not much, just that you are in some kind of new business deal with Cami's father."

"Aye. That was what I meant to tell you on the boat yesterday, only we got sidetracked—" He paused and took in Grace's unabashed grin and the tension seemed to ease in him. He ducked in and bussed her fast and hard on the mouth.

"What was that for? Not that I minded. I just want to make sure I do it more often," she said, echoing his earlier words.

"For being open and honest. No games with you, Grace. If you feel it, you show it. It's a help to me, a small guidance, perhaps, since I'm sure I'll screw up more often than no'. And you came here and are giving me the benefit of the doubt. I'm certain you've more than a few doubts where I'm concerned. But you always ask first before you decide what's what, and then you listen to what I have to say. It's a rare commodity, to be sure. It doesn't go unnoticed."

She didn't blush but she might have glowed a bit more brightly. "Well . . . thank you. I—maybe it comes from what I used to do for a living. Listening was oftentimes ninety percent of the battle. Figuring what's really important to people. So that's . . . thank you."

He laughed then, tugged her more fully into his arms and to hell with his messy shirt. He smiled down at her as she tipped her head back to look into his eyes. "You confound me, Grace Maddox. All ballsy straight talk one moment, then flustered the next, as if you're no' used to hearing about your good points."

"It's not that, it's just . . . well, maybe I'm not used to caring about who it is I'm hearing them from." She grinned then. "Now who's blushing?"

He just shook his head, kissed her lightly on the tip of her nose, then her forehead, then drew her against him and wrapped his arms around her fully. She tucked her cheek to his chest, not caring or even noticing the sawdust, too caught up in the soap and sweat smell of the man. Her man.

Hmm. My man. Is he?

She wanted him to be. *I think I really do.*

"About the deal with Winstock, and Cami . . . I hadn't the heart to wake you. Then you had work issues. After so much in one day, you looked a bit flat on your feet. I thought we could talk of it later today. I was going to make you dinner. I should have known in twenty-four hours someone else would mention it before I could. I'm sorry you heard of it that way. I'm guessing you have questions."

She lifted her head and looked up at him. "Delia mentioned there was a business deal with Cami's father, but when she saw I had no idea what she was talking about, she stopped and said it would be better coming from you. She also mentioned that Cami has a grudge of some kind with you, which I took to mean she might not be so happy with me now, either. Brodie, honestly, I'm not worried about any of it. I just . . . it sounded like it might be something I should know."

"It is. And I should have told you about why Cami sold you my boathouse in the first place, straight out. I just . . . didn't think it had so much to do with you as with me. But then we weren't an *us* and now—"

Grace wove her hands around Brodie's neck, aware in a way she'd never been before of the statement she was really making, standing out in the open as they were in plain sight on the main Monaghan pier where more than likely several sets of eyes were on them, intentionally or not. She'd meant what she'd said about not caring who knew she was spending time with him . . . but hearing him say the same thing was also something she wanted. "And now we are." She didn't make it a question, but held his gaze as she said it all the same.

"Aye," he said on a short breath as if he'd been holding it. "That we are." She saw relief, a sort of abashed pride, a bit of stunned happiness . . . and still a thread of concern. She took that last bit to be about whatever it was he had to tell her—not about them personally or where they stood—and her trembling new confidence in wanting to be part of an *us* grew a little steadier and stronger.

"Whatever it is, we'll deal with it," she said. "I thought I'd give that together part a try," she added with a laugh.

"Together." He held her gaze, then his handsome face split into that sexy grin that made his dimples wink out and his eyes twinkle. "I know this was my idea, but hearing you say it . . . any other time in my life, that word would have scared me senseless."

"And now?" she asked, thinking that just because she wanted it, wanted him, didn't mean she wasn't still scared. Maybe more so now. But that's what risking it was all about.

"Now I'm still scared out of me mind . . . but it's all for a greater good, so what choice to I have but to go with it?"

"Exactly what I was thinking. You know," she added, marveling a bit at the step they were trying to take toward each other, toward being together. "Langston has been married a bunch of times, and yet he's constantly giving me relationship advice, encouraging me to go for it, to take bigger risks. He claims he's been head over heels every time he's said his vows, as hard and deep as if it were the best thing he'd ever had. I didn't really get how that was possible, though I believed he felt that way. But he said something to me that I understand now. He said, 'if you're not scared out of your mind, then you're not really in—' " Too late she realized what she'd been about to say and broke off. Not that saying it was saying she loved Brodie, but he might think that's what she was saying.

Would that be such a bad thing? Do I love him?

She looked at him, blinked, certain she looked a bit poleaxed. Sensible or not, rational or not . . . she was pretty sure that even if she couldn't say those words to him right that second, she was well on her way to a place where not saying them would be almost impossible.

Chapter 20

Brodie was glad Grace stopped speaking when she did . . . because his heart pretty much stopped beating right at that point. He had no idea how he'd feel if she'd said those words to him. And he wasn't ready yet to find out. From the look on her face, she wasn't ready yet, either. *Thank the saints.*

He didn't know what else to do, so he kissed her. She took the out. Quite fervently, if the way her fingers dug into the back of his neck was any indication. He was smiling as he lifted his head. They were a pair, that they were.

"Let's go up to the boathouse. I'll show you the plans for the schooner I'm to build for Brooks Winstock." He turned, arm around her shoulders, and headed up the pier.

She slid her arm around his waist, leaned into him, matching his stride, as if they'd walked many a mile together. "Schooner. Like your two-master, you mean? Wow, that will be quite some undertaking. Where would you build it? Will you renovate the main boathouse for that?"

He shook his head. "The main boathouse isn't really a boathouse, it was the lumber mill, amongst other things, for the shipyard. Part of why the company ended up failing was because when the shipbuilding shifted from wood to steel, they didn't shift with it."

"Aren't you planning on building wood-hull boats as

your new business? I mean, what you're building out in your workshop is wood hull."

"Aye, I am. But my focus will be entirely different from my ancestors'. I'll be going more for small, specially designed pleasure craft. Boats, mostly sail, for owners who want the art put into the design as much as the finesse and polish of the finished product."

She grinned. "I was thinking that same thing when I stepped into your workshop today—that what you do is truly art. It's a bonus that it happens to be functional art."

He looked down at her, inordinately pleased by her compliment. "Thank you."

She laughed. "Don't sound so surprised. You know you're good."

He chuckled, then squeezed her briefly against him and bumped hips. "I know my worth, but it's good to know ye see it, too."

She rolled her eyes and nudged him back. "So, will you build this on your own? I know you did your two-master, but you said you had help. Even then it had to have been an enormous undertaking."

"She's what I truly learned it all on, aye. She'll always be me first love. They're the most special." As soon as he said the words, he experienced momentary brain freeze. *Gawd, can I not just steer clear of the L word today?*

Instead of reading anything into his remark, or making some kind of joke, she answered quite honestly. "I didn't build my scull by hand, but after renting them for years, the day I bought my very own . . . yeah." She leaned her head against his shoulder, her voice softening. "It's a standout moment that you can't really repeat. Something about firsts, I guess."

That was his moment. With nothing more important going on than walking the short steps to his boathouse and sliding open the panel door, fate didn't care what you were doing when the inevitable sank in. When she'd said "something about firsts, I guess," Brodie's instinctive, gut reaction was *aye, like how I feel about you.*

"Well, I'm about to tackle a very different kind of first." He winced inwardly again at the double meaning as he stepped back and let her enter before him. "I'm no' quite sure how as yet, and we've not finalized the deal." He wasn't entirely sure that was because Brooks needed to look over the plans longer . . . or whether it was because he needed to consult with his daughter, and let her know that Brodie had been less than enthusiastic about her role in their deal. In fact, he'd made it rather clear she would have no role in their plan.

If they still had one.

Grace glanced at him expectantly. He motioned her over to his drafting table, and as soon as he lifted the cover sheet on the plans, she gasped. Her gaze immediately flew to his, then back to the scale drawing of the eighteenth-century, three-masted schooner.

"Brodie," she said on a hushed breath. "This is . . . are you serious?" She looked at him again. "I—how would you even do that?"

He smiled. "Well, my ancestors did it. Many times. Right out there on that hill. Someone built those ships, you know."

"I mean, of course, but . . . I guess I never thought about how they did it. This is, it's . . . stunning. I've seen paintings of tall ships and models of them, but that . . ." She trailed off, shook her head, and went back to looking at the drawing. Really looking at it.

Brodie felt a simultaneous swell of pride . . . and gut-notching fear. Because he was still wondering the very same thing. *How in the hell am I going to build that ship?*

"What is Mr. Winstock going to do with it?"

Brodie's mind was still on the enormous challenge in

front of him and answered absently. "He wants to run day tours out in Pelican Bay. There are other port towns that use modern-day versions of historic tall ships for tourist purposes." He looked at his plans. "This will have some minor modifications for modern facilities, auxiliary power, communication, for safety and comfort purposes, but the ship itself will be an exact replica of the wood-hull schooners my ancestors built right here in Blueberry Cove. The modernized ones used today are usually built with a steel hull. Winstock realizes there will be longevity issues with such an actual replication, but is willing to make the investment in order to have something no one else has. I—" Brodie broke off as he glanced up and caught her looking at him. Staring at him.

"Brooks Winstock is going to run tours in Pelican Bay. Tourist-type tours." She spoke as if she were trying to get that to sink in.

Brodie grinned. "It won't be happening anytime soon, but the time it takes me to build the ship will allow him months to plan and market the business, so, in the end, it all dovetails nicely. And yes, allow you time to finish your inn. To be ready made for the influx of visitors."

She was still staring. "He's going to run it out of Half Moon Harbor," she said. "Right? Where else could a ship that size go, anyway?"

"We're still discussing those particulars, but yes, it would have to be here."

"Here," she repeated, then pointed downward. "As in *here,* here."

"Aye." He was realizing that her shock wasn't actually one of stunned excitement. More simply stunned. He wasn't sure exactly why, but she didn't look very happy.

"It will be great for your boatbuilding business as well." She was almost talking to herself. She looked back at the plans, and even in her current state, her expression melted a little. "You're going to build this here, too. Right here," she added faintly.

And then he realized where she was going with this. He'd thought about it while talking to Brooks, but so many things had happened since then, that part had gotten lost in the shuffle. "Aye."

"How long?" She looked from the plans, to him, to the plans. "Wouldn't this take . . . years?"

"No. Back during the time when they built such schooners, when the shipyard was running at full capacity, they could build this in under nine months."

Her gaze swung to his; she was gaping. "No way."

He nodded. "That won't be the case with this ship, but once the actual building is underway, assuming I can get the right labor, I've got it scheduled out for fourteen months, from the laying down to the launch. Eighteen tops. It can't start right off, as I need to do a complete renovation and reinstallation of the lumber works and ironworks in the main boathouse and"—he blew out a breath on a half laugh—"so many other things." He touched her arm. "But no, it will not be a peaceful and serene environment here. I know you probably have this idyllic vision of this place, but you bought a building that is part of a shipyard."

"A shipyard I thought was defunct and abandoned."

"For a day. Then you found out it wasn't."

"I didn't know what you planned here. I thought it was going to be kind of like what you're doing out on the pier boathouse. Just . . . not huge. And certainly not that." She gestured to the plans but didn't look at them.

"I never dreamed I'd have the opportunity to truly bring the yard back to its former glory."

"Were you going to relaunch a full lumber mill and ironworks as part of your original plan?"

"A far more limited version of it, yes. I had hoped to

section off part of the building and add on more space up the hill for actual indoor construction to allow us more months of the year to work."

"Us. Who is us?"

He shrugged. "Whoever I hire or bring on to work with me. I don't want to bring all this back and have it be only about me. It can't be. You're talking about heritage and building something. My ancestors already did that. But I'm not going to go through all of this simply so I can personally build a few boats. I could have stayed in Ireland and done that."

"So . . . you dream of having a bunch of little Monaghans and seeing them take this over?"

He looked at her quizzically, unsure of what she meant by that; it hadn't sounded like a ringing endorsement. "I don't know. Perhaps someone from back home will want to come over. I don't know what my personal future holds, but my sisters have no compunction about procreating. As I said, we Monaghans are overachievers in that particular arena. My three older sisters are all married and have started families. I realize that their children don't bear the Monaghan name, but they have Monaghan blood, and for me, that's enough. If not a relative, then perhaps someone who comes to work here will take up the passion. Mostly I don't want the craft of wood shipbuilding to die out. The business doesn't have to bear the Monaghan name, but I do want what my family spent generations building to continue in some form or fashion." He paused and took a breath, realizing he was going from passionate to defensive and that wasn't what he wanted. "You yourself called it an art. Well, I agree. And it's a dying one. I'm trying to resurrect it."

She listened, she took it all in, then she turned back to look at the plans, staying silent. He didn't know what was going through her mind.

"This is a once-in-a-lifetime opportunity, isn't it?" She lifted a hand, signaling it was a rhetorical question. "I can't even begin to imagine how excited you must be. And that is . . . well, it's awesome in the truest meaning of the word. I am happy for you, thrilled for you."

But. He heard the word; she didn't even have to say it.

"You say eighteen months, tops, so, not forever, not much longer than it will take to get the inn built and open, and no time, really, in the bigger picture of things. Even the building phase will be a huge tourist draw, so I get that it's good for me, too." She was talking herself through it. "But . . . lumber mills and shipbuilding and . . ."

"Things that aren't peaceful and serene and quiet," he finished gently. He turned her to him, hands on her arms. "Not the romantic, picturesque, seaside inn of your dreams, perhaps?"

She shook her head, then surprised him by making a *but, what are you going to do?* face and shrugging.

No pouting, swearing, whining, though he suspected if she were in private she'd have done all three. He knew she was quite adept at that second one, at any rate. Ultimately, though, she was simply, well . . . taking it. He wondered how often she'd had to do that. She was rather too good at it.

"Where did the urge for this inn come from?" he asked, knowing he should be thankful she was handling the disappointment, perhaps even feeling a modicum of smug satisfaction that her dreams were being a bit tainted as his had been when she'd bought his property out from under him. But he wasn't feeling either of those things. He wanted her to want her dream so strongly that she'd be, well, angry if it wasn't going how she wanted. To fight for what she wanted. If she wasn't willing to get angry and fight for this big dream of hers . . . what was to say she'd fight for their relationship? Because no way was that going to be always smooth going. "You want a foundation for future generations to be proud of, so why not your own law offices or something? Why an inn?"

"It's not so much that I want future generations to be innkeepers; I think it's more . . . making a place they can call home. A place that they'd think of, identify themselves with, think back on fondly if they move on to other paths." She looked at him starkly. "I didn't have that. I have—had—a condo in Alexandria, a city I wasn't tied to except by its proximity to my job, which I took because it was a good offer. The city was okay. D.C. is certainly striking in history and architecture and all that. But the only real connection I ever felt to it, the only one that was personal to me, was the river. My time on the water."

"So what makes Blueberry Cove different?"

"Ford," she said simply. "He's the only connection I have left to anything. If I got here and hated it, or if the situation between us made staying in the same place untenable—though I couldn't see how it could be any worse than it was, considering it was nothing—I'd have done something else, figured out something else. But I got here . . . and I loved it. I connected immediately to the water, the coast. I knew right away that I wanted my inn to be on the water. It's not like the river, and it's not about sculling. But I quickly realized it's more about my connection to the water, to the . . . I don't know, the primal element of it. So that, plus Ford . . ." She trailed off, lifted a shoulder. "It's not just as good a place as any. It's a specific place that has meaning to him, and now meaning to me. Hopefully, if I'm lucky, I can create something to pass down to whoever comes next."

"Because you plan on makin' a bunch of babies, do ye?" he teased, but gently.

She took it as intended, making a quick, but cute face at him. "Or maybe Ford will. Or maybe the Maddox clan will simply die out here. But it won't be without me at least trying to leave something meaningful behind. Meaningful to me. And that's not a job, not even the inn. It's just . . ."

"Home," he said, knowing what she meant. Intimately. Something else twinged in his heart. "I know something of that."

She looked into his face, and he realized from her expression that he'd let some of the plaintive emotion home evoked in him come out in his voice. "Do you miss Ireland?" she asked more quietly. "Do you miss home, your family? Are they proud of you even if they think you should be doing what they're doing?"

He nodded. "I think they believe this is foolhardy and I will give up eventually and come home, but, in their own way, I think they do support me finding my own way. Much as they'd rather it be their way. But miss them? Miss Ireland? Oh, aye. That I do."

"Why not start a Monaghan's Shipbuilding there?"

"I thought about it, but this place was already here, with history that called to me, and . . . I knew I'd have a much better chance of making a go of it if they weren't all looking over my shoulder, trying to talk me away from it with every breath. I didn't know the place was in the shape it was, but even so . . . I wanted to make my own mark. Not in the way you do, not necessarily by making a home, but the bigger goal is the same, I think. Finding a place to belong, a place that has a bigger meaning than merely occupation or location. Something that extends beyond that, connects all of that."

She nodded. "Exactly."

"So, you know why I'm here and why boats. I know why you're here, but why the inn?"

Her cheeks went instantly warm and that surprised him. His quiet smile edged out wide again. "Well, well . . . do

I detect something perhaps not rooted in rational planning and educated risk-taking?"

"Oh, I educated myself about it. As much as anyone can. It was actually a fantasy, a sort of pie in the sky, if I ever won the lottery kind of dream, and that's all it was ever supposed to be. Somewhere along the line, as my life wasn't going as planned, or the plan wasn't as satisfying as I'd thought it would be, the dream suddenly, somehow became a goal. And then I couldn't stop thinking about it, like what would happen if I just . . . did it. Went for it. You know? What it was suddenly wasn't as important as what it represented—which was doing something that I wanted to do, versus what I thought I should do. It was the first thing I've ever really, really just . . . *wanted* to do."

He nodded in understanding. "That tells me not at all why it is that innkeeping ended up being that thing."

She gave him a rueful smile and nudged at him, which just made him tug her more deeply into his arms.

"You're going tell me?"

"Or?" she said, the playful lightness coming back into her voice. With it came a bit of the energy, the verve she always seemed to have so naturally, so effortlessly that had winked out when she realized her dream wasn't going to go off quite as she planned.

"Or I carry you up to my lair and find a way to make you confess all."

She gave him a considering look. "I'm almost tempted to call your bluff, just to see what mad skills you think you are going to employ to make me talk."

He grinned. "That's the spirit." He back-walked her until she was pressed against the large picture window that looked out over the slope of the hill and the water just beyond his boathouse and leaned down to nip at her chin, running his hands up her sides, brushing ever so lightly over her nipples. Reveling in the way his touch made her gasp and her body go all soft and pliant, he cupped her face with both hands and tipped her head back, which arched her hips more fully into his. "Have I mentioned how much I love that you wear your hair down so often now?" he said against her lips, sinking his fingers into it and gently tugging.

She moaned against his mouth and opened under his questing tongue. He'd thought to tease her more, but ended up as lost in the moment as she was. He finally left her mouth damp, her lips puffy for a breath of much-needed air and continued the rain of kisses along her jaw, pausing at the pulse spot just beneath her ear. She groaned, letting her head roll to the side, and he turned her, so her back was pressed to his oh so aching front. He groaned as she pressed the soft curve of her bum against the very hardest part of him. He drew her hair aside and kissed her neck, his body twitching hard as he felt the shiver of pleasure race through her in a delicate shudder. He grinned against her skin, happy to have found yet another of her pleasure triggers. He drew his hands up her hips, fingers splayed over her stomach, then inched them up higher, taking her shirt with him, exposing her soft, pale skin until he could cup the gentle swell of her breasts.

She pressed her head back against his shoulder, arching as he played with her nipples through the soft white fabric, then pressing back against him as he leaned around and kissed the edge of her jaw. She moved against him, and they found their rhythm so easily. He realized it was like that for them in all ways. A match of ebb and flow, need and want, thought and process.

He nudged her head forward, caught up in the moment with this woman—his woman—and feeling as if everything was converging for him in that one moment. "Open your eyes and look out there," he said in a heated whisper against her damp neck. "See the slope of that land, how it runs naturally straight to the water?"

She murmured, "Yes," her breath coming in short gasps as she reached down and grabbed his arm, keeping it tight around her waist as she pressed back against him.

She made him want to howl at the moon, everything was so primal with her. "See the deep curve"—he moved against her—"dipping in, then playing out way across the other side?"

"Yes," she gasped as he dipped her back against him and pressed his hips in.

"That's where they built the great schooners, the massive clippers, right there on that ground . . . and then rolled them down into the sea. We Monaghans were brilliant at finding just the right lay of the land. Did ye know that's where the term came from?"

She moaned softly, letting her head roll left to right in a slow shake, her eyes still open, still looking, seeing, taking it all in, even as her body was lost to his touch.

"Now I get to build one, Grace, right on that very same spot. I have no idea what I'm doing, I know it as concept only, but och, the dream of it, the chance of it. I want to try, need to try. Do ye ken?"

She nodded, and he felt her body catch, her throat work under his questing fingers, which curved around her collarbone as he turned her cheek to his mouth. He turned her fully in his arms and saw her eyes were shimmering and felt his belly clutch again. "No, no, I didn't say it to make ye sad, but to show you that it's the right thing." He brought her mouth up to his. "As is your inn. Yer out of your depth, but it's what ye want and ye know it. Ye see it in your mind's eye, your heart's eye, and ye want it to be all that ye imagined." He pulled her close. "I know I'll have to make compromises with my ancestors' design for all sorts of reasons. As will you, concerning the idyllic setting you envisioned. But we'll do it, Grace, that we will, to get to the grander goal, and it will be none the less satisfying for it. I want my dream and I want you to want yours, to fight for it. Dinnae give up on it because it's no' perfect." He knew what else he was saying. *Don't give up on me, for I'm far from perfect, too.*

She nodded, and the shimmer turned to glass. "I never cry." The words were hardly a whisper. "I do want it, Brodie. For you. For me."

He tipped up her chin. "For us?"

She held his gaze, even as hers swam. "Yes. Yes, I do."

"Then have it we shall, aye?"

She searched his eyes, his face, her fingers sliding around his waist, then holding on by fistfuls of his T-shirt. "Aye."

He grinned, and felt, in that instant, that the world was his to claim and conquer. He took her mouth fiercely, confidently, and urged her to take the same. And that she did. But just as he thought to take her up to the loft where he'd imagined her so many times, where he'd wondered how it would be to wake up to her scent on his pillows every morning, she ducked out of his arms and stepped away.

Drawing in breaths in deep gulps, she dipped her chin, one hand propped on her hip, the other scooping her long hair away from the heated skin of her face.

He knew better than to go to her, crowd her any further. There should be something he could say . . . but he'd said it all. It was up to her now—which was terrifying, really. He knew she was of like mind with him, but still wasn't quite certain she would see it through.

"It's . . . a lot," she said when she'd gotten her breath

back under control, her back still to him. "And it's good. So good. I just . . ." She finally turned to him. "I need to be better at trusting it will always be good." She lifted a quick hand. "I don't mean smooth, no bumps. I mean—"

"That I won't up and abandon you," he said, understanding as much as he could just how deep those scars ran. He honestly couldn't fathom the rootlessness she felt, knowing it had been caused by people making active decisions to put her in that place. She'd overcome so much of her past. On the surface, she could be considered a success. Smart, educated, good career, better head on her shoulders. Bright, funny, forward thinking. Strong. So damn strong. And yet . . . this was her soft white underbelly. And the power that her fear of abandonment had over her wasn't to be underestimated.

"It's stupid," she said.

"On the contrary. It's the very opposite of that. Self-protection has it all over self-destruction."

"Until one becomes the other," she said quietly.

"Och, Grace. Ye see that's where I have faith in you. You're too stubborn, too independent, too strong, and too damn smart to let yourself be doomed by your own fear. You might hate it, you might want to run from it . . . but in the end, you won't."

"What makes you so certain of that? You're so certain, but you don't know me. You don't know—"

"Don't I?" he countered. "Has anything I've just said to you shown that I don't understand you? You're here, aren't you? That took courage." He took one step closer, but that was all.

"Since you know so much," she countered, "you'll know that I need time." She laughed, more a short hiccup. "Isn't this kind of hilarious? The ladies' man and perennial bachelor is the guy preaching about grabbing what you want and holding on tight . . . and I'm the one needing to step back, take a breath. You know, I wondered once, when I realized that you had so much more depth than your swagger and charm—"

"When was that?"

"When you first mentioned Alex to me, that very first day. I saw that look in your eye, that emotion, that she'd meant something special to you. And I thought 'huh, who would have thunk it?' Then I learned that she'd chosen someone else, and I wondered how that was possible. To have someone like you actually fall . . . only to turn you down. I thought that would take a strength I wasn't sure I'd have. I'd be too locked into the fairy-tale ideal of it to say no, even if maybe I should. Only now, here I am, and here you are, and it's all of that and so much more . . . and I'm the one, in the end, who isn't strong enough to say yes. To take what's being offered."

"Grace—"

He was interrupted by the sound of the panel door being slid open. Or opened wider. Apparently his visitor had been standing there for a while, unnoticed in the heat of the moment.

Cami strolled into the room and walked right up to Brodie. "Well, that's your loss," she told Grace. Then she smiled at Brodie. Every hair on his neck lifted at the barracuda gleam in her dark eyes before she turned back to Grace. "Just as well you bow out now, and bow out *gracefully*." Cami laughed at the little pun, and there wasn't the slightest bit of warmth in it.

Brodie hadn't completely recovered from the shock of Cami's sudden appearance, so he didn't react in time, didn't calculate her next move.

"What this man needs is a woman who knows exactly what he has to offer." Cami turned her hot chocolate brown eyes on him and her smile twisted wider still. "And exactly what to do with him." With that, she wrapped herself around him and kissed him.

His body was still hard from being wrapped up with Grace and leaped, quite declaratively, at the physical contact, separate and apart from his brain, which had instantly recoiled.

But it was enough for Cami. Eyes wide with a dark thrill at his apparent response, she turned while still draped all over him and leered at Grace. "Happily, I know just the woman for that." She looked back to Brodie and raked her long nails through his hair. "Besides, what with you and Daddy working together, my powerful connection to the town council, and"—she rubbed up against him, her pupils all but drowning her eyes when his damn body jumped right back—"the firestorm we're about to start, we'll be one unstoppable force."

It was as if he was in a horrible bad dream, his feet in quicksand, his body immobile as all of his brain synapses fired at once and he couldn't seem to force them to regroup against the more primal responses of his body.

She leaned in and whispered loud enough for Grace to hear, "You did tell her about our little deal, didn't you, darling? She knows all about us, right? Maybe she's simply not cut out to be the kind of . . . understanding partner you really need. But then, so few women are."

Over Cami's shoulder, Brodie's gaze was locked directly on Grace's. Her expression had gone completely blank.

Chapter 21

It was The Moment. The one Grace had been wondering about. The one when she'd know, when she'd figure out what she really wanted, or more to the point, what she was willing to do to get it. And there it was. Right in front of her. Wearing a tight melon suit and designer heels.

She'd never thought Cami Winstock would be the final piece to the puzzle, but then, did that matter? What mattered was, in that moment, when Cami threw down her overly tweezed and made-up and Botox-enhanced gauntlet, Grace didn't even have to think twice about snatching it right up and taking a big ol' swing with it.

"Cami—" Brodie said, teeth gritting, at the same moment Grace stalked—*stalked*—across the short space between her and the melded twosome. He didn't even have time to peel Cami off before Grace took care of that little matter for him.

"Excuse me," she said, taking Cami by the shoulder and spinning her around.

Only because Cami had been stunned by the move was she yanked and spun so easily. Well, that and the fact that the tottering heels she was wearing didn't do very well on bare cypress planking. She wobbled quite a few comical steps before gathering herself and her swinging little matching purse. She whirled back around, her gaze set-tling on Brodie, not Grace. "You're going to let her *man-handle* me? Since when do you let a woman fight your battles?"

Brodie stepped forward, apparently freed from his frozen statue status. He switched easily and swiftly to an-gry protective male and appeared to have every intent of escorting Cami from the premises.

But Cami whirled on Grace and it was her turn to stalk. *She got her sea legs quickly,* Grace thought, reacting a split second too late as Cami swung a hand and slapped her square across the cheek with the open flat of her palm.

Brodie launched himself toward them, but Grace lifted a hand. "No." When he looked as if he was going to do what he damn well pleased anyway, she said, "No! This isn't your battle." She turned to Cami. And smiled. "It's mine."

Once again Cami turned her gaze to Brodie, apparently fully expecting him to defend her, only to gape when he looked at Grace, then lifted his hands and stepped back. "You only get one swing, Camille," he warned quietly.

Deadly quiet, Grace thought.

"And you've used that one up." He glanced at Grace, winked, and motioned for her to continue.

Cami swung back to Grace, putting her purse into the motion. Though Brodie reacted on instinct to leap in and snag it, Grace was closer. And faster. She grabbed the purse and twisted it, which torqued the chain handle, then used that leverage to spin Cami into her body—two moves that Cami definitely hadn't seen coming. Grace yanked Cami's bound arms up behind her back and planted her chin on the shorter woman's shoulder.

Pressing her mouth close to Cami's ear, Grace said slowly and distinctly, "I'm only going to tell you this one time. I don't appreciate how you used me to play some twisted game of cat-and-mouse with Brodie. We've come to terms with it, and now I'm going to come to terms with you. I definitely don't appreciate a woman—any woman—coming in, unannounced and uninvited, to the private quarters I'm sharing with my significant other and draping herself all over him like some cheap whore." She leaned closer and tightened her hold when Cami struggled at the insult. "The next time you think about sticking your tongue where it doesn't belong, you better pray I'm not around anything with a sharp edge on it."

Cami's face had initially gone beet red with fury. Now it was pale white.

"Do we have an understanding?" When Cami didn't reply, Grace gave a little jerk to the chain.

Cami nodded, then through gritted teeth growled, "Let . . . me . . . go."

"Sure. But then it's do not pass go, do not cop so much as another gaze at this man, and head straight to the exit." She released the chain, stepping back at the same time.

Cami stumbled at the sudden shift, but righted herself quickly. She kept her gaze on Grace, her eyes hot coals. "You think you've scored some hot piece of ass by playing Buffy the Vampire Slayer or something in front of your little boyfriend here." She paused. "Emphasis on the word *boy*. Letting you fight his battles. It's pathetic. You deserve each other." She all but spat the last words out. "However, if you think there will be no repercussions, She-Ra, that's where you are sadly mistaken."

"Okay, I'm done," Brodie said matter-of-factly. He took Cami's arm, held on tighter when she tried to jerk it free, and double-stepped her straight through the open panel door, where he promptly let her go, then wiped his hands on his pants, as if needing to clean them. "Don't threaten me, don't threaten Grace. Before you run to Daddy so he can fight your battles— If you want to talk pathetic, getting your own father to pimp for you?" He made a *tsk*ing sound. "That's not only pathetic, it's disgusting."

"The only schooner you'll be building will be the kind they shove in a glass bottle," Cami said, shaking with rage and indignation.

"Now, now. That sounds like a threat. And you're standing on my property." He looked over his shoulder. "Grace, darling? Where did I put my gun?"

Cami made a smirking face; then, when he swung a cold smile back at her, seemed to reconsider how serious he might be and took several steps down the short path to the docks. "It won't be your property for long. Mark my words. Daddy will take his business elsewhere, and if I can't sell the rest of this godforsaken place out from under you, I'll buy it my goddamn self." She looked past him to Grace. "You two have made yourselves the wrong enemy here. I'll see to it that neither of you earns so much as a single dollar from anyone in Blueberry Cove or anywhere else. When you run back to Ireland with your tail between your legs, please take that two-bit—"

That was as far as she got. Brodie moved so fast even Grace was amazed. His hand went over Cami's mouth and his face was up in hers so fast both women's eyes went as wide as they could go. "Enough," he bit out.

"Yes, is this Chief McRae?" Grace said loudly into her cell phone. "We have a trespasser here. She's making personal and physical threats and refuses to leave. Could you send a cruiser please? Who is it? Camille Weathersby."

Grace paused and went to stand in the open panel doorway. "Sirens?" She smiled as Brodie kept a lock grip on Cami's arm, and let his hand off her mouth just in time for a string of exceedingly foul language to erupt . . . straight into the receiver Grace held out so helpfully. "Yes, yes she is definitely dangerous. We're afraid here. Very afraid," she added calmly. "Don't be worried about causing a scene.

Just get here fast. And with great force." She paused. "Yes, Chief. We appreciate it. Yes, I'll hold."

"How *dare* you?" Cami said. Since Blueberry was a very small town and the sirens were already echoing in the distance, she made a quick retreat. "You haven't heard the last of this," she screeched over her shoulder as she took quick, tiny little steps over the planks, then the gravel lot at the far end of the property.

"Oh, but at least I've had the last of you," Brodie said under his breath.

Grace ducked under his arm and he pulled her tight up against him. Once Cami had peeled her little Audi coupe out of the lot, spinning gravel and shouting more epithets at them, he turned and wrapped Grace in a fierce hug.

"Don't ever do that again," he demanded, and she could feel his heart pounding hard against her chest. Then he leaned back and shot her a grin so wide and so wicked, she could only grin back. "Where the hell did you learn that maneuver? And thank you, by the way, for demonstrating on someone else before you were forced to use it on me."

"From Ford after his first tour. I begged him to show me some of the close-quarters combat maneuvers and he finally gave in. At the time, I thought it was just to shut me up, but I think he realized the situation I was in, and that it wasn't stable. He'd already re-upped and was going back overseas, so . . ." She lifted a shoulder.

"Well, I owe him a debt of gratitude for giving you what he could to help you protect yourself." Brodie looked as if he was uncertain about what he wanted to ask, but then he relented. "Was it like that for you? Did you have to defend yourself? Physically?"

She shook her head. "I mean in school, sometimes. Bullies love the new kid, and I was always the new kid. But no, I wasn't so much a victim of any kind of physical abuse as I was just neglected. Completely."

"Ah, Gracie," he said, pulling her in, bussing her on the forehead. When she stiffened, he pulled immediately back. "Dammit, your cheek. Let's get some ice."

"No, it's not that. She really didn't get that much contact. I—Ford taught me how to absorb a hit, to move with it and not deflect it, so it looked a lot worse than it was. It wasn't that, it was . . . Ford used to call me Gracie. Well, I guess he still does because—" She looked off, then laughed and looked up, and blinked a few times. "It's nothing, it's okay."

"No, it's his. I can respect that." Brodie tucked her close and they went inside and closed the door. The ringing of Grace's phone still clutched in her hand startled them both. She'd forgotten she was holding for the police to arrive. "Hi. I'm sorry. Yes, she's left the premises. I'm not sure where she went. No, no, we don't need to file a report. Thank you, though. Yes, I promise to call back if she comes back on the property. You have my absolute word on that." She hung up and looked at Brodie. Now that the adrenaline was wearing off, she felt mildly queasy and a bit shaky. "Do you think I really screwed things up for us? Her family is pretty powerful."

"I don't know. But I do know that she's not well liked. No one has run against her husband for town council because of his connections to the Winstocks, but no one likes him, either. Brooks, I think, is more respected, but if word were to get out that he was actually trying to facilitate his daughter's extracurricular liaisons—"

Grace gaped, then winced. Maybe her cheek was a little more bruised than she'd thought. Along with the adrenaline leaving, the feeling was coming back to her face. "You weren't kidding about that?"

"Oh, I would never kid about anything like that."

"I mean, I'd heard, you know, the gossip about her, but her own *father*? Really? That's sick."

"I think they see it purely as business leverage."

"Which is even more disgusting." She turned and pulled Brodie around to face her. "If I ruined your chance to build that schooner—"

"Shh." He leaned down and kissed her gently on the mouth, then tugged her over to the kitchen and pulled out a chair. "Sit. I'll make an ice pack." He pulled a bottle of painkillers from the cupboard and a bottle of water from the fridge. "Here." He set about making the cold pack, talking over the rattling sound of the ice. "It wouldn't have mattered. I had no intention of allowing her anywhere near me, despite the arrangement I had with her father, and I'd already let him know that. So she was either going to sneak around and do her evil deeds to get back at me or do what she did today. I have to say, that while I didn't much care for the first part, the second part"—grinning, he wheeled around from the counter and handed Grace the ice pack—"that part pretty much kicked ass. Literally."

Grace pressed the pack to her cheek, winced at the cold, then sighed in relief as it started to soothe the bruised skin.

He grimaced as he looked more closely at her cheek. "You could press charges."

Grace shook her head. "I think I've made things bad enough." She smiled with half her mouth. "Besides, I think we're pretty even. I wasn't particularly kind with that arm maneuver."

Brodie smiled, but there was a look of serious concern there, too.

Grace reached over and put her hand on his arm. "I really am sorry about that part. I know you say it was inevitable, but no way is this not worse than it would have been."

"You know, I don't know about that. Maybe it was going to take something like this to finally get through her head. Like I said, they're not well liked. The fact that you called the police means that word will get out."

"But I didn't tell them anything. I mean, not anything juicy."

"Won't matter. I'm sure the town gossips will take great pleasure in filling in the blanks." He glanced at her. "If you happen to have a conversation with someone on your phone, say Langston . . . or even the dial tone . . . and you mention some of the details in private, only within hearing distance of even one of your crew? You're a town legend overnight."

"My crew? But they're a bunch of guys."

Brodie gave her pitying look. "Worst of the bunch. Have you met Fergus McCrae? He's second only to Delia." He snapped his fingers. "There you go. Talk to your new friend Delia. Woman to woman."

At that, Grace whipped her head to the brass clock on the wall. "I forgot she's coming over to talk to me about Ford after she gets the dinner shift done and night shift started."

Grace relaxed when she realized that was still a few hours away yet. "I don't know if I'm up to that tonight. It's been . . . a hell of a day." She glanced at Brodie. "So, this thing with Cami. I take it this isn't the first time she's tried to have her womanly way with you. You rejected her. That's why she screwed you over with the boathouse deal."

"It's as good a guess as any. She more or less confirmed it."

"She said you were going to use the contract money to get up to speed on the taxes and clear up the ownership on the rest of the property."

Brodie nodded.

"So what happens if your deal with her father falls through?"

"It hasn't yet, no matter Cami's histrionics. Winstock really wants this, and I'm not so sure he's willing to let his spoiled brat of a daughter ruin it for him. If he wants the schooner here, he's going to have to work with me to gain deep-harbor access and docking, even if someone else builds the boat. I may not have cleared the remaining buildings with the tax office yet, but the big docks are mine. I took care of that when I made sure my boathouse was secure. He'd have to go to Blue, and I don't see that happening. Blue won't have any part of that deal, especially when he finds out what else Winstock wants."

"Which is?"

"A yacht club." Brodie motioned in the direction of the bigger boathouse. "He wants to turn the big place into some high-dollar boys' club, but I've already got a way around that. He can run the schooner trips here, and have his little club around the cove where it's quieter. Plenty of places to tie up the kinds of boats his mates will be sailing. I need the big house for the lumber mill, so if he wants his schooner, he can't have the boathouse. It's as simple as that."

Grace took in all this information, then decided it was just too much to sort through and shelved it for later. "You think there's still a chance you'll build it?"

"I honestly don't know. It will all come down to whether Winstock wants to be a businessman or a father. I'm pretty sure that even as spoiled as his daughter is, he didn't get to be the powerful man he is by letting his own interests take a backseat."

"You trust him? To deal squarely with you?"

"I trust the attorney I'll hire to do the contract." Brodie slid a glance at her. "How are you at contract law?"

"Not my specialty," she said with a wincing smile. "But I know folks who are very good at it and can possibly recommend someone up here. If my former coworkers don't,

I'm sure Langston can." She snapped her fingers. "Wait, that's it!" She looked at Brodie and put the ice pack down. "Langston is college buddies with Brooks Winstock. They went to Harvard together. I don't know how close they were or if that was just Cami being Cami, but Langston could definitely bring some leverage to the table." Grace sat back, inordinately pleased with herself. Then she realized Brodie wasn't smiling. He was looking at her with something close to a stunned expression. "What? I'm not kidding. Langston's clout makes Brooks Winstock's power look like—"

"No no, it's not that. In fact, that's bloody brilliant."

"So, what is it then?"

"You'd do that? I mean, this is your chance to get back to that idyllic setting you were hoping for. No big schooner, no big shipyard."

"Yes, well, you're assuming Cami won't just burn my place down." Grace leaned forward when his expression instantly tightened. "I'm kidding. Maybe you're right and we should spread the word a little on Cami's threats, just so the local authorities are on their toes." She looked back at him and her smile faded. "I know my initial vision is going to change. But what the heck? Everything has changed since I've gotten here. I don't recognize a single thing about my life. And every bit of the change is in the very best way possible."

She stood and held out her hand. He took it, and she tugged him up, then walked into his arms. "I have no idea where the ship deal and the inn deal will go after Cami's fury and Langston's possible intervention—which he will relish by the way. *Relish.* I don't know what's next. I do know one thing, though."

Brodie tugged her in closer, then wrapped his arms around her. "What is that?"

"The moment Cami put her hands on you, I wanted them off." Grace deliberately put her hands on his chest and smoothed them slowly to his shoulders, then around his neck, and raked her fingers up into his hair.

He groaned. "You have all day to stop doing that."

"I was hoping for a lot longer. Not only did I not want her hands on you, but I'm pretty sure I don't want anybody else's hands on you, either." She tipped up on her toes and kissed his mouth, then nipped at his bottom lip. "Except mine," she whispered against his lips.

"And here I thought having Cami over was a really bad idea," he murmured, then laugh-winced when she rapped him lightly in the shins with her booted toe.

He spun her around, lifting her feet off the floor before she could aim another kick, then pulled her in and kissed her soundly, deeply . . . and quite confidently. When he lifted his head, Grace saw that same deep sparkle she'd noted once before, only there were no shutters on it holding back even a sliver of what he was feeling.

"You know what? I don't care if you say it," he told her.

Her whole body started to shake. She knew, without a doubt, where he was going. And she didn't even try to stop him.

"I don't care if you ever say it, which is an utter lie even as it trips right off my tongue. I sure as hell never thought I'd be the first one to say it, but God almighty, Christ in heaven, I love you, Grace Maddox."

The sensation that shot through her straight to her toes was unmitigated joy. Grace had never once heard those words in her entire life. And she was thrilled about that fact . . . because she'd saved the best for first . . . and last.

Part of her wanted to gush the declaration right back, but it was his moment. She kind of liked that he'd gone that far out on a limb for her. She knew from the broad grin on his handsome, sexy face that he was pretty damn proud of himself, too. So she let him keep all the thunder. And simply reveled in it.

"Well," she said, toying with the hair on his neck, reveling also in that little shudder of pleasure she felt ripple over him every time she did it. "Next time, it would help if you'd at least look like you wanted to fend her off. Or even, you know, actually physically did that. She's fierce, but if I can take her, I'm pretty sure you could, too. You know, not in the biblical sense, but"—she whooped out a laughing squeal as he scooped her over his shoulder—"like that!" She crowed. "Only maybe more in a dragging her out by her ankles kind of way. Or by her hair."

"Bloodthirsty little wench," he said, sounding fairly approving about it. "I was just about to do . . . something. Honest. I just couldn't switch gears fast enough and she—"

"Was all up in your very aroused business, I know. You men, so controlled by that one little thing."

"Little, ye say? Really?" He made his way up the iron steps to the loft without once hitting her head on anything, then laughed when she smacked his ass.

"So sensitive. Frail ego. It must be such a challenge, having to—" The rest went in a whoosh of breath as she found herself flat on her back on his bed, with him right down on top her.

"I know a wee bit about sensitive parts." He pinned her wrists to the bed. "And my ego isn't one of them." He leaned in, nipped at her chin, then sucked her bottom lip into his mouth, making her groan and squirm under him. "Here, let me show you."

He left her arms pinned by her head, and started a very delectable, intensely detailed journey down her torso.

"You know"—she gasped as he pulled her top off in one swift tug—"we're never going to get an inn or a ship built because whenever we're together for more then two minutes, we end up—"

"Doing this?" He tugged down the zipper of her pants, wasting no time pulling them down just far enough to put his tongue right—oh sweet goodness—right where she wanted it most.

She bucked hard against his mouth and climbed straight up, then straight over, in the fastest, most intense orgasm she'd ever had. Shuddering and panting, she said, "Okay. So . . . maybe you have that sensitive part thing down."

He leaned in again and she all but dragged him up by his hair and shoulders.

"So impatient," he said, chuckling and grinning, his green eyes dancing.

It was in that moment, staring into his handsome face with that wicked grin, mischief alight in his beautiful Irish eyes, that she knew she'd do more than fight to keep him. She'd do whatever it took to never lose him.

That was the real Moment.

She cupped his cheek when he would have leaned in and rendered her incapable of speech. "At the risk of ruining this delightful interlude or being forever accused of speaking in the heat of the moment . . ." She trailed off until her words sank in and he slowly lifted his head, his expression sobering in almost fearful anticipation. If she hadn't known it before, she definitely did just then. He was so strong and bold, and yet, at his core, just as vulnerable as she was. "Brodie Monaghan, I love you right back."

Chapter 22

A knock on the side of the open panel door had Grace jumping guiltily and thrusting behind her back the catalog she was looking through.

Delia walked in and gave her a wondering look, clearly having seen the quick dodge. "Catching you at a bad time?"

"No, no." Grace felt her cheeks heat even as she acknowledged how silly she was being. She pulled the catalog out.

"Sex toys?" Delia shook her head and made a *tsk*ing sound. "Here I always thought Monaghan could back up the charm with the goods."

Grace laughed and blushed for real. "No, it's bed-and-breakfast porn."

Delia's eyebrows climbed. *"Really,"* she said, drawing the word out. "I've never heard of it. Share." She held out her hand and wiggled her fingers. "Come on, I'm the one not getting any, not you. Have a heart."

"Not fictional B&B porn," Grace said laughing. "It's a catalog to order decorating items for small inns and B&B's. I found one online with nautical items, and it just came in the mail today."

"Um, Grace"—Delia leaned in, waving away the catalog—"I hate to tell you, but it's not porn if you actually *have* an inn. Then it's just business. Nothing to feel guilty about." When Grace just gave her a *really?* look, Delia continued. "Okay. My porn is kitchenware catalogs and pamphlets full of really sharp knives. Hell, it's one of the few fun things about being a business owner."

Grace clutched the catalog to her chest and beamed. "I know!" She fanned her face. "It's just, now that we're actually going to start the renovation, there's even a longer list of things to be done beforehand. I have no business wasting time on future dreaming and drooling."

"Well then, you should make time. It's important." Delia looked around and whistled. "Wow, I can't believe how much you've accomplished in such a short time. Well, you and your manslaves." She grinned at Grace. "Shouldn't we all just have a ready crew of manslaves? I tell everyone they should try it. I know I couldn't get through the day without mine." She tapped her finger to her chin. "You know, maybe I'm being shortsighted by only having them actually work for me. Maybe they should really, you know, *work* for me."

Grace barked out a laugh, then winced a little, her cheek still tight. "I'm sorry about the other night, I was—"

"Being all femme fatale, I know. I heard." She leaned over and took a look at Grace's face. "Quite the shiner you've got there."

"You should have seen it two days ago. How did you know? Brodie said you were good, but—"

"I'm Delia. All knowing, all seeing." She reached out, but didn't touch Grace's cheek. "I'm not so sure I wouldn't have pressed charges on that."

Grace shook her head. "Next time you see Cami, pat her on the shoulder." She let out a little smile. "Her left one. Maybe put some oomph in it."

"Ah." Delia's grin was approving. "I take it back, Grasshopper. You have learned many useful skills."

"I have Miyagi Ford to thank for that," Grace said, laughing and striking a pose. "Wax on, wax off." She noted the flicker of . . . something . . . cross Delia's face and sobered. "Delia, you know you don't have—we don't have to talk about Ford. I mean, at some point I'd like to, but you can pick your time, or—"

"No, it's not that. I was going to back out, make the excuse that it was his story to tell, but then I realized it's just as much my story as his, and I was just being a chickenshit. I'm never a chickenshit, so why start now?"

Grace snorted as Delia looked around again.

"We're alone," Grace told her. "The guys are done for the day."

"I heard Langston deVry was back in town."

"You heard right." Grace tilted her head. "You want to meet him?"

Delia made a *who, me?* face of innocence, then cracked a smile. "Sure. You know, if it works out without looking all staged or anything." Then she grabbed Grace's arm in mock urgency. "I'll pay you. Name your price."

Grace just laughed. "Wow. If I'd known, I'd have arranged something sooner. So, are you an older guy kinda gal, or . . . ?"

"I'm a guy who can show a girl a good time kinda gal. Especially when there's private jets involved."

"Yeah, well, with Langston, there's often quickie weddings. How do you feel about that?"

"I've managed to avoid those shackles since I was nineteen, so I think I'm bulletproof there."

Grace just shook her head, murmured, "Sucker," under her breath, and grinned, which made Delia laugh. "Don't say you weren't warned. Don't go primping now. He and Brodie and Brooks Winstock are out at the Point house having a powwow."

Delia dropped her hands from where she'd been fussing

with the hair she'd swept up in a quick knot on the back of her head. "I heard Langston leased out Proctor's old place. Nice digs." She looked at Grace consideringly. "Why aren't you out there? This is about the schooner deal, right?"

"How do you even know that?"

"I'm Delia. I know everything," she repeated.

"Sensei Delia," Grace said with a mock bow, not sure how they'd slipped so easily into a fast friendship, but very glad they had.

"If only the rest were as aware of my greatness as you." Delia sighed. "So, what, they didn't invite you because they were afraid of your Wonder Girl superpowers?"

"Privately, that's what I think," Grace said, checking her nails with studied calm. "Men . . . can't handle a girl who can manhandle other girls."

"I know. You'd think they'd be all over that."

"Right?" Grace said with mock outrage.

They both laughed until Delia wheezed and Grace was holding her cheek in pain.

"Well, even though they are inherently weak of mind, they are strong of body, so we forgive."

"We do." Grace sighed. "It has its benefits."

"Don't gloat." Delia reached in her pocket. "Do you have a Kleenex?"

Grace went off to her little room area in the corner and came back with a box. "The dust in here is awful."

"You're still sleeping here?"

Grace knew they were well past any kind of shyness or embarrassment, but her relationship with Brodie was still new, at least to the townsfolk. To her, it felt like she'd known him forever "Define *still*."

Delia laughed. "Good. I'm glad. Breathing all this in couldn't have been good for you. And his loft space is amazing."

Grace shot her a quick look, but she knew damn well Brodie hadn't lied about never sleeping with Delia.

Delia hooted, anyway. "Boy, if you could see your face right now. I know why Cami was scared." She lifted her hands. "Don't hurt me. I never touched him. Alex is a friend, and she snuck me in when she was done with the remodel so I could see it. I love what she did." Delia paused. "You're really okay with all that, aren't you." It wasn't a question.

Grace nodded. "Of course, I haven't met the great Alex yet, so maybe I won't feel so confident when she's like, awesome, but I trust Brodie."

"You should. So that's good."

Grace agreed. "He's a good man. He has my back."

"He even trusts you to kick ass all on your own when necessary."

"Oh God. Is everyone saying that? I mean, are they going to tease him about it?"

"Every day for the rest of his life," Delia said, smiling. "Myself included." She held up her hand. "We kid because we love, and he knows that. But yeah, he's totally screwed there. To his credit, he's handling it quite well."

Grace gaped. "It's already happening? To his face?"

"Well, honey, it's no fun unless he's there to hear it." Delia patted Grace's arm. "He's been by. He takes the ribbing and he defends your honor as well as giving you total props. Personally, I think he loves it that you kicked Cami's ass, and so does everybody else. You know he's head over heels for you, right? I mean, he's a goner."

Something flashed across Grace's face because Delia snatched her arm right up and pulled her a step closer. "He said it, didn't he? Oh my God." She didn't wait or apparently need confirmation. "Did you say it back?"

Grace figured there was no point in trying to dodge the

question. "It's possible I might have said something like that."

Delia spontaneously pulled her into her arms and gave her a big hug. "I'm thrilled for you, honey." She set her back. "Don't you worry about the ship deal."

"What? You know what's going to happen there, too? That's impossible. Brodie wasn't sure if they could make it happen. I asked him if he even wanted to do any kind of deal with a guy like Winstock, but he said that where business is concerned, Winstock is a pretty straight arrow. Brodie did his due diligence, checked out his other business dealings." Grace casually lifted a shoulder, then gave Delia a little grin. "And when I did my own, I found out the same thing. Can't endorse his parenting skills, but for all he appears to be aggressive in business, he's fair."

"Easier to do when you own every damn thing," Delia said, but she was nodding in agreement.

"See, that's my bigger worry. I mean, the deal between the two men might be fair and square, but you know Cami won't let things go. I don't know her well, but I got to see her eyes up close and personal, and she's not simply going to pick a new target. Heck, she's had it in for Brodie for almost the entire time he's been here."

"He told you about all that. Good."

"Yes, he did."

"Well, as I said, I think some of the Winstock power is going to shift. Building the tall ship and holding true title and deed to the property where Mr. Winstock wants to park his little boat is going to give Brodie back the kind of clout that his family used to have back in the day."

Grace groaned. "But Ted still has the council in a stranglehold, and I imagine Cami has more than a little clout there. I still have a long laundry list of things I'll need permits and licenses and inspections for. I'm dreading it all the more now. She could keep me buried forever just with that."

"Till the fall maybe, but I wouldn't be so sure after that."

"What happens in the fall?"

"Elections. Ted has been positioning himself to run for mayor. Davis is finally retiring, so now he has a chance. He's never made any secret of the fact that he eventually wants to move on to a bigger, grander political arena, above and beyond our local politics. State at least, maybe bigger. Why do you think he and Cami picked each other? He wanted her clout and she wanted to ride his political aspirations."

"Why not just pursue politics on her own?"

"I don't know. Personally I think she's a misplaced Southern belle. She loves all the attention, but doesn't really want to do the work."

"She's apparently pretty successful in real estate."

Delia gave Grace a look. "Where else is anyone going to go when she can offer smooth sailing with all those permits and inspections you were talking about?"

Grace wasn't surprised. "True. Small-town stranglehold."

"Pretty much."

"So, what would change that?"

"Someone else running for Ted's council seat . . . although I'm trying to talk the candidate I have in mind into running straight at the mayor's office. He'll have final say over Ted and can rein him in. Hell, if we can get someone to run for Ted's old seat on the council, he could lose both races and lose his clout entirely."

Grace perked up. "Who do you want to run for mayor? Is it someone I know?"

Delia nodded. "Owen."

"Hartley?" Grace was somewhat stunned until she

thought about it for a moment. "He's lived here his whole life, I know that. And he's smart. Folks seem to love him."

"They do."

"And respect and admire him."

"In spades."

"But is he, you know, a leadership kind of guy? He seems pretty unimposing. Can he hold his own in a conflict?"

"Oh, he can take action, all right. Ask him sometime about staking out his own store and catching old Mrs. Darby breaking and entering, then locking her in a storage closet."

Grace's eyebrows climbed straight up her forehead. "Owen?"

Delia nodded, respect clear on her face. "It looks like Lauren has decided to go to college closer to home, in Bangor. She says she wants to come back and use her business degree to help run the family store. Owen had all these big dreams and ideas for her, but she's really a homebody at heart."

"I met her. She really seems like a great kid. I could see her doing bigger things, too."

Delia shrugged. "Well, she's got her heart set on following in the family footsteps. For all she has cover girl looks, she knows her hardware. She literally grew up in the business. So, I wouldn't count her out."

"Oh, me either. That's great."

The conversation dwindled and Grace shook her head in wonder. "Owen Hartley for mayor. I hope he does go for it." She glanced over at Delia, who was lost in thought, her hand stuck in her jacket pocket. "Is everything okay? Is there something else?"

Delia nodded. "You have no idea how badly I wanted to cheat and read this . . . for reasons that go well beyond my usual nosiness." She pulled out a folded and somewhat crumpled envelope. "It's for you. From Ford. He sent it in with one of Blue's guys, who brought it to me." She pulled it back when Grace gasped, and Grace knew she must have gone a little pale.

Delia looked concerned. "Okay, I think we need to talk first. Let me tell you what I know about your brother, then you can read this. No matter what it says, you'll at least have a shot at understanding where he's coming from. Okay?"

Grace couldn't talk past the instant lump that had formed in her throat, so she just nodded.

"Where can we go and still be private? I think we need somewhere we can sit down."

"End of the dock?" Grace managed, swallowing hard. "I drink my coffee out there every morning. But I don't talk. I guess our voices would carry. Wait, I know. Brodie's boat."

"The big one? *Godspeed?*"

Grace nodded. "Why? Are you not fond of boats? It's tied up. It doesn't rock that much."

"No. I've just—ever since he sailed in to the harbor when he first arrived I've been dying to get an up close inside look."

"He sailed into Maine?" Grace asked.

Delia tilted her head to the side. "How did you think he got his boat here?"

Grace laughed. "I don't know. I mean, I know he built it, and he's here and it's here, but I never put it all together. He has the sloop, too."

"He built that here as a calling card of sorts, to get the ball rolling. As for *Godspeed,* I don't think he came straight across. I think he went south, to the islands, then came up the eastern seaboard." She smiled at Grace. "Intimidating to you, or sexy as hell?"

Grace managed to smile past the dozen other things her

brain was spinning around. "Both. You've never been on it? You mean, I know something the great Delia doesn't know?"

"Only for as long as it takes to get us out there. Come on. And bring the tissues."

Grace gulped, but she grabbed the box. Knowing that Whomper loved the Point house as much as the docks, she hadn't minded when he'd jumped into Brodie's truck with him, but she was thankful it was going to be just her and Delia. She wasn't sure she was ready for Delia's revelations, but what other choice did she have? She wanted to know about her brother. She hoped she didn't regret wanting to know.

Once Delia had oohed and ahhed over every inch of the boat, Grace rolled open all the windows and they settled belowdecks in the lounge area between the galley and the passageway to Brodie's stateroom.

"So . . . I'm not sure where to begin," Delia said.

"You sent me the note, asking me to come see Ford." Grace settled herself more deeply into the cushions, kicking off her boat shoes and tucking her feet up under her legs. "It's funny. I had a hundred different stories I came up with about who you were and who you were to him. Good ones," she added. "Because I didn't doubt you were trying to do a good thing."

"Why didn't you come, then?"

"Because he didn't ask me," Grace said simply. "And I knew he didn't know you had. I compromised and sent him an invitation to my college graduation. He never even acknowledged it, so I didn't regret not coming. I mean, of course I did. I second- and third- and forty-fifth-guessed it, but in the broad scope of things, I felt I'd done the right thing and protected myself. When I saw him out on Sandpiper, he told me he never got it."

"Then I'm sure he didn't," Delia said so matter-of-factly that Grace didn't question her belief. She just didn't know where that trust came from.

"He also said you weren't his girlfriend. So . . . who were you to him? Who are you now? I guess I should have asked that before we jumped right into girl talk. I had planned to, but . . . that just felt . . . I don't know."

"Personal," Delia supplied. "It's right that you want to know. And I like that it was easy for us, natural."

Grace nodded.

"It wasn't like that with Ford, but it might have been, under other circumstances."

"So, tell me how you know him. Are you why he came to Maine? Or did you come here for him?" Grace knew Delia's diner was a long-standing business in the Cove, but had never asked about her backstory or heard talk of it. "No one has talked to me about Ford. They still don't. But I'm pretty sure everyone knows I'm his sister. They seem to respect him, so . . . I guess I'm surprised. They don't mind telling me every last thing about Brodie's history and Cove history, but—"

"They were being respectful. More toward Ford, you understand, than for your benefit. They want to see him happy, or at least more . . . settled, or . . . I'm not even sure what the right word is. They wanted to make sure you were here for good reasons, good for his well-being, anyway. You seemed to pass that test easily enough, putting down roots and being very open about wanting to honor the history and legacy of the boathouse. Until the two of you spoke and things moved forward, folks just kept a step back."

"Thinking I'd talk to him, he'd push me away, and I'd run?"

"Something like that, maybe." Delia gave Grace a considering look. "He didn't do that, did he?"

"I'm not sure what, exactly, he did. I didn't give him much choice about talking to me. And we didn't leave it with a time or date to see each other again. Not that I thought we would. I told him to invite me or I'd just keep inviting myself. That I wanted to see what he did and just . . . find a bridge back to him."

"And?"

Grace lifted a shoulder. "I'm not sure what his take on our estrangement is. I was . . . pretty ugly to him the last time we saw each other."

Delia reached out, but let her hand drop just shy of taking hold of Grace's arm, leaving her a little bubble of self-containment and self-control, for which Grace thanked her profusely. "Oh, honey, that's not it. That's not near to being it. Trust me, he's been far, far uglier to himself about his role in your life than you could ever be to him, even if you tried."

"You weren't there. You don't know." Grace didn't say it accusingly, simply stated it as fact.

"I wasn't, no. But I have the benefit of hearing his side of that story."

Grace's gaze flew to Delia's. "He told you? About that day?" Part of her felt betrayed to think that anybody else was privy to one of the most intensely personal, intensely private, and utterly shameful moments of her life. The other part felt an immense relief that it really wasn't some deep, dark secret only she bore, and bore alone. Still, she was afraid to ask what he'd said.

"You know, we're coming at this sideways. Let me tell you how I know Ford. Tell you our part of the story. The rest, well, that really is up to him." She lifted a hand to stall Grace's reply and added, "I reserve the right to change my mind about that if he doesn't pull his head out of his ass and do the right thing, but I have to give him that chance."

"That's fair. For what it's worth, he did seem to be taking on all the blame for us being apart." Grace settled back into the cushions again and admitted to still being a little hurt that someone—anyone—could know her brother so well to talk about him so . . . familiarly. "So, when did you meet him?"

"The first time? When he was twenty-two."

Grace shot her a look again, stunned silent.

"Yes, right after his first tour."

"He came—" Grace had to stop, clear the tightness from her throat. "He came to Maine back then?"

Delia nodded. "He'd re-upped, so he was going back. That I knew. I learned before he left again, that he'd gone to find you, had seen you, spent some time with you, made sure you were okay."

"Why did he come here?" Grace asked, not wanting to hear about how Ford thought she was okay. She hadn't been okay. No way could he have thought she was okay. But that had been her perspective at the time. Given what he'd seen, experienced, suffered, her life must have seemed like a cake walk, a safe stroll in the park. The very fact that she was in the States, and not where he was going, that she had a roof over her head and food in her belly, meant she was doing better than great. Understanding that so clearly was difficult. It meant she had to let go of the deep-seated anger she thought she'd let go so long ago . . . and very clearly had not. Not the deepest part.

"He came to see me," Delia replied. "He'd never met me, didn't know me . . . though he apparently knew a great deal about me. He'd served with my brother. Tommy was almost four years older than me, signed up when he was twenty-one. Your brother had just turned nineteen when they were assigned to the same unit. Tommy was older, but Ford . . . well, Tommy only mentioned him once or twice in his letters, but then he sucked at sending letters, so once or twice was fair to gushing. Apparently Ford was being groomed for special forces."

"Ranger school," Grace said, and Delia nodded.

"I think Tommy sort of wished he was cut out for that, but he knew he wasn't. He admired your brother. They were battle buddies. You know, where—"

"I know. They protect each other in combat."

"In everything."

Grace had a sick feeling in the pit of her stomach. She knew where this was going. Delia confirmed it in her next sentence.

"I lost my brother a week after he turned twenty-four. He'd been over there for three years and with Ford for most of it." She looked up and held Grace's gaze. "He was killed by one of those roadside homemade bombs. Destroyed their tank, injured Ford pretty badly. Tommy risked his life to drag Ford and two others back to safety, then got hit himself. Ford held him, even though he was already past saving, until their unit came and got them all out. He, uh . . ." She shook her head. "I've told this story before and . . . I'm sorry, it doesn't usually . . ."

"Delia," Grace said, her own voice choked with unshed tears. "It's okay."

Delia shook her head, regrouped. "Ford came back home to recuperate, but, like I said, had already decided to re-up. He came here to accompany Tommy home, to talk to me and my grandmother, to tell us about him, about how he died a hero. Ford wanted us to know that Tommy had been a good man, a good soldier."

Grace just sat there and took it all in, contrasting the story Delia was telling her with the brother who'd been a stranger to her after that first tour.

Ford had sent postcards, short notes, that first tour. She supposed she'd always imagined his life overseas the way you picture a war movie or something. She'd tried to picture the things he'd done and seen . . . except she couldn't. Not really. Not even close. She was only nine years old that first time. Then he'd been gone again. The cards and notes trickled to a stop during the next tours of duty.

"He did two more tours after that," Grace said. "Spent a lot of them overseas. He made it to the Rangers. I knew that much, but by then he'd largely left behind his life before the Army. Including me. The last time I saw him was when he'd gotten out for good. He was twenty-nine, I was sixteen. We hadn't connected, spoken, not so much as a word for—" Grace cut herself off. "It's . . . you're right. It's our story. It's not that I wouldn't tell you, but—"

"No, I agree. I mean, if it's ever something you want to let out just to let it out, I'm here. But . . . otherwise, like my stories about my brother, my feelings about him, they're mine. So I get to pick and choose. And so do you. No harm, no foul."

Grace nodded, thankful for Delia's no-nonsense, clear-cut attitude. "So . . . when did you see him again after that first time?"

"I-I'm not trying to hurt you, but I suspect this will, and I'm sorry for that. When . . . when he came here with Tommy, he stayed briefly after the funeral, and we spent some time together. When he went back overseas, he kept in touch. It was infrequent and always brief, but just when I suspected the worst had happened, some card or note would show up."

Grace ducked her chin. Delia was right. It was hard to hear. "I certainly don't blame you. You two are close to the same age. You shared a different kind of bond that connected you to his world in a way I never could."

"I am trying not to speak for him," Delia told her. "Just trying to give you information about him and let you draw your own conclusions, but I need to at least say to you that . . . the longer he stayed in the service, the more, well, damaged he became. What happened with him and Tommy was just the start. As a Ranger, well, Ford was very good at his job, which means he handled some very, very bad stuff. I know that after a while, he felt he was some kind of war machine and didn't fit in back here. I know he felt he was keeping you safe by letting you find your own life without him because he simply saw no way he'd ever fit into it." She lifted a hand. "It's a stupid guy way of thinking, and while that doesn't excuse it, it was where his head was, or where he put it, anyway."

Grace didn't say anything to that. Ford had tried to tell her much the same thing in what little he had said out on that pier. It was a lot to take in, and it was going to change things. But that's why she had come to Maine, wasn't it? She opted to not talk, to simply listen, and begin to absorb.

"When he and the Army finally parted ways for good, he came here because I guess it was the one place he knew he'd be accepted for who and what he was, by me anyway. And so, what happened between the two of you is my fault, I guess. I told him he had to find you, make things right with you. I knew how desperately I still missed my brother, and I knew you two had lost both your parents and had only each other, so I begged him to go find you, reunite with you, be your brother and let you be his sister. He . . . he wasn't in any shape for that, but he went. I know that's when you had that last blowout because he lashed out at me for begging him to go. He blamed me for a long time . . . because it was easier than blaming himself." She looked at Grace until she looked up. "He never, not once, blamed you."

"I know he said you weren't his girlfriend, but were you two . . . ?" Grace just let it trail off. She knew Delia knew what she was asking.

"No." Delia paused, then took a breath. "But . . . when

he came here with Tommy's remains, that first time, my husband had just left me and I'd lost my brother. Ford was hurting, too . . . and . . . there was one night when we . . . weren't just friends. It was grief and alcohol and a lot of other things that weren't smart or . . . entirely stupid, but we did what we did. We never did it again. After that, going forward, it was more that I was his connection to Tommy, to the person who'd died in his arms. I became something of a talisman, or a connection to home, or maybe to reality, or even sanity. But no, Grace, we were never lovers again . . . or really at all. Not in the way you mean."

Grace had looked down to where she was shredding tissues in her lap, but something in Delia's voice had her looking back up again. "Did you want to be?"

Delia opened her mouth, then closed it again. "My stock answer to myself and to the world is no. But that's probably a lie. Your brother is like no one I've ever met, before or since. Our relationship isn't normal, and I'm pretty sure it isn't healthy, or at least not in any way that I can make sense of. So, while I might have harbored a fantasy or two back in the day of being the one who would magically fix him, I grew up and got past that. The only one who can fix him is him. For all intents and purposes, I think he's done that."

"So, no regrets?"

"No," Delia said immediately, quietly, and quite sincerely. "We would not have been good for each other."

"Then. What about now?"

"When he came here after he got out and decided to stay here, we spent a lot of time together. Talking mostly, sometimes not doing anything. He just . . . I was a safe person for him to be around, so when he couldn't stand being alone, he'd be around me. But not in a sexual way, just . . ."

"Friends."

"I guess. Of a sort. I don't know how you'd describe it. He'd decided to go to school on the Army bill, to figure out what he was going to do, what he was going to be. He seemed to find his place there, which surprised the hell out of me. Not because he was really smart, I knew that, but that he'd conform to the world of academia the way he did. Maybe there was something of the military lifestyle in it that spoke to him. Except, in that world, he could be a complete loner, and he didn't have to save anybody."

Or kill anybody, Grace thought, but kept that to herself.

"That's when I sent you the note. I knew he kept track of you. Actually, I didn't know it from him, but in one of my weaker moments, I sort of snooped."

Grace was shocked to find she had a smile in her, she felt so emotionally swamped. It was real, and that felt good. "Not you."

"I know, right?" Delia smiled and it remained, though it was a bit sad . . . or maybe it was wistful as she continued. "Anyway, I snooped, realized he'd been keeping track of you all that time, or at least since he'd settled in Maine. I guess I felt like he was doing okay and that he clearly cared about you, so big stupid me sent you that letter. I guess I wasn't as past that fix-him fantasy as I thought I was."

"And when I didn't come?"

"Well, frankly, I didn't blame you. He might have kept track of you, and I might have understood all his twisted reasons for staying away from you and out of your life, but I couldn't find a single shred of evidence that he'd actually communicated with you in any way. So . . . no, I definitely didn't blame you. I just chalked it up to trying and hoped you'd maybe get some peace out of knowing he was okay. I'm sure I was as dead wrong about that as I was about the rest, but . . . my heart was truly—"

"I know." Grace stood and winced as the blood rushed to her feet. She'd needed her little cocoon of space in order to handle the information being shared. She held out her arms.

Delia all but lunged up off the couch, hopping a bit when the blood didn't flow quickly enough to her feet, either. She took Grace in a bear hug. "I feel like we're family, you and me," she said almost fiercely. "I mean, maybe not sisters, but just—"

"I know," Grace whispered just as fiercely. "I do, too. I have since you sat down across from me in that booth."

They hugged each other for another long moment, then finally broke apart, sniffling, then laughing a bit as they took in each other's rather emotionally ragged appearance.

"Thank you," Grace said. "I know that wasn't easy for you, either. And . . . you've given me a lot to think about."

Just then a scrabble of feet sounded on the dock above them, followed by a series of yips. Whomper. That meant—

"Grace?"

"Down here," she replied in response to Brodie's shout.

"Whomper just took off, so I figured you were here."

Grace and Delia took a moment to mop at their faces and wipe their noses with fresh tissue, then rolled their eyes in unison and gave up. Grace climbed above deck first. "Hi, I came out to—oh!" She broke off her explanation as soon as she saw who was with Brodie. "Hi, to you, too!"

She turned instantly back around and stopped Delia from climbing up behind her. She mouthed *Langston is here.*

Delia flushed a bright pink, which was exactly what Grace needed to pull herself together.

Head? Delia mouthed.

Grace pointed past her to the bathroom, then turned when Brodie bent down to see what she was doing.

"Everything okay?"

"Yep!" she said brightly . . . way too brightly. "I was just out here talking to Delia."

Brodie's face immediately smoothed and softened. "And? You good?" He held out a hand to help her over the rail and up the ladder to the dock, which was above them as the tide wasn't fully back in yet.

"Very good, yes." She knew that he knew there was a lot more to it, but he didn't press further since they weren't alone. "And the meeting?" She looked past Brodie to Langston, who beamed at her. Then his expression faltered when he saw her face and noticed she'd been crying.

"Very good," Brodie answered.

"You won't be having further issues with Winstock," Langston assured her. "Father or daughter. Is . . . everything okay?" He then turned his attention past Grace, his face instantly wreathed in a huge smile. "Oh my, now who is this lovely creature and why haven't we been introduced?"

Grace laughed when Langston's big muscular form almost sent Brodie headfirst into the harbor as he leaned past him to extend a hand to Delia.

Grace glanced over her shoulder. "This is—" She broke off and did a double take at Delia, who looked as if she'd just stepped out of a spa. "How did you—?" She leaned in and whispered, "You are *so* sharing those secrets with me. I mean, I'm as close to a sister as you'll get, right?"

"Honey, when you work in kitchens all day, you learn quickly how not to look like a stewed tomato. Now, are you going to introduce me or what? I'm not getting any younger here."

Introductions were made and Langston and Delia made their way down the dock. Since they clearly didn't care if

Brodie and Grace followed them and given the laughter floating back through the air behind them, probably preferred they didn't, Brodie held Grace back, then turned her to face him.

"You okay, luv? Truly?"

Her heart tipped right over. "I'm . . . it was a lot. But I'm okay. I have a lot to think about, and to rethink about." She reached into her shorts and got the envelope Delia had pressed into her hand as she'd climbed up above deck. "Ford sent me a letter."

"And?"

"I haven't read it yet. I think . . . I need a breather first. To clear my head. He came here because he'd served with Delia's brother. Her brother died in Ford's arms and he brought him back and helped bury him here. It was a long time ago, well before he came to live here full-time. Did you know that story?"

Brodie shook his head. "I didn't, no." He pulled her into a hug and just held on to her. "That's a lot."

"It is. There's more. It's insight I didn't have. And it will matter. It's just . . . I've had a lot of years to feel one way and I can't flip a switch."

"It takes time, luv. And that's okay. You have that."

She fingered the letter she had clutched to Brodie's broad back. "I know. But I also don't want to lose any more of the time I do have with him. I've lost too much already."

She straightened and stepped back, looking down at the letter.

"Do ye want me to take a look? Let you know if it's going to be a good thing or a hard thing?"

He's so earnest, she thought. *He so wants to do the right thing.* Impulsively, she leaned in and kissed him hard on the mouth.

"What was that for? Not that I mind, but I'll want to know so I can encourage it again."

She smiled, thinking of the other times they'd said that. "Just for being you."

"Well then, lucky me, eh?"

She laughed, and it felt . . . cathartic. Grounding. She realized that he really was her anchor, her port in the storm. She didn't have to figure out if she could trust him . . . she just did. It was a strong foundation they had, something to build on. She realized her newfound happiness wasn't Maine. It wasn't location, it wasn't occupation, or any of those things. Even what she was starting to build with her brother was only part of it. Getting to where she wanted to be with Ford would be better, stronger because she had Brodie supporting her along the way. And that was what she'd really come looking for—the love they were sharing and building with each other.

She slipped her arm around his waist and turned them to start down the dock. Whomper had raced ahead and was racing back. Seeing they were finally coming, he raced off again, which made her smile. Home. Family. Heritage. A future.

She leaned her head against his shoulder. "No, lucky us."

Epilogue

Brodie watched from the deck of the *Mary Margaret* as Grace zipped toward the dock on Sandpiper Island in the skiff. Ford stood on the end of the pier, waiting.

His note had asked Grace to come whenever she wanted. That was all he'd said. *Come out whenever you want.*

That was all she had needed to hear. She'd sent word out with Captain Robie that she'd come the end of the week, then had driven Brodie batshit crazy every day, worrying to death about it until it was finally The Day.

He smiled, happy she was finally getting to take the next step. She knew more, understood more, and was better prepared because of it.

He lifted the binoculars to watch. Not that he didn't trust Ford to welcome her. He'd asked her out there after all. But Brodie just . . . needed to. Grace had teased him about his protective nature with her. And he supposed he was. But then, you protected what was important, what was yours.

And Grace Maddox was his.

As if reading his thoughts, Whomper whined and leaned more fully against his ankle.

"She's all right, mate. She'll be fine."

Through his binoculars he watched as Grace tied up and climbed to the pier, then brother and sister fell into step and started to walk back to the island. Brodie knew she was worried about how to conduct herself with Ford, now that she knew more about his background. She'd had a hard couple days sorting through her feelings. She'd shared everything—about her childhood, about Ford, all of it—over the course of one long, sleepless night. Brodie understood as best he could where her conflicts and demons came from.

He also knew her. Her heart was huge and she was just beginning to understand that. She'd kept it tucked away so long, protected so long, it was a bit petrifying now that its power—and vulnerability—had been unleashed. He knew something of that, how sobering it was to be part of something bigger than only himself, to consider more than his own path, his own goals.

Knowing her as he did, he knew her anger would recede, even the parts that were tucked away deep in those recesses that had nothing to do with being rational, or even right. He also knew those pockets would empty because her heart had fully stepped in and stepped up.

Like Delia, he knew Grace would want to fix her brother. There was likely a long road ahead for her in learning, as Delia had, that it wasn't her job. It was Ford's job . . . if he thought there was something in him that needed fixing.

In the meantime, Brodie hoped brother and sister could forge something meaningful that was at least bare bones functional.

He watched them walk, then grinned. Always pushing and so impatient, that was his Grace. She might take a while to trust, to commit fully, but once she did, there was no holding back.

True to that, Grace made it only as far as the end of the pier before she slid her arm through Ford's and leaned her head on her brother's shoulder.

Brodie knew exactly how that felt. It was the best damn feeling in the world. "Be smart, man, and admit defeat now," he murmured. "You'll be happy you did."

How to Make a Vintage Suitcase Table

Supplies:
Vintage suitcase
4 table legs, same size/length
4 straight top plates w/screws
Power drill
Measuring tape or yardstick/ruler

Possible optional supplies:
Plywood or particle board
Paint/wood stain
Sandpaper
4 washers, wing nuts

1. Find/purchase vintage suitcase or trunk. If you don't have one in your attic, check out local flea markets, antique shops, auctions, yard sales, or go online and look at eBay, Craigslist, etc. The suitcase *must have* hard sides. Preferably the old suitcases made from plywood sides or Masonite.
2. Find/purchase four table legs. You can use the same sources as above. Look for legs already separated from the table, sold in a bundle, or look at old tables and simply unscrew the legs. You can also go to your local hardware store and purchase new table legs. These can be any length or angle, but all four must be the same. The length will determine the kind of table

you'll have—highboy or cafe table, end table, nightstand—short legs will create a coffee table.

Important note! If the legs have already been unscrewed from a table, check the screw tops to make certain the threads aren't stripped.

Optional: sand down and paint or stain the legs. I preferred to keep mine vintage and rugged looking. (By rugged I mean peeling paint, scuffed wood, to match the aged, somewhat worn look of the suitcase I am using.)

3. There are two methods you can use to attach the legs to the bottom of the suitcase, You can use a power drill to drill holes in the four corners of the bottom of the suitcase, insert the screw tops of each leg through the holes, then fasten them on the inside of the suitcase with washers and wing nuts. The problem with this method is it puts a lot of pressure on the attachment point and oftentimes suitcase sides aren't strong enough for that.

   My preference is to purchase four top plates from the local hardware store and attach them to the bottom of the suitcase. (Make sure to get the correct plates for the kind of legs you have—straight top plates or angled top plates, depending on how the legs screw in.)

   For top plates: Turn the suitcase upside down, measure and mark out the four corner areas to place the hardware, then get your power drill and attach the four plates.

4. *Option:* If you feel the bottom of the suitcase is too flimsy or old to withstand even this method, purchase a piece of plywood or particle board and cut it down to fit inside the bottom of your suitcase. Then attach the plates to the exterior bottom of the suitcase so the hardware goes through the suitcase bottom and into the plywood for extra support.

5. Screw on your table legs . . . and you're done!
6. If you plan to use your new table for storage, or have it open on display, find compatible fabric to put in the bottom of the open suitcase or trunk to hide the hardware or plywood. Depending on the size, a folded old quilt or fabric remnant, folded table cloths, even vintage place mats can be used to line the bottom and retain the vintage feel. If your suitcase already has a fabric lining, you can also carefully remove the lining before attaching the hardware, and/or inserting the plywood, then simply reattach it once the hardware and legs are installed.
7. It's time to find just the right place for your new table and decorate!

Check out this link for a full, downloadable instruction sheet including photos!

Read on for a peek at Delia's story, coming this September.

If you ever truly cared about her, you need to do something.

Ford Maddox stared at the message that had popped up on his laptop screen and scowled. When, exactly, had he lost command of his oh-so-carefully controlled world?

He looked away from the screen, but it wasn't so easy to look away from the request, which only served to deepen his scowl. There was no question whom the note referred to. Not because he was aware that Delia was in need of something, particularly something he might be able to provide, but because, with the lone exception of the person who'd sent the message, there simply wasn't anyone else it could be about.

He'd come to Maine to get a grip on his life and on himself. At the time, those two things had been synonymous. He'd arrived in Blueberry Cove having narrowed his life down to one person who required his care, one person whose well-being he was responsible for—himself. At the time, he hadn't been at all certain he could even pull that off.

That had been thirteen years ago.

In the intervening years, he'd done everything in his power to keep that list from growing. He'd been marginally successful where his work was concerned, given the number of flippered or feathered endangered sea creatures that relied on him for their continued existence. But where people were concerned . . . that population he'd maintained strict control over. No one got close, no one got hurt. Or dead. Simple math for the not so simple life he'd lived.

Granted, the only thing bombing him these days were bird droppings, but it had been the real deal for enough years that he could no longer be the go-to guy when things got rough. Not personal things, anyway. He had no problem being the guy in charge on Sandpiper Island. Out on his strip of rocky soil at the outer edges of Pelican Bay, the only battle he fought was the one against the relentless forces of nature.

Other than the ten weeks every summer when the annual crop of interns invaded to help with the various nesting populations, it was just him, the wind, the sea, and the tides. His troops consisted of a few thousand migratory seabirds and whatever harbor seals found their way to his rocky shores. That he could deal with. That was what he preferred to deal with. The animals he'd devoted himself to were simple creatures, relatively predictable, and, most important, minded their own business. Human animals . . . well, that was an entirely different story.

Getting involved in the personal matters of that particular breed of animal, especially in a small town like Blueberry Cove, and even more particularly in matters of any kind that involved one Delia O'Reilly? "Pass," he muttered under his breath, steadfastly ignoring the twinge in his chest. The Cove had saved his life, no argument there, and he was giving his life back to it in the only way he knew how, the only way he could.

Of course, if he were being honest, Delia O'Reilly had played a pivotal role in his rescue. He was, to a fault, honest—most critically with himself. In this case, the truth was that he definitely wasn't the man for the job. Or any job that had Delia's name on it. He was pretty damn sure she'd be the first one to agree.

He went back to the painstaking and often frustrating task of deciphering his notes on the recently completed nesting season, reluctantly looking up again when a ping indicated another incoming message.

I've only known her a few months, Ford, but I can already state with fair certainty that she's never going to come out and ask for help. Not from me, and most definitely, not from you.

"My point exactly," he retorted. He and Delia had a past, a distant one, some might say a complicated one. They weren't on bad terms. More like they weren't on terms of any kind. Hell, he hadn't seen or talked to her in . . . longer than he cared to figure out, much less admit. Figuring it out would mean admitting he'd been intentionally avoiding her—which meant there was something between them that needed avoiding. Except there was nothing between them. Good, bad, or otherwise. Nothing except for her brother, and Tommy had been gone a very, very long time.

That didn't stop a mental scrapbook of photos from flipping through his mind's eye. Over the past several months, memories of his friend had popped up on more than one occasion. Tommy on his first day out of boot camp being assigned to Ford's small platoon, and to Ford personally as his battle buddy. Tommy had been a few years older, but in all other ways, Ford was the mature one, the one with more experience. In battle and in life.

Despite coming from a small town in the northern coastal reaches of Maine, and being about the most unworldly person Ford had ever met, Private O'Reilly had been cocky around his fellow grunts. Around Ford, however, he'd been almost tongue-tied. Ford remembered how annoyed he'd been by that, especially since he'd done his damndest to be more—how had his C.O. put it?—

accessible. Less threatening. Ford had had enough self-awareness even then to know he was intense, focused, motivated. It was why he'd been groomed almost from day one for the Army's special forces unit, the Rangers. But he'd never threatened anyone. Well, not anyone on his side of the trigger, anyway.

He forced his thoughts away from Tommy, away from the grinning kid who'd weaseled his way under Ford's skin, and even into his good graces. More shocking, Tommy O'Reilly had managed to do the impossible. He'd found a way to be a friend. Ford hadn't had many of them—a choice he'd made very early in life. Life was simpler when you didn't need people . . . or even like them all that much. Especially in his line of work. Didn't mean he wouldn't have risked his life for O'Reilly. He had. More than once. Tommy had saved his sorry ass, too, ultimately sacrificing his own while doing just that.

It was for all those reasons, as well as the ones that, to this day, he'd been careful not to examine too closely, that he'd accompanied Tommy's body home to Blueberry Cove, intent on making sure his family knew he'd not only died a hero, but a damn good soldier and an even better human being. Those last two things didn't always go hand in hand. Ford knew that to be true every time he'd looked in the mirror.

Ford? I know you're reading this because the little green dot is next to your name. If you don't want me messaging you, then make yourself invisible.

Ford tossed his pen on the desk, leaned back in his chair, and scrubbed a hand over his face, wishing he could scrub away the message screen and the voice he heard behind it just as easily. He'd spent the past thirteen years being invisible, goddamn it. He wasn't used to anyone caring whether or not he was accessing the Internet, much less feeling compelled to communicate with him whenever the mood struck. The folks he communicated with as part of his work knew when information and data needed to be shared he did so via e-mail and responded in kind. Suited them, suited him, don't fix what's not broken.

Don't make me come out there.

"Dammit, Grace." Even as he barked the words, he felt the corners of his mouth briefly twitch upward. She was impossible to ignore when she wanted something. Got right in his face until he responded, too. She was a lot like him . . . in more ways than he wanted to admit or even think about.

One thing was certain, that name flashing on the screen next to the message bubble was exactly the reason he'd lost control of his carefully contained world.

Grace Maddox. His baby sister. Not that there was anything baby about her. She might be thirteen years his junior, but she was thirty-two, had a law degree, and was the proud new owner of an eighteenth-century boathouse she was converting into an inn. In Blueberry Cove. Where she'd moved to—lock, stock, and stray dog—four months ago, specifically so she could be near her only family. Namely, him.

Grace was one of those things he'd carefully removed himself from. He'd told himself at the time he'd done it for her own good. He supposed even then it was something he half expected to come back and bite him on the ass. It was one thing to join the Army at age eighteen, certain he was doing what was right for himself and that his five-year-old only sibling would understand and even be better off without him.

It had been quite another to see just how wrong he might have been on his first return home . . . but he'd already re-upped for another four and was heading into the type of training that was best done solo, so there hadn't been a damn thing he could do to fix it. By the time he and the Army had parted ways . . . hell, he could barely fix himself. By then it had been too late for him to mount any kind of rescue. Even if he could have, she'd hardly needed it, not from the likes of him, anyway. She'd gotten herself through grade school and high school, four years of college, and on into law school. She'd made something quite good out of the crap deal life had handed her.

Staying away, letting her start her life on her terms, do things her way had been the right thing to do. He'd abandoned her, for God's sake. Why the hell would she want anything to do with him? He'd taken the only chance he'd had, gone down the only path he'd seen available to make a life for himself. She'd deserved no less than the chance to do the same. So, he'd kept track, but he'd stayed away. For her own good.

You're so full of shit, then and now. He reached out to flip the screen off, but his hand paused mid-reach.

Both Maddox siblings had made their way in the world, chosen their own paths, but only Grace had had the balls to reach out for what she really wanted, for what really mattered—family.

He curled his fingers into his palm and let his hand drop to the top of the desk, her words still staring him in the face. What he saw wasn't the words, but her face, those eyes, that stubborn chin, the way she lifted one eyebrow as if to say *Seriously? You expect me to buy that?*

Grace was his one weakness. When they were face-to-face, there was no way he could deny her anything she wanted. Even if what she wanted was to rebuild a relationship with him. But that didn't change the fact that he sucked at it, that he was supremely uncomfortable with it. Allowing even the tiniest chink in his damaged and beat-up armor to be revealed was the single most terrifying thing for him. Being vulnerable in any way, on any level, put his carefully constructed new self at risk. He'd survived more than most men could and still lay claim to their sanity, if not their soul. He wasn't sure he could survive letting her down. Again.

She'd given him no choice in the matter. She'd simply shown up, making it clear she wasn't going away . . . and then she'd wrapped her arms around him, hugged the life out of him, and told him she loved him. Loved him. After all he'd done. After all he hadn't done.

How was that possible? He didn't even know what the hell love was anymore.

He only knew he couldn't tell her no.

Now she wanted to drag him into other people's lives. Namely Delia's.

Ford owed a debt he could never adequately repay to his one and only sibling, but he and Delia were square. He would figure out how to continue managing his world and have his sister be part of it, but he'd be damned if he'd open himself up to anything—or anyone—else. Delia knew better than anyone—*anyone*—even Grace, that was by far the best for everyone concerned.

He shoved his chair back and stood, too restless to simply sit there and let thoughts and memories dive-bomb him like he was a sitting duck. He strode across the corner of the open loft space he used as an office and climbed down the ladder to the open area below that comprised kitchen, dining, and living area. He crouched down to check the pellet stove that squatted, fat and happily chugging out heat in the center of the home he'd built himself, but it was going along just fine, which he'd known it would be since he'd just reloaded it that morning.

Swearing under his breath at his uncustomary restlessness, he straightened, then, skirting the corner area that was both kitchen and dining area, he gave the rough bark of the tree trunk that formed the far corner an absent rub with his palm before pushing open one of the triple-paned doors. He stepped out onto the side deck. The dense, coniferous tree canopy provided year-round shade as well as protection against the elements. The unseasonably brisk late August breeze blowing inland through the treetops didn't bring him the peace of mind it usually did.

When he'd been working toward his degree, he'd spent almost every minute of his spare time researching alternate living spaces. Initially, it had simply been a brain puzzle, a way to keep his thoughts occupied when he wasn't studying so they wouldn't veer into territory better left in the past. But that particular puzzle—off-grid living—hadn't been so easily discarded. In fact, it had captured his attention so completely that he'd eventually admitted it was more than a casual interest, more than momentary mental distraction.

The first time he'd laid eyes on a drawing of a sustainable, livable tree house, he'd known instantly that that was what he'd been searching for. In that moment he'd understood that in addition to studying environmental habitats of various endangered species, he'd also been studying his own environmental habitat. Being endangered himself, he'd needed to find the right home where he could, if not thrive, at least survive.

He'd already begun his work on Sandpiper as an intern to Dr. Pelletier, a man he'd greatly admired and whose wisdom and guidance he missed very much. It had been his first summer out on the island when he'd discovered the exact right spot deep in the white pine forest that filled the center of the heart-shaped surge of boulders, soil, and rock that comprised Sandpiper Island. The whole of it was like a kind of fortress, hugged almost entirely by a rocky, boulder-strewn shoreline. There in the tall, old forest heart of it, he'd found his home.

By the time he'd graduated and taken over operations on the island full-time after Dr. Pelletier had taken ill, Ford had figured out every last detail of how the tree house would be constructed. Multileveled at the core, then spread out through a sturdy group of perfectly matched pine, naturally spaced, so as not to overly burden any one of them. It had taken him eighteen months, and that was with a mild Maine winter in the midst of it. He'd added to it over the ensuing years, with connected outbuildings, most connected by a combination of decking and rope bridges, others only by swing rope. He'd hewn every log, driven every nail, so he knew every last nook and cranny. It was his aerie and his bunker. It had given him the one thing he'd known he needed to survive—the freedom to feel completely safe for the first time in his life.

Even his safe haven couldn't save him from the entirely different set of images that flashed through his mind as he stood under the tree canopy. Images he'd kept tightly sealed, away from all conscious and subconscious thought. They weren't filled with horror, weren't the seeds of endless nightmares suffered while asleep and while wide awake.

No, he'd kept these particular memories under lock and key for entirely different reasons. Polar opposite reasons. He'd learned to live with his past, with the things he'd done. He'd made a certain kind of peace with himself, a deal of sorts, that he was giving back, balancing a score that could never be measured, much less rectified. It was carefully constructed with the knowledge that his work was where he funneled whatever passion he had left in him, where he gave whatever might resemble a heart, if not a soul. It was the only place he could allow himself the luxury of caring, of wanting, of being needed or necessary to something other than himself.

The flip side of that deal was that he'd never allow those same parts of himself to be touched by another person. He would never let someone in, allow them to rely on him, to need him, or, God help him, want him. He'd most definitely made certain he'd never want those things for himself. He didn't deserve them, for one, and he sure as hell hadn't earned the right to them.

Images of that long-ago night roared in—the storm lashing the windows of the small rooms above the tiny restaurant on the other side of Half Moon Harbor, the lightning strikes illuminating the walls, the twisted linens on the fold-out bed . . . and the woman astride him, gloriously naked, her red hair glowing in the light flashes like some kind of flaming, otherworldly halo. She was completely unapologetic about taking her pleasure from him, wrenching his release in return. Mother Nature relentlessly pounded the shores of the harbor, unleashing her fury, while the two of them pounded just as relentlessly against each other as if the delirious pleasure of release could somehow liberate them from the ripping grief threatening to drown them both.

Delia, sinking because she'd lost her brother, her only sibling, her only anchor. And Ford, going under because he'd known even then that his grip on what made him human, maybe his grip on his very soul, had already begun to slip away. Tommy was gone . . . yet Ford had been left to live another day so he could take more Tommys from the world, so he could cast more families into the devastating throes of grief he was witnessing firsthand on Delia's beautiful, heartbroken face.

She'd been gone when he'd woken up the next morning. When he'd made his way downstairs, she'd already been hustling in the kitchen. Her grandmother had been the one to push his breakfast plate onto the bar, her expression neither open nor shut, but simply vacant. She'd lost a grandson . . . but there was work to be done, one foot in front of the other. Delia hadn't so much as looked

his way, so he'd stayed out of hers. He'd eaten his breakfast, paid the bill, said his good-byes . . . and gone back to
hell.

He'd returned to the Cove nine years later far more
broken and damaged than he'd had any awareness was
even possible. He wasn't even sure why he'd ended up
there, except . . . there just hadn't been . . . anywhere else
to go.

Delia had her own place by then, her grandmother having gone on to her peaceful reward and their old restaurant having burned down. She hadn't seemed all that
surprised to see him. Her eyes were the color of the deep,
sparkling sea and her hair still a fiery halo. Her grin
seemed more naughty angel than pure, but he'd noticed
straight off that it was a natural part of her, simply how she
took in the world around her . . . not something private,
something reserved specially for him. She'd asked after
him, friendly, sincere, caring, and yet quite clearly one
step back, all the while looking into his face, into his eyes,
and finding far more there than he'd wanted her to find.
He'd been unable to hide from her the way he'd long since
learned to shield himself from everyone else.

He'd known then that while the Cove had felt like the
only safe harbor he knew, Delia O'Reilly could be part
of that safe place only as past memories. The kind that
needed to stay in the past. She never mentioned that night,
and he'd been quite content to leave it at that. He'd eventually moved out to the island and turned his attention forward, always careful not to look back.

He heard the ping from the other side of the door he'd
left open behind him and headed back inside, up to his
office, drawn inexorably to the screen, feeling fate wrapping its long, clever fingers around his neck . . . except the
tightness he felt was in his chest. He sat down, intending

to find the words to explain to Grace that while he understood her concern, and appreciated her trying to help Delia, that he wasn't going to be of any help, not because he wasn't willing so much as he had no help to give. Only instead of typing, his fingers closed into fists instead as he read the words on the screen.

She reached out to help me before she even knew me. Because she cared enough about you to want you to have what you really needed. Family. We both should have listened to her then. We both need to help her have what she really needs now.

He reread Grace's latest message, unable to find a single thing that wasn't perfectly true with what she was saying. Another ping came, making him almost viscerally flinch. Memories, so long held at bay, roared in like thundering waves, breaching any and all walls, drowning his futile attempts to block them. Not just of that night, but of all the long mornings, afternoons, evenings, he'd sat in her diner, wallowing in the energy, the vitality, the *life* of her very presence. Her smile, her loud laugh, listening as she alternately goaded a smile out of a gruff fisherman or a grudging apology from a short-tempered townie. He'd lost count of the number of times she'd leant an ear, offered a hug or a free meal, scolded, sympathized, lectured, loved, bussed cheeks, and even pinched the occasional ass. Dozens, hundreds of moments he hadn't even been aware were there for the recalling.

Through the torrent, he read Grace's final message. This one was simply a cut and paste of a news story in the local Cove newspaper. He clicked on it, trying—failing—to keep his mind blank, open, and noncommittal.

Local Diner Owner Losing Battle
With Town Scion Over Land Rights

He skimmed the article, and the tight clutch of dread in his gut was replaced with two fists clenched in anger.

Hasn't she lost enough in her life? "He has every other god-damn thing. Why can't he just leave her the fuck alone?"

The *he* in this instance was Brooks Winstock. Descended from one of the oldest families in the Cove, he owned most of it and was richer than Croesus. He wanted Delia's diner. Or more specifically, the piece of prime harbor front property it sat on . . . for, of all things, a yacht club.

What in the fresh hell would Blueberry Cove do with a damn yacht club? It was a town with a three-hundred-year legacy of lobster fisherman, shipbuilders, and sailors. Hardly the yacht-club type.

The diner, he knew, just as Brooks Winstock damn well knew, was all she had. Not just to earn a living. It was the center and focus of the rich full life she'd carved out for herself with her own blood, sweat, and tears. She loved that life, and the town loved her right back. She had earned the right to enjoy it. Delia's was a Cove landmark . . . the diner and its colorful, saucy, outspoken owner.

Ford couldn't imagine her taking it lightly or well, much less going quietly. If he hadn't been so pissed off, the image of her taking on Winstock might have gotten what passed as a smile out of him.

He punched the screen dark, then went back down the ladder, stalked to the other side of the kitchen, grabbed his boat keys from the hook of the pot buoy attached to the wall, and took the fast exit, shimmying down the knotted rope to the forest floor below. He was halfway down the path that led to the only pier on the island before he realized what the hell he was doing. *Just what in the hell* are *you* *doing?*

"Dammit, Grace," he muttered again as he unknotted the ropes and jumped onboard the old lobster boat he'd bought off Blue years before and kept running with a combination of spit and sheer power of will.

So, he'd been wrong. There were apparently two people in the world he couldn't say no to. *Not that Delia asked me to stick my nose in her business.*

In fact, he'd be lucky if she didn't bite it off and hand it back to him, wrapped neatly in a take-out box. Hell, he wasn't even sure what he thought he could do. But he'd stayed on the sidelines once before in his life. Every time he looked into Grace's pretty hazel eyes, he knew what his choice had cost her. He might not be able to do a damn thing to help Delia, but sitting on the sidelines wasn't going to be an option.

God help us all.

GREAT BOOKS, GREAT SAVINGS!

When You Visit Our Website:
www.kensingtonbooks.com
You Can Save Money Off The Retail Price Of Any Book You Purchase!

- **All Your Favorite Kensington Authors**
- **New Releases & Timeless Classics**
- **Overnight Shipping Available**
- **eBooks Available For Many Titles**
- **All Major Credit Cards Accepted**

Visit Us Today To Start Saving!
www.kensingtonbooks.com

All Orders Are Subject To Av
Shipping and Handling Char
Offers and Prices Subject To Change